The American Agent

a&b

THE AMERICAN AGENT

A Maisie Dobbs Novel

JACQUELINE WINSPEAR

Allison & Busby Limited
11 Wardour Mews
London W1F 8AN
allisonandbusby.com

First published in Great Britain by Allison & Busby in 2019.

A CIP catalogue record for this book is available from
the British Library.

First Edition

HB ISBN 978-0-7490-2460-4
TPB ISBN 978-0-7490-2475-8

Typeset in 11/18 pt Sabon by
Allison & Busby Ltd.

The paper used for this Allison & Busby publication
has been produced from trees that have been legally sourced
from well-managed and credibly certified forests.

Printed and bound by
CPI Group (UK) Ltd, Croydon, CR0 4YY

In Memory of Don
One of 'The Few', the young men of the Royal Air Force who fought the Luftwaffe in the skies above England during the Battle of Britain. He was killed in June 1940, age twenty-two

The radio will be for the twentieth century what the press was for the nineteenth century. With the appropriate change, one can apply Napoleon's phrase to our age, speaking of the radio as the eighth great power. The radio is the most influential and important intermediary between a spiritual movement and the nation, between the idea and the people.

FROM A SPEECH BY JOSEPH GOEBBELS GIVEN ON
18TH AUGUST 1933, AT THE TENTH ANNUAL RADIO EXPOSITION

AGENT. *Noun: a person who works secretly to obtain information for a government or other official body. A person or thing that takes an active role or produces a specified effect.*

DEFINITION FROM *THE OXFORD ENGLISH DICTIONARY*

PROLOGUE

I am going to talk to you three times a week from a country that is fighting for its life. Inevitably I'm going to get called by that terrifying word 'propagandist'. But of course I'm a propagandist. Passionately I want my ideas – our ideas – of freedom and justice to survive.

VERNON BARTLETT, 28TH MAY 1940, DURING THE INAUGURAL
BROADCAST OF THE BRITISH BROADCASTING CORPORATION'S
NORTH AMERICAN SERVICE

The RAF's brilliantly successful week raised the public's spirits enormously. It was hoped that the number of German planes destroyed by the British fighters would be duly noted by a section of the American press which appears to people here to act as though mesmerised by the achievements of the Luftwaffe. Many astonished

Britons, taking time off from the war to read how American editors think it's going, have felt like protesting, like Mark Twain, that reports of their death have been greatly exaggerated.

THE *NEW YORKER*'S LETTER FROM LONDON BY
MOLLIE PANTER-DOWNES, 12TH AUGUST 1940

Each time I entered a new shelter people wanted to know if I'd seen any bombs and was it safe to go home. At one shelter there was a fine row going on. A man wanted to smoke his pipe in the shelter; the warden wouldn't allow it. The pipe smoker said he'd go out and smoke it in the street, where he'd undoubtedly be hit by a bomb and then the warden would be sorry. At places where peat is available, it's being consumed in great quantities at night. I have seen a few pale faces, but very few. How long these people will stand up to this sort of thing I don't know, but tonight they're magnificent. I've seen them, talked with them, and I know.

LONDON CALLING BROADCAST BY EDWARD R. MURROW
TO AMERICA, 26TH AUGUST 1940

In September 1939, the talk was of the Navy, the ring of steel that was to starve the Germans. Today the Royal Air Force has captured the respect and admiration which has traditionally been given to the Royal Navy. On the day war was declared any man who predicted that after a year of war, including only ten weeks of battle, Britain would be without effective allies and faced with the prospect of invasion would have been considered mad. Invasion is now one of the favourite topics of conversation. These Londoners know what they're fighting for now – not Poland or Norway – not even for France, but for Britain.

LONDON CALLING BROADCAST BY EDWARD R. MURROW

TO AMERICA, 3RD SEPTEMBER 1940

BLITZ BOMBING OF LONDON GOES ON ALL NIGHT

Two buses hit: hospital ringed by explosions

EAST END AGAIN: MORE FIRES

Goering restarted his great Blitzkrieg on London last night promptly at blackout time – one minute to eight. Half an hour before that time he made a gloating, boasting broadcast to the German people. 'A terrific attack is going on against London,' he said. 'Adolf Hitler has entrusted me with the task of attacking the heart of the British Empire.'

THE DAILY EXPRESS LONDON,

MONDAY 8TH SEPTEMBER 1940

London still stood this morning, which was the greatest surprise to me as I cycled home in the light of early dawn after the most frightening night I have ever spent. But not all of London was still there, and some of the things I saw this morning would scare the wits out of anyone.

HELEN KIRKPATRICK, REPORTING FOR

THE CHICAGO DAILY NEWS, 9TH SEPTEMBER 1940

CHAPTER ONE

REPORTING LONDON, BROADCAST BY CATHERINE SAXON, LONDON, 10TH SEPTEMBER 1940

Tonight I joined the women of the London Auxiliary Ambulance Service as they rushed to the aid of civilians caught in the relentless bombing of this brave city. Herr Hitler's bombers have been swarming in for the past three nights, raining down terror on the men, women and children of London as if to pay the country back for the success of Britain's Royal Air Force as they fought the Luftwaffe over England's south-eastern counties throughout the summer. Resilience and endurance have been the order of the day and night for the citizens of this country – an experience we Americans should be grateful we have not yet encountered on our soil. Pray to God we shall never see the shadows of those killing machines in the skies above Main Street.

I was aboard an ambulance with two women – both

Mrs P and Miss D served their country in the last war: Mrs P with the First Aid Nursing Yeomanry, and Miss D as a nurse at a casualty clearing station close to the front line. I later discovered Miss D is, in fact, a titled member of England's aristocracy, a sign that everyone's pulling together on Britain's home front. As Miss D drove through the streets at speed, her way lit only by fires either side of a thoroughfare strewn with scorched and burning rubble, the flames threatened to take us with them. When we reached our destination, a street I cannot name and would not know again, Miss D braked hard, and before the ambulance came to a stop, Mrs P had leapt out and was gathering the kit needed to aid bombed-out families. The men of the fire service were hard at work, directing wide arcs of water into houses destroyed by the bombing. Flames rose up as if to spike the heavens, the remaining walls like broken teeth leading into the mouth of hell. Beyond I could see searchlights as they crossed each other scouring the skies for bombers – and many of those searchlights were 'manned' by women. The constant ack-ack-ack of anti-aircraft guns added to the ear-splitting sounds of a night with London under attack. Within minutes an injured boy and a girl were made stable and placed in the ambulance. I'd watched their grandmother pulling at fallen masonry even as it scorched her hands. 'My girls, my girls,' she cried, as she tried to move bricks and mortar away from the untimely grave that had claimed her two beloved daughters. Miss D gently put her arms around the wailing grandmother and led her towards the ambulance, where she bandaged her hands and reminded her that two small, terrified children were counting on her strength. Minutes later, firemen carried away the bodies of the deceased, the grandmother's 'girls' – the mother and aunt of the two children. This report cannot include a description of the remains of those two women.

The Civil War is still remembered by the elders in our American hometowns. Those men and women were children during a terrible time in our country's history, and some saw what trauma cannon fire and machine guns will inflict upon the human form. The volunteers who fought with our Lincoln Brigade witnessed Hitler's Blitzkrieg in Spain – they too know the terror of a bombing raid. We who have seen war know the children in that ambulance will never forget this night – it will be branded into their young minds for ever. And it will be branded into the memory of those two women of the London Auxiliary Ambulance Service, and into the heart of this reporter. The children's father is at war. If he comes home, it will be to what's left of his family – as will many men who believed they were fighting for the safety of their loved ones.

This is Catherine Saxon, courtesy of the British Broadcasting Corporation in London, England, on the night of September tenth, 1940. God bless you all, and may peace be yours.

'Well, Miss D – what do you think of that?' Priscilla Partridge leant towards the wireless set and switched it off, then reached for her packet of cigarettes and lighter. 'I thought she was quite good. That broadcast went out live last night – New

15

York is five hours behind, so I daresay they heard it at dinner time over there – carefully planned to tear at the hearts of happy families as they sit around the table.'

'I wish she'd held back on that bit about the aristocracy. It was rather much, and I'd like to tell her, "See these streets? I know my way around Lambeth because I was born here!"'

'She would probably have missed the irony, Maisie,' said Priscilla, drawing on her cigarette. She blew a smoke ring into the air. 'Americans don't quite understand the many distinctions between one person's station and another here in Britain, as I am sure we don't understand theirs – though they know rich and poor. We're a mystery to each other, if truth be told.'

'Anyway, I'm just glad she didn't give out our full names. She must have whipped over to Portland Place and recorded that report immediately she left us last night. Apparently she had been pursuing an opportunity to broadcast for a while. In fact, she told me it was an uphill battle because reporting is a boys' game.' Maisie stifled a yawn. 'Oh dear, I'm worn out, Pris. It was a long night and I'm going home to bed for a couple of hours before I start my day.' Maisie Dobbs pushed down on the arms of the chair, stood up and leant towards her friend, kissing her on both cheeks. 'What Miss Saxon didn't say was that we all need a bath.'

'I thought she was a good sport,' said Priscilla.

'She was,' said Maisie. 'She didn't get in the way and helped when she could. I would imagine she has to walk a narrow line between telling Americans what she's observed, and not scaring them so much they don't listen.'

'You're right – you wouldn't hear her describing the poor baker who went out to find out why his drain was blocked, only to find a decomposing foot in it.' Priscilla paused. 'It's only eight in the morning and already I would like a drink.'

'Do me a favour, Pris – settle for another cup of tea. And some toast. I'm going home now.'

'All right, Maisie. We're both fit to drop – it's just as well you only live up the road.' She paused. 'I wonder about those children – the ones we picked up on that run with the Saxon woman.'

'The girl will pull through, but I wouldn't put money on the boy's chances,' said Maisie. 'Miss Saxon rather understated their wounds.'

'Douglas says that truth is always a victim of war.'

'"No kidding," as our new friend from the Colonies might say. I'll see you later, Pris,' said Maisie. 'We're on duty at five.'

Maisie had just begun to draw back the blackout curtains at her Holland Park flat when the telephone in the sitting room began to ring.

'Blast!' She had a mind to ignore the call, but thought better of it – she had not been able to return to her property in Kent for several days, and as much as she would like nothing more than to sink into a bath filled with hot water, the call might be about Anna – and there were many things to concern her about Anna.

'Good morning,' said Maisie.

'Busy night?' The voice was unmistakable.

'Robbie MacFarlane, you should know better than to ask, and in that tone – it was a terrible night, and it's not a bloody joke you know.' Maisie knew her reply was uncharacteristically short, but at that moment she was too tired to deal with Robert MacFarlane.

'My apologies. Yes, you're right. I heard you were out on more than a few runs to the hospitals last night. I'm sorry.'

Maisie chewed her lip. It wasn't like MacFarlane to request forgiveness. She knew him only too well, and if he was rude, it was generally by design, not an error.

'Why are you calling me, Robbie? You've let me know you're keeping tabs on me, but I am bone-tired and I want to rest my weary head before I try to get some work done today, and then take my ambulance out again.'

'It's about an American. One of those press people over here on a quest to keep our good friends on the other side of the Atlantic informed about the war. Name of Catherine Saxon. In fact, Miss Catherine Angelica Saxon, to give the woman her full moniker.'

'Angelica?'

'No accounting for the Yanks, Maisie.'

Maisie rubbed her neck, following the path of an old scar now barely visible, and shivered. 'No, it's just that . . . well, she was with us in the ambulance last night, just for a couple of runs because she had to make her first broadcast – she told us that she had previously only had her reports printed in the newspapers. I can't remember which papers she's working for. More than one. Anyway, I was just listening to her on the wireless at Mrs Partridge's house – her report was broadcast for the Americans last night. In fact, she told us she was very excited because it was also going out in London this morning, and she hoped she would get to be as popular as Mr Murrow, who is as well known here as he is over there in America. I've heard him a few times myself. Anyway, it's just that she didn't strike me as an Angelica, that's all, even if it's only a middle name.' Maisie was aware that she was rambling, staving off whatever news MacFarlane had called to convey. She'd wanted to escape war and death if only for the time it took to wallow in a hot bath.

'Well, hold on to your seat, Maisie, because she's with the angels now.'

'Robbie? What's happened? Was the poor girl caught in the bombing on her way home? Or were her lodgings hit?' Maisie felt a chill envelop her. She knew the gist of MacFarlane's response even before he spoke.

'No, lass. She's been found dead in her rooms at a house on Welbeck Street this morning. And we can't lay this one at Hitler's feet – she was murdered. Twenty-eight years of age and someone saw fit to slit her throat.'

Maisie felt her own throat constrict, her voice cracking as she spoke. 'And why are you involved, Robbie?' Robert MacFarlane worked in the opaque realm between Scotland Yard and the Secret Service. 'Why not someone like Caldwell – murder is his job.'

'Maisie, I know you can hear me, even if you've almost lost your voice. Get yourself some sleep, then go to your office. I'll see you there at two this afternoon and we'll discuss the matter. There will be plenty of time for you to find your way to the ambulance station before tonight's blitzes start. And they will come back again, those bastards. They won't leave us alone until we've beaten them. See you this afternoon.' Maisie stood for a moment, holding the receiver, the long tone of the disconnected call echoing into the room – MacFarlane was known to dispense with a formal 'goodbye'.

She slumped into an armchair and thought about the young woman who had joined them in the ambulance when they'd reported for duty at five o'clock the previous evening. Saxon was almost the same height as Maisie, with shoulder-length, sun-kissed hair – she looked as if she'd spent the summer sailing. At one point she'd twisted it back and pinned it in place with a pencil. Maisie could see her now, laughing. 'Gotta use the tools at hand,' she'd said. She'd worn a pair of dark khaki trousers, with a fawn blouse tucked into the waistband – both seemed freshly laundered. And she had brought a brown tweed jacket, though she soon took it off. Her worn but polished lace-up boots were a choice Priscilla had seen fit to comment upon. 'No one could accuse her of overdressing, could they? That girl could be a mannequin with those looks, yet look at her – she's almost ready for the trenches!'

Maisie remembered the scuffs of ash and dirt across the blouse as Saxon clambered over hot bricks to talk to a fireman, and later she explained to Maisie and Priscilla, 'My mother always says that no matter what happens, one should always make a good first impression – hence the pressed blouse, which is now fit for the rubbish! I never told her how I'd let everything go when I was in Spain – there wasn't time to look as if I'd just returned from a shopping expedition to Bonwit Teller!' And Maisie had told her that she too had been in Spain, but they'd let the words hang in the air, as if neither wanted to recall or discuss – and there was no time anyway, because now Saxon was reporting on Hitler's blitzkriegs in another country, and Maisie was drawing upon skills she'd honed in two wars. Saxon had only mentioned that, while her mother seemed to admire her choice of occupation, her father did not approve. 'In fact, he doesn't want me to be occupied at all – he'd rather I just sort of languish until a good man finds me. My mother, though, is secretly proud, I think – and sometimes not so secretly, to my father's chagrin.' Maisie had shaken hands with Catherine

Saxon – Catherine Angelica Saxon – only nine or ten hours ago, bidding her farewell and expressing hope that her first broadcast went well. She'd added that she also hoped her parents were indeed proud of their intrepid daughter. And now she was dead.

'Miss, you look all in,' said Billy Beale, Maisie's assistant. 'Terrible night, wasn't it? What time did you get home this morning?'

'Just after seven, but then I stayed and had a cup of tea with Mrs Partridge. I suppose I climbed into bed at about half past eight.' Maisie rubbed her forehead. 'And now it's past noon. How about you, Billy? You must have been out there on patrol too.'

'Wish I could go back to the Bore War, when all I had to think about as an Air Raid Precautions man was knocking on doors and telling people to make sure their curtains were closed properly during the blackout. Anyway, I'm going to make a cuppa.'

'Wait a minute.' Maisie reached into her desk and pulled out a small brown bag, twisted at the top and secured with a clothes peg. 'I think I would like a very strong coffee, Billy. Just put a couple of heaped teaspoons into that other pot I brought into the office last week, add two cups of water and strain it like tea after it's brewed for a few minutes.'

'That sounds a bit too strong, miss. That bad, is it?'

'MacFarlane will be here later on, so I need to be awake.'

Billy took the bag of coffee. 'What does he want?'

'It's about a young woman who came out in the ambulance with us last night. An American correspondent – a reporter. Apparently, she had been given a stab at doing a broadcast by that man – oh dear, I'm so tired, I've forgotten his name again. You know – the American.'

21

'Mr Murrow?'

'Yes, that's it. Anyway, she had been writing for various newspapers in America – some quite important ones, by all accounts – and had been invited to see Mr Murrow. She said something about becoming one of "Murrow's Boys" – the American reporters based here in London.'

'She's not a fella though, is she?'

'Apparently there was already one woman working for him, and I've remembered her name – Mary Marvin Breckinridge. She was married in June, so she's not working for the broadcaster any more, which led Catherine Saxon to hope that if she made a good account of herself, she would be in the game, reporting from a woman's point of view. That's what she said. "In the game".'

'So, what's happened?' asked Billy as he opened the bag and lifted it to his nose.

'She's dead, Billy. Murdered. And MacFarlane wants to see me about it.'

'Sounds like she got into the wrong game.' Billy closed the bag. 'Mind if I have a cup too, miss?'

'Not at all – I think we're going to need all the energy we can get.'

'Why do you think MacFarlane wants to talk to you about it? Sounds more like Caldwell's alley to me.'

'My thoughts exactly, Billy. My thoughts exactly. Now then, let's get that coffee down us and have a look at the cases in progress.'

At exactly two o'clock, the doorbell rang.

'That'll be him, Billy.'

'I'll go down. Do you want me to make a pot of tea?'

'No – if he has tea, he'll be here longer than he needs to be and half of it chatting. Let's see what he wants first. Probably a statement from me.'

Billy stopped by the door. 'Miss – don't kid yourself. He'd have called you down to his gaff and had a clerk take a statement. Nah – be prepared. He wants you working for him again.' He grinned. 'I've told you before – he's sweet on you.'

'I wish you'd stop nibbling on that bone, Billy.'

'Your Ladyship. Looking in fine fettle, all things considered – though a little powder under the eyes might not have gone amiss.'

'Robbie, Billy is quite capable of throwing you out of my office, you know.'

'Aw, just pulling your leg, Maisie. Just pulling your leg. In dark times, a bit of light never hurt anyone. English rose you are – an English rose.'

'All right, stop there,' said Maisie. 'Let's sit down and you can tell me what's going on and why you want to talk to me about something the Murder Squad should be investigating.'

'In your office, Maisie. With doors closed.' Robert MacFarlane turned to Billy. 'Ah, the faithful Mr Beale. Couldn't rustle up a cuppa, could you? No sugar – easier to give up than cut down, if you ask me.'

'Right you are, sir.'

As Billy left the room, MacFarlane followed Maisie into her private domain. She closed the doors leading from the outer office.

'Shall we get down to brass tacks?' said Maisie, taking a seat at the long table where she would usually sit with Billy to discuss a case. She pulled out a chair for MacFarlane.

MacFarlane unbuttoned his jacket, and sat down.

'The American woman was murdered, Maisie, and I want you to play a part in the investigation.'

'Why me?'

'Because you're qualified.' He held up his hand, as if to prevent Maisie interjecting, but sat back when Billy knocked on the door, entered the office and placed cups of tea in front of his employer and MacFarlane.

Maisie nodded her thanks, then turned to the Scot as Billy left the room.

'How am I qualified for this case in particular? You're going to have to work hard to persuade me, Robbie.'

MacFarlane drank the entire cup of hot tea in several gulps, placed the cup on the saucer, pushed it away from him on the table and brought his attention to Maisie.

'You'll scorch your gullet if you keep doing that.'

MacFarlane waved away the comment. 'It's like this. We have a delicate situation – American correspondents in Britain, citizens of another country telling their fellow countrymen about our war over here. They're walking a fine line, taking what we're going through with Hitler and his bloody blitzkrieg, and putting it into the homes of their fellow Americans.' He lifted his tie and rubbed at an invisible stain. 'You could say that Murrow and his ilk are probably the best propaganda tool we have to get the Yanks on our side.'

'But they are on our side,' said Maisie.

'You're being deliberately obtuse. You know very well what I'm talking about. Yes, they are on our side – but they don't want to be in any wars over here or anywhere else in the world. It's not that we want to twist anyone's arm, but a little support from the citizenry for the help the American president wants to give us would be handy. Money, materiel, that sort of thing. A bit of sugar.' He sighed. 'Their reporters are doing a good job, and so are ours. Anyway, back to the delicate situation. Catherine Saxon was murdered. She had been reporting here for a press concern in the USA, and she was about to be a lot better known than she was – Murrow had her pegged to do more broadcasts to appeal to women, and as you know, she was pretty good at that. Didn't gloss over anything, but as you no doubt heard, she went to the heart with that broadcast last night.'

'You still haven't answered my question,' said Maisie. 'Why me, and why the secrecy?'

'We're keeping the lid on the story inasmuch as there will be a limited announcement in the press, and though her death will be reported in the USA it will be very low down in the papers. Here are the problems. Her father is a politician. A senator. Last thing he wanted was a daughter running towards trouble – and that's what Miss Saxon did. France, Spain, Berlin. You name it, she's been there. Now London. The good senator is what they are calling an "isolationist" – he's built a following by pointing out that one hundred and twenty-five thousand doughboys were lost in the last war, and saying enough is enough, and that Americans want to stay out of foreign wars. The second thing is the way we have to play this one. The American embassy is involved, so is their Department of Justice. They want someone on the investigation from their team, and we don't think Caldwell or anyone at the Yard can quite do what is really a job requiring the skills of a detective and an ambassador.'

'Of course they can, Robbie – they know what they're doing,' said Maisie.

'They do, but we – and the Yanks – want to know there's absolute confidentiality, and we want someone who can work with their investigator.'

'What makes you think I can work with one of their investigators?'

'You've worked with him before.' MacFarlane stared at Maisie. 'In fact, you almost killed him.'

Maisie was silent. She met MacFarlane's gaze.

'Well, that did the trick,' said MacFarlane. 'Never thought I'd be the one to strike you dumb.'

'There are other investigators you could call upon,' said Maisie.

'But he doesn't want to work with the others. He wants to work with you. He's a lot more important now than he was in Munich, and he's here, in London. And it's not a flying visit.' MacFarlane looked at his watch. 'In fact, any minute now—' He was interrupted by an insistent ringing of the doorbell. 'As I was about to say, any minute now he'll be here in your office.'

Maisie was silent. She heard Billy leave the office, followed by voices in the entrance hall and on the stairs, and then a knock on the door of her private office.

'Robbie,' she whispered. 'It's Anna's adoption panel in a week's time – I can't put a foot wrong. I cannot get into any trouble, and I cannot be mentioned in the press.' She felt tears rise.

'Don't worry,' said MacFarlane. 'I know. I won't put you in any situation that would risk little Anna's future.'

Maisie nodded, then called out, 'Yes, Billy?'

The door opened, and Billy entered, followed by a tall man of about forty-five years of age. At over six feet in height, with dark hair and pale blue eyes, he wore a charcoal grey suit, a white shirt, and a tie with diagonal stripes of black and grey. His black shoes were polished, and he carried a grey fedora with a black band, along with a well-worn nutmeg brown briefcase.

'Thank you, Billy,' said MacFarlane. He turned to Maisie. 'I believe you know Mr Scott.'

Mark Scott smiled as he held out his hand to Maisie. 'I hope you're not going to hold a gun to my jugular this time, Maisie.'

She took his hand. 'Hello, Mark. Lovely to see you again.' Feeling the colour rise in her cheeks, she turned away and took up the file that MacFarlane pushed towards her. She drew a hand across her forehead. 'Well then, we'd better get on with business. Gentlemen, please sit down.'

CHAPTER TWO

'Tell me who found her – and the circumstances,' said Maisie. She tapped a pencil against her left palm, glancing at Mark Scott before bringing her attention back to MacFarlane.

'According to her landlady, Mrs Doris Marsh – who lived in the ground-floor flat – she heard Miss Saxon come in at about half past one-ish this morning, which seems about right, considering her broadcast and the time it would have taken to walk home. It's not that far from Broadcasting House to Welbeck Street. Marsh heard a noise and ignored it – apparently Saxon sometimes pushed a note under the door, asking Marsh to wake her if she hadn't heard her stirring by a certain time. She was, according to Mrs Marsh, always a little worried about sleeping through the ring of an alarm clock.'

'Do you know if that concern was warranted?' asked Maisie. 'Did she often sleep through her alarm?'

'Interesting question, Maisie,' said Scott.

She turned to the American. 'She's reported on war, Mr Scott. If you're used to being so close to battle, you don't sleep – you catnap. And there were bombs falling last night, yet she went home – not to a shelter – and her landlady was there too.'

'Yes, I know about war, Maisie – remember, I was also in France last time around,' said Scott. 'Anyway, she might have felt safe enough – after all, she wasn't exactly close to the river, was she?'

'Neither were some of the bombs, though the Luftwaffe were definitely after the docks,' replied Maisie. She looked at MacFarlane. 'I was just wondering about the note, and her fear of oversleeping.'

'And the answer is we don't know – but I'm sure it's because you ask these questions that our American friend requested your presence on the investigation.' MacFarlane winked at Scott.

'Do that again, and I'll have Billy see you both out,' said Maisie. As soon as she'd spoken, she regretted her tone – it was brusque and smacked of arrogance. She could have ignored the conspiratorial joke between the two men. Lack of sleep and concern regarding the child she wanted so very much to adopt had taken their toll upon her. And now a young woman she had admired was dead.

'Nothing meant, lass. I'm sorry,' said MacFarlane. He cleared his throat and continued. 'You'll doubtless be speaking to Mrs Marsh, Maisie, and I am sure she will tell you more than she might have been willing to reveal to a man.'

Maisie nodded. 'Thank you, Robbie – and I'm sorry. Please continue.'

'Marsh heard the creaking of floorboards as Miss Saxon entered her rooms. She heard the tap running, then Saxon left the room, walked along the corridor, used the WC and returned to her rooms.' MacFarlane looked from Maisie to Mark Scott. 'I should add that sound can carry in some of these older houses. And to give you the lay of the land, the door from the upstairs passageway to Miss Saxon's rooms led into what she used as a sort of sitting-room-cum-study – there's a settee, an armchair, desk, bookshelves. Looks more like the lair of a university don than a reporter. She had a small typewriter, of the portable type you can carry in a case. Another door led through to the bedroom, and there's a sink in there – all-purpose, as she also used it to wash up her crockery. There was a small stove in the sitting room – gas, with a couple of rings and a tiny oven. You wouldn't get the Christmas turkey in there.'

'Thanksgiving,' said Scott. He looked up from his notebook. 'She's an American – more likely to have turkey at Thanksgiving. Guess you don't have Thanksgiving here.'

'No, that's just for the Colonies,' said MacFarlane. 'Our Thanksgiving is on July the fourth.'

'Aw, Mac – you think I've not heard that one before?' said Scott, landing a playful punch on MacFarlane's arm.

'Aye, you take it well, laddie,' said MacFarlane, though his smile evaporated as he continued. 'The landlady said she heard Miss Saxon's footsteps again, crossing the floor into the bedroom. Then Mrs Marsh went back to sleep herself. She rose at quarter to six, and though Miss Saxon liked to be up and about by six – in the past few days she'd been rushing out early to take photographs of the night's bombing, and talk to people on the streets – Marsh thought she'd give her another ten or fifteen minutes because she knew the lass was very tired, given the hours she'd been keeping since the bombings began. She went up just before quarter past six, knocked on the door. No answer. She knocked again three or four times before trying the master key and realising the door wasn't locked anyway. There was a kettle on the stove almost boiled dry, and Miss Saxon was lying on the floor – dressed in the clothing she'd worn the night before and decidedly deceased.'

'Therefore time of death might have been within only an hour before she was found,' said Maisie.

'Depends upon how much water there was in that kettle,' said MacFarlane. 'As I said, it was boiled dry and burnt – could have been put on the gas a couple of hours prior to Marsh going up there.'

'So, the police were called and very quickly – very quickly indeed – you were involved and Mr Scott was informed, plus you had time to telephone me at roughly half past eight.'

'That's correct, Maisie,' said MacFarlane. 'The nature of Miss Saxon's work, and her status as a foreign national indicated that I might be interested.'

Maisie nodded. 'I see – so Caldwell *was* at the scene after all. He's the only person I could imagine who would know it was important to alert you.'

'Correct again. And he has enough to be getting on with; he doesn't need complications of this sort. I was duty-bound to contact the embassy, and Mr Scott – who was already at work – assumed responsibility for the "problem" and various diplomatic steps were taken from there.'

'Nevertheless, that was all very fast,' said Maisie, looking at Scott.

'Like Mac said – I was already here, on an assignment in London.'

Maisie nodded, then consulted her notes. 'Do you have information on Miss Saxon's friends, associates, and so on?'

MacFarlane tapped the folder he'd passed to Maisie. 'What we know so far is in there – it's your starting point. Now then – anything else, before I leave you good people to demonstrate the very best in Anglo-American collaboration?'

'Yes, there is,' said Maisie. 'What about her father? And mother?'

'What do you want to know?' said Scott. 'They're about three thousand miles away. Her father's in DC – Georgetown – and her mother is currently in Boston.'

'Be that as it may, Mr Scott, but I understand people are still coming here from the United States, so I wondered if they had been informed and were on their way.' She shrugged. 'Let's just say I'm interested – very much so, because Miss Saxon indicated that her father was not terribly happy with her choice of profession.'

Scott leant back, balancing the chair on two legs, then came forward so there was an audible scrape as the wooden legs landed. He sighed. 'Here's how it is – Senator Clarence Saxon is not exactly a fan of Britain. He is averse to any suggestion that might have been put on the table by the president, to the effect that the United States might come to the aid of the old country. President Roosevelt leans towards some sort of financial assistance over and above that which has already been promised. Saxon is what you might call an "isolationist". He does not want any entanglements with the Nazis, and if that means leaving Britain to fight the good fight alone until the invasion – so be it. He is on the side of doing business with Herr Hitler if it comes to that. Regarding his family, he has two sons – a few years older than Catherine – who are up and coming, and will most likely follow him into politics. One's a government employee in Washington, DC, and the other is in banking, in New York. There's some hefty money in that family. Catherine was expected to toe the line, flutter her debutante eyelids and marry well after graduating Vassar, one of the Seven Sisters, so—'

'One of the what?' interrupted Maisie.

'I was wondering myself,' said MacFarlane.

'Women's colleges – top notch, as you might say. For the young ladies of the very well-off. And they're not for the academically unfit either – you need a brain to get in and to get on.'

'I would have assumed so – Catherine struck me as a very bright young woman,' said Maisie. 'Anyway – please go on.'

'Where was I?' said Scott, leaning back in his chair again. 'I was about to say that after she graduated Vassar, the senator wanted his daughter to enter into what you might call a dynastic marriage. But much to old Clarence's dismay, our very smart little Miss Muffet ditched the fiancé, scion of a powerful family of industrialists – and hoofed it off to Paris. Five years ago. And that was the very visible start of Catherine Saxon doing exactly what she wanted. Next thing you know our debutante is doing a bang-up job of reporting the news from Paris, then Spain. She saw what was happening there, so she went all out on Hitler and the Nazis. And then it was off to Berlin, then back to France. She got out of there just in time, soon after the invasion. And I think you might know the rest.'

'So to go back to my earlier question – have her parents received word of her death?' asked Maisie.

'Yes, they were informed by the president this morning,' replied Scott.

'Pretty high up bearer of bad news, don't you think?' said Maisie, continuing without waiting for a response. 'Will they come here?'

'And risk the senator getting slaughtered by a U-boat or the Luftwaffe? I doubt it. We understand that Clarence Saxon Junior – eldest son – might try to fly from New York via Canada to Lisbon, and into Croydon from there. The embassy might not advise it, given what's been going on in the air over Britain. And the senator says it's not necessary – already there's talk of a quiet cremation here in London, followed by a private memorial service in DC at a later date – when the dust has settled on her murder.'

Maisie nodded. 'I see.'

Scott shrugged. 'The motivations of a grieving family aren't my business, but finding the man who murdered an American citizen is. So, Maisie – when do we start? Ready to go tomorrow morning? It'll give you a chance to read through the files.'

She looked at her watch and turned her attention to MacFarlane. 'I have to be at the ambulance station no later than half past four today, which means I've got about an hour and a half – may I see Catherine's body?'

'Catherine?' interjected Scott. 'You two became "pally" – see, I'm picking up the language – kinda fast.'

'Not really, Mr Scott – but I thought she was brave, and I thought she conducted herself with a certain grace, considering the job she had to do, and in the midst of what we encountered last night.' She paused. 'If I call her "Catherine" I'll be reminded that she was a living, breathing, feeling human being, and not simply the headstrong daughter of an important man on the other side of the Atlantic who even as we speak might change his mind and choose to make political hay from her death, when really it sounds as if she disappointed him by following her own path and not his. And there's another reason – and the most important, to me – I thought she had heart, that she was compassionate, and those qualities were demonstrated in her broadcast. That's why I want to stand at her side and show my respect.'

After dropping MacFarlane at his Whitehall office, his driver took Maisie and Mark Scott to the mortuary where Catherine Saxon's body was being held until released by the pathologist. As soon as the vehicle moved off into traffic, Scott turned to Maisie.

'I'm going to tell you right now, that the reason I asked for you on this case is because I am not an expert when it comes to murder. I know how to conduct an investigation, but I'd be the first to admit that murder isn't exactly what I excel at.'

'I thought so,' said Maisie. She glanced out of the window, then back at Scott. 'But thank you for putting my name forward, though the timing's a bit awkward.'

They were silent for a few moments as the driver manoeuvred past a series of bombed buildings surrounded by barbed wire.

'So, what's all this I hear from Mac about you and a kid?'

Maisie sighed, rubbing the top of one hand with the palm of the other. 'It's all very delicate at the moment. An evacuee – Anna – was billeted at my house in Kent, and it transpired that she was not officially at the school being sent to the village, but instead she was put onto the evacuee train by her ailing grandmother – her only relative. Anna wasn't even five years of age at the time. After a good deal of searching, we found the grandmother gravely ill in hospital. In order to have some control over Anna's future – I didn't want her to end up in an orphanage – the grandmother signed papers for me to become her guardian, although my promise was to find her a family home.'

'Sounds more like you were trying to place an unwanted puppy!'

Maisie gave a half-laugh. 'Mark, any other time I might be offended by that comment, but I confess, I sometimes think dogs are treated better than children. Perhaps not any more though, because so many animals were put down when people were told to expect the invasion and bombings. Anyway, one thing led to another, and I decided to adopt her. We have a hearing soon with a panel of officials. There will be someone from the Ministry of Health and others from the local council, plus a magistrate. It'll be held here in London.'

'Jeez, all that officialdom. How good are your chances? Pretty good, I would have thought – you've got connections, if I'm not mistaken.'

'I have some good references, yes. But I must be careful not to do anything that might draw attention to my work.'

'And will you still work, if you officially become her mother?'

'I'll work, but just do things differently – spend more time in Kent, which I have been doing anyway. The plan was for my father and stepmother to stay at my house from Monday morning until Thursday evening each week, though since the summer they've been there all the time. Believe it or not, that timetable was not due to my work, but the roster for my volunteer position with the Auxiliary Ambulance Service. Strangely, the adoption authorities like the volunteer aspect, despite the fact that it's the most dangerous thing I do. After all, everyone in Britain has been instructed to do their bit.'

The motor car slowed.

'Looks like we're here,' said Scott.

The driver pulled over to the kerb. Scott stepped onto the pavement and held out a hand to Maisie. He looked at the sign indicating the mortuary.

'You're probably better at this than me,' said Scott.

'You can always wait here, or just outside the laboratory – or we can speak to the pathologist in his office.'

Scott opened the door, and they walked together towards an office with a window above which a sign instructed callers to 'Ring Bell'. Maisie pressed the brass button on the wall where indicated. The glass window was pushed aside, and a young woman asked Maisie to state her business. Maisie asked to see the duty pathologist, who she said was expecting her.

'Yes, of course, Miss Dobbs. I have your name here,' said the woman, lifting a telephone receiver. 'Dr Ferguson will be with you shortly.'

A portly man wearing a white laboratory coat pushed his way through double doors into the waiting area. He was an inch shorter than Maisie, with thinning grey hair swept away from his face in strands. Grey bags under the eyes suggested a man who had not slept well in days.

'Miss Dobbs. I'm Dr Ferguson. MacFarlane said to give you all the help I could. I'll be square with you – I wasn't happy because I thought I'd have to scrape a silly woman off the floor; however, when he told me you'd been Maurice Blanche's assistant, I changed my mind.' He looked at Scott. 'Not sure about him though. Green around the gills.'

'I beg your pardon – I should have introduced you. This is my colleague, Mr Mark Scott,' said Maisie.

'And I'm happy to stay right here, Dr Ferguson,' said Scott, shaking hands with the pathologist. 'I've seen my fair share of dead bodies, in France, back in '17, but I just don't like to see them after you good doctors have been at them with a scalpel. Can we ask you a few questions first, before Miss Dobbs goes in?'

'Ah, an American.' Ferguson looked as if he was about to make a comment, but thought better of it. 'Of course – please go ahead.'

'Do you have an indication of the weapon used to take Miss Saxon's life?' asked Maisie.

'Something very sharp, and very fine. Not your average carving knife, for example. A stiletto, perhaps, though only one side was sharpened. And it didn't have a serrated edge – it was slick, and the murderer cut her throat with a right-to-left motion. It seems to have been done with speed and with a good deal of power.'

'So the man was right in front of her,' said Scott.

'That would be my first thought, but it could have been done very fast by someone standing behind her – then of course he would be right-handed, given the weapon's point of entry. If he were in front of her, I would imagine he would have killed her thus.' Ferguson stood back, took a pencil from his pocket and held it out as if he were grasping a knife. He then made a lateral movement from right to left.

'Interesting,' said Maisie. 'You've used your left hand – are you usually left-handed?'

'No, though I lean towards a conclusion that whoever killed Miss Saxon did so standing in front of her and was left-handed. Take into account that it's entirely possible I'm wrong in my supposition.'

'Time of death?' asked Scott.

'Hard to say, but I would put it at between two and four in the morning, given the level of rigor mortis when I received the body into the mortuary. I was told she took precedence, and I must admit it was with a sigh of relief that I started work.' Ferguson shook his head and looked down, pressing a hand against his forehead, and sweeping back his sparse hair. 'They're going to have to find other ways of dealing with the dead from these bombings. I can't keep having unidentifiable remains brought in here to me when it's quite clear what killed a human being – every morgue in London must be full by now. And the tragedy is, when I say "remains", I really do mean "remains".'

Maisie drew a deep breath. 'Shall we go in, Dr Ferguson? I must report for duty at half past four.'

'Report for duty?' said Ferguson.

'Yes – I drive an ambulance with another woman.' She turned to

Scott. 'Perhaps you'd like to remain here in the waiting room – I shan't be long.'

'Happy to,' said Scott, turning to sit down on a wooden bench.

Ferguson drew back a white sheet covering the body of Catherine Saxon, folding the fabric just above the dead woman's breasts, as if he were about to tuck a child into bed. Maisie remembered how Maurice would demonstrate the same respect for the dead, handling a body as if the ability to feel pain and discomfort were still present. She recalled him saying once, 'I do my job as if the soul were looking on.'

'May I have a moment to myself?' asked Maisie.

'I'll just be over there,' replied Ferguson, pointing to a desk at waist height upon which a stack of papers was placed alongside a series of bottles and jars.

Once alone, Maisie swept a stray tendril of hair away from Saxon's forehead and began to study every aspect of her face and head, down to the wound that had ended her life. The lightly freckled facial skin was now tinged with a pale bluish-grey sheen, and she could see that Saxon's hair was more of a sun-streaked coppery brown, rather than blonde. She looked behind her ears, and at bruising above and below the place where her flesh had been torn apart. Lifting the sheet, she drew it back just a few inches at a time to focus her attention as she inspected the body. She stopped to study the gentle rise of her belly, and then her legs. Maisie assumed the bruising to Saxon's calves was a result of clambering over rubble and bomb sites. She paid special attention to the ankles, and then to the spaces between each toe. And after she had reached the little toe, she drew the sheet up slowly, taking account of those places that had caught her attention, before she folded the sheet as Ferguson had done before her. She reached under the sheet and took Catherine Saxon's hand.

'Thank you,' she whispered. 'Thank you for speaking the truth about what you saw, as far as you could. Thank you for being brave in all those places where you travelled to tell stories of the people. You will not be forgotten, Catherine. And I will find out who took your life. Bless you, and may you know peace.' Maisie closed her eyes, and remained still for a moment, before resting the dead woman's hand alongside her body, and pulling the sheet over her head. She walked across the room to Ferguson's desk.

'Any questions?' asked the pathologist.

'Yes, I do have a couple.' She paused, considering how to couch her observations. 'First, I wonder if the assailant might have attempted to strangle Miss Saxon before resorting to a weapon – I know you would expect to see evidence of ruptured blood vessels in line with a swipe with a knife, but just below the ears there seems to be evidence of a contusion due to greater pressure, and I wondered about that. Secondly – and this is a delicate point – it appears to me that Miss Saxon might have been delivered of a child in recent years. Perhaps two or three years ago. There were some faint stretch marks, though she might have experienced a loss of weight – perhaps whilst she was in Spain, reporting on the war. I believe she was there about the same time as me – 1937 or thereabouts. And finally, she has a very small tattoo, barely visible between the big and first toes on her left foot. I had trouble discerning the letters, but I think they form the initials "JT". Would you have a look and tell me what you think?'

Ferguson removed his spectacles and pressed into the corners of his eyes with the thumb and forefinger of his right hand. 'Good Lord, I can't think how I missed a tattoo – or anything else.'

'I could be wrong, Dr Ferguson. Like you, I am not exactly on top form due to lack of sleep, and . . . well, you know. But if you've a moment—'

Ten minutes later, Maisie met Scott outside. He was leaning against the building, smoking a cigarette and talking to the driver, who returned to his seat in the motor car when he saw Maisie.

'I discovered I don't really like the smell in there. It oozes out of that place where they do the . . . well, where they do whatever they do,' said Scott. 'But the smell out here isn't exactly fresh – smoke and dust in the air, and I don't want to think what else I might be breathing in. Anyway, how'd it go?'

'I have some more information. Catherine Saxon's murderer likely tried to strangle her first – I noticed some other bruises I thought were suspicious, and Ferguson agreed. She also had a small tattoo, so someone with the initials JT might be of interest.'

'Anything else?' asked Scott.

Maisie nodded. 'Yes. She gave birth, probably around three years ago.'

Scott whistled as he opened the door for Maisie to climb into the back of the vehicle. 'Well, that puts an interesting slant on things.'

'It does,' said Maisie, leaning forward and tapping the driver on the shoulder. 'I must get to the ambulance station now, and I'm running late. I believe Mr MacFarlane gave you the address.'

'Right you are, miss. I'll get you there.'

The driver sounded the vehicle's warning bell and sped off. Traffic parted for them to pass at speed.

'I was just thinking, while you were in there speaking to the dead,' said Scott.

'And what were you thinking?' asked Maisie.

'I was thinking that, really, this here adoption panel has only one important question to ask, and it's the most important question you have to answer.'

'And what's that?' asked Maisie.

'Do you love this child?'

Maisie looked out of the window.

'Well?' asked Scott.

'Well what?'

'That's the important question. Do you love her?'

Maisie held Mark Scott's gaze. 'I adore her, Mark. I love her as if she were my own. And I would give my life for her.'

For a moment she thought she had seen tears well in Scott's eyes, but he turned away. 'That's all you need to say, Maisie. That's all you'll ever need.'

'I don't know if you realise this, but you've never really talked about anyone you meet during the course of your work.' Priscilla flicked ash out of the passenger window as Maisie drove the ambulance towards the docks, where they would be ready to help any wounded from the air attack when it came – they had ceased to consider the possibility of *if* it came. 'So, you've been tagged to work with this American.'

'I mentioned it because you met Catherine Saxon last night.' Maisie sighed, turned the steering wheel to the left, and drove the ambulance along a narrow street. 'I cannot believe she's dead.'

'You of all people should be used to death,' said Priscilla. 'And we're all pretty used to it by now. I am only shocked that someone feels inclined to murder another person, when we're onto our fourth night facing nothing short of carnage, and we had months of the

Luftwaffe bombing airfield targets and everything from market towns to small villages to get us ready for Hitler's blitzes.' She threw the cigarette stub out of the window. 'Well, are you going to tell me about this Mark Scott?'

'I'm quite sure I've told you everything – I met him in Munich. He's with the American embassy – well, the Department of Justice, Bureau of Investigation. I was quite surprised to see him in London. He happened to be here, and so Catherine Saxon's death landed on his desk, and he asked to work with me.'

'For old times' sake? You probably impressed him.'

'I don't know why,' said Maisie. 'He was the one who saved my life, not the other way around.'

'So, what's he like? Tall, handsome, matinee idol type?'

'I couldn't say – I wasn't really looking at him from that perspective,' replied Maisie, aware that Priscilla was staring at her.

'Well, well, well. You weren't looking at him from that *perspective*,' said Priscilla. 'Personally, I think it's about time you looked at someone from that perspective.'

'No, really – the most I've done is consider what it's going to be like working with him. I think it'll be all right, though he has a bit of a cheeky side to him,' said Maisie. 'He can be funny, but not always.'

'Given that you owe your life to him, you should invite him to your flat – discuss the case, you know, lay down the plan of attack.'

'I'll stick to the office, Priscilla. He's an American agent, and I'm not going to enter into a social milieu with him.'

'Hmmm. A *social milieu* eh?' Priscilla was silent for a moment, then began again. 'Are you all prepared for your panel?'

Maisie nodded, changing gear as she slowed the ambulance. 'You ask me that every day. I've gone over every possible question with Mr

Klein, and Dad and Brenda have been gently talking to Anna about it – I cannot believe it's been stipulated that she should be present in case they want to level questions in her direction.'

At that moment a siren began to wail, starting low and then winding up to an ear-splitting crescendo.

'Here they come, the bastards,' said Priscilla, reaching down to the floor for two tin helmets. 'Put this on, and let's get to the depot for instructions. We'll be back out here soon anyway.'

Maisie allowed Priscilla to fasten her helmet's chin strap. 'One thing Mark Scott told me – he said the most important thing the panel could ask is if I loved Anna.'

'Those stuffed shirts will never ask that sort of question, Maisie, though it tells you something about Mark Scott, doesn't it?'

'What's that?'

'He has a soft side.'

'Or he wants me to think he has,' said Maisie, looking up at the sky. 'Priscilla—'

'If you were going to ask about Tom – don't. He telephoned home this afternoon. He's on ops – probably right now, in fact. The "all-clear" can't come soon enough. But then it never can, can it?'

CHAPTER THREE

I know something about these Londoners. They know that they're out on their own . . . These black-faced men with bloodshot eyes who were fighting fires and the girls who cradled the steering wheel of a heavy ambulance in their arms, the policeman who stands guard over that unexploded bomb down at St Paul's tonight . . . they're busy, just doing a job of work, and they know that it all depends on them.

EDWARD R. MURROW, BROADCASTING FROM LONDON,

12TH SEPTEMBER 1940

Once again a late night left Maisie tired and tardy, though her ten o'clock arrival at Fitzroy Square was not unexpected.

'Good morning, Miss Dobbs,' said Sandra as Maisie entered the office. 'You look all in – it was a nasty night again. Let me make tea – Billy's been here, but had to go out again to visit a new customer.'

'Strong coffee this morning, Sandra,' said Maisie. 'It seems to help get me going more efficiently than my usual cuppa. Anything you can tell me about the new enquiry?'

'Older couple in Primrose Hill. Apparently they believe someone is going into their home while they're out, but the police think they're imagining it, that it's "blitz nerves". Their names are Mr and Mrs Horne and they sent a message on a postcard to us yesterday afternoon – came with the early delivery this morning. Billy's gone out to see them, to find out what's going on.' Sandra held up the morning's mail. 'I'm amazed the post office is managing to keep up, but they're getting the job done.'

'Indeed, they are,' said Maisie, leafing through a sheaf of papers on her desk. 'Right, I just have to read through some information before I do anything else today – I should really have done it before now – then let's have a chat about your work today. I was hoping to get the twenty past four train down to Tonbridge, so I can be at Chelstone for supper. In any case, I'll try to meet Mrs Partridge as usual so we can make the journey together.'

'I bet Anna's excited – she must love Thursdays, when you go back down there.'

'She does indeed love Thursdays, but now the schools are back after the summer, getting her into her uniform and off to school on a Friday morning is tricky. We had tears last week because she wanted to stay at home with me and Emma, who also hates her going to school – that dog waits at the gate for her to come home.'

'At least the child knows she's loved,' said Sandra. 'I'll just pop in to get the bag of coffee from your desk. Oh, and I almost forgot – an American telephoned. Mr Mark Scott. He said he'd meet you at the Welbeck Street address at one. He said you'd probably be finished speaking to the landlady by then. And he'll have spoken to a – just a minute.' She reached for her notebook. 'Yes, he said he will be talking to a Mr Murrow this morning.' Sandra looked up at Maisie. 'Is that the same Mr Murrow who—'

'Yes, it is. And Sandra – I'd love that coffee,' said Maisie, glancing at the clock. 'I must be on my way in half an hour.'

'Oh, and there's another thing to consider,' said Sandra. 'Charing Cross Station was bombed last night, and Victoria's had some damage too, so you should probably think about getting the coach.'

Welbeck Street brought back bittersweet memories. When Maisie was first apprenticed to Dr Maurice Blanche almost twenty years earlier, his office was situated farther along the street, on the floor below his private rooms in a Georgian building typical of the area. It was only later, following his death, that she learnt the property was in fact part of his estate and was therefore now hers. She had not visited the house since, but had given instructions for it to be leased until such a time as she saw fit to sell. In truth, when told the extent of her legacy, she had been in a state of some shock, and had not wanted to return to the area. Now, after all these years, she was coming back to the place where she had learnt her craft at the feet of a master, for Blanche was not only a formidable investigator, but a highly regarded doctor of legal medicine – the science of forensic enquiry. As she made her way along Welbeck Street to the house where Catherine Saxon had died, she remembered her first day at work with Blanche, her nerves and her excitement at being chosen to be his assistant.

'Let's hope I can demonstrate that I know a little more now than I knew then,' she muttered to herself as she arrived at the house. She lifted the door knocker, formed of a brass ring woven through the nose of a lion, to signal her arrival.

There was no answer, so she stepped back, and at that moment saw the closed curtains at the downstairs window move back an inch or so. There was another pause, and she was about to lift the brass ring again when the door opened.

'I'm terribly sorry, my dear – I was just having a quick forty winks, and didn't hear you knock.'

Maisie smiled at the woman, who was about seventy years of age, not tall – she was a good five inches shorter than Maisie – and clothed in a floral day dress fashionable some ten years earlier. She wore a pale blue cardigan unbuttoned, and a pair of slippers on her feet. Her stockings had gathered a little around her ankles.

'I think we could all do with a nap today – it was a terrible night. Are you Mrs Marsh?'

'Yes, that's me. What can I do for you, dear?'

'My name is Maisie Dobbs, and I'm here to ask you a few questions about Miss Catherine Saxon. Would you be so kind as to spare me a few minutes?'

The woman stepped back, and for a second it seemed she might close the door. 'Are you with the police?'

'I'm here at the request of the police department dealing with the official enquiry into Miss Saxon's death. The American embassy is also involved in the investigation.' Maisie paused, studying the look on Marsh's face. The woman was frightened. 'And I knew Catherine,' she added, as she reached into her jacket pocket and took out a calling card, which she gave to the landlady.

'You knew her.' It was not a question, but a statement. 'Then you'd better come in.'

The design of the house mirrored that of so many in London. Built in Georgian or Victorian times, and sometimes a blend of both as later additions to the property followed, there was a passageway leading from the front door, with rooms to one side – first the parlour, then the dining room, followed by a kitchen and scullery. In some houses the kitchen areas were downstairs at a lower level, which could also be accessed from outside, so servants – in the days before many such houses had been converted to flats – could go straight to the kitchen without entering the domain of their betters. Servants who lived in would share accommodation at the very top of the house, often with only a small window from which rooftops and a postage stamp square of sky were visible.

Mrs Marsh opened the first door on the right and led Maisie into her parlour. 'The room through those doors was once the dining room, when this was a whole house, but now it's my bedroom. I've got a kitchen and scullery past that, and I can go into the garden, though the tenant downstairs uses it too. She works in an office, so she likes to come home and sit out there. Catherine would join her sometimes – she'd go out and they would chat, and if they saw me they'd ask me to come out and take a seat, never mind that they were girls and I'm getting on now. "Come on out, Mrs Marsh," Catherine would say. "Take a load off and tell us tales of Albion's yore!"'

'It sounds as if you get on very well with the tenants here – especially Miss Saxon.'

'She sort of brought people out of their shells. Made it seem more like a girls' club than a house with rooms rented out.'

Maisie nodded. 'Who owns the property?'

'I told the first policeman all that,' said Marsh.

'I know, and I have his notes. But sometimes when someone else asks the same question, a person remembers something new, or it refreshes their memory. So some of the questions will be the same – as will some of your answers.'

'It's owned by a couple. They inherited it – a lot of the property along here is inherited. But not everyone's that well-heeled. These houses have gone through good times and bad over the decades. And there are what they call fixed rents too – due to old land laws going back centuries, when the Dukes of Portland built this whole area. But even over in Mayfair, you can get a flat cheap if you're lucky – they usually get passed on by word of mouth. It's like a lot of things, it's down to who you know. Anyway, Mr and Mrs Tucker own the house – not the land, but the leasehold. They live down in Sussex, just outside Haywards Heath.'

'Mr and Mrs Tucker. And do they come here to inspect the property?'

'Not very often. In fact, only about once a year, even though Mr Tucker comes up to the City for his business, and of course he came over yesterday to talk to me, and he's spoken to the police, being as it's his property. He's in banking. Well, it's something to do with money – I've known Mr Tucker for many a year, and I'm still not sure what he does. I look after everything to do with the flat, and there's an accountant who comes once a month to collect the rent monies, which the tenants pay directly to me – and I'm the one who has to keep knocking on the door if they're late. If there's a water leak or something like that, I make sure it's mended.'

'I see. I once worked on this street, and I believe the man who owned the property had a similar arrangement with tenants after he retired and went to live in Kent.' Maisie scribbled a note on one of the index cards she had taken from her shoulder bag. 'Tell me more about the residents. You have the young woman downstairs, who works in an office – what's her name, and do you know where she works?'

'That's Miss Isabel Chalmers. She's a secretary, and she works somewhere in Whitehall. Not really sure where, and she doesn't say much about her work. Whenever I've asked her – by way of making conversation – she just says, "Oh, Mrs Marsh – I've had work all day, I don't want to talk about it now!" She's a nice girl – about the same age as Miss Saxon, or perhaps a year or two younger. She's got a bed-sitting room and a WC down there. And, of course, you know Miss Saxon lived above me. She did her best to keep quiet, so I didn't hear her clomping around – took her shoes off as soon as she was in, that sort of thing. But these old houses, you know what they're like – if I sneezed, I'd hear Miss Chalmers say "Bless you."'

'Tell me about the other lodgers.'

'Above Miss Saxon is Mrs Lockwood. She's older – a widow from the last war. She was only young when her husband died. They'd got married and a couple of weeks later, he went over there – she was eighteen and he was twenty. It wasn't long before the Armistice that she received the telegram. Poor girl.'

'So she's forty-three, forty-four, something of that order.'

'Yes, that's about right. Apparently, after the war she went to night school, learnt to use a typewriter and also do bookkeeping, and now she works for one of the big shops – Derry & Toms, I think. Or is it Debenham & Freebody?' She shook her head. 'Anyway, she works in the offices, and I'm sure it's Derry & Toms. She's done well for herself, though she never married again – didn't have much chance, I suppose.' She looked at Maisie and put a hand to her mouth. 'Oh dear, I hope I haven't—'

'Not at all. Please go on.'

'I'm always putting my foot in it. Anyway, I'll be quick – on the third floor, the one above Mrs Lockwood's rooms, there's Miss Polly Harcourt. She's on the stage. West End. She says she wants to go to America, to Hollywood. Miss Saxon laughed at that. Not that she didn't think Miss Harcourt could act – she went to one of her performances, and said she was good – but she told her that Hollywood was the abyss of broken dreams, that it's full of people who end up working dead-end jobs just to make it from one week to the next. Mind you, as Miss Harcourt said, at least no one is bombing the place and the weather's nice all the time.'

'Yes, I believe it is,' said Maisie. 'And on the next floor?'

'Couple of students sharing the rooms. Elizabeth Drake and Helena Richardson. I'm not sure how long they'll stay – one has already taken some tests to join the Wrens, and seeing as they go everywhere together, I think the other one will too.'

'I know something about the geography of these houses, and it would appear that "rooms" is rather an understatement – each of the women has quite a large flat at her disposal, it would seem.'

'But they've not got kitchens, only small stoves at most, and I don't put out a dinner for the residents – though once a month I'll make a stew and get all the girls together for supper, and I know some of the tenants will make a bite to eat to share with the others, though they are all working very hard – and Miss Saxon was always at her job, even when she wasn't. She said a reporter is never at rest, that there's always a story, even in the most ordinary conversation.' She shook her head again, taking a handkerchief from her pocket which she pressed against her eyes. 'Now she is the story – though I was surprised not to see anything much about it in the papers.'

Maisie smiled and held out a hand towards the door. 'May I see Catherine's room now, Mrs Marsh?'

Marsh showed Maisie to the room, leading the way up a creaking staircase before unlocking the door – upon which an official police sign indicated that there should be 'No unofficial access' – and standing aside for Maisie to enter. As she stepped into the room, Maisie felt the full force of Catherine Saxon's personality, as if she had only just left, having first sprayed her neck and wrists with an atomiser. But there was no fragrance in the room, only a certain essence to which Maisie was sensitive.

'I wonder if I might have some time alone here, Mrs Marsh – I shan't be long.'

'Yes, of course, Miss Dobbs – I'll be in my rooms when you've finished.' She held out a key. 'If you wouldn't mind locking up when you leave. Save me walking up the stairs.'

Maisie took the key. 'I'll be down soon.' She closed the door behind her and leant back against it. 'Right then, Catherine – what's been going on?'

She remained in that position, not moving for two full minutes. She had closed her eyes and imagined Catherine Saxon in the room, sitting at her desk, going through her notes and crafting her report, whether that work was for a newspaper, a journal or something she would broadcast as one of 'Murrow's Boys'. At once the room, which had felt chill when she entered, seemed to have become warmer. Maisie moved towards the desk.

If someone had looked through the files, notebooks and papers on the desk, they had taken care when replacing them. Maisie sat at the desk, pulled a notebook towards her and began to leaf through the

53

pages. Each series of notes was dated, so she leafed to 10th September.

Arrival at ambulance station, 5 p.m. Crews check ambulance, supplies, and receive briefing before waiting for the air raid warning and their orders. Tonight there will be searchlights and anti-aircraft fire – not on previous three nights.

There was a gap, and a slash along the page.

Joining Miss Dobbs and Mrs Partridge, who take over from previous crew at 17.30 hrs (must get used to 24-hour clock). Told on the QT . . . Dobbs the widow of an aristocrat. Doesn't use title. (Part of story?). Mrs P – very outgoing, ordering people around. Elegant, even in boiler suit and tin hat. Son in RAF – has lost lot of pals; based in Kent – most dangerous place!

Another slash.

D & P are older than some of the girls, and both served in last war. Told they are the best. Dobbs quieter – personal note – she seems the observant sort. Was in Spain in '37. Find out why.

The notes went on to describe the air raid siren, and the subsequent rush to Lambeth, and rescuing the children. But what had touched Catherine Saxon more than anything, it would seem, was the grandmother plunging her bare hands into burning hot rubble and masonry as she called for her daughters, who had been buried by the blast. Maisie closed her eyes. She had learnt only this morning that one of the children had died. It was when she opened her eyes that she saw a personal note in brackets.

(Can imagine it if it were me under there – the senator pulling mother off the bricks, saying, 'Oh come on, Amelia, it's only Catherine – there's a cocktail party to go to.')

And Maisie wondered how many times each day Catherine Saxon's thoughts had lingered upon her parents, and the reaction of her father, especially, to her work. She slipped the notebook into her bag.

The drawers held various items one might have expected in the rooms of a reporter – blank notebooks, sharpened pencils, erasers, two fountain pens. She closed the drawer, then moved to the wardrobe. Saxon's clothing suggested a woman who had a garment for every occasion – though it was not an extensive collection. A drawer held several clean blouses, and two pairs of trousers of the type she had worn to accompany the ambulance crew. Several pairs of socks were tucked into a corner, and three brand-new pairs of stockings, unwrapped. There was underwear and two light cardigans, plus one Aran pullover, of the type that a fisherman would wear. Shoes were lined up underneath the hanging clothes; Maisie had to push back a dress to see what Catherine Saxon wore on her feet. There was a pair of heeled shoes of the type that might be worn to a formal event, along with leather walking shoes and a pair of black ballet slippers, plus another pair of plain brown lace-up shoes. The boots that she had worn on the night she died had been cast off alongside the wardrobe – one on its side, as if it had keeled over from the work of scrambling across burning bricks and mortar.

Saxon owned a pair of woollen trousers with a matching jacket and skirt – Maisie suspected the coordinating trio had been tailored to order. A long black dress indicated Saxon liked to have something glamorous in case the occasion arose, and there was a summer dress and two summer skirts. Three silk blouses of the same design but in different pastel colours were hanging in the wardrobe. Maisie thought that at a push, most of the clothing could be squeezed into the suitcase which had been placed above the wardrobe, though she suspected Saxon would think nothing of leaving pieces behind if they did not fit in the case. She thought her books would come first if she had to move on; there was quite a collection shelved on a bookcase on the other side of the desk, next to the window.

Maisie had done her best to ignore the livid red stain on the almost threadbare carpet, but now she stopped to regard it in the way that one might linger to appreciate a work of art one had looked forward to seeing for many a year. She knelt down and touched the stain, then came to her feet and imagined how the attack might have happened. She walked to the window in front of the desk – Saxon was able to look out at the street, perhaps to gaze in search of inspiration if words failed her at any point. Maisie moved the desk so she could view the street, and then opened the window. It was at this point she realised the handle securing the window didn't work very well – the window was held closed by the pressure of one frame against the other, and she thought that to open the window, Saxon would have had to thump the frame to get it open. To close it she would have had to pull hard, though she was never able to secure it properly.

The blackout curtains would have been drawn when Saxon arrived home – though Maisie would check that point with Mrs Marsh. She pushed against the window until it opened, and then leaning against the railing that formed a brace to stop someone falling – there was no balcony as such – she stared down at the street and at the railings below, their fierce spear-like points aiming upward. She thought the railings would soon be requisitioned, as had so many in the quest to build a stockpile of metal for military use.

Maisie turned back into the room, but instead of stepping forward, she stood by the window. The blackout curtain brushed against her arm as she looked towards the place where Catherine Saxon was killed. And she suspected that Catherine Saxon might well have been attacked from behind, though she could have turned at the last minute? 'No,' she spoke aloud. 'You weren't fast enough. But why the bruises? When did someone put their hands to your throat?'

And at that point she felt a breeze from the space between the window and the frame as it whistled into the room, lifting papers on the desk. She nodded. 'I know – I was right – you just weren't fast enough.'

She stepped across to the corner on the other side of the door, where a small stove sat atop a cupboard with a curtain in front. She inspected the kettle, which remained on the cold gas ring – it was scorched, with burnt limescale rattling around inside. Behind the curtains were some Jacobs cream crackers, a small earthenware pot with butter, and a solitary egg. A half-empty jar of marmalade stood next to a tin marked 'Coffee' and another labelled 'Sugar'. Maisie lifted the latter – it was about half full. She closed the curtain.

Moving into the bedroom, she noticed a bowl under the sink, and pulled it out to reveal a pair of cups, saucers and plates inside. Along with a collection of cutlery, they had been washed and dried. On the shelf above, a pot of cold cream, lipstick and rouge seemed to lie in wait for a fresh face to colour. A hairbrush was balanced on top of the cold cream next to a mirror marked by age, with brown spots that seemed to reflect the skin of an older woman. She thought it interesting, then, that a mirror could age in the same way as the person who checked her hair and skin every morning. Perhaps it was best – the wearying reflection becomes disguised by the cloudy, ageing glass. She smiled and looked away, across to the simple counterpane on the double bed, with an eiderdown folded at the foot. A cardigan and blouse had been thrown over the back of the only chair. A pair of black shoes had been pushed underneath. A bedside table held several books and another notebook and a pencil.

She skimmed pages of a notebook devoid of any pencilled thoughts. But there might once have been something – she ran her finger down alongside the stitching, and felt the jagged papery teeth of pages torn away. She slipped the notebook in her bag, and took up the nearest book. *101 Things To Do In Wartime*. It was brand new, and had not been opened, though there was a small sheet of paper sticking out.

Possible article for women's page? Wire Jane at McCalls, or Sue at GH. British grit, etc., etc. Should I pass on to Jenny?

'British grit?' Maisie laughed. 'Yes, Catherine, the grit you get in your teeth after you've ground them down to nothing wondering when a bomb's going to land on you!' And she wondered who 'Jenny' might be.

She was about to return the book to its place, when she stopped and leafed through a few pages, then placed it in her bag with the other items she had taken. Before leaving the bedroom, she felt under the pillows, pressed down on the mattress and lifted it to check underneath. And she knelt down to look under the bed. But it was as she turned around that she noticed two photographs pinned to the wall. Not framed, or properly positioned, but pinned – it was as if Catherine had wanted the images in her room, but did not want to accord them respect. Love, but not regard or admiration. Only love, perhaps, because no more had been earned. She leant closer. The photographs had been taken a good number of years earlier – perhaps when Catherine Saxon was no more than, say, eleven or twelve. Even then there was a strength to be seen in her stance, and a resolve in her eyes. In one photograph she was standing between a man and a woman, and on either side of the trio, two young men were smiling at the camera. Catherine was offering only a half-smile, as if having this photograph taken was a game she would not play. The woman smiled – and Maisie could see where the girl who became the fearless reporter had garnered her strength of character, for there was something in the way the woman's gaze met the lens that suggested she too was playing a game. The father's eyes were disguised by a pair of dark glasses, but there was a smile – though it was directed at the young man next to him, who was of similar height, and wore identical glasses. It was as if he were a more slender version of the older man, whose arm was around his shoulders, and he stood with arms crossed in a way that Maisie thought suggested confidence, as if he were the prince who would succeed the king.

Maisie cautioned herself. Time and again in her work she had embraced the challenge of interpreting a person's motivations based upon a smile, a lifting of the chin, a brushing back of a stray hair, or that glance away from the camera at the crucial second the scene is captured. Now she must be careful – it was folly to try such a translation when she'd already learnt that all was not well between father and daughter, and possibly between husband and wife. And the man was, after all, a person of some importance. Or considered himself so.

The second photograph was more interesting. It was a portrait of Mrs Amelia Saxon as a younger woman. It might have been a photograph taken at her engagement, because it was clear there was once another person in the shot – a man – but he had been neatly snipped out of the photograph, so all that remained was an elbow.

Having taken one more walk around the rooms, Maisie was about to leave when she did two things. First, having noticed that all Catherine Saxon's pencils had been whittled to a point with a very sharp blade, she wondered where the reporter had kept her penknife, or whatever tool she'd used for the task. She found nothing – no blade, no knife. Second, she chose the heaviest tome from the bookcase, walked to the centre of the room and dropped it on the floor. She picked up the book and put it back on the shelf. Then she made her way downstairs after locking the door.

'Hello! Mrs Marsh!' She knocked on the parlour door. There was no answer, so she called out again and knocked once more. It took one more call before Mrs Marsh opened the door.

'I am so sorry – I dropped right off again!'

'Forgive me for waking you – you wanted me to pop in with the keys before I went on my way.'

'Will you be coming back, Miss Dobbs?'

'Yes, I'm sure you'll see me again, as I want to talk to the other ladies in the house, though I will get in touch with them separately. And I will be giving instructions for nothing to be disturbed in Miss Saxon's rooms. They must be left as they are for the time being – though there's one egg left on the shelf under the stove, plus some tea, coffee and sugar. There's some marmalade too. No point in letting anything go to waste.'

'Right you are,' said Mrs Marsh. 'And I've got something for you.' She stepped back into the room and took a sheet of paper from the table. 'I wrote down the names of the lodgers, and – as far as I know – where they work. And I've added the hours they usually keep – just in case you need it. Mind you, nothing's been "usual" for days now, what with the air raids.'

'Thank you all the same, Mrs Marsh. I'm grateful to you.'

'I'll see you out, then.'

'Oh, just one more thing – did you hear anything, while I was upstairs?'

Marsh shook her head. 'Quiet as a mouse, you were. I usually hear things, as a rule, but what with all this bombing business, I drop right off again. Happens in the morning – I wake up, and the next thing I know – I'm asleep! I hate to admit it, but I'm so tired.'

'Oh, I know the feeling,' said Maisie. 'Me too!'

She left the house and crossed the street to look at the opposite property.

'Looks like I'm just in time.'

'Oh, Mr Scott—' Maisie glanced at her watch. 'In fact, you're bang on time.'

'Never keep a lady waiting. And you can go back to calling me Mark. Sounds better, because I'm not going to keep shouting "Miss Dobbs" into the distance.'

Maisie was about to respond, but Scott turned and pointed along the street. 'I think if we go down there, and then turn right, we can wander over to Marylebone Lane. I know a nice little restaurant along there, so let's go eat. I'm starving, and you can tell me everything you've found out today.'

'You can tell me what you've found out too,' said Maisie, falling into step alongside Scott.

'Not everything I'm doing is connected to Catherine Saxon's death, you know.'

'No, I didn't for a moment think it was.'

CHAPTER FOUR

The small Italian restaurant was busy when they walked in, but Maisie was surprised to see the owner approach Mark Scott with a warm smile.

'Marco! Good to have you back – when was it, last Wednesday?' The man, wearing a white shirt with a bow tie, and black trousers topped with an almost ankle-length apron, slapped the American on the back.

'Pete – got a nice quiet table for the lady and me?'

The man bowed to Maisie. 'Madam. It is my pleasure. A friend of Marco's is a friend of Pete's.' He turned to Scott. 'We're busier than ever – it's the bombings. People are leaving the shelters hungry, and they keep coming in – a lot of them don't even have time to go home to have a wash and change their clothes before they go to work again. So we're dishing up breakfasts and it has helped us and them – we thought we would lose everything in the summer, when we had bricks thrown through the window. But I am about to clear a table over there, in the corner – usually the last table to go, but today everyone wants just a seat and something hot. Look at the time – it's the afternoon already, and we haven't stopped since eight this morning.'

'Wherever you want to put us will do, Pete – thanks.' Mark Scott held out his hand to Maisie, and she followed the owner to the table.

'The usual to drink, Marco?' asked Pete, pulling out a chair for Maisie, then taking up the table napkin and dropping it into her lap.

'Just a glass of water today, thanks – I'm working,' said Scott.

'And you, madam?' Pete turned to Maisie.

'Yes, please – a glass of water.'

'And to eat? We're short of a few things today – but I can still offer you a wonderful spaghetti with tomato sauce and my home-made bread.'

Maisie felt her stomach rumble, and was grateful when Scott looked at her and raised both eyebrows, querying her preference without speaking. She nodded.

'Then let's have two of your spaghetti, Pete.'

The man gave a short bow, and stepped away in the direction of the kitchen, stopping to talk to another waiter on the way, whereupon he looked back at Maisie and Mark, pointing to them. In short order, the waiter came to the table with glasses of water.

'Thanks, Ricky,' said Scott.

The waiter smiled. 'Nice to see you again, Mr Scott,' he replied in a rich Cockney accent, before leaving to attend to patrons at another table.

'You know everyone here, Mark – how long have you been in London?'

'Oh, a little while now.' Scott glanced out of the window, then brought his attention back to Maisie. 'It's not far from my flat, so I come in a lot – they're generally open late, and I keep long hours at the embassy – it's over at number one Grosvenor Square. You know the one, it's a fairly new building, courtesy of the Duke of Westminster. The guy owns a lot of land around here, doesn't he? Anyway, the embassy moved in a couple of years ago. I can just walk to and from work – and I know my way pretty well, which is good because most of the time I'm out in the blackout.'

Maisie was about to ask Scott about his accommodation, when he volunteered the information.

'The embassy found me a flat – around the corner from Manchester Square. I got to London, set down my bags and that was that. Don't see much of it.'

Maisie nodded, then looked at her watch.

'Need to hurry?'

'Not yet – but I must get back down to Kent later this afternoon, and what with the blitzes, the stations were closed when I last checked – my secretary reminded me I might not be able to get my usual train. So, I've been thinking I might try to get the earlier one at twenty past three. I'll probably just have to go along to one or other station and take my chances.' She reached for her glass and took a sip of water. 'But don't worry about my commitment to the investigation – I'll be working whilst I'm in Kent. I've some notes to read regarding Miss Saxon's endeavours in London. And on Monday I'll be interviewing her fellow lodgers – it seems she was very friendly with them.'

'So you lifted a few things in the flat,' said Scott.

'A couple of items – I'll list them if you wish.'

'I trust you, but I'll need anything important as soon as you're finished with it.' He looked up as Pete returned to the table, placing plates of steaming spaghetti with tomato sauce in front of them.

'Ricky is behind me with the bread – just out of the oven. Just as well I have some olive oil – no butter today.' More pleasantries were exchanged, the bread was delivered and the conversation between Mark Scott and Maisie resumed.

'Pete told me that until he brought in some olive oil from Italy, the only place you could get the stuff around here was in a chemist – tiny bottle, and they only kept it for ear pain.'

'He looks like an Italian, but he doesn't sound like one,' observed Maisie. 'Probably to his advantage, otherwise he'd be in an internment camp on the Isle of Man by now.'

'His mother started the restaurant – she was Italian – and his dad is as London as they come. That's why Pete is still here – London boy with a British name and blue eyes, though where I come from an Italian with blue eyes means the mob. His mother died a few years ago, and Dad is out back, in the kitchen. They had some windows smashed when Il Duce threw in his lot with Hitler, but Pete and his brothers sorted it all out, and they've been left alone. And as you heard, they're scoring points by dishing up food early in the morning for people coming out of the shelters. Pete said it's costing them, but not as much as it would if they'd had to close. Before he was "Pete" he was "Pippo". I think his real name is Giuseppe – Joseph – but Pete sounds more like Pippo, so that's his name now.'

'I'm amazed they've remained in business, but good for them – Churchill said he wanted every Italian in Britain rounded up and sent away. Frankly, I think our love of ice cream might overcome our desire for retribution.' She looked around the restaurant, and at the line outside. 'But back to Miss Saxon's death. One thing I am curious about is the way the—' Maisie looked around to ensure no one could hear. She lowered her voice. 'How the murderer gained access to the room. It might even have been from the street. It's perfectly possible for someone to climb up onto the railing below, then the small balcony outside the upper window. It could then be pushed open. Those windows are floor-to-ceiling, so an intruder wouldn't exactly have to crawl in.' Maisie turned her fork in the long strands of pasta. 'And on the other hand, if the killer had already gained entrance to the house, then all he or she would have to do is knock at the door. Which reminds me – where was the key to Miss Saxon's rooms? The door wasn't locked when Mrs Marsh found her, so I'm curious about it.' She lifted a forkful of spaghetti. 'Bit sloppy, isn't it? Trying to eat this and discuss the case.'

'Just tuck the table napkin into your collar – it's not very ladylike for an English rose, but it'll save that silk blouse.'

Maisie raised an eyebrow at his comment, but followed the advice. 'The other thing is the sharp pencils, because—'

'Sharp pencils? Saxon wasn't killed with a pencil, Maisie, despite Dr Ferguson's demonstration,' said Scott.

Maisie looked at him, drew the edge of her napkin across her lips and set down her fork. She leant forward on her elbows. 'Mark Scott – whilst I know you are a very good agent, and from experience I know you can break into just about any room to find what you want, I also think you hit the nail on the head when you said you knew nothing about a murder investigation. But surely even you can see the link between a sharp pencil and the whereabouts of the blade used to bring the lead to a point?'

'Very funny,' said Scott, taking a mouthful of his food. 'This is the best spaghetti.'

'Have you tried Bertorelli's?'

'No – but let's have lunch there next week,' said Scott.

Maisie cleared her throat. 'I wasn't trying to be funny, Mark – she used a very sharp knife or blade, and it's missing. It could be the murder weapon.'

'Right, yes.'

'So we have to find out what happened to it.' She reached for her glass of water. 'Did Mr Murrow say anything of note?'

'Just what we know already – that he was considering her for his crew here in London. He liked what she'd done before, her reporting from Spain and the stories she'd filed from London for various newspapers in the States. He said she had a strong voice when it came to human interest – and that's what he needed.'

They ate in silence for a few moments, Maisie gauging Mark Scott's remarks.

'Did he know of anyone who was put out by her work – had she upset anyone?'

'Frankly?' Scott took a spoon and scooped up the last of his tomato sauce, then reached for a slice of bread and tore off a piece, holding it above the plate as he spoke. 'Murrow's reporters could have been upsetting a lot of people – but not here. The tide is beginning to turn in America – the statistics show that more people are becoming sympathetic to what Europe is enduring and how Britain is fighting back. It's a compelling story – poor little Britain is holding the fort against the Nazis, and her boys in the air have been giving the Luftwaffe a run for their money. Or as you Brits might say, they've "given them what for".'

'How would that upset people – our RAF doing their bit, or your statistics?'

'There's a new organisation – called America First. Well, it's not exactly new, but let's say it's been given a new lease of life. Charles

Lindbergh – you know, the hero aviator – he's at the forefront, along with other big names. They are set against helping Britain, and they advocate taking America's isolation even further than it is already. The president is facing another election, so he has to watch his step. He's with Churchill all the way – well, all the way as far as he can venture right now, though on a personal level, I'm not sure he likes the guy. But every time another of those broadcasts is heard in American homes, the America First sympathisers get upset all over again.' He folded the slice of bread, drew it through the last of his sauce and popped it into his mouth, wiping his lips with his napkin before speaking again. 'Then you get Catherine Saxon telling the story of a woman burning the flesh off her hands as she cries out for her daughters who have just been blown to shreds, and on one hand you have more and more Americans with a deep sympathy for the old country weeping into their dinner, and on the other there are those who believe that it's all a fabrication to draw us into another European bloodbath and they're yelling, "Lies!"' He looked across to Maisie's plate. 'Gonna finish that?'

'Go on – I hate to see food wasted, and I've lost my appetite.'

Scott reached for Maisie's plate, swapping it for his. 'You could say I am here to monitor communications between my country and yours. I have a job at the embassy that involves . . . it involves diplomacy.'

'Given that it's an embassy, one would hope so,' said Maisie. 'But I have to say, you're a funny kind of agent.'

'Takes all sorts.'

'Did you find out if Miss Saxon had any particular friends among the other correspondents here in London?'

'I have a couple of names – here.' Scott reached into his pocket and drew out a folded piece of paper. 'One was a sound engineer guy at the BBC. Apparently she'd known him before her interview with Murrow – don't know where they met, but you can find out. He's an Australian. Been over here since the end of the last war – married an English girl and decided to stay.' He looked up at Maisie. 'And I bet it was the weather that did it!'

'Oh, very funny,' said Maisie. 'Who else?'

'The other one is a woman, a friend from home. Lives in London and is married to a banker. They were at Vassar together. Jennifer Barrington, formerly Jennifer Standridge of Greenwich, Connecticut.'

'Very nice indeed,' said Maisie.

'Know the place?' asked Scott.

'I was in Boston a few years ago – just for a short time, and I travelled a little, though I don't remember much about it.'

'That was after—' Scott stopped speaking. 'Sorry.'

'Yes, I almost forgot you knew,' said Maisie. 'You were going to say, "After your husband was killed."' She looked at her watch. 'I really must be going soon. I'm meeting a friend for the journey down to Kent and we've got to find each other!'

'A gentleman friend?' Mark Scott grinned.

Maisie rolled her eyes. 'It's Mrs Partridge. Her son, Tim, was wounded during the Dunkirk evacuation, so she and her husband rented a cottage not too far from my house. Tim's still there – trying to come to terms with his disability, though he's rather in the doldrums at the moment. She goes back and forth to London because we are on an ambulance crew three or four nights a week.'

Scott waved to Pete, who came with the bill, which he paid with a single note. He pushed back his chair, not waiting for change.

'Come on, let's get you to Charing Cross or Victoria, or whichever station you want to try.'

'Wait a minute,' said Maisie, turning to Pete. 'May I use your telephone?'

'I'll show you where it is, madam.'

Maisie returned to the table a few moments later. 'I just telephoned my friend, and we're going to try to catch a train at Victoria Station after all. Apparently there's not too much damage to Charing Cross, but the trains have been affected – and to make matters worse, the bomb that went into the Thames has made it difficult to use the Underground. Anyway, I can catch a bus and—'

'Not a chance – I'll get a taxi.'

'Really, Mark – it's not—'

'I hate to keep interrupting you, but I insist.'

'All right – I'll take a cab. By the way, you know we mostly use the suffix here. You say "taxi" whereas we say "cab".'

'Maybe I'll hire you to be my interpreter every time I need a taxicab then,' said Scott.

'Oh, I think you're doing well enough on your own,' said Maisie, as she climbed into the cab, which had screeched to a halt as soon as Mark Scott raised his hand outside the restaurant. 'Shall we speak on Monday afternoon? I should have more to report.'

'No, you go ahead with the investigation. I'll be in touch – I'm on embassy business for most of next week. Here's a number where you can reach me if necessary.'

Scott handed a card to her, and without further ado slammed the door. Maisie looked back just as Scott was lifting his hat by way of farewell, and the driver moved out into traffic. She turned away and brought her attention to the road in front: to the sandbagged buildings, to the barrage balloons overhead, and as they neared the station, to buildings rendered nothing more than smoking rubble. She considered Mark Scott. Yes, he was amusing. Yes, she knew he was clever, and a very accomplished agent. But she was curious about his remit in London – in fact, she continued to wonder if the death of Catherine Saxon wasn't providing Mark Scott with some sort of useful camouflage.

'I thought I would never catch this bloody train!' said Priscilla, clambering aboard and taking a seat alongside Maisie. 'Elinor walked in just as I was about to leave, so of course I had to find out what she's been up to with the First Aid Nursing Yeomanry. I don't think it's much like it was in our day – mind you, I was in France, driving ambulances through the mud.'

Elinor was the former nanny to Priscilla's three sons. Such was the bond between the family and their former employee that even after she had joined the 'FANY' for her national service, Priscilla had insisted the house remain Elinor's home, and her room was always ready for her return. Having bumped into Elinor earlier in the spring as she was leaving the building where Robert MacFarlane's office was located, Maisie suspected Elinor was involved in work that had the potential to be every bit as dangerous as Priscilla driving ambulances across the shell-erupted landscape of Flanders during the last war.

'And I almost went to Charing Cross,' continued Priscilla. 'Then I remembered we'd just agreed it was best to come to Victoria, though I think this train will take ages. At least it's early enough so we won't be moving along in the blackout.'

'I don't know about you,' said Maisie, 'but I'm feeling guilty already about not being on duty tonight.'

Priscilla sighed, and looked out of the window towards the

platform. The train was still not moving, even though the guard had sounded his whistle to signal the locomotive was about to begin its journey. 'Me too – but we did the right thing in going back to London last Saturday, as soon as we knew it had started.' She looked down at her hands. 'And don't forget we said we'd return on Sunday, after lunch, to relieve another crew – I would imagine we might not get back down to Kent for days now, the way things are going, so we'd better make the most of it. And for me, that might not be such a bad thing, given Tim's mood when I'm there. I really hope he's a little better disposed to having his mother in his midst for a few days. And thank heavens Douglas has been able to work from the cottage, though we're like ships that pass in the night, both of us making sure Tim isn't alone in the house. It's been four months since Dunkirk, but sometimes I wonder if he will ever truly recover. And needless to say, I'm always the one who seems to rattle his cage.'

'Andrew says it will take time,' offered Maisie, referring to Andrew Dene, the orthopaedic surgeon – and Maisie's former love – who had operated on Tim Partridge.

'That's what his father said – and he should know, having lost an arm the last time around! But Douglas wasn't given the chance to take time to get over his wounds. He had to buck up and get on with it – which seems to be the best way, if you ask me.'

'Priscilla, perhaps this is the moment I should remind you that you met Douglas in Biarritz, where you had both gone to leave the war behind. Your husband was probably in the same state of distress as your son, but you didn't realise it at the time, because you'd just met each other and had fallen in love.'

'Oh, don't be too kind, Maisie – let's be truthful. I was sozzled, in an almost constant drunken state because I had lost three brothers to the war and my parents to the bloody "flu". If anything, saving me probably helped Douglas save himself. But Tim is not cut of his father's cloth. Sadly, he is more like me.'

'He's the very best of both of you. He just needs to find his place, now that his dream of going into the navy has been shot to pieces.'

The guard sounded his whistle again, and the train began to move.

'Oh, thank goodness – we're off.' Priscilla glanced out of the window again, then back at Maisie. 'Anyway, I shall brace myself and do my best not to rise to any bait my son throws into the waters of otherwise household calm. I feel as if all he wants to do is pick a row with me.'

'And that's exactly what he wants, Priscilla – you must be able to see it. He won't fight with his father, because Douglas is so easy-going. Tim reveres Tom, because in truth he not only adores his older brother, but he's his hero – so he won't goad him. And Tarquin is keeping his distance – which isn't surprising for a younger brother who has not one, but two brave older brothers to look up to. So, you are the only person upon whom he can vent his anger.'

'I'm the one who comes out wounded though. I just want my toads back, my three little toads who used to be so much fun! And as for Tarquin, well, what can I say? He's become the quiet one, when I always thought he would be the holy terror. My mother's instinct tells me he's up to something – fourteen is not a good age to be up to something. I should have spotted that with Tim, when he began going off to sail – but I was just grateful not to have him picking arguments with me.'

Maisie reached out and took the hand of the friend she had known since girlhood, when they met as students at Girton College, in

Cambridge. 'Let's all have an early Sunday lunch at the Dower House before you and I have to go back on duty. Anna loves our big Sunday lunches. And I'll invite Lord Julian and Lady Rowan. I think they would like a break from entertaining Canadian officers.'

'All right. Good idea. We might as well have some fun before venturing back into the fray.' Priscilla looked out of the carriage window, tilting her head to the sky. 'They'll be here soon enough, filling the sky. What do they call a flight of crows? That's it – they're like a *murder* of crows, those bloody Germans with their bloody bombs.'

'There's a letter for you here, Maisie,' announced Brenda, waving the envelope in front of Maisie before she even had time to take off her jacket. 'It looks important – from the Ministry of Health.'

Maisie dropped her bag and took the envelope from her stepmother. She ripped it open and removed the letter.

'Oh dear. I don't know whether this is good or bad.'

'What is it?' asked Brenda.

'The adoption panel has been cancelled due to the bombings. They've assigned me a new date – which they are saying will be "in October".' She folded the letter and returned it to the envelope. 'And I bet it gets pushed along the line again and before you know it, we'll be into November and lucky if it's sorted out before the new year.'

Brenda was thoughtful. 'Let's just imagine it's good news – I mean, let's face it, the way this war is going, those people will have more to worry about than one child's adoption.'

At that moment, the kitchen door crashed open, and Anna, now almost six years of age, rushed into the house with Frankie and two dogs in her wake.

'You're home, you're home, you're home!' she squealed as she jumped up to be swept into Maisie's open arms. 'Uncle Frankie says we must go down into the cellar now – they're coming back from London, and we don't know if they're going to lay their spare eggs!'

'Their what?' asked Maisie, smiling. She kissed Anna on both cheeks, then her nose.

'I'll explain when we're down there. Maisie,' said Frankie. 'Bren – come on, down into the cellar now.'

'I've got the flask and sandwiches ready,' said Brenda.

Still holding Anna, Maisie grabbed a flask from the table, and called the dogs to heel. The cellar door was beyond the kitchen, in the recess leading to the scullery – Maisie opened the door, switched on the light and began to descend the stone staircase. A single electric light bulb hung from a low oak-beamed ceiling, revealing a cellar the size of a cottage drawing room. A shaft of golden late summer evening light shone through a small window. In one corner a pile of coal had landed underneath double doors that opened to the ground alongside the house – each week the coalman would open the doors to shoot in two one-hundred-weight sacks of coke, and perhaps more in winter, for the stove and fireplaces. It was fuel that would have to be conserved now, because coal was needed for factories and power stations first. Brush marks were evident where Frankie had swept back the dust before constructing a wooden barrier between the coal and the rest of the cellarage – for good measure he had placed a tarpaulin over the mound so they would not breathe in the dust. At the opposite end of the cellar, three mattresses had been laid on the floor with blankets and pillows on top, covered with dust sheets to keep them clean during the day. Maisie drew back and folded the dust sheets, before taking her place on one mattress, with Anna alongside her. Frankie settled the dogs on blankets in the corner, and

Brenda set three flasks of tea and a picnic supper on the table.

'I reckon they came from another direction today,' said Frankie. 'I didn't see as many going over, but they could have flown in from the east so they can follow the river in towards the docks again. Whoever planned this blitzing business was nobody's fool, but our boys have been up there, taking them on, doing their level best to stop them before they reach London.' He paused and held out his hand to his daughter. 'I didn't want to ask about it, Maisie – but we've been on tenterhooks since you went back last time. We went upstairs on Saturday night – could see the red light of fires across London as we stood there at the bedroom window. It was like watching the sunset on fire across the horizon.'

'I'm here now, Dad – and feeling bad. I should be there – I should have taken another shift.'

'How long are you staying?'

'Well, as you know they've been changing the roster a lot lately. Priscilla reminded me on the train down that we're on duty from Sunday night until Thursday. But we should have a nice lunch before I have to leave. Pris and I have already talked about it.' Maisie looked up at the ceiling as a droning sound reverberated overhead. 'The papers say they've been dropping bombs on Kent as they make their way back to France – I've been so worried about you all.'

'That's what I meant by laying their eggs – that's how old Avis, the gardener, put it. "They're laying their rotten eggs on the way home," he said the other day. And they're doing some damage – the shop in the village caught it last night. It was a miracle though – the bomb bounced off the roof and left a blimmin' great dent.'

'It's like an egg cup!' interjected Anna. 'We were sent home from school – the army men had to come to make it safe.'

Maisie looked from her father to Brenda, and as a deep groaning echoed from the sky into the cellar, all four souls cast their gaze to the ceiling again. *A murder of dark crows*, thought Maisie.

'Right, who's for a cup of tea and a sandwich?' asked Brenda, reaching for the tin she'd placed on the table. 'We've got cheese, ham, or egg. What'll it be, Anna? And then we'll do a jigsaw puzzle.'

Despite the air raid continuing throughout the night, and the sound of bombers flying to and from London passing overhead, Frankie and Brenda were able to sleep, which Maisie attributed to their age and the fact that her father, especially, had become a little hard of hearing. She often had to repeat a question or raise her voice so that he might hear her, and she realised the same thing was now happening to Brenda. Anna had dropped into a deep sleep halfway through the story of *Blossom, The Barrage Balloon*, confident that the dear balloon would save them all from the wicked Luftwaffe aircraft. Maisie moved so she was close to the light, and pulled out the notes from her bag. War might be waged, the German Luftwaffe might be trying to destroy the city she loved, but she felt a duty to the young woman who had risked her life to tell London's story. And she wondered, not for the first time, whether it was Catherine Saxon's decision to paint a picture of Britain's plight in the minds of people living thousands of miles away that had led to her death.

'We've been called back early, Maisie,' said Priscilla.

'What's happened?' said Maisie.

'Mr Keene, the supervisor on duty, has just telephoned – last night's blitz was terrible and a couple of drivers are in hospital, so they need us back there immediately. I thought it was too good to be true, being able to stick to the plan of only working certain shifts – all very well when you're practising, but not when the bombs come raining down. Douglas is here, so Tim will not be alone – and apparently Tom will be back on a twenty-four-hour leave tomorrow. He's been on ops around the clock, so has just been given rest time. I'll be dashed to miss him, but duty calls.' Maisie heard her friend draw from her cigarette – she always knew when Priscilla smoked using a holder; the hiatus before she spoke again seemed to extend for ages. 'Douglas has looked up the coach timetable, and he telephoned to check – it appears we're in luck, because a coach is leaving Tonbridge at half past twelve. We'll be back in town well before our shift at four. Just in time for the bloody Luftwaffe to start coming in.'

'All right – I'll let Brenda and Dad know. Anna will be disappointed about lunch – but tell Douglas to bring the boys over in any case. Just because we're not here doesn't mean life shouldn't go on.'

'Righty-ho. Excellent idea. Keep on going, that's my motto – though let's face it, Maisie, if I'm not there, the entertainment goes downhill.'

Maisie smiled, recognising her friend's need to make light in dark times. 'Don't flatter yourself, Pris,' she teased. 'They'll do very well without us.'

'But you can't leave!' Anna screamed, clutching Maisie's skirt, then rushing towards Priscilla, holding on to her arm. 'Auntie Pris, you can't go. You mustn't go. You've got to stay here.'

Maisie knelt down, pulling Anna to her. 'Now, now, Anna, everything's going to be all right. We won't be long – you'll see both of us again soon. And Tim's coming tomorrow for lunch!'

'In fact, I know he'll come today, to watch you ride Lady.' Priscilla ran her hand through Anna's long dark hair. She looked at Maisie, and nodded her head towards the door.

'Come on, Anna, it's time for us to go down to groom Lady,' said Frankie. 'And look at Emma – your tears are upsetting her. She's sad because you're sad. Come on, darlin'.'

Upon hearing her name, Emma, the large Alsatian dog – who had been standing next to the child she followed as if she were her shadow – pushed her nose against Anna's arm.

'Go away, Emma – go away!' cried Anna.

'You'd best just leave now, Maisie,' said Brenda, stepping forward. 'She'll get over it. She's just having a little paddy – she thought you'd be here for a few days.'

Maisie pressed her lips together, fighting her own tears.

'Come on, Maisie – let's go,' said Priscilla.

'But, Auntie Pris – you can't. You mustn't go away.' The child reached for Priscilla's sleeve, trying to pull her back again.

Maisie picked up Anna and walked towards the sitting room. 'Come on, let's go to your crying chair, and you have a good weep until you're ready to help Uncle Frankie with the horses.'

She lowered the child into the plump armchair, feeling the heaving sobs wrack Anna's small body as she began to relent, curling up on the chair, her head down on her knees. Maisie pulled a blanket and cocooned her charge, kissing her forehead before stepping towards the door. Emma took her place alongside the chair, and Frankie put an arm around his daughter.

'Don't worry about the little one, love – we'll look after her.'

'I've never seen her like this. She's barely ever cried, and it was only a few tears over a scraped knee, or if she saw an animal hurt.'

'It'll be better when the adoption's over. She's not a stupid child –

she knows what's going on, and how important it all is. It's just the waiting now. Anyway, you get on your way – let us know when you're off shift. You two are the ones *we* worry about.' He nodded towards Priscilla, who reached out to Maisie.

'George has been enlisted to take us to the coach station in Tonbridge, Maisie,' said Priscilla. 'It appears Lord Julian still has use of his motor car and there's petrol in the tank, so that saves us waiting in the village for the local bus.'

Sitting at the back of the London coach – a long-distance motor bus with only a few stops on the way into the capital – Priscilla lit a cigarette, snapping the silver lighter as she blew a smoke ring and turned to Maisie. 'I've never seen Anna like that before – she was terrified. And what's all that about a crying chair?'

'Oh, that was Brenda's doing. Anna came from the garden after finding a dead bird, and was weeping about it. So Brenda told her it was best to get everything sad out and cry until she couldn't cry any more, so she took Anna into the drawing room, put her in the chair, covered her with a blanket and said she could always come to that very chair for a good cry if she felt sad, because crying helped get all the bad feelings out. Anna has rarely used it for crying – and when she does, as I mentioned to Dad, it's generally about animals. She cried when James's big hunter had to be put down, and when one of the sheepdogs was caught on a wire and needed stitches, she went to the chair to cry about it. But this is a strikingly new behaviour – and it wasn't directed only at me.'

Priscilla lit another cigarette and snapped shut the flame on a lighter embossed with the initials PE – her maiden name was Evernden. 'I would imagine she's very upset with me because I'm the one who came to the house to take you away.' She drew on her cigarette. 'But don't worry, I've become quite used to getting it in the neck from children.'

'Tim giving you some lip again?'

'Well, it transpires I'm a dreadful mother because I've kept him back. You would have thought I'd tied him to a stake in the garden – mind you, that might not have been such a bad idea. I might do it yet – and light a fire underneath the boy.'

'Pris – come on, that's not how you feel.'

Priscilla wiped away tears that had emerged as she spoke. 'No, it's not. And I'm not arguing with him – I'm just trying to absorb every swipe on the chin. And yes, I understand everything you've said about me being the one he's putting all his angry venom into, but sometimes I don't know if I can take it. Anyone would think I was cruel to my children.'

Maisie reached for her friend's free hand. 'There's something my mother used to say when I was a girl – when she was so ill. She always said, "Don't worry – it'll all come out in the wash." Of course, she meant that everything will come right in the end, but as a child I imagined I'd see the sickness come out of her body to be swept down the drain when we did the laundry. But she was right in a way, because the washing always gets done, the laundry aired and folded – life goes on, though it might never be quite the same.'

The women looked out of the window at homes where walls had been torn off by explosions, revealing bedrooms with beds still made, sitting rooms with furniture still in place, yet curtains and clothing falling across torched bricks.

'It's like looking into dolls' houses with the sides taken off, isn't it?' said Priscilla.

Maisie nodded. 'But all the dolls are gone.' She drew her gaze down to the remains of another home, at the still-smoking rubble, and in her mind's eye she could see Catherine Saxon again, clambering across to speak to a fireman, her notebook in hand. At least in leaving Chelstone early, she would be able to immerse herself in the work of finding the woman's murderer.

CHAPTER FIVE

It didn't require a bombing of Buckingham Palace to convince these people that they are all in this thing together. There is nothing exclusive about being bombed these days. When there are homes down in your street, when friends and relatives have been killed, when you've seen that red glow in the sky night after night, when you're tired and sleepy – there just isn't enough energy left to be outraged about the bombing of a palace.

EDWARD R. MURROW, BROADCAST TO AMERICA,

15TH SEPTEMBER 1940

'Surprised to see you here on a Monday morning, miss,' said Billy, looking up from his desk.

'Morning? I'm so late, it might as well be afternoon,' replied Maisie, taking off her jacket and slipping it onto the hook at the back of the office door. She picked up the document case she had set on the floor upon entering the room. 'I think I'd like strong coffee to get me going again today – and I'm sure you could do with one too. We were on duty Saturday night and last night – we don't get home until past eight in the morning after a fourteen-hour shift – and it'll go on all this week, I'm sure. But it's the same for everyone, so we mustn't grumble about it.'

'You all right to work on the case today?'

Maisie nodded. 'Mr Scott is away for a few days – well, I don't know if he's technically "away" but he told me he's otherwise occupied, which is probably just as well, because I can get on with talking to various people, especially the other women lodging in the house where Catherine Saxon lived.' She looked at Billy, pausing as if to take stock of progress on the case.

'What is it?'

'Billy, I have an odd assignment for you – and you'll need to be very careful as you go about it.'

'All right, miss – you know me, careful as they come.'

'It's not dangerous – at least I don't believe it is – but you must take care not to be seen or apprehended.'

'I think I know what you're about to say – it's that American, isn't it?'

'Yes, it is. Look, when I haven't been roaring through the streets in an ambulance, I've managed to read through some of the files I was given on the case and reflect upon a few things. Apparently Scott lives on a street close to Manchester Square, but I don't know his exact address, and I think it would be a good idea to have the information to hand. Could you find out? He might even be living on the square itself, but decided to tell me a half-truth. Remember he is a very clever man, an experienced agent for the American government's Justice Department – he may know you're looking for him before you even get a whiff of the scent. Be watchful and stay in the shadows, so to speak – but if it's possible to follow him without being seen, then do just that.'

'You don't trust him, do you?' said Billy.

Maisie was thoughtful. 'I'd trust him to save my life, and that's basically what he did in Munich. But something else is going on, and I want to know what it is – it may have nothing to do with me, this case or Catherine Saxon's death. Or it may have everything to do with it, and he's not been fully honest and open with me, or with Robbie MacFarlane. Mind you, I don't think you can pull the wool over Robbie's eyes – but on the other hand there might be an alliance between the two of them, one kept from me when I was asked to work with Scott. I want to know the ground I'm treading on, Billy – so find out what you can. And take care – that's the most important thing, always.'

'Right you are, miss.'

'And as soon as I've had that cup of coffee, I'll be off to see if I can talk to some of the other women at Catherine Saxon's lodgings.'

With the coffee in front of her, Maisie placed a telephone call to Robert MacFarlane.

'Good day to you, Your Ladyship. To what do I owe this intrusion to my very busy day?'

It seemed MacFarlane was in a jocular mood, which wasn't such a bad thing, as far as Maisie was concerned.

'I'd like some information, if you can get it for me.'

'Go on,' said MacFarlane.

'I'm curious about one of Catherine Saxon's fellow lodgers, and I wonder if you might know – or be able to find out more about her. She's a civil servant employed in your neck of the woods. All I know about Isabel Chalmers so far is that she works at an office in Whitehall and she doesn't talk about it, and never answers questions about her job.'

'And that's exactly what anyone who works for the government is supposed to do – not blether about it.'

'That's not very helpful, Robbie. I want to talk to her, and if you want this investigative alliance between us and our American friends to come to a satisfactory conclusion, I'm going to need a bit of assistance – because by the time she gets home to her rooms on Welbeck Street, there will be a blackout and she'll be in a shelter, and I'm going to have trouble talking to her. In fact, she'll probably be in one of your bomb-proof government shelters that I'm not supposed to know about. Can you lend a hand here?'

'I'll look into it, lass, and I'll do my best to make arrangements for you to talk to her. Will someone be in your office to take a telephone call from me?'

'Sandra's coming in shortly and will be here until half past two – I want her home and safe before the blitz tonight.'

Polly Harcourt was in her rooms when Maisie called at the house in Welbeck Street. Mrs Marsh answered the front door, then called up the stairs several times until the young woman leant over the banister and called back.

'What is it now, Mrs Marsh? It's only just gone one o'clock, not time for the blackout.'

'Visitor for you, Miss Harcourt – so get yourself decent.'

Maisie raised an eyebrow, and made her way up the stairs to the third-floor accommodation rented to the actress. She introduced herself and gave Harcourt a calling card.

'Psychologist and investigator? This must be about Cath.' Polly Harcourt wore her dark hair shorter than was fashionable, though it drew attention to her pale skin and hazel eyes. She was already 'decent', wearing navy blue trousers with an embroidered cotton blouse tucked into the waistband and topped with a yellow cardigan, but had no shoes on her feet. 'Come on in, then – but excuse the mess. I was late last night, and as you can see, I haven't even bothered to put a pair of slippers on.' She placed the calling card on the desk and began to pick up a few items of clothing from the back of an armchair as Maisie entered, hanging a jacket and dress in the wardrobe. Maisie used the moment to look around the room. It was similar in size to Catherine Saxon's quarters, and – somewhat to Maisie's surprise – another element of similarity was a desk with papers laid out upon it, and to the right a series of shelves filled with possibly more books than Saxon had acquired. 'You seem surprised,' said Harcourt, looking up at Maisie as she closed the wardrobe door. 'The way you're looking at my room.'

'I thought Miss Saxon was the only writer in the house, but perhaps not.'

'Catherine always said I should try to write a play.' She sighed. 'And a couple of days ago I thought I might as well, seeing as the theatre has closed until this spate of bombing is over. A few have stayed open, but probably not for long – and naturally not the play I was in. Anyway, I was only the stand-in – but all the same, it means I'm back to leaning on my savings.' Another sigh. 'And thank heavens I've got something put by for a rainy day. But I'm off to work in a few hours – one thing that hasn't changed is the nightclub where I'm the barmaid when I haven't anything else lined up. The club's in an old cellar, over near Paddington, and believe me, there's quite a few who've discovered it's not a bad place to sit tight until the bombing stops, because we've got a fair amount of beer, gin and whisky stashed out the back. And it's work that pays the rent.' She paused, looking down at her stockinged feet. 'I suppose I started writing the play because I miss her. I miss Cath. She was a real live wire, even though she said I should stay away from any idea of getting into those Hollywood pictures. She said the films only give a sunny impression of what it's like over there.'

'Perhaps she was right. But you say she encouraged you to write?'

'Oh, she was always encouraging us to write. Truthfully? I think it was to try to find out more about Isabel – she lives downstairs in the basement rooms underneath Mrs Marsh's flat. Cath hated not knowing more about her, even though we said it was probably boring office work. She just liked to ask people questions – she said it was her job to be nosey.' Harcourt pointed to the small stove in the corner. 'Would you like a cup of tea? I can put the kettle on – doesn't take long to boil; these little gas rings work very well, you know.'

Maisie was about to decline, but changed her mind. 'All right – yes, I will.' She pulled a straight-back chair away from the desk and sat down as Harcourt lifted the lid from the kettle to check the water level, then replaced it on the burner, which she lit with a match. 'Why do you think Catherine was so curious about Isabel?' she asked.

'I suppose because she didn't say much about her job. She wasn't one to natter about it, and only ever said that she was a civil servant – and we all know how boring that is. Cath probably didn't understand, being an American. Perhaps working for the government over there is more exciting, because you only have to look at Isabel to know how tedious it is. Not that she isn't fun when she wants to be, but I would have thought it was obvious she is one step away from turning into stone, she's so fed up.' Harcourt paused, turning back to the stove. 'Not long now – kettle's almost boiled.' She took a teapot from a shelf above the stove and set it on a cold burner. 'I've no sugar, but I have dried milk, if you can bear it.'

'A teaspoonful of the milk, thank you,' said Maisie. There was no more to be gained from asking about Isabel Chalmers, so she stood up and moved to the window – Polly Harcourt's desk was smaller than Catherine Saxon's, so she was able to stand next to the window without moving furniture. She ran her finger down the frame, noticing it suffered the same warping as the window in the reporter's room.

'I read there's going to be a sort of National Dried Milk available soon – mainly for mums doing their national service, so they can leave their babies if they're out on war work in the factories. But I thought you couldn't feed that sort of milk to a baby – it's bad for it.' Harcourt turned to Maisie. 'Oh, you've noticed that window frame. They're like it all over the house – bending with the years, if you ask me. Cath said the windows were like rickety old gentlemen not able to stand up straight.'

'It sounds as if she had something to say about everything,' observed Maisie. She watched as Harcourt warmed the pot, tipping the water into a spare cup before putting just one teaspoon of tea in the pot, and pouring on water she'd brought to the boil again. She set cups on a tray, placed a small tin of powdered milk between them, and carried the tray to the desk. Another straight-back chair was brought from the bedroom, and she took a seat at the desk opposite Maisie. She began speaking again when they had cups of tea before them. The fact that Harcourt's hands were shaking as she poured tea did not concern Maisie to the extent it might have before the bombings began. In a peacetime investigation she would have viewed shaking hands as an indicator of something amiss. But since the onslaught of daily blitzes, she had noticed that no matter how much people seemed to be coping with the onslaught of death and destruction, fear was revealed in other ways – shaking hands, an overly sunny disposition, or perhaps its opposite: a snapped response to a simple question. At the very least, a lack of sleep was catching up with so many residents of Britain – it wasn't only London being targeted by German bombers.

'Miss Harcourt – Polly – can you tell me what you remember about Catherine's last hours? Did you hear her return from the studio after midnight? Were there any sounds from the floor below that you were not used to hearing? Let's start there, and we'll work backwards.'

'I wasn't home until after she'd been taken away to the mortuary, Miss Dobbs. You see, I was at the club. We stopped serving about half past two – long after last orders should have been called, but people needed a bit of Dutch courage that night. Then everyone just sort of bedded down until it was safe to go home again. I went out the back where Nick, the landlord, kept some blankets, and I just wrapped one around my shoulders, lay down on the floor and went out like a light. I hadn't slept since it all started.'

'What time did you leave the house to go to the club?'

'I left about four in the afternoon – I wanted to get to work before the sirens began, and when I got to work, Nick said I shouldn't go home until after the all-clear sounded.' She took a sip of tea. 'I last saw Cath before I went out – I knocked on her door, because I knew she was going out too. She'd told me she was joining an ambulance crew and would likely be over in the East End. I was worried about that – the East End has been getting it really bad – I mean, look at all those poor people killed in Canning Town when that bomb dropped on the shelter. A bus was supposed to have evacuated them – but it went to bloody Camden Town instead. I mean, excuse my language, but that's like the old joke – you know, the one from the last war, when an officer sent out a message, "Send reinforcements, we're going to advance," and someone got it wrong and passed it along as "Send three and fourpence, we're going to a dance." Except it wasn't a joke for hundreds of poor souls in Canning Town, was it?' She shook her head. 'Anyway, sorry about going on like that. But the thing is, I was worried about Cath – she took chances, if you ask me.'

'What sort of chances?' asked Maisie. 'Do you mean beyond being out during the bombing?'

'That's the main thing.' Harcourt paused. 'If I'm to be honest, perhaps it wasn't that she took chances – it was that I always knew she was the type who would take a chance if she thought there would be something in it for her work. I knew she was that sort of fearless.'

'Did she have visitors? Men or women?'

'Her friend from America came 'round a few times. Cath said she was having a difficult time with her husband. I suppose all couples go through their ups and downs, and they were going through a down.'

'Do you mean Mrs Jennifer Barrington?'

'Jenny – yes, that's her. We were all sitting out in the garden one day – you have to go through Isabel's rooms to get there, but she's good about it – and Cath brought Jenny out to join us. Jenny said it reminded her of when they were at college in America – you know, all girls together, chatting.'

'What sort of things did you talk about?'

'Oh, anything and everything! The first time Jenny joined us, we talked about men. That was after Cath introduced me as "Polly the actress". Cath thought it was funny, Isabel laughed, Elizabeth and Helena blushed, Pamela rolled her eyes, and Jenny said "Say no more," as if she'd already made up her mind about actresses. Fortunately Mrs Marsh stuck up for me and said, "Our Polly is a good girl." I liked her for that, because a lot of people think that if you're an actress, you're "that sort of woman". But I always thought Jenny was a nice person – she and Cath made us laugh with stories of the things they got up to when they were younger. Even Pam couldn't help but smile.' Harcourt shook her head, and wiped a hand across her eyes. 'Cath could make a stone laugh.'

Maisie nodded. She knew the importance of not peppering a possible witness with too many difficult questions; however, once a subject had begun speaking with ease, it was time to increase the pressure.

'Tell me, Polly – can you think of anyone who might have had some sort of grudge against Catherine? Or did she ever indicate a problematical relationship?'

Polly Harcourt shifted her seated position and looked out of the window, casting her gaze away from Maisie. For her part, Maisie began to mirror her actions, and wondered if she was about to tell a lie.

'I don't know anyone who had a grudge – she was such a lovely person,' said Harcourt, turning back to Maisie. 'She worked hard, and she was ambitious – she really wanted to work for that American man who's on the wireless. Mr Murrow. It was her big dream to play the game with the big boys – that's how she put it anyway. Perhaps someone didn't like that ambition – you never know, do you? And about problematical relationships? Well, do you know a woman who hasn't had a problematical relationship at some point? Unless you get

93

yourself up the aisle with the bloke of your dreams at nineteen, you're on the way to a problematical relationship or two. And I daresay there's many a woman who has a problem with her husband.'

'I see your point,' said Maisie, though she wondered if such a harsh summation was the result of disappointment in love. Perhaps it was something the two women had in common.

'Did Catherine have a broken heart, do you think?'

Harcourt nodded. 'I think she did. But don't we all?'

Maisie did not respond to the question, thrown down like a glove as if to mark the start of a duel. Instead she shifted her questioning.

'Would you let me know if you think of anything that might be of interest to me?'

Harcourt stood up, taking Maisie's calling card from the desk. She looked at it again. 'I'm glad a woman's looking into Catherine's death.'

'Why do you say that?'

'Because men don't care, if you ask me. It's just another woman dead – and they always jump to conclusions, don't they? And because it happened here, in her home – yes, only a couple of shabby rooms if we're being honest, but it was her home – there's those who will point the finger at the victim and say, "She knew the killer – must have invited him in," and the next thing you know, her name's dirt.' Harcourt took a deep breath, wiping the palm of her hand across each eye in turn. 'You should have known her, Miss Dobbs. Catherine Saxon was one of a kind. She might have been well-to-do – and if you saw her friend, and what she was like, you'd know she was better off than most – but she had no side to her, and was just a good human being.'

Maisie reached out and placed a hand on Polly Harcourt's shoulder. 'I knew her, Polly. I knew Catherine. It was only for a short time, but enough to get the measure of her. I was driving the ambulance she came out with, that last night of her life. It's one of the reasons I accepted the request for my help on this case.'

'You knew her?' Harcourt looked into Maisie's eyes. 'If it's only one of the reasons you're here, what are the others?'

'I liked her. I saw the goodness in her. And when it came down to it, I wanted to make sure the killer of a woman who made truth her business was found.' Maisie pointed to the card. 'I'm in Fitzroy Square if you remember anything of note – no matter how seemingly insignificant.'

Harcourt nodded, but as Maisie turned away she spoke again. 'She had a lover, you know. I would hear them come in late sometimes, whispering on the stairs. They'd be giggling, you know, like people who are trying not to make a noise.'

'Is that all you can tell me?'

'I think he was an American. It was the rhythm in the way he spoke – I couldn't hear the words, exactly, but people from different places speak with a different cadence and he had the same sort of sound as Cath. I'm a trained actress – I can hear these things. So yes – I reckon he was another American. Or someone who'd spent a lot of time there.'

As Maisie left the house, she looked across the road, focusing on the building Polly Harcourt glanced at when she thought the woman might be about to lie. But was it a lie? Having learnt that Catherine Saxon was involved in a romantic relationship with a man who could have been an American, Maisie wondered now whether Harcourt had been staring out of the window in thought, or if she had been looking at something specific. And Maisie knew that sometimes what appeared to be a lie might simply be an avoidance of the truth, the uneasy demeanour that comes with dodging an obvious fact. Maisie walked across the road, and noted the names on a series of separate brass plaques next to a blue door with a similar lion's head brass door knocker, though there was a button alongside each plaque to summon a secretary. The men were all surgeons, an obvious distinction, given that each man was listed as 'Mr' – the accepted title of a British surgeon. In her experience, some physicians adopted an air of superiority when elevated from 'Dr' to 'Mr' upon qualification as a surgeon – indeed, the fealty accompanying their status meant they might not be open to questioning by an investigator. One of those men – Mr G. Chester – was also a Fellow of the Royal College of Physicians, an affiliation that suggested he might also be an obstetrician. She was somewhat curious about him more than the others.

Maisie looked at her watch and wondered if MacFarlane had been able to smooth the way for her to see Isabel Chalmers. Catherine Saxon's curiosity about the downstairs neighbour had piqued Maisie's interest – even though she was in a job others considered boring.

CHAPTER SIX

Could she have made an error, perhaps jumping the gun when she saw Polly Harcourt gaze across the street? The counsel she'd received from Maurice in the early days of her apprenticeship – that coincidence is a messenger sent by truth – often served her well; however, she had also learnt that coincidence could be the trickster, the Loki among Maurice's cadre of maxims. Then again, it was always worth considering. In her estimation, when Harcourt looked to the house opposite, it was not an idle glance – there was something more. But what was it? Maisie stopped walking so abruptly that the person on the street behind almost bumped into her.

'I am so sorry – I do beg your pardon,' said Maisie.

'My goodness – Maisie! What are you doing here?'

'Andrew! I could ask you the same question.'

Andrew Dene leant forward to kiss her on the cheek. 'I'm just on the way to my consulting rooms in Harley Street. I'm usually at the hospital, but I have a couple of appointments this afternoon –

want to get them finished before the air raid warning sounds.' Dene smiled, reaching for her hand. 'And what about you? Back on the old stomping ground?' He smiled, nodding towards a house farther along the street. 'Every time I walk past that house, I think of Maurice, how he took me under his wing and made a doctor of me – not an easy task with a Bermondsey boy.'

'He could see your talent, Andrew, when you ran errands for him at the clinic in return for caring for your mother. He saw your curiosity, and your innate compassion with patients.'

'Speaking of Maurice's clinic, Maisie – we should discuss matters soon. It's destined to come under compulsory government control because there's so much casualty care going on since the bombings started. People are coming to the clinic in droves – I've been down there, and I think it's time to think about the next step. The Comptons are not getting any younger, and Maurice wanted them both on the board, plus there's already talk in the coalition government that when this is all over, we'll have some sort of welfare service founded. Could all be hot air, but I think the days of charity clinics might be coming to an end.'

'Is that something to be celebrated, Andrew? Do you ever think the government can pull off something like that?'

'I hope so. There will always be the people who can afford Harley Street, but I see a lot of what goes on because I'm working between two worlds – the "nobs" who come to the posh clinics, and all the rest in the big hospitals. I see it here in London and down in Sussex too – I never could give up my links to the hospital there. Think about it – you can't charge people who've been so badly wounded in the bombings, and it's unfair to have hospitals that have a good budget at their disposal and others dependent upon any crumbs that fall off the table, to coin a phrase. I think a better system will come out of this war.' He glanced at his watch and shook his head. 'Isn't young Tim Partridge due to see me for a check up soon? It feels like a month since I last saw him.'

'Yes, I believe so. He's being a bit of a handful at the moment.'

'Not surprising.' He looked at Maisie's hand, which he was still holding, and released his grip. 'You must tell Priscilla and Douglas that they cannot give him any quarter – if they mollycoddle him, he'll be a mouthy monster in no time. He's struggling with a handicap now – but if he wants to see disability, bring him to the London Hospital. In fact, that mightn't be such a bad thing. I know it sounds harsh, but it's high time he realised it's not the end of the world, losing an arm. He can still walk, talk, eat and think.'

'I'll pass that on – but I think Priscilla is rather weary of the arguing.'

'That's what happens, and then the parents just give in, and *voilà*! There's your monster youth.' Dene looked at his watch again. 'Better be off now – I'm late.'

'Andrew – I wonder if you could do me a favour – I've a very quick question.'

'Go on – I've always got an extra five minutes for you, Maisie.'

Maisie smiled. 'Thank you, Andrew. Do you know many of the doctors around here? It seems a veritable village of physicians.'

'I only know them if they're in orthopaedics. Or the vascular and anaesthetics men – they're the ones I have to liaise with on a somewhat regular basis. Then there's old Chester, who has consulting rooms just along the street there. I know him because he delivered our first – personally telephoned me at the hospital to give me the news, so I was able to rush straight over there. First-class man. It's a pity he couldn't deliver the other two, but they were born at home in Sussex. Now then, I should be off – and we must talk about the clinic soon.' He kissed Maisie on the cheek once more, and began to walk at a brisk pace towards Harley Street. Maisie was about to call after him, to give her regards to his wife, but realised she had forgotten her name. She wondered too if Loki was at large, tricking her with a coincidence she should perhaps ignore.

'How did MacFarlane sound, when he telephoned?' asked Maisie, pulling a chair up to Sandra's desk.

'How does he always sound? Like a bull with a sore head. He said you could speak to Miss Chalmers, but he would be in the room with you.'

Maisie chewed her lip. 'Hmm. I suppose that's better than nothing, but I would prefer to be alone with her – MacFarlane is enough to intimidate anyone.'

'Unless she already knows him, or she's quite important herself, so she won't be distracted by that oaf.'

'He has a good heart, Sandra – he's just a bit gruff.'

'And rough around the edges.'

Maisie looked at her secretary, a woman she had known since she returned to the Ebury Place home of Lord Julian and Lady Rowan Compton more than ten years ago to live in rooms she had once cleaned as a maid in that same mansion. Sandra was a maid then, but had left Ebury Place upon her marriage. Following the death of Sandra's young husband in a suspicious accident, Maisie had encouraged the grieving woman to continue her education. Sandra later married her employer at the publishing company where she had found suitable work, and now with a child, she had returned to help Maisie with the administration of her business for a few hours each week. Maisie suspected Sandra's patience had been stretched by sleepless nights in a cellar with a baby not yet a year old – who was currently dozing in his carrycot in a corner of the office.

'I'd better go over to Whitehall to see MacFarlane and Miss Chalmers. In the meantime, Sandra – take Martin and go home now.'

'But I've still got—'

'No. You haven't got anything. This work will all wait – just a few invoices and a report to type up. If a bomb drops on the building, it will all be lost anyway. Go home, try to get some rest in the hour or so before the air raid warning, because you'll be hard-pushed to sleep tonight, if they come again.'

'Lawrence can sleep through anything. And he says I should go to the country.'

Maisie nodded. 'Sandra – I think he's right.' She pushed back the chair and came to her feet. 'What about staying with Lawrence's aunt?'

'That'd be worse than a bomb!'

'Then I'll see what I can do. Mr and Mrs Partridge are living in a cottage on one of the Chelstone estate's farms. It needed a bit of work and a lick or two of paint, but it seemed to be just the ticket for Tim to continue his recovery. Tarquin's there too. It's nothing like the size of house they're used to, but there are three bedrooms, a small sitting room, dining room and kitchen. I could ask if there's another cottage available in the area.'

'That would be lovely – the train station's not far, and there's also the coach stop in Tonbridge, so Lawrence can get back into town for work easily enough, though the coach does rattle along the road a bit.'

'All right – I'll see what I can do. I must go – I've to question this woman before reporting for duty. Go home now, Sandra – just leave things as they are and get on your way. I am sure Billy will be doing the same.'

'At least he doesn't have a boy in the air, like Mrs Partridge. They must be relieved that young Billy is now in Singapore – sounds like a jammy posting to me.'

'I think a few more of the boys who were stuck on those Dunkirk beaches could do with a jammy posting, don't you?'

'Miss Chalmers, it's very good of you to agree to see me. I'm sure Mr MacFarlane brought you up to date with the details. I'm currently looking into the death of Catherine Saxon – given her status as an American citizen in London during a time of war, her murder is being investigated as a joint case with a representative from their embassy.' Maisie looked at Isabel Chalmers as she spoke, taking in the woman's demeanour and the way she presented herself.

Chalmers was of average height, around five feet, four inches. She wore an austere navy blue costume comprising a tailored jacket and a skirt that draped to two inches below her knee. She had dark hair pulled back into a French pleat, and secured with a tortoiseshell comb. Her black shoes had been polished to a bright shine.

Chalmers smiled, but said nothing. Maisie thought it was the ready smile of someone quite nervous, someone who was fearful. She endeavoured to put the young woman at ease – for she was probably no older than twenty-two or twenty-three years of age, and somewhat younger than Mrs Marsh had suggested.

'Anyway, thank you very much for putting your work to one side to see me.' She glanced at MacFarlane, then brought her attention back to Chalmers, who was staring at Maisie, her eyes wide. Maisie suspected Chalmers had hardly absorbed a word of her introduction, so she repeated her connection to the enquiry. 'I know you must be terribly upset about Miss Saxon's death – it's so unsettling. As Mr MacFarlane has no doubt informed you, I am the investigator personally working with the American embassy to find the person who took her life.'

Chalmers nodded, her right hand massaging her left elbow, as if all feeling had gone from the limb.

Maisie drew her chair an inch or two closer to Chalmers, and leafed through a file of papers on her lap. She had no need to consult the report, but wanted to give the woman a chance to settle. She looked up and smiled. 'It's all right, Isabel – you can breathe in here.'

Chalmers swallowed as if her mouth were dry. 'I can barely think about it – that someone came in and did that to her while we were all there, while we were all asleep. Though I suppose, when I think about it, we weren't all there, were we? Because of the bombing.'

'It's very unsettling, I know. But perhaps by putting together snippets of information from her friends and colleagues, we can find out who took Catherine's life.'

As Maisie uttered the victim's Christian name, she noticed Chalmers' shoulders drop, almost as if Catherine Saxon had entered the room and said, 'I'm all right really. Don't worry.'

Maisie consulted the papers again, and looked up, meeting Chalmers' eyes. MacFarlane remained seated behind a desk close to the window about six feet away from the two women.

'Isabel – I take it I may call you "Isabel" and not "Miss Chalmers" – it makes these conversations a little easier, in my experience.'

'Yes, that's perfectly all right.'

'Good. Now, could you tell me how long you've worked here, in Whitehall?'

'Since the war started. I applied to join the Civil Service straight from Oxford – I'd done a secretarial course afterwards, and then the Civil Service examination.'

'What did you study at Oxford?'

'PPE – Philosophy, Politics, and Economics.'

'Not for the faint-hearted, that choice,' said Maisie, again smiling, putting the woman at ease.

'It was a bit hard. But great fun at Sommerville.'

'Ah, those idyllic days at college! I was at Girton. I studied the Moral Sciences – long before your time though.' Maisie's smile was brief. She consulted her notes before asking the next question, looking up again as Chalmers cleared her throat. 'Are you at liberty to tell me what you do here?'

Chalmers turned to MacFarlane, waiting for him to nod his accord.

'I'll let Miss Dobbs know if any question is too close to the mark.'

'Thank you.' Maisie drew her attention back to Chalmers. 'Your role here?'

Chalmers seemed to sit straighter, as if her job bestowed a greater level of importance upon her shoulders.

'I'm in a department concerned with our work in the United States of America.'

'Can you describe that work?'

MacFarlane looked at Maisie, holding up his hand with his thumb and forefinger just a quarter of an inch apart. *Be careful – you may go too far.* With a single nod, Maisie indicated she had understood his silent instruction.

Chalmers cleared her throat. 'Informally, we deal in what we call "soft propaganda". For example, we have sent a group of men to Washington, pilots who have been wounded – they're walking wounded, so almost recovered. They're acting as sort of ambassadors for what we've endured here. They're attached to the embassy, and their job is just to be there, in Washington, so that when the ambassador holds parties or any sort of function with American politicians and men of commerce and influence present, they're there too. And it's very important when these powerful men have their wives with them, because women can see the human side, can't they? Our pilots talk informally about what they did, and how we sent the Luftwaffe packing over the summer. That's why we're being bombed now – because Hitler thought he could destroy our fighters and then invade. Our boys in Washington are letting people know that Hitler's trying to wear us down now, and that we're holding the fort against his ambitions to take over the world – that we stand between him and America.'

Maisie did not give in to the desire to look at MacFarlane, but instead inclined her head as she took a moment to compose her next question, all the while keeping eye contact with Chalmers. 'Yes, I think I have the picture. Essentially, your department has selected young men – probably rather dashing young men, I would imagine – who currently cannot fly or otherwise be engaged in combat due to wounds sustained during an altercation with the enemy. Those men have the necessary experience, bearing and intelligence to become tools of propaganda on the other side of the Atlantic, indeed America's seat of power.'

'Yes. They're hand-picked. Very bright. Very engaging.'

'And I take it they all have the required level of security credential.'

'Yes.'

'And what part do you play?'

'I receive their reports – sometimes it's over the telephone line, or in a cable, coded of course, and sometimes I receive a handwritten letter in a diplomatic purse. I type the reports, and I am authorised to give priority to certain items if I consider them more important – which only means I type that bit first. I also make arrangements for them to get to and from the United States, invariably by aeroplane from Croydon via Lisbon.'

'This sounds like very important work to me, Isabel. Why do you think you were selected for this job?'

'It's only clerical, Miss Dobbs.'

Maisie shook her head. 'Not quite, Isabel – it's a bit more than that. You are supporting a plan devised at a high government level to effect the possible entry of America into the war, via her citizens. Who do you know?'

Chalmers looked at MacFarlane, who was staring out of the window – he did not meet her gaze. She cleared her throat. 'My father is with another government department, and he spoke for me. But I still had to pass those exams, and be good enough for the job of liaising with our people in Washington.'

'Yes, of course. I just wanted to know the connection. Can you tell me which department your father works in?'

'No, she can't. That's not on the table.' MacFarlane spoke without turning to face the women.

Maisie smiled again at Chalmers. 'Tell me about Catherine – start where you like.'

'What do you mean?'

'When did you first meet her? Were you already living at the house when she moved in?'

Chalmers nodded. 'Yes – I've been there since just after war was declared last September. Polly moved in a month or two before me, I think, but Pamela – Mrs Lockwood – had been there for some time, probably about ten years. Yes, that's it – she was living with her parents in Surrey following her husband's death in the last war, and then came up to London after they upped sticks to live by the coast due to her father's bad chest. She goes down on the train once a month to see them. The girls at the top of the house – Elizabeth and Helena – are both students, and they'd been in rooms for about a year, I think. They might not be there for long, because they're joining the Wrens, if they get in. They're like Siamese twins – they go everywhere together.'

'Yes, I'd heard that might be the case.' Maisie leant forward. 'And I understand Catherine was particularly interested in your job.'

Chalmers laughed. 'She was like a little terrier. She wanted to know everything, and she kept picking, picking, picking. I never wanted to tell her outright to mind her own business, though I tried to make a joke of it – telling her it was too boring to discuss. Or I'd say, "Pushing paper, Cath – your job is so much more exciting, got any room for me at Broadcasting House?" That's what she was after, a job on the wireless.'

'On the other hand, I suppose she might have been useful to you in a way – after all, she was also telling Americans at home what the battle has been like over here. Different job, same end in sight, I would imagine.'

'Oh no, what I do is very different, I mean, I have to instruct our men—'

'That's enough, Miss Chalmers,' MacFarlane interjected. He raised his chin. 'Miss Dobbs, another tack perhaps?'

'Right you are, Mr MacFarlane.' Maisie turned to Chalmers again. 'Can you describe any visitors Catherine might have had in recent weeks, or anyone who ever visited or who she talked about, perhaps, who caught your attention?'

'Cath knew so many people. She was always busy, most often out getting a story or up in her rooms writing. From the time I knew her she said her ambition was to become one of the "warcasters". Apparently, that's what they call themselves, the reporters who get on the wireless. Once she was in with the American wireless people, she would be over at Broadcasting House, or down at the post office sending a telegram to a newspaper somewhere. She was often off interviewing people too. But people coming to the house?' Chalmers brushed a stray hair from her face. 'There was her friend from home, the woman she was at college with. Her name's Jenny. Then there was the RAF fellow – but he was an American.'

'Really?'

'Yes, there are quite a lot of them here – well, more than just a few.' Chalmers looked down. 'That sounded terrible – I didn't mean that, after all, Mr Churchill said we owed so much to "The Few". But a lot of people don't realise there were Americans up there fighting with our boys over the summer. Some joined the Canadian air force, and some just came over to fly with the RAF. They were all aviators at home, perhaps for the postal service, or on a farm or something. This one was based in Kent somewhere. Cath met him when she was writing about Americans over here who are already doing their bit.'

'Do you remember his name?'

'We nicknamed him "Johnny". That was because Polly bumped into him outside once and said, "Hello, who's this – a stage-door

Johnny?" He was on leave and came up to see Cath, only she was out working, so he was waiting until she came home.'

'You say he's based in Kent? Any idea which aerodrome?'

Chalmers shook her head. 'Careless talk costs lives, doesn't it? Before I was transferred, I worked in the department where they drew up the anti-gossip campaign. The American had seen the posters, so when I asked him where he was based, that's what he said. "Careless talk costs lives." I had to laugh – it was so funny, coming from a foreigner – and, of course, he could have been a spy himself, for the Americans. But that would be ridiculous, wouldn't it?'

Maisie raised an eyebrow, smiled, and continued. 'And you don't know his real name?'

'No. He was "Stage-Door Johnny" from the time we first knew him – and it's not as if I saw him loads of times. Just once or twice. After all, let's face it, he was in the air more than on the ground. For all I know, he could be dead.'

'He could indeed.' Maisie closed her file. 'To recap – Catherine wanted to know what your work entailed, yet you did not tell her. You were friends, but you know only two of her associates – is that correct?'

'There was another man came once, but she never invited him in. I know because I have the downstairs rooms – the one that leads out into the garden. You've been to the house, so you know I can see up into the street from my downstairs front window. I was just home from work and heard voices coming from the front of the house. I looked up and saw a man standing there talking to Cath. She had one arm across her middle, as if she would have folded her arms had she not been holding a cigarette in the opposite hand. It wasn't a jolly conversation – she was frowning. Then she took one last draw on the smoke, threw it down and stepped on it. She turned and went back in, but he stayed there, then lifted his hat and walked off down the street.'

'Could you describe him?'

Chalmers shrugged. 'He was just ordinary. An ordinary man, with an ordinary suit – grey, and you don't get more common and ordinary than grey – and an ordinary hat, and ordinary shoes. He was carrying a mackintosh, which was a bit odd, because it was a warm evening and didn't look like rain at all. But you never know. Could have been another one of those Americans, being careful!'

'It could indeed,' agreed Maisie. 'Now, I understand you had nothing really to report regarding the day Catherine's body was found.'

'I was asleep. Sometimes I have to work late because there's a time difference between Washington and London, and a report might come in after six o'clock. I'm the one who has to type it up and forward instructions. I didn't come home until after the all-clear, and I think that wasn't long before the police came. I'd put cotton wool in my ears so I'd get some sleep when the other girls came in again, but I wasn't asleep for half an hour, and that's when I knew something terrible had happened on account of the voices, and the black van outside. I thought something had happened to Mrs Marsh at first, then I heard her crying. To be honest, I was worried she might have had a heart attack or fallen on the stairs. Would have served her right – she creeps around at all hours, standing outside doors, listening in case you've got a man friend in there with you. I think she only keeps away from Liz and Helena's rooms because she thinks they're best friends of a different order, if you know what I mean.'

MacFarlane cleared his throat. When Maisie looked in his direction, he was staring out of the window again, as if determined not to turn.

'Isabel, I have taken much of your time today. I appreciate your assistance, though I would like to emphasise that this meeting must be held in the strictest confidence. Certainly I am as much accountable to the government and the Official Secrets Act as you are, so I will not be discussing anything you said unless it is directly with one of the other two people responsible for this case.'

'So, if Mr MacFarlane is one, who is the other?'

'I'm not at liberty to say, Isabel.'

'Of course. As the poster says, "Keep Mum, She's Not So Dumb".'

With that, Isabel Chalmers came to her feet, shook hands with Maisie, and left the room without acknowledging MacFarlane.

'She's an interesting study,' observed the Scot. 'And you came a bit too close a couple of times.'

'Having more information in the file might have helped.'

'You always say you like to form your own impressions, Maisie – I took that into account and minimised our briefing before she came in. And I wanted to hear if she told you anything she hadn't already told the police when they first went to the house. Not that they had a chance to conduct a full investigation.' He stood up and walked to the other side of the desk, and leant back against it, crossing his arms. 'What do you think?'

'I think she is a young woman with a good deal of responsibility, working in a wartime government office that is probably more interesting than others. I mean, she's not trying to get people to give up sugar.'

'Yes, but what else do you think?'

'I'd like to see her again on her home turf, but I'm not sure it will be possible, given her working hours and the fact that she can also use the government shelter.'

MacFarlane paused, and once again looked out of the window. 'It's seeing the fires still burning, even from here, that gets to me. And that smell in the air – the ash, the smoke, and that hint of burning flesh.'

'I know . . .'

MacFarlane turned to Maisie. 'I trust you. If you feel the need to see her again, don't go any further than good sense and your fine reputation with me takes you.'

'And there's another thing,' added Maisie.

'Yes? Just as long as it's not more money.'

Maisie laughed. 'You're doing nothing for your fellow Scots with comments like that, Robbie.' She shook her head. 'No, it's not money. I believe I will need an official form of identification in order to interview some of the people on my list. I managed to do well earlier in the year when I took on that case where I had to visit the aerodromes, but Lord Julian smoothed the way. There's a doctor, especially, whom I would like to speak to, and given his work, I will definitely require documentation to bolster my position of investigator working with the government.'

'It'll be delivered to your office by tomorrow lunchtime. I'll see to it. Now then, anything else?'

'Soft propaganda? Is that a real government department?'

'It most certainly is. Remember that case you had a few years ago – you know, Eddie Pettit? You came across the business of getting stories into newspapers and books about our wonderful Britain, that sort of thing?'

'Yes, I remember – it was designed to build a sense of national pride, so that if the balloon went up, people would know what they were fighting for, what they were up against and would be more likely to stand together before the foe. That was the plan, I believe,' Maisie paused, thoughtful, adding, 'and I looked over a book I found at Catherine Saxon's flat – *101 Things To Do In Wartime*. One page is dedicated to what we should be reading – and every book listed harks back to those things we hold dear in Britain. I suppose you could say our "heritage".'

'Well, as I said – it's the same sort of thing – only now we're doing it on the other side of the Atlantic. We're quietly walking round and round the walls of Jericho – weakening the pillars of dissent against us over there. We'll bring them down, eventually, and not a moment too soon.'

Maisie said nothing at first, though she consulted her watch before continuing. 'Mr Scott is unavailable for a few days. It's a very strange situation I'm in, Robbie – I am supposed to be working with him, yet he admits he's never investigated a murder before. He leaves me to my own devices, but I almost feel he's breathing down my neck and he isn't here. Tell me, Robbie – is there something I am not being told about this case or about him?'

MacFarlane shook his head. 'Not on my part, lass – though there are some things I cannot tell you, but not directly about Mark Scott.'

There was another pause. Maisie weighed up whether to raise more doubt. She would take a chance on trusting Robert MacFarlane.

'Robbie, when I knew Scott in Munich, he was using John Otterburn's daughter, Elaine, as an informer. She was most unsuitable for the job, though heaven knows she demonstrated immense bravery when I asked it of her, and she was calm in the face of what could have been a terrible death. He might have saved my life, but at one point he risked hers.'

'You know what this work is like, Maisie. Sometimes we just do what we have to do, and bugger the outcome.'

'Be that as it may. But I wondered if the ordinary grey man in the ordinary grey suit carrying the ordinary mackintosh who came to see Catherine Saxon might not have been Mark Scott. And if so, what was she doing talking to an agent working at the American embassy in London? Was he transferred for a very specific reason and we just don't know it? Or do you know something about this and you're not telling me?'

'No, I don't know anything about his business at the embassy. You have my word, Maisie.' MacFarlane sighed. 'You must continue the investigation in accordance with your brief and everything you know about conducting an enquiry.'

'And if that compromises Mark Scott?'

'Just continue. I'll tell you if I want you to pull back.'

'I don't like it, Robbie.'

'No more than I, lass. No more than I. But I trust you.'

It was as Maisie left Whitehall, bound for the ambulance station, that she wondered if she trusted MacFarlane any more, because she certainly did not trust Mark Scott. And she wondered too if she trusted Catherine Saxon. Had there ever been a time in her work when she had not trusted the dead? If only Maurice had left her with some wisdom to draw upon in such a circumstance.

CHAPTER SEVEN

'I told Douglas about Catherine Saxon, so we started talking about the wireless, and how it's really caught on in the past fifteen, twenty years or so.' Priscilla placed her bag in a locker and took out her helmet, upon the front of which had been painted a large white A.

'I like listening to the wireless when I'm at home – though I quickly turn it off on a Sunday if that Lord Haw Haw comes on. It's not just what he says, it's his voice – everything,' said Maisie.

'Hitler trying to undermine our morale with one of our own,' added Priscilla.

'That's why I turn the dial.' Maisie slipped on her helmet, and pushed her bag into the same locker, along with her clothing. She rolled up the sleeves of her boiler suit, then checked the laces on her boots. 'Mind you, Brenda thinks he's nothing more than a bit of a laugh.'

'I need a cigarette,' said Priscilla.

'There's ti—' Maisie looked up as the air raid warning sounded. 'Here they come. We'll get our first call soon.'

'Let's go out to Bunty and wait there,' said Priscilla. 'At least I hope it's Bunty – she's the best set of wheels in the whole place.'

'You know how it is, Pris – we'll get a different one, because we're seen as the older crew, more experienced. I think the younger women have enough hours under their belts though – these past few days have been hell for everyone.'

'Ladies, you'll be the first out tonight.' Mr Blake, one of the supervisors, pointed to the first of several ambulances lined up alongside a wall. 'You've got Alice.'

'Oh, she's not a bad old girl,' said Maisie.

'Heavy on the turns,' said Priscilla.

'Nothing my two stars can't manage, eh, ladies? I'll be out as soon as we get the call. Give her the usual once-over so you don't have any surprises.'

Maisie and Priscilla set about the 'once-over', with Maisie checking medical supplies, blankets, and the necessary items they would require to stabilise bombing victims for what could be an arduous journey to the hospital, while Priscilla checked the engine, making sure the oil and water levels were sufficient, and the tyres still roadworthy – not that they had time to change a tyre if it was found wanting. With their task complete, they leant against the ambulance, Priscilla speaking as she lit up a cigarette without her customary long holder.

'Anyway, back to what I was saying about the wireless – Douglas thought you might be interested in this, from *Variety*.' She reached into her pocket and took out a folded page torn from a newspaper. 'Not something he usually reads, but for his work with the Ministry of Information bods, he's digesting all sorts of things he would normally never consider. Here you are – have a look at it later, when you're safely at home.'

'So how was Tom's visit? Have you heard?' asked Maisie as she slipped the paper into her pocket.

'Oh yes, I've heard all right. It transpires my eldest son took it upon himself to give his brothers – and I mean both brothers – a proverbial smack on the rump, if you know what I mean. He'd borrowed a motor car and came down to the cottage with one of his air force friends. They'd already decided they wanted to visit some of their pals who had been shot down and, due to their wounds, transferred to a hospital in East Grinstead – it's where they're sending the serious burn cases.'

'Yes, I've heard about it – the Victoria Hospital, isn't it?'

'What most people don't know is how bad the burns can be.' Priscilla drew on her cigarette. 'Tom tells me that a number of men have managed to land their aircraft even when it's on fire, but the hood – I think it's called a "hood" – can become stuck when it's hot, so they get horrible burns to their hands and faces. And I mean terrible, with their skin melting against the bone. Anyway, number one son and friend took sons two and three to the Queen Victoria Hospital to visit those pilots, and it seems to have made Tim wind his neck in. They saw boys not much older than themselves bearing up with the most dreadful wounds, doing their best to be cheery, making light of their pain and disfigurement to keep up everyone's morale. There were no moaners, according to Douglas, when he recounted the whole episode to me – the story came via Tom when he brought his brothers home. There's apparently a doctor at the hospital who is doing amazing work, you know, not only giving them back their faces – inasmuch as he can – but he's allowing them to wear their own clothes, not uniforms, and those who can are allowed to go out. Can't remember his name, but he's from New

Zealand.' She pushed back her helmet and scratched her forehead where it had left a red welt. 'And Tom told Douglas the local people have been marvellous, just marvellous – not staring or being otherwise objectionable when they see the boys on the street.' She continued, dropping the half-smoked cigarette on the ground before pressing her boot into it. 'Makes you wonder, really, what it means to lose your face. I suppose you lose something of who you are, and it takes someone else to remind you.'

'It all seems to have come a long way since the last war, when young men found that being in hospital with others with the same wounds was one thing – it was when they left to go back to the outside world that life became so very difficult. I remember—'

'Shoreditch, ladies. Shoreditch now. Here's where you're going.' Blake pressed a piece of paper into Maisie's hand.

No more words were spoken. Within seconds the ambulance had left the depot and they were on their way, looking in the direction of smoke, of barrage balloons, searchlights and fire, and the dark shadows of bombers above London.

'A murder of crows,' said Maisie.

'Just watch old Alice on this corner,' warned Priscilla.

'Pris—'

'All right. I'll shut up.'

Maisie could not stifle a yawn as she entered the office the following morning.

'Last night was a terror, wasn't it, miss?' said Billy.

'Another long one, though we were able to get off duty earlier than we expected – around five.'

'So you managed to have a few hours' kip, then?'

'Sort of – I keep thinking about Catherine Saxon. There's so much bothering me, so much to find out and it's hard to get hold of possible witnesses when they aren't able to return home after work, but instead are in shelters and you don't know where they are.' She rubbed her eyes. 'Give me a minute – I must make an appointment to see Jennifer Barrington – Catherine Saxon's best friend – and then come on into my office. It's past time that we had a case map underway.'

Maisie walked into her private office and took out the note Mark Scott had given her with Jennifer Barrington's telephone number. She placed the call, and when the housekeeper answered, asked to speak to Mrs Barrington.

'I'm afraid she isn't at home, madam, and not expected at the residence until tomorrow afternoon. May I tell her who called?'

'Yes, indeed.' Maisie gave her name, and informed the housekeeper of her reason for calling.

'I see – Mrs Barrington would most certainly wish to see you soonest – she has been most upset since she heard the news of Miss Saxon's death.' There was a pause, and in the background Maisie could hear the unmistakable rhythmic *tick tock* of a grandfather clock. 'I'm going to take the liberty of asking you to come on Thursday. I know she will be at the house all day. Might you be able to make a firm appointment?'

'Yes, of course. May we say twelve o'clock?'

'I've added it to Mrs Barrington's diary for Thursday, September the nineteenth.'

Maisie thanked the woman and sat back in her chair and stared out of the window. As a rule, she liked to pay a visit unannounced to those associated with the dead, but the bombings had made it difficult. As much as people made the effort to retain life's rhythm, it seemed only the clocks met with any success.

'Right you are,' said Billy as he entered the office, his notebook in hand. 'I've got something that might interest you.'

'Good – but first, has Sandra telephoned? I want to know if they're all safe,' said Maisie, turning towards her assistant. 'I heard there were some bombs in Pimlico last night.'

'Sandra, Lawrence and Martin are all chipper, miss. She was able to use the blower at the flat – I took the call only five minutes before you walked in. In fact, she said Lawrence was just off to work. But she mentioned they're hoping you can find them a cottage around Chelstone somewhere.' He paused. 'I sent Doreen and Margaret Rose back to her aunt in Hampshire – I want my girls safe. I mean, my boys are both safe enough – Billy in Singapore now, probably square-bashing in the golden sunshine, and Bobby's still at that college.'

'Sorry, Billy – I should have asked before. Is Bobby getting on all right?'

'A bit too all right. Now he's going on again about applying to be an engineer on the blimmin' aeroplanes. Says that's his ambition. And there's me hoping he'd forget all about that idea.' He took a roll of wallpaper from a basket in the corner, stretching it out on the desk with the plain side up, pinning it to the surface so they could write on it. 'I tell you, miss, if a boy of his age talks about having an ambition when there's a war going on, it gives you the shivers. When he first started to take an interest in engines, I thought he'd do well to work up to being a mechanic on Rolls-blimmin'-Royces, perhaps one day having his own business, not setting his eye on sitting in the engineer's seat with a bomber crew. And that's what he talked about – how he's heard there are plans in the works for a new bomber, and it sounds really exciting. Really exciting? I tell you, there are times when I feel like getting him by the scruff of the neck and giving him a piece of my mind about what's really exciting. Really exciting is when every day is the same and verging on boring. That's a thrilling thought, as far as I'm concerned.'

Maisie placed a jar of coloured crayons on the table in front of two chairs. Billy took a seat and watched as she wrote Catherine Saxon's name in the centre of a circle, and then drew lines coming from that circle, each leading to another name. One of those names was Mark Scott.

'Billy – tell me what you've found out.'

'For a start, I still don't know where Mr Scott lives. I went over to Manchester Square and I walked around, down a street here and a street there, and I looked at the names outside front doors of the ones converted into flats, that sort of thing. I didn't want to start asking, just in case – I didn't have a very, you know, positive feeling about that course of action.'

'Not like you, Billy. But I respect your judgement. We'll find out soon enough – although this case should move faster, and I'm hoping "soon" is just around the corner.'

'Speaking about 'round the corner, that's what happened yesterday.'

'Go on.'

'Well, as I said, I wore out shoe leather around Manchester Square, and I followed a route I imagined he'd take to work of a morning, then I thought I should get over to see Mrs Van Larsen, you know, the Dutch lady who lives over in Kensington. She's the poor old girl who everyone keeps thinking is German, but she's from Holland, and she asked us to check her doors, and such like. To be honest, I think she just wants people to see that a man is coming to the house.'

'Let's not charge her – a woman on her own deserves to feel safe. But tell me what happened.'

'After I'd visited, I was walking along the road to catch a bus, and was coming up to Prince's Gate – and who do you think I saw?'

'You're going to tell me it was Mark Scott.'

'You're right, it was!'

'What was he doing? He couldn't have been just standing there.'

'That's the funny thing – he was. Just standing there. I had to stop a bit sharpish, in case he saw me. I pulled my cap down a bit, and went on slowly to have a proper gander. He was standing on the other side of the road, just looking at the building as if he was weighing up a few things. Then he turned and walked away into the park – Kingston Gate was right opposite.'

'He was just looking at a house? Do you know who lives there?'

'I do now, because I found out – asked a copper I saw down the street. Turns out it's the residence of the American ambassador. Joseph Kennedy. I remember when he got the job, and it was all over the papers, what with him and all his family coming over there. There wasn't anything about that family they didn't report on.'

'Hmm. I'm not sure Scott being in that area is something to be surprised about – after all, he works at the embassy.'

'Nothing to be surprised about, perhaps. But the way he was looking – he was thinking. He was looking and thinking. And it seemed to me he looked like you or I might look at a gaff when we're wondering about the people in there.'

'Billy—'

'You want me to talk to my mate down on Fleet Street, don't you?'

'I do. Saves us going through a mound of newspapers on a dig to see what we can find. See what he says about the American ambassador. He might be at some risk and Scott is reviewing safety measures in place around his residence. Or maybe he's responsible for someone who was at the house. I daresay the authorities have increased surveillance around all embassy and consular buildings, given the bombings and so on.'

'Consider it done, miss – I've got to say, even though he was outside, it was as if he didn't want to be seen, yet at the same time he couldn't care less if he was. I daresay the ambassador himself was not at home – he was probably at the embassy – but Mr Scott looked like a man who was . . . I dunno, sort of . . . what's that you've said once or twice? Yeah – that's it. He was hidden in plain sight.' Billy shrugged. 'I hope I was – wouldn't want to think he'd seen me.'

'If he had seen you, you're in the clear because you had just left a client's residence. If he mentions it, then tell the truth. At that moment, you were in the area in connection with another job. Anyway, you talk to your friend the newspaperman, and in the meantime, I'm going over to Derry & Toms. I want to have a word or two with Mrs Lockwood, the woman who lived on the floor directly above Catherine Saxon. Oh, and could you find out if your friend has ever heard of her father, Clarence Saxon, or Catherine's brothers? It's probably nothing, but I'd like to know if their names have cropped up in the press over here for any reason. I'm sure all these reporters keep tabs on each other, and they read the *New York Herald*, and other international newspapers, so you never know, there could be a snippet someone's heard somewhere.'

'I'm leaving now, miss.'

'Good work, Billy – oh, and Billy—'

'Yes, miss?'

'Look, I cannot promise anything, but Dad and Brenda are spending all their time at the Dower House now, because we have a cellar and they like to know they can get down there when the bombers go over. They feel safer, given their age, and it's better for Anna, so she has all three of us when I'm there. If you'd like Doreen and Margaret Rose closer but still in the country, I could ask if they can stay at the bungalow. The pub along the street has a big cellar that people in the village are using as a shelter, so it's handy. There's a tunnel leading from it that was used by smugglers in the 1700s, and they've put mattresses in there for the children – making it into an adventure of sorts.'

'Much obliged, miss. I won't say anything until you let me know though.' He pushed back his chair, but lingered at the table, fingering the edge of the wallpaper. 'Some blimmin' adventure though, ain't it?'

'Yes it is, Billy – some blimmin' adventure. I'll be back here before I go on duty again at five, so perhaps I'll see you.'

They were about to leave the office, when Billy reached back to his desk and took up an envelope.

'Sorry, miss, almost forgot! This was delivered by messenger this morning, before you got here – looks like it's from MacFarlane.'

Maisie took the envelope, ran a finger under the sealed flap and looked inside. She smiled. 'Just what I was waiting for, Billy – this will come in handy today.'

Stepping out at Kensington High Street Underground Station, Maisie stopped to look at an advertisement for Derry & Toms, then made her way to the department store, housed in a fairly new building Maisie thought was somewhat austere from the outside; it was in the art-deco-style, with bold architectural details reminding her of buildings she'd seen in Munich. Her sojourn in Munich was not a time she wanted to reflect upon, but as it was where she had first met Mark Scott, there seemed to be no escaping the memory. She asked an assistant to direct her to the offices, and made her way to the realm where Mrs Lockwood worked.

It transpired Pamela Lockwood was a supervisor, and quite a senior one into the bargain. Maisie had no difficulty in asking if she might spare her a few minutes – Lockwood was not required to ask permission of a superior, and Maisie had a new identification card from MacFarlane to support her request. To her surprise she was shown into a private meeting room, where Lockwood asked if she would like a cup of tea.

'Thank you for the offer, Mrs Lockwood, but I don't want to take any more of your time than necessary.' Maisie took a seat at the table, while Lockwood sat opposite.

Pamela Lockwood wore a costume of pale rose pink, with a cream silk blouse under the jacket. Her hairstyle was neat and practical, and was similar to Maisie's – cut to just below the ears, her hair was brushed away from her face in soft waves, then held in place on both sides by silver combs. She wore plain light brown court shoes with a low heel. Maisie wasn't sure why, but she had imagined her as a woman who would not wear cosmetics, and was a little surprised to note that Pamela Lockwood wore make-up with powder, rouge, mascara and a hint of red lipstick applied to maximum effect. The result was a woman in her mid-forties who would pass for a thirty-year-old with ease.

'First of all, I'm so glad you were able to see me, Mrs Lockwood – what with the blitzes, everyone vanishes into a shelter as soon as the air raid warning is heard, and it would have otherwise taken me days to speak to you.'

'I'm happy to offer any help I can. I gave a cursory statement to the police, mainly because they didn't ask me much. I was rather surprised, because even though I might not have had any helpful answers, they didn't exactly ask a lot of questions.'

'Indeed,' said Maisie. 'They're very busy, which is why this case was handed over to another department fairly quickly. I work on assignment for Scotland Yard, and on this occasion I am required to liaise with a representative of the United States consular service.'

'That makes sense, seeing as Catherine was an American,' said Lockwood. 'Now then – fire away!'

'Right. First of all, I want to confirm that you are Mrs Pamela Lockwood, and you are resident at the same address as the deceased, Miss Catherine Saxon.'

'Yes.'

'And you are a widow.' Maisie looked at her notes, though she could have continued without referring to them.

'My husband was killed in 1918, Miss Dobbs. One day before he was due to come home on leave. Just one day. October 1918 to be precise.'

'I am so sorry – how very sad. So close to the Armistice.'

'Just before the finish line. A single bullet to the right temple, from a sniper. I am inclined to think he was so excited about coming home, he stopped paying attention, as if he'd imagined it so many times, he was already here, so he became careless.'

'I can imagine that. I remember that frisson of anticipation as leave drew near – and feeling as if you were home before you'd even left.' She looked at Lockwood, and as their eyes met, she added,

126

'I was a nurse in France, at a casualty clearing station close to the Belgian border.'

'I rolled bandages in the evenings in the local town hall, though I was helping out with the accounts and orders for my father's business – well, I should say my parents' business, because they both worked in the shop. Fortunately, I was able to get a better job after I'd managed to get some proper qualifications under my belt, and then came up here as soon as they moved closer to the coast.'

'Yes, of course.' Maisie cleared her throat. 'Tell me when you first met Catherine Saxon.'

'When she moved in – first day, actually. It was a Saturday, so my half-day, and I reached the front of the house as a man was unloading her belongings from a van. I think she'd just come from Spain, or France. Might it have been Berlin? I'm not sure. But she told me that many of her things had been stored in the cellars at a friend's house – another American. Mrs Barrington – Jenny. Both very nice girls.'

'I'll come to Jennifer Barrington in a minute. Can you describe your first impressions of Miss Saxon?'

Lockwood nodded. 'She was standing outside the house holding a box of books, and laughing with the driver. I don't know where she'd lived before finding the rooms – I think she spent a few days in a hotel, just a cheap one, when she came from overseas, and she might have stayed at Jenny's too. She seemed very forthright – put down the box when she saw me, and said, "I'm Catherine Saxon – your new neighbour." I was a bit taken aback. So my first impression was of someone very confident, as you might expect with an American.'

'Do you know any other Americans, Mrs Lockwood?'

The woman shook her head. 'Only from the pictures. She sort

of reminded me of that actress – you know, the one who was in the picture *Holiday* with Cary Grant.'

'Katharine Hepburn?'

'That's it. And Cary Grant – he's British, you know.'

'I didn't see that picture. I only usually go with my godson, and I don't think Katharine Hepburn and Cary Grant are quite up his alley. But I know who Katharine Hepburn is. Do you like to go to the pictures?'

Lockwood smiled. It was a broad smile, and Maisie realised it was the first hint of true enthusiasm or connection she'd noticed in the woman. 'Oh yes, I do – go as much as I can, usually on a Saturday afternoon, when the shop closes, though with the bombing, you never know what's going to happen. It's like stepping into another world at the pictures – away from all this.'

'Yes, I suppose it is,' said Maisie. 'Would you say you had a friendship with Miss Saxon?'

'Not really.' Lockwood looked away, her gaze directed out of the window. 'We were cordial, but not pally. The woman on the lower ground floor, under Mrs Marsh – Isabel – she would sometimes invite us all down to her flat for a cup of tea on a Saturday or Sunday afternoon, and of course it was very nice, having a chat. But Catherine would badger Isabel – Miss Chalmers – about her job, and she pushed it a bit too far if you ask me. In fact, I had a word with her about it once, on the way back upstairs. I said, "Cath, you should just wind your neck in. Isabel works for the government, and even if she's only licking stamps, she wouldn't be able to tell you if it was a penny stamp or a ha'penny stamp." She just laughed and said, "Oh, I'm only teasing her." But I don't think she was teasing at all. She was looking for something to write about, or after getting someone on the inside of government to bring her information that no other reporter could get, and she thought a secretary was the way to go about it. She was ambitious – and she wanted so much to be on the wireless. That's why she picked up with that engineer, I would imagine – she thought she could get in that way. But as it happened, that American man gave her the chance she wanted anyway. And then she was dead.'

'Yes, the engineer,' said Maisie, looking at the notes Scott had given her at lunch. 'Do you mean Bob Walkinshaw? Australian?'

'That's him. Came over in 1915 with the ANZACS and ended up staying because he'd married here. Nice man – met him once when he came to see Cath. And before you ask, I don't think they were having an affair, though he might have had a bit of a crush on her. He was very chummy – like they are, the Australians.'

'Did you get the impression he might have wanted more from Catherine?'

Lockwood shrugged. 'I think if she'd been game for it, he wouldn't have looked back. Not that she wasn't nice to him – when I saw them a few times, she always had her arm through his, and she was giggling like a schoolgirl. I'm told men like that sort of thing, but I've always thought it demeaning for a woman.'

Maisie regarded Pamela Lockwood, the set of her jaw as she completed her observation. 'Demeaning' was a word she uttered as if she could see it inscribed in capital letters before her, and had underlined it to emphasise a point.

Lockwood continued. 'Cath seemed to have a few men friends. But she wasn't flirty.' She tapped the table, as if to emphasise a point. 'She wasn't *that* sort of girl. But she had a light about her, and a person with that light attracts all sorts, wouldn't you agree?' She didn't wait for Maisie to answer, but went on. 'And I've got to give it to her, she really worked hard. I heard her on the doorstep one evening saying, "Scotty, I don't have time to talk to you now. I have to work – it's really important. I'll call you tomorrow."'

'Scotty?' Maisie looked up at Pamela Lockwood.

The woman shrugged. 'Didn't see him and didn't hear him, so I don't know who he was. Just another stage-door Johnny.'

'Stage-door Johnny?' repeated Maisie.

'Oh, just something Polly said about Cath's admirers – the stage-door Johnnies, she called them. And being an actress, she would know, though I think she spends more time serving drinks than treading the boards!'

'Can you tell me anything else about her friends, or anyone else who visited her?'

Lockwood shook her head, then seemed thoughtful, gazing out of the window again. 'Not that he was an admirer – well, I suppose he might have been – but she was very excited about the American airman she'd interviewed. Apparently there are quite a few over here, and she wanted to write about them, just to let people know at home that there are some Americans who are doing their bit for us.'

'Do you know his name?'

Lockwood shook her head, then glanced at her watch.

'Just a couple more questions, Mrs Lockwood.' Maisie consulted her notes, then met Lockwood's eyes again. 'On the morning of her death, did you hear any noise coming from Miss Saxon's flat? After all, it was just below yours, and it seems sound travels a fair bit in that house.'

'It does, but I wasn't there – I'd gone down to the shelter here at work. I wasn't going to be blown out of my bed by the bloody Germans.'

'Of course.' Maisie closed her notebook. 'Mrs Lockwood, I wonder, would you be so kind as to get in touch if you think of anything pertinent to my investigation? I am sure you want to see Miss Saxon's killer brought to justice. And I might have to return to you to ask a couple more questions.'

'All right.' Lockwood came to her feet, turning to pull away her chair and stepping towards the door.

'Thank you for your time,' said Maisie.

Lockwood nodded, though this time their eyes did not meet. 'Follow me – I'll show you to the lifts.'

As they reached the lift, Lockwood pressed a button on the wall, then paid attention to her cuff, brushing her fingers against it as if to remove a speck of lint.

'I do have one more question,' said Maisie. 'Do you have trouble with the windows in your rooms? Do they stick, or not close properly?'

She nodded by way of reply. 'Cold in winter, with that draught coming through. But it's an old house. I bought some tape last year to try to keep the wind out. Did a fairly good job. Offered some to Cath, actually, and she said, "Oh, Pam, how can I let the guys in if my windows are taped!" She always had to make something of it, that she attracted men – even if she wasn't a big flirt. She had to let you know she was special.' Lockwood looked up at the series of numbers above the lift. 'Here you are. You'll know your way from here.'

Maisie watched Pamela Lockwood walk away along the corridor, then stepped into the lift bound for the ground floor.

The Underground station was just a few minutes' walk along the street, but Maisie wanted to sit and think, to consider the interview she'd just conducted, so having consulted her watch she decided to go to a nearby cafe instead. She ordered a strong coffee, though she knew it would not be quite the same flavourful blend she bought from the importers in Tunbridge Wells. This coffee would be laced with chicory, and would require hot milk to render it drinkable. Maurice's love of good coffee had spoilt her from an early age, but she felt a need for sustenance if she were to have the energy required on the ambulance runs this evening. The coffee came with hot milk, along with her order of a round of Welsh rarebit and an Eccles cake for something sweet before she set off again.

The questions levelled at Pamela Lockwood were innocuous enough. Her answers offered a mix of information Maisie had to hand. In Catherine Saxon, she already had a picture of a woman set on adventure, yet tempered with a certain understanding of the reality of her work, and the compassion to tell a story created to touch the hearts of her readers – or the listeners she wanted to reach. Maisie leant against the back of her seat by the window, watching passers-by as she sipped the coffee and reached for the Eccles cake. Silver barrage balloons swayed in the sky above, sandbags protected people from broken glass should a window be blown out by a bomb blast, and gas masks in their shoulder-strap boxes bumped against the hips of those who remembered to bring them to work in the morning. Pamela Lockwood was busy in her office, immaculate in her rose pink costume, and with her coiffed hair. It was clear she had both regard for Catherine Saxon and an accompanying disapproval. But then, didn't the characters Katharine Hepburn brought to the silver screen also draw an element of disapproval? The widowed Lockwood would know, being an enthusiastic follower of the pictures who would go on Saturday afternoons to escape loneliness. Maisie had felt Lockwood's isolation as if it were a vapour that enveloped her; it was a solitariness, an aura of abandonment she sensed in one who had imagined a future with a husband and children, a family home with a dog, and a garden with swings.

It was while she was sipping the bitter coffee that Maisie remembered the snippet of an article in *Variety* Priscilla had given her to read. She rummaged in her bag and found the folded sheet; opening it, she read:

Radio exposes nearly everybody in the country to a rapid, bewildering succession of emotional experiences. Our minds and our moral natures just cannot respond to the bombardment of contradictions and confusion.

'You can say that again,' said Maisie, at once realising she had spoken aloud, for a couple at a nearby table had looked up. Maisie smiled back, and stared out of the window again. The people of London were most certainly on a carousel of emotional experiences, and due not only to the gamut of BBC broadcasts, but the onslaught of bombs every single night, along with families divided by war, children sent to the homes of strangers, and the task everyone had taken on – of acting as if nothing in the world bothered them when there was everything to bother them.

Had Catherine Saxon's work bothered someone to the extent that they had wanted to silence her? Or had someone just wanted to scare her? Was there reason to believe that a visitor came to her room to talk, but emotions ran high, a sharp knife was taken up and Saxon was killed in the heat of emotional confusion?

Maisie looked down at the dregs of her unsatisfying beverage, and pushed the cup away. She took out her notebook and began to record her impressions about the meeting with Pamela Lockwood. As she reflected upon the conversation, there were two points of interest deserving of immediate investigation. Who was the American airman? And more than anything, she was determined to discover the identity of Catherine Saxon's 'Scotty'.

CHAPTER EIGHT

As she stepped into the nearest telephone kiosk, Maisie looked at the telephone number on the card Mark Scott had given her. A man answered the call, but did not identify himself.

'May I speak to Mr Mark Scott, please?' asked Maisie.

'Mr Scott is not available, ma'am. Who shall I say called?'

'When do you believe he will be back in his office?'

'I don't have that information, ma'am. Your name, please?'

'Maisie Dobbs. M-a-i-s-i-e. Tell him I telephoned, and that I would like to speak to him at his earliest convenience.'

'Thank you, ma'am.'

'And thank you too,' said Maisie, once again listening to the long tone of the disconnected call echoing into the telephone kiosk. 'I'm getting a little too used to this.' She replaced the receiver, stepped out of the kiosk, and joined the crowd of people funnelling through the turnstiles down into the Underground station.

*　*　*

'No need to huff and puff,' said Priscilla, as Maisie arrived at the ambulance depot, running in as Priscilla was taking off her hat and gloves. 'The siren's only just sounded, so we've time to check the wagon – we've been given Bunty tonight, and thank goodness. I could do with some positive news.'

'Oh dear,' said Maisie, changing into her dark blue overalls. 'Don't tell me it's Tim again.'

'He telephoned from the cottage to inform me he's had enough of being down in the countryside, and he's sure there's something useful he could be doing for the war effort in London. I said I thought that was most noble of him, but there were already a number of soldiers thanking their lucky stars that he didn't mind giving up an arm to rescue them from the German army in Dunkirk.'

'Priscilla—'

'I know – my words might have had a little edge to them, but in the meantime, I wanted to remind him that he's done his bit. I'm not sure Tom did any good at all taking him to that hospital. Tarquin is now even more determined to be a conscientious objector – for which every night I am getting much closer to being grateful rather than experiencing a smattering of humiliation – and Tim is still having hospital appointments to check his arm, or lack thereof. I also reminded him that studying for Oxbridge entrance exams mightn't be such a bad idea in the circumstances. And at least he'll have an edge on the other young men – and, of course, young women, I might add – in that he's already served his country in a rather stunning fashion. I find that mentioning young women to my young men often has a most positive effect.'

'And how *was* the Oxbridge suggestion received?' Maisie pushed a handkerchief into her pocket, picked up her gas mask and helmet, and nodded towards the door.

'Went down like a lead balloon,' said Priscilla, following Maisie, her own gas mask and helmet in hand. 'All he does is listen to the wireless and get upset about everything, when the people who are in the thick of it are soldiering on.'

'He's young, Pris – we've already talked about it, and he's just having a very difficult time adjusting.'

'He's not the only one.' The women stopped alongside the ambulance, and threw their helmets and gas masks into the cab. 'I'll check Bunty under her bonnet, if you check supplies in her nether regions,' said Priscilla.

Following two easy runs, transferring patients from one hospital to another, Maisie and Priscilla returned to the depot for emergency instructions. Already German bombers had followed the Thames in towards London and both the East End and areas south-east of the river were under attack. Ambulance staff were warned that the Luftwaffe were dropping heavy bombs along with incendiaries, a combination designed to cause maximum damage and uncontrollable fire.

'We've got injured in Laddington Street. It's in Lambeth – know where to go?' said Priscilla.

'Yes, I'll drive,' replied Maisie.

Gripping the wide steering wheel, Maisie manoeuvred the ambulance out of the depot, the engine groaning, the bell ringing to warn any traffic out of the way. Taking a route along the Embankment, she drove at speed towards Lambeth Bridge, sounding her horn and swerving around a delivery cart.

'Don't worry, you'll get him on the way back,' said Priscilla, as she tried to hang on to the leather strap alongside her head, while at the same time lighting a cigarette.

'If that were my father, once the air raid warning had sounded, he would have had his horse in a place of safety.'

'Perhaps that poor man's trying to get there,' said Priscilla, who gasped as she leant forward, pointing across the water. 'God help us all – look at that. Lambeth is burning. I hope those people are in the shelters – anywhere but their houses.'

'According to our briefing, there are wounded and the firemen weren't managing to stem the fire. And there's an unexploded bomb in the area.'

'That's all we need – UXB! One look at me, and I reckon the thing will just go bang!'

'Don't even joke about things like that, Pris – hold on.' Maisie swung the ambulance around a corner, and onto Lambeth Bridge. 'Four streets along I go right, then a left and another right, and we'll be there.'

Priscilla donned her helmet, and with her cigarette in her mouth, reached sideways to position Maisie's helmet and fasten her chin strap.

'I suppose a bit extra smoke up my nose won't matter, will it?' said Maisie.

'I bet this reminds you of that gypsy funeral you went to – I remember you telling me about it.'

And in her mind's eye, even as she drove on, Maisie could see the gypsy caravan in flames, the sound of a violin being played with greater and greater intensity as the dead matriarch's home was consumed by fire.

'The difference is, Pris, that her home was empty, and the fire was a ritual everyone understood.'

Pressing on through streets flanked by fire, they reached Laddington Street. Maisie braked hard, and the women leapt from the cab. A series of bodies had been laid on the ground to one side.

'Them ones are gone, love,' shouted a fireman. 'But the other three are still with us. There's another ambulance along the street, and the WVS ladies are coming in with blankets to cover the dead.'

'Right you are,' said Maisie, as Priscilla opened the back of the ambulance to gather supplies they would need to stabilise the wounded for transportation.

The women set to work without speaking, each knowing their next move as if they were cogs in a machine, turning this way and that to save human beings torn apart by the weapons of war.

'Bloody hell!' one of the firemen cried out. 'There's kids upstairs in that house.'

Maisie looked up as she finished applying dressings to a woman's head wound. Priscilla had already run to the fireman, who began directing the volley of water from the hose towards the walls surrounding the window where two small children stood screaming.

'What the hell are they doing in there?' shouted Priscilla.

'Now I know what that poor girl was talking about – she kept going on about the children, then she just went. Passed out and died.' The fireman pointed to one of the blanket-covered bodies. 'She ran into the street when the bomb came down – Lord knows how she managed to move, she was that wounded. I reckon she's a relative, a cousin or something, supposed to be looking after the kids.'

Leaving the woman she was tending with a member of the WVS, Maisie ran towards Priscilla, who seemed to be wrestling with the fireman.

'I told her she can't go in,' said the man.

'Get your bloody hands off me, or I'll knock your teeth out!'

shouted Priscilla, but before Maisie could stop her, she had pushed the fireman back.

'I'll go,' said Maisie. 'Stay here, Pris.'

'No!' Priscilla pushed against Maisie, who failed to grab her as she ran into the burning property.

'Bloody hell – is your friend mad?' said the fireman. 'One of us men should have gone in.'

'Get a blanket – come on – and hold the corners,' shouted Maisie. 'There's no time to waste – she'll throw the children down for us to catch, and then she'll jump.'

Three firemen took corners of the blanket as Maisie held on to the fourth, looking up at the screaming children, their hands banging against the window. Glass cracked and splintered with the heat, causing the blanket-bearers to look away as shards fell around them. When Maisie looked up again, it was to see a window frame being kicked open and one child held out.

'Let her go, Pris. Let her go!' shouted Maisie.

The men and Maisie braced as the child landed on the blanket, to be snatched off by one of the WVS women and carried away, screaming. They braced for the next child as Priscilla held him out of the window and allowed him to drop. He landed without crying and scampered off, cursing the 'effing bombs' as he did so.

'Nice turn of phrase for a nipper,' said the fireman, turning back to look up at the window.

'Come on, Pris – jump!' Maisie screamed to her friend. 'Jump now!' Priscilla wavered.

'She'd better get out of there – the main beam's ready to go down in that roof.'

'For God's sake jump, Pris!' Maisie screamed out again.

And then Priscilla was gone, turning back into the house.

'Blimey, she's going to try the stairs – what is she, scared of heights?'

Maisie didn't wait to hear any more, but ran to the front door carrying the now sopping wet blanket. Holding up her hand to shield her face, she walked into blistering heat generated by the burning house. Ahead, Priscilla had fallen on the stairs, and Maisie was about to run to her when a beam crashed from the ceiling, coming down across part of her friend's body. Maisie pressed on.

Kicking the beam over the side of the staircase and onto the passageway below, Maisie was now surrounded by flames, by the intense heat and the terrible smell of burning hair and flesh. She wrapped the blanket around Priscilla and began to lift her.

'Come on, Pris, help me out, my love, help me out. I know you've got some energy in there – try to get up and help me.'

Priscilla pushed against the floorboards as two firemen came to the bottom of the stairs, aiming the hose around the women. Another fireman ran forward to assist Maisie.

'Come on, love, come on, my darlin' – you saved them kids, now let's get you out of here.' The fireman lifted Priscilla, and carried her out of the house.

'Straight into the ambulance,' said Maisie.

'There's another one coming along for the others now – you get her to the hospital. She's saved two little children – bloody foolish thing to do, but she did it.'

Before taking the driver's seat, Maisie sat alongside Priscilla in the ambulance – she was drifting in and out of consciousness and moaning.

'I'm bloody hurting, Mais – I feel fried.'

'You'll be all right, Pris. This won't take a second.'

Maisie opened a bag carrying medical supplies, and took out a vial of morphine and a syringe. She measured a small amount of the drug into the syringe, enough to quell Priscilla's pain – and the additional pain she was about to cause. Ripping back the sleeve of her boiler suit – Priscilla's arms were not burned – she slipped the needle into Priscilla's flesh and injected the painkiller. Working with speed despite her own pain – the backs of her hands had been burned – Maisie steeped lengths of gauze in clean water with a small amount of Dettol antiseptic liquid, enough to ward off infection. She wrapped the cloths across the left side of Priscilla's face and where her hair had been scorched, and then wrapped her hands. Priscilla whimpered as the cloths were applied.

'I'm sorry, my darling, I'm so sorry,' said Maisie. 'Not long now. Not long now – you won't feel a thing in another second or two.'

Maisie poured the remaining water over the backs of her own hands, biting her lip as the antiseptic made her want to cry out. She strapped Priscilla to the cot so she would not move on the way to the hospital, then ran to the cab and started the engine.

'Here we go, Pris. Here we go, my love.'

Maisie put her foot on the accelerator and drove off as fast as circumstances would allow.

'I'm taking you to St Thomas' Hospital, Pris – they're the best of the nearest. It won't take me long. God help me – it won't take me long.'

Maisie pressed the ambulance to its maximum speed, taking turns as fast as possible while giving consideration to her precious patient, to whom she spoke during the entire journey, though Priscilla could not hear. Above her, bombers droned across the skies on their mission of death and destruction, and before her she could see only burning, the back-and-forth glare of searchlights reaching into the sky, and in her ears the echo of her own heartbeat and the constant *ack-ack-ack* of anti-aircraft fire. London was on fire again, and her friend might die if she didn't get help soon.

The ambulance screeched to a halt at the casualty entrance. Maisie heard herself shouting for assistance; even as orderlies ran to the ambulance, she was still shouting. 'She's my friend. My best friend. For God's sake help her!'

Maisie followed the orderlies as they carried Priscilla on her stretcher into the hospital.

'I want to stay with her – I was a nurse, I know what I'm doing,' said Maisie.

A casualty department sister appeared next to the bed where the orderlies were transferring Priscilla.

'Then give me the important details. Name. Age. Injuries at site and treatment applied,' said the woman.

'Her name is Mrs Priscilla Partridge. She's forty-four years of age. She's had morphine for pain already and as you can see, I've covered the most serious burns with Dettol-soaked gauze. I applied only minimal diluted antiseptic liquid to the gauze, enough to keep out infection until I got her to the hospital. You must get a drip into her – she must have fluids, or she will suffer organ failure,' said Maisie, knowing she was shouting but unable to stop. 'I saw it in France you know, men with terrible burns but no one knew about giving them enough fluid and they died.'

'It's all right, we'll take care of her from here,' said the sister. 'For a start you're in my casualty department and you're filthy. Get yourself cleaned up, and perhaps you'll be able to see your friend when she's out of theatre. She's just been bumped along to the front of the queue so we can get her on an even keel.'

'And I forgot to tell you,' said Maisie, wiping blood, tears and black smears across her face. 'She's very brave. She's the bravest women I've ever met. When she's in there, in the operating theatre, just . . . just save her.'

Wearing a pair of khaki trousers of the sort donned by porters – but held up with a length of string – and a man's clean white shirt brought to her by a young nurse, Maisie had washed her face and hands, wincing as she did so given the blistering burns she had sustained. She had already telephoned Douglas at the cottage in Kent by the time Priscilla was brought out of the operating theatre and transferred to an isolation ward. Douglas would come to the hospital as soon as he could get to London, and in the meantime, he would leave a message for Tom at Hawkinge aerodrome.

Having been furnished with a mask and gown, Maisie sat alongside Priscilla's bed and reached out to lay her hand alongside one of Priscilla's bandaged hands. She sat in silence wondering what had happened at the burning house. Why hadn't Priscilla jumped when given the chance? Why did she run back inside? She thought back to college days, and remembered Priscilla having no qualms at all about escaping through a bedroom window to go to a party. But that was more than twenty years ago – perhaps a fear of heights had overtaken her since then.

'We're going to have to ask you to leave soon, Miss Dobbs.' The young nurse, her eyes smudged with grey from many sleepless nights, tapped Maisie on the shoulder. 'Sister made an allowance for you, on account of your having been a nurse, and on the ambulance with Mrs Partridge. Sister was a nurse in the last war too.'

'But what about when Mrs Partridge wakes up? I don't want her to be alone.'

'She's not going to wake up for a while – we'll be keeping her sedated. Don't you worry – she'll be all right.'

'But look at her. She's not going to be all right – look at her.'

Priscilla's thick chestnut hair had been shorn along the right side of her head. Half of her face was now bandaged, and the dressings on her hands made it seem as if she were wearing a pair of giant snowy mittens. One leg was bandaged – Maisie remembered the beam falling along her thigh, and seeing it touch Priscilla's head. The beam had knocked aside her helmet before Maisie was able to kick it to the floor below. She looked down at her own hands, at the layers of gauze the sister had instructed a nurse to apply after cleaning the burns. She had a cut over one eye, and another dressing on her calf where the flames had caught her boiler suit.

'I'll stay, if you don't mind,' said Maisie.

'Miss – you should really go home now. Get some rest and come to see your friend in a day or so. Visiting hours start at ten, but I doubt we'll be on time.'

'How old are you, Nurse—' She looked at the name badge on the nurse's apron. 'Nurse Simpson?'

'I'll be twenty next week. Only another year to go and I'll get the key to the door! Isn't that what they say, that when you're twenty-one your dad gives you the key to the door because you're a free woman?' Nurse Simpson smiled.

Maisie smiled in return, acknowledging the expression that all nurses seemed to be able to slip on like a mask even at the worst of times, as if it were a promise that all would be well. 'I think you get that key a lot sooner in wartime – I was younger than you when I was a nurse in France, but . . . but you seem so very young to be working here, and with a war going on.' Maisie put a bandaged hand to her forehead. 'Oh my dear – I'd forgotten about that bomb – the one that hit the nurses' home. I am so very sorry.'

145

Nurse Simpson held out her hand to support Maisie. 'It's all right, miss. Five of the nurses were killed, but – well, there's work to get on with, so none of us are running home. And like I said, miss, it's time you left – you've been here for hours, and you're not well yourself. Besides, a gentleman's waiting downstairs; he's come to collect you. He arrived almost an hour ago.'

Maisie looked up at the nurse, at her young, unlined face. At once she felt quite light-headed.

The nurse smiled again, and placed a hand on Maisie's arm. 'Come along, miss, the gentleman—'

'But I don't know anyone here, and certainly not a man.'

'Well, he knows you, Miss Dobbs. And he's an American.'

Maisie stared at the young woman. 'An American?'

She nodded. 'Yes, and I don't think you should keep him waiting.'

Maisie turned to Priscilla, leant across the bed and kissed her beloved friend on the forehead. She stepped away and took the nurse's hand in her bandaged fingers. 'Look after her, Nurse Simpson. Please look after her.'

'Don't worry – I haven't lost a patient yet, Miss Dobbs, even though I haven't got the key to the door! Now, let me show you where to go – I'll get a porter to help you out.'

Maisie allowed a porter to take her arm as they made their way along the corridor, passing nurses on the stairs running from one ward to another, carrying supplies or sustenance. The bombers might have returned to their bases across the Channel, perhaps refuelling for another attempt at breaking the back of London, but the work of the doctors and nurses would not stop. As she reached the entrance hall she saw Mark Scott leaning against a wall.

'Maisie!' Scott began to walk towards her.

'How did you know I was here?'

'I called in at that ambulance depot and they told me where you were. I heard you wanted to talk to me.'

'I didn't expect you to come looking for me during a blitz though.'

'They told me you were here – I was worried about you.' He stared at her, placing his hands on her shoulders, looking at the clothes she wore, the dressing above her eye, and then her bandaged hands. 'You look all in and you're going to have some bruising around that eye tomorrow. Come here.' He pulled her towards him and held her in his arms. 'How's your pal?'

Maisie opened her mouth to speak, but could not. Instead she began to weep.

'OK, Maisie, let's get you home.'

Scott led her outside, where a black motor car was idling along the street. He whistled to the driver, and the vehicle drew up alongside them. Scott opened the back passenger door and held Maisie's arm as she climbed aboard. He took the seat next to her and instructed the driver, giving him Maisie's home address in Holland Park.

'How do you know—' began Maisie, before adding, 'Oh, never mind.'

As he put his arm around her, she felt a heaviness descend upon her, and within a minute she was asleep, her head against his shoulder.

CHAPTER NINE

Today I talked with eight American correspondents in London.
Six of them had been forced to move – all had stories of bombs
and all agreed that they were unable to convey through print or
the spoken word an accurate impression of what's happening
these days and nights.

EDWARD R. MURROW, BROADCASTING FROM LONDON,

18TH SEPTEMBER 1940

Maisie awoke fully clothed on her bed. In the distance she could hear someone banging on the French doors that led from the sitting room of her garden flat, out on to the lawn. She tried to rub her eyes, but as she lifted her hand she remembered the bandages. She swung her legs around to the side of the bed, and with her feet on the floor she stood up, remaining in place until she felt steady enough to walk. She moved one step at a time towards the corridor, and then along to the sitting room. Emerging into the room, she was in the dark – the blackout curtains were still drawn. It took a minute for her to reach the curtains and pull them back, revealing Sandra at the door with her baby son, Martin, held on her hip. Under her arm she was clutching a pale blue blanket.

'Miss – thank God you're all right! Let me in – I've come to help you.'

The door was a struggle to open, but soon Sandra was in the room. She laid out the blanket on the floor and placed her son on top, along with a teddy bear and rattle to keep him occupied.

'Sandra, how did you know I needed help? And what time is it?'

'It's gone ten o'clock. And Mr Scott telephoned me at home early and asked if I would be able to assist you, because if I couldn't he would send a woman from the embassy. Funny how he knew our telephone number. Anyway, I knew you wouldn't like a stranger in here, so I went to the office first, and then came right over in the motor car. Now, I'll just make a cup of tea, and then we'll get you washed and dressed in clean clothes – I'm not sure that costume really suits you.'

Maisie looked down at the trousers, and at her hands. 'Would you telephone the hospital – St Thomas' – I must find out how Priscilla is faring.'

'And I know all about that too. A lot's happened since you arrived back here last night. But she's in very good hands – I'll tell you as soon as I've made you some tea and toast. I hope you've got some jam, because you look like you could do with some sugar in you.'

Maisie sat in the armchair while Sandra pottered in the kitchen. She looked down at Martin, Sandra's son, and she thought about Anna, and her father, and Brenda. She thought about everyone in her firmament, and knew, then, that something akin to a movement of the earth had happened. Everything in her life was about to change, and the war had started the ball rolling. At that moment, the telephone rang. Maisie reached for the receiver, but fumbled with it in her bandaged hands. It was a few seconds before she retrieved it from the floor.

'Maisie! Rowan here. Look, I know about Priscilla – Douglas came over very first thing this morning, long before breakfast, and George ran him to the station. Your father is terribly worried about you, as are we. Are you all right?'

'Yes, Rowan. I have a couple of small burns, nothing much.'

'Oh my goodness. Look, shall I send George up to town? You should come back to the Dower House. Anna has been beside herself for days now; she's been most upset. I don't know if it's the bombs or what, and yesterday afternoon apparently she was sent home from school because she was not very well at all.'

Maisie closed her eyes and held a bandaged hand over the cut while pressing the telephone against her ear with the other. Her mother-in-law saw Maisie as the last link to her son, and her concern for her late son's wife had escalated during the past year since war was declared – and she had come to look upon Anna as if she were the grandchild lost years before, when Maisie's baby was stillborn.

'She'll be all right, as soon as I'm home,' said Maisie. 'And I'll take her to see Priscilla in hospital, of course, when she's on the mend.'

'Right you are.' Rowan paused. 'You know, friends of ours have arranged for their grandchildren to go to Canada to get away from this blitz business. As much as they will miss them, they know it's for the best, and even as we speak they are on their way. As Anna's guardian, you can petition to send her to safety through the Children's Overseas Reception Board. Have you thought about it? We have good friends there, and you could go too – I mean, we would absolutely hate to see her go, but—'

'Anna remains at the Dower House, Rowan. I'm not sending her overseas on a ship, and I'm not going either. We all stay together, as family. Anna's had enough disruption, and I believe she'll settle down now. She was upset because it seemed to her that people she loved were leaving her – but I'll be home very soon.'

'Yes, good. You're absolutely right, Maisie. We all must stick together. And as soon as Priscilla is at the Queen Victoria Hospital in the care of a burns expert, so much the better.'

'What?'

'Didn't you know?'

'I went to bed very late last night and have been awake for only half an hour. What's happened?'

'I'll tell you, miss.' Sandra had entered the room with a tray set with cups of tea and buttered toast with jam.

'It's all right, Rowan – Sandra's here, she'll give me the details.'

'Do take care, my darling. You may be my daughter-in-law, but you're more like a daughter to me – even more precious since James died.'

'Yes, I know.' Maisie faltered, then spoke again. 'And you are part of my family. I'll see you soon, Rowan.' She returned the telephone receiver to its cradle.

Maisie turned to Sandra. 'It's not lunchtime yet and I've just heard that my dearest friend isn't in the hospital where I left her last night – one of the best hospitals in London, even with bombs falling on it.'

'It's all right, miss. Sit down and I'll tell you all about it. And Mr Scott will be here in about an hour.'

'Oh dear – I don't want him visiting.'

'Don't worry – I'll get you looking respectable.'

'I don't care about respectable, Sandra – I just want to finish this case and it's probably best if I don't see Mark Scott. And yesterday the case became a lot more complicated. But first – tell me about Priscilla – what's happened?'

Sandra explained that Tom Partridge had rushed to the hospital almost immediately upon hearing of his mother's injuries. Taking a twenty-four-hour compassionate leave, he had arrived at six in the morning, with his father joining him a couple of hours later. The two younger brothers had been left at home and not yet informed of their mother's condition – Douglas had thought that, with emotions running high in the household, it was best he told them when he had more information. Sandra added that she believed Douglas was himself tired and had a desire to see his wife without disturbance, though she wasn't sure he'd made a good decision – in particular where Tim was concerned.

'I mean, he must be worn-out, that man – he is the backbone of the family, the rock they all knock up against – but at the same time, if those younger two keep thinking they're big men, then it's time they acted like it, especially Tim.'

'But what's happened to Priscilla? Sandra, tell me!'

'Tom got there and asked to see the doctor, who wasn't available, so Tom told the sister that he was going to arrange for his mother to be transferred to East Grinstead, because they are better at dealing with burns there, and he should know because half his mates are in there and getting better.'

'That doesn't sound like Tom – he's not usually so bossy, and how on earth could he arrange something like that?'

'He loves his mother, and it turns out he was right – that is exactly where there's a lot of airmen recovering from burns. They're not perfectly well, but better than they would be anywhere else. Anyway, Mr Partridge arrived – Mrs Partridge was still sedated – and by that time, Tom had already taken over. Mr Partridge just went along with it – I think it was shock, to tell you the truth, seeing his wife like that. This flying business seems to have turned Tom from a boy into a very strong man, I'll say that for him. And apparently, as soon as patients are stable, they're being sent out to hospitals away from London to free up the beds for more emergencies, so it's all working out all right.'

'So where is she? Is she actually at this hospital in East Grinstead?'

'On her way by lunchtime, apparently. Tom sorted out an ambulance to take her, and she's being transferred to the Queen Victoria Hospital. And it's only family who can visit, just for now.'

'But—'

'Don't worry – Tom says you'll be considered family.'

'And how do you know all this?'

'Tom telephoned me – I told you, I've already been to the office this morning. I went in after that Mr Scott telephoned. Tom called the office looking for you – I don't know why he didn't telephone you here.'

'He might have tried. I cannot think why I slept like that.' Maisie rubbed her forehead with a bandaged hand.

'Don't do that, miss – you'll mess up that dressing.'

'These annoying bandages are coming off my hands soon. I'll put on cotton gloves – I can't get anything done like this.'

'Miss—'

Maisie finished her tea and set the cup on the saucer at an awkward angle, causing it to rattle. 'I don't want to see Mark Scott today – please telephone his office and tell them it was very kind of him, but Miss Dobbs will be in her office later. I want to see Billy and I want to get to work – I've got to take steps forward with the case today, even if it's only a few.'

Sandra picked up Martin, who was now sleeping soundly, and wrapped the blanket around him.

'Can you make those telephone calls before you go home, Sandra?' Maisie began to rub her eye again, but pulled her hand away. 'And Sandra – the bombings are getting worse. We'll find room at Chelstone for you as a matter of urgency now – the blitz was terrible last night – terrible. And Priscilla—' Maisie closed her eyes, again seeing her friend's body caught under the burning beam.

'She's going to be all right, miss – she'll pull through. Mrs Partridge is a fighter.'

'I know – but what with Tim's injury, and now this—'

'And from what I know of Tim's attitude lately, I wouldn't want to be in his boots right now. I bet that lad feels terrible, considering what he's put his mother through.'

Maisie travelled by taxicab to her office as soon as she was dressed and ready to leave the house. Sandra had removed the bandages from her hands and, following instructions from Maisie, had replaced the bulky padding with a softer dressing of gauze, which Maisie followed by slipping her hands into a pair of white cotton gloves with as much care as she could muster, though she could not help wincing in pain.

'I'll get you an aspirin powder, miss – that'll take the edge off,' said Sandra.

'All right – thank you, Sandra. I hate aspirin, but I have a lot to do today.'

'At least you don't have to rush into the depot – you can't go back to driving the ambulance, can you?'

'I don't think they'd have me, Sandra. Anyway, I'll be all right – I'll walk to the end of the road to get a taxi. You should go home now – you've done enough for one day.' Maisie paused to lock the door as they left the garden flat. 'Will Billy be in the office?'

'Saw him just as I was leaving – he had some visits to make, but he'll be there by the time you arrive, miss.'

'Right you are, Sandra – and I'll let you know about accommodation at Chelstone.'

'Thank you, miss – I'm so grateful, especially as we've been living in your old flat.'

'Just make sure you're in the cellar as soon as the air raid warning goes off.'

Maisie was at the office by half past twelve, and after fielding questions from Billy about the events of the previous night, Maisie asked him to lay out the case map so they could ascertain their next moves.

'What did your friend in Fleet Street say?'

'Well, miss,' said Billy. 'Turns out this ambassador bloke has voiced some not very popular opinions.'

'Go on.'

'For a start, when war was declared, he apparently said that Hitler would be in Buckingham Palace within two weeks, and even before that he was being very friendly towards old Adolf, making what they call "overtures". He never expected our boys to beat the Luftwaffe in the air, so that's another strike against him. And he's said some nasty things about different sorts of people, if you know what I mean – really, miss, it makes my skin crawl, and I never would have claimed to be one of the most, you know, tolerant people in the world – though I know right from wrong. But if the ambassador had his way, all those East End Jewish bakers and tailors would be sent out to Africa and out of the way – that's what he said about the Jews; send them all to Africa.'

'Not very ambassadorial,' said Maisie.

'And that's not all. He was not exactly on the up and up before that – they reckon he's well in with the underworld.'

'You sound like Mark Scott.'

'No, I'm not kidding, miss – there's all sorts of things people say about him, which is surprising, don't you think?'

'Perhaps . . .' Maisie began the sentence before her words seemed to vanish back into her thoughts.

'Perhaps what, miss?'

'No, nothing, Billy. Anything else?'

'Not at the moment, but—' Billy looked around at the door. 'There goes the doorbell – I bet that's Mr Scott.'

'Better let him in, Billy – pity he's on time; I wanted to talk to MacFarlane before he got here.'

'You want me to keep him occupied?'

Maisie shook her head. 'No – he's not stupid. Oh – and Billy, if he mentions seeing you over in Kensington, just say you were in the area to see a client, and say, "Why didn't you give me a shout?" Or something like that. And before you go down, help me roll up this case map.'

156

'Right you are, miss.'

With the case map rolled up and put away, Maisie waited for the men to return to the office, and was looking over her notes when she heard Billy say, 'Well I never – sorry, I didn't see you, Mr Scott. Mind you, I had something on my mind – new client just along the street. The poor old lady had been getting some aggravation from people on account of her Dutch name, which everyone thinks is German. Ain't that terrible? You know, Miss Dobbs had a case some years ago, similar situation—'

Maisie stepped into the outer office. 'Hello, Mark. It sounds as if Billy was on the verge of telling you about one of our former cases.'

'Don't worry. He's not revealing your secrets.'

Maisie smiled. 'Cup of coffee? Or tea?'

'What's the coffee like?'

'The real thing – from an importers in Tunbridge Wells. My former employer swore by his good cup of coffee.'

'I'll make it, miss,' said Billy, leaving the room.

'Thanks, Billy,' Maisie called after him.

'Tunbridge Wells – not far from your country seat, is it?' said Scott.

'I would hardly call it a "country seat" but it's a very nice house.'

Scott nodded. 'Don't mind me asking, but shouldn't you be resting?'

'No, I shouldn't. It's already taken too long to get this far, and I am still only picking at the edges of the investigation – the blitzes have made it harder to see the people I want to talk to.' She paused, wincing in pain as she moved to take up her pen. 'Anyway, as we know, I won't be driving ambulances for a while, and I'm going back to Welbeck Street this afternoon. In the meantime, I have some questions for you, if that's all right.'

'Fire away.'

Maisie extended her hand towards a chair next to the table. She sat down opposite him as he was seated, and continued the conversation.

'There are a number of American men here in Britain who have come over to help with the war effort, and I understand quite a few are aviators. Some are attached to the Canadian air force, others to the RAF. Do you have a list of them? Is that information the embassy has to hand?'

Scott sighed. 'As citizens given leave to remain, they should register with the embassy upon arrival in Britain, but of course, these are young men and most want to just get on with the job. I can request a list of names we have on file, though it might not be complete. Do you have anyone in mind?'

'I don't have a name, but—'

'You're not planning to see every single American aviator in the country?'

'No, of course not. I have some of Catherine's notebooks and have not finished going through them, so I would hope to have a name or two by tomorrow. But there is one I'd like to locate in particular – an airman who visited Catherine, and I believe more than once.'

'Anyone else?'

'I'm also planning to talk to Mr and Mrs Tucker, the owners of the building, and there's another person.'

'I figured there might be.'

'Really?'

'There's always one more person, and they're usually important and the last to be mentioned.'

'"Scotty".' Maisie looked directly at Mark Scott. He did not flinch.

'Scotty?'

Maisie rested her elbows on the table as she leant forward. 'You know very well what I'm getting at – did you know Catherine Saxon? Are you her "Scotty"? Are you the man who turned up on her doorstep and she didn't really want to see, who went by the name of Scotty?'

Mark Scott waited just a second before shaking his head. 'No. I did not know Catherine Saxon before being assigned to the case, and I am not the Scotty she was referring to.'

'Do you know who is?'

'Scott might not be a popular first name here in the sceptered isle, but there are quite a few Scotts where I come from. And I guess it might be kind of popular in Scotland – you should ask Mac.'

'I have quite a few questions for Mr MacFarlane.'

'Don't go all Englishy-maid-proper on me, Maisie – I came to find out how you are, and how your friend is doing. She's pretty badly injured.'

'Mr Scott – Mark – I'm not going proper on you, though I suppose I have to be more formal in my work than you might imagine. But I am frustrated by this case. However, I intend to get to the bottom of it, and seeing as you're supposed to be in on the job, I'd like some help. And—'

'Coffee's up,' said Billy, returning to the room with a pot of coffee, two cups and a small jug of milk. 'Sorry it took a bit longer – had to nip across to the dairy for some milk. Here you go.' He set the tray down on the table. 'Miss, I've got to be getting along – seeing a new client, down near Soho Square.'

'Go home after that, Billy. I know you'll be on patrol this evening, but no need to linger here.'

'Right you are, miss. Make sure you're down the shelter on time.' He turned to Mark Scott. 'Nice to see you, Mr Scott.'

'Likewise, Billy.' Scott turned to Maisie as her assistant left the room. 'And?' he asked, taking his cup of coffee.

'And what?'

'You were about to say something more when Billy came in, then you stopped.'

Maisie rubbed her head, grazing the dressing above her eye. 'I can't remember now. Anyway – I should be going soon. I have a lot to do before this evening.' She took two sips of her coffee and set down the cup.

'Need a ride anywhere? I have a driver along the street.'

'No, it's all right – the walk will do me good.'

Maisie packed up her bag while Mark Scott finished his coffee, before accompanying her out to the square.

'Let me know as soon as you have a name, Maisie.'

'I will – and it will be by tomorrow, I hope.' She looked at her feet and then back to Mark Scott. 'I can't remember if I thanked you, Mark – you were so very good last night. I had no idea you knew where I lived, or – indeed – how you got into my flat, but thank you for . . . for . . . for looking after me.'

'Isn't that what a gentleman's supposed to do?'

'Yes, but—'

'I'll talk to you tomorrow – will you be going down to your country seat?'

'Later in the day, and of course I must see Priscilla. I'm anxious to know how she is – I would have gone to see her sooner, but she's being moved to another hospital.'

Mark Scott nodded. 'Take care, then – and brief me tomorrow.'

As Scott turned and walked away, Maisie waited before stepping out across the square on her way to Welbeck Street. It would be a fifteen-minute walk at a clip, but Maisie did not have the energy to move with any speed, and her hand had begun to hurt as she carried her bag. Yet it was not the pain that was on her mind, or how she might have extended the time she would take to heal by removing the hospital dressing – instead she felt torn about Mark Scott. Every time she thought about him, she felt conflicted. She trusted him with her life, but did not trust his word. She considered him to be loyal, yet could not count on his presence in the investigation. And while she felt he was a man of integrity, there were moments when she wondered if he was pulling the wool over her eyes. And given the overheard conversation with Billy, it would seem he saw her assistant while he was in South Kensington. It was an interesting exchange, because she had assumed he would have kept that piece of information to himself, as one might be careful not to show an ace in a game of cards.

'Hello, Mrs Marsh,' said Maisie, as the landlady held open the front door. 'Do you happen to know if Miss Harcourt is in her rooms?'

'I believe she's home – learning lines for a new play, apparently. I'm not sure where it'll be running, but I suppose the show has to go on!' Marsh looked at Maisie's hands. 'Oh my dear, what have you done? I can see blood seeping through those gloves.'

'Oh, it's nothing – I just sustained some burns last night. The ambulance auxiliary aren't supposed to be the ones who get hurt, but I slipped up and let the side down. I'll sort it out as soon as I get home. Anyway, do you mind if I just go up?'

'Of course not – you know where to find her.'

Maisie made her way up the stairs, pausing alongside Pamela Lockwood's door as she passed, noticing the door was ajar. She continued on.

'Come in,' said Polly Harcourt.

'Hello, Miss Harcourt – Polly – it's me, Maisie Dobbs.'

'Oh, Miss Dobbs.' Harcourt pushed back the chair at her desk, and stood up to greet Maisie. 'What can I do for you – have you found out who killed Cath?'

'Not yet, I'm afraid. But I thought I might ask you a couple more questions.'

Polly Harcourt moved a jacket that had been thrown across the armchair, and hung it on a hook behind the door so Maisie could sit down, then pulled her desk chair closer to Maisie.

'Would you like anything to drink – tea?'

'No thank you – I can see you're busy. I understand you're learning lines for a new play.'

'Christmas panto. It's *Peter Pan*, and I'm Tinker Bell – the fairy. Not exactly Oscar Wilde or Shakespeare, but it's a part, and I'm grateful. It's going on tour, because so many children are away from London now, though you would be surprised about the number who are back here because the parents don't want to be separated any longer. I heard a woman in a shop yesterday saying, "If we go, then we all go together." And I can't say I blame them – who wants to think their children might be orphaned? But on the other hand, you can understand those mums and dads who go so far as to send their children to Canada, or America. My sister's neighbour's children left to go to Canada a few days ago – on a ship from Liverpool.'

'The parents must feel such a wrench having made that decision, even though it's to keep their children safe.'

'They won't know them when they come back though, will they? I read in *The Stage* that there are Hollywood actors and actresses taking in our evacuees. Can you imagine it? There you are, just a nipper and you get used to living out there, and then you have to come back here? They could be grown-ups by the time they're home! Mind you, I was thinking of signing up as a chaperone on one of the evacuation ships, just to get over there to America. Even though Cath told me not to, I still think I'd like to go. Anyway – thank you for asking about the play. I'm lucky they gave me the part.'

'Polly, I understand from Miss Chalmers that you saw Catherine with a man – an American airman. Can you tell me anything about him?'

'Yes, though I don't know his name – she probably told you I called him "Catherine's stage-door Johnny". For a while he seemed to be hanging around every time he was on leave, even if he only had a twenty-four-hour pass. And he was probably the one I heard, though I thought that man was older.' She shrugged. 'I should have given you more details but . . . but I didn't want you to think Cath was running around with lots of men. And Catherine never told me his name – not that it was a secret, but it never came up. She brushed it aside. Maybe she even brushed him aside. I believe they met when she was writing about the Americans over here, what they think of the war and so on.'

Maisie considered Harcourt's response. There was no guile in the woman before her, no sign of reticence when being questioned. She seemed the sort of person who took people as she found them, accepting who they were – but given her experience working as an actress and behind the bar at a club in Paddington, she suspected Polly Harcourt was no pushover either.

'Have you any idea where he was stationed?' asked Maisie.

Harcourt shrugged. 'Must have been within about an hour or so of London, or he would never have been able to get up here and back so easily if he only had twenty-four hours before he had to return to his aerodrome. If I had to pick somewhere, I would say Biggin Hill or one of those other places between us and the English Channel – but that's a lot of ground to cover.' Harcourt pressed her lips together and seemed to study the floor, as if more information had been dropped there. Then she looked up. 'You know who could help you – Jenny, Cath's friend. They'd known each other for years. I bet you she knows everything about Cath. A girl always tells her best friend everything, after all.'

'I was hoping to see her today, though I think at this point, it will be tomorrow morning.'

'I'd wait until the morning, Miss Dobbs,' said Harcourt. 'I mean, I've met you before, but Jenny hasn't, and I don't know if you've looked in the mirror, but that's a nasty cut over your eye. And here – let me help you with your hands. What happened to you anyway? I mean, I didn't like to ask, because it seemed rude, but I thought you might have got caught in an air raid.'

'Yes, that's what happened. I was hit by some debris.'

'Come on – I've got some antiseptic in the bedroom, and believe it or not, I have some bandages – I fell over in the street last year and cut my knee, so I've got a first-aid kit now. And I've a pair of white gloves you can use – you'll need to soak yours in bleach when you get them home, or they'll stain.'

Polly Harcourt proved to be proficient with the contents of her first-aid kit, bandaging Maisie's burned hands, and with a gentle touch slipping on a pair of white gloves to protect the dressing. It was as Harcourt was putting away the antiseptic, that Maisie heard a noise from the rooms below – from Pamela Lockwood's quarters.

'Did you hear that?' asked Maisie, standing up from the chair and inclining her head.

'Yes – it's probably Mrs Marsh. Nosy old woman, that one. She'll be snooping into Pamela's things, probably looking to see if she's left any money lying around. If I'm at home and I know she's in there, I'll tiptoe down and ask her if Mrs Lockwood's all right, or something like that. I've let Pamela know she's going into her rooms, but Pam doesn't seem to worry – she says there's nothing worth stealing. And you know what? I think she also just likes to look at Pamela's clothes. She's a very well-turned-out woman, and she has good costumes, quality skirts and dresses, very well tailored, and I think Mrs Marsh likes to just look at them. Funny old bird, that one.'

'And does she go into all the rooms?'

'She's got a master key, so I bet she does – though Liz and Helena are probably safe enough, because not only are they right on the top floor with the gods, but Mrs Marsh keeps them at arm's length, though she wouldn't let anyone say a word against them. No, she's a bit like a mother hen in that regard. Protective, but reserves the right to put her nose in whenever she wants.'

'I think I might drop in on her while she's on the prowl,' said Maisie, gathering her bag. 'Thank you, Polly – I appreciate your time, and your nursing skills. You should volunteer, you know.'

'I'm doing my bit every evening in that club, keeping people's spirits up. And I'll be doing the same when we take the panto on the road – making people laugh. Hitler can do a lot of things to us, but if he stops us laughing and having some fun, then the wicked old sod has won, hasn't he?'

* * *

Maisie stopped outside the door to Pamela Lockwood's rooms, leaning forward to listen. She could still hear someone shuffling around, so she knocked, then opened the door. She was in time to see Mrs Marsh opening a drawer in a desk by the window – again, the room had an almost identical configuration of furniture to the rooms of Catherine Saxon and Polly Harcourt.

'Hello, Mrs Marsh – I thought that might be you. I just wanted to let you know I'm leaving now.'

'Oh . . . oh, right you are, my dear.' Marsh stepped back as if she had been pushed. Still flushed, despite having regained some composure, she began to explain. 'Mrs Lockwood likes me to come in and push the duster around, tidy up a bit for her. She's such a busy woman – like all my ladies, they're all busy. But Mrs Lockwood likes a clean room, and it's a bit extra for me every week, you know.'

'Of course – if I lived here, I would be delighted to have a landlady like you.' Maisie took another step towards Marsh, and began to look around the room. 'It's so very nicely decorated, isn't it?'

'Mrs Lockwood is my oldest tenant – well, old because she's lived here the longest, and to be fair, she is older than the others. She's a very elegant lady, very particular, as you can imagine.'

'And she was a beautiful bride,' said Maisie, pointing to a framed photograph on the desk. Pamela Lockwood was in her wedding dress, standing next to a young man in the uniform of an infantry officer.

'Geoffrey, his name was.'

'Geoffrey?' repeated Maisie. 'How tragic, to lose your husband so close to the Armistice.' She leant towards the photograph, paying particular attention to the bride. 'And she seems so very happy there.'

'I don't think I've ever seen her smile like that,' said Marsh, folding her arms while studying the photograph. 'Well, perhaps once or twice.'

'Can you remember the occasion?' queried Maisie.

'There was one time when Miss Chalmers had invited everyone out to the garden – lovely sunny day it was, in the summer. It was after Dunkirk, I remember that much. Catherine was telling some sort of story, and Mrs Lockwood was laughing, and you could see a little spark in her eyes. Yes, it's coming back to me now – Catherine had received a man visitor the evening before, and Mrs Lockwood was asking her about him, because they'd passed on the step. I'd looked out of my window when I heard them speaking – not to be nosy, mind, but I like to know who's coming and going, because I have to think about these things with a houseful of women. Mr and Mrs Tucker wouldn't like any funny business and their property being known as a house of ill repute. And that was the other time I saw her smiling. Didn't see the man's face though, but I could see Mrs Lockwood, and she seemed very happy that day.' Marsh shook her head. 'Funny, isn't it, the things you remember?'

'It certainly is,' replied Maisie.

'I see you've had your dressings done – that would be Miss Harcourt. Mind you, you'd expect her to know a thing or two, because both her parents are doctors. Can't imagine what they must have thought, having a daughter who could have gone to medical school and instead trained to be an actress and is serving behind a bar!'

'No, I didn't know that,' said Maisie, adding, 'perhaps she chose acting because it's so different.'

'Well, it's all theatre work, isn't it? Her father's in an operating theatre, and she's on the stage, so you could say they're both in a line of business where they have to get every move just right and remember what comes next,' said Mrs Marsh. 'And I'm sure I don't know why a girl from a good home would want to tread the boards.'

Marsh moved towards the door, with Maisie following her out onto the landing. Marsh locked the door and together they made their way down the staircase. Maisie thought it interesting that a woman tasked with cleaning Pamela Lockwood's rooms was not wearing a pinafore, and carried neither dusters or a broom, no bucket of water, no mop, polish or other cleaning materials.

'Will you be coming back, Miss Dobbs?' asked Marsh as they reached the front door.

'Yes, I believe I will. I still haven't spoken to Elizabeth Drake and Helena Richardson, and I'd certainly like to speak to Mrs Lockwood and Miss Chalmers again.' Maisie's eyes met those of Mrs Marsh. It was another second before she spoke. 'Mrs Marsh, now that several days have passed, I wonder, in your thoughts – for I know the death of Miss Saxon must be at the forefront of your mind – do you have any idea who might have wanted Miss Saxon dead? I am sure you saw many things in this house, and I am equally sure you would have protected your ladies, both in terms of their personal well-being and their reputations, but can you think of anyone who might have had cause to take Catherine's life?'

Marsh clasped her hands together, and began to knead her fingers. The question unsettled her, and she took a minute before answering. 'Miss Dobbs, I have turned this over in my mind time and time again. I've thought about every one of my ladies, every one of their friends who came to visit – and believe me, I turned a blind eye more than once, though I liked them to think of me as if I were a very strict headmistress. Didn't do any harm to let them believe I'm a bit stricter than I am – I remember what it was like to be a young woman. Now I look at every man who passes me on this street and I wonder if he could have followed Catherine home in the blackout, and I wonder if she was tired and accidentally left the door on the latch so a killer could get in. I've been asking myself if someone was agile enough to climb up to that window – goodness knows, I've asked the Tuckers to pay for repairs to the windows often enough, but these rooms aren't that dear, and my ladies can afford the rent, though probably not much more, so I don't push too hard. I've thought about everything, and each time I think of Catherine – Miss Saxon – I keep hearing the words my old Jack used to say, God rest his soul. He would say, "Doris, take a bit of advice from a soldier. If you put your head above the parapet, someone is going to take a potshot at you and blow your noddle off." And he said it was good enough advice for life too – keep your head down, get on with your job, mind your own business and you'll be all right.' She sighed, placing her hand on her chest, as if winded by her own soliloquy. 'I think that's what it comes down to. Catherine had taken up a job where her head was above the parapet all the time. It was what she had to do, wasn't it? She couldn't mind her own business, because she had to poke her nose into other people's to get her work done. So, if you ask me, that's what's gone on – she poked that nose somewhere it wasn't wanted.' She shook her head. 'Or I could be wrong. Someone could have killed her just because they didn't like her, or she upset their apple cart. I wish I knew more, so I could help you.'

Maisie nodded, placing a gloved hand on Mrs Marsh's shoulder. 'You've been a big help, Mrs Marsh – thank you. I daresay I'll see you again very soon.'

As she departed the house and walked along the road, Maisie looked back once. Doris Marsh was standing on the doorstep watching her leave. She looked back one more time to see Marsh turning and stepping back into the house. Her plan was to walk a little farther before crossing to the other side of the road and retracing her route so she could, with luck, slip unseen into the doctors' surgeries opposite the house where Catherine Saxon was murdered.

CHAPTER TEN

Maisie pressed her thumb against the button next to Mr Chester's name. She waited, pressed again, and was about to press one more time when a middle-aged woman opened the door.

'Mr Chester has finished seeing patients for the day – he's about to leave. And he's not a general practitioner, so you'll have to go to the hospital about that eye – or if there's any other reason for your visit.' The woman seemed to sneer as she made the suggestion – and Maisie did not care for the unspoken inference suggested in the woman's raised eyebrow.

'I wonder if Mr Chester might be able to spare me a moment or two. My call is nothing to do with my health – I've already seen a doctor about my eye – but it is in connection with a police enquiry.' Maisie reached into her bag and took out the identification card given to her by MacFarlane. She felt a certain pleasure in seeing the woman wrong-footed. 'As you will see, I am a special investigator, and I have been assigned to a case you may be familiar with – the death of Miss Catherine Saxon, who lived just across the street. Someone took her life over a week ago now, and following her murder, certain aspects of the case suggest to me that she may have seen Mr Chester at some point.'

The woman wavered, looking at the card again, then at Maisie. 'You can come in and wait while I talk to him.' She drew back the door, locking it behind Maisie after she'd crossed the threshold. Already Maisie knew the answer to her first question – had Catherine not been a patient, the woman would have said as much, and would in all likelihood have added that the doctor is beholden to keep a patient's medical history private, so he could not talk anyway. She was now sure Catherine had visited the doctor.

The woman, who she assumed was Chester's secretary, led the way up a staircase to the first floor, where she opened the door to an office. Another door beyond was ajar, allowing Maisie to see a bespectacled man at a desk, his head down, his hand holding a fountain pen which he *tap-tap-tapped* on a sheet of paper, as if not quite sure what to write.

'Just a minute – you can sit there,' said the woman, who pointed to a wooden chair with a tapestry-covered seat, before crossing to Chester's office and closing the door behind her.

'And how very polite of you,' whispered Maisie, taking a seat as instructed, while looking around the room. On the desk she noticed a wooden sign indicating that the secretary's name was Miss Handle. Maisie smiled. 'And I expect you can handle almost anything.'

A low mumble coming from the adjacent room indicated a somewhat intense conversation in progress, which furthered Maisie's curiosity – how long could it take to enquire whether the doctor could see an investigator regarding a now-deceased patient? Perhaps the doctor and his secretary were looking into the legal position of a physician whose patient had been murdered.

The door opened, and Miss Handle beckoned to Maisie. 'Mr Chester will see you now.' She held out Maisie's card.

Maisie nodded as she replaced the card in her bag. 'Thank you, Miss Handle,' she said, walking past the secretary and taking care to close the door behind her. She turned to the doctor, a portly man who wore a tweed jacket over a plain brown waistcoat, with a white shirt and a brown tie. His red, bulbous nose seemed livid above a grey moustache; his hair was the colour of graphite streaked with white and was parted from the centre in a straight line. 'Mr Chester – it's so very good of you to see me.' She extended her hand, adding, 'I had hoped to visit you before now; however, I know you're a very busy man – in fact, you delivered the first child of very good friends of mine.'

'I did?' replied Chester, who seemed taken aback by the personal connection – which Maisie had planned. A wrong-footed secretary, and a wrong-footed doctor might nudge open otherwise closed doors.

'Yes, Andrew Dene and his wife. Dr Dene and I have known each other for many years through our connection to Dr Maurice Blanche.' She shook hands with Chester, and took a seat opposite him without waiting for an invitation, adding, 'I suppose I should really call him "Mr", given that he's now such an eminent orpthopaedic surgeon, though for some reason I've always thought of him as "Dr" Dene.'

Chester nodded. 'Yes, he once told me that being Dr Dene made him feel more like the family physician, which was something he thought helped calm his patients when they were anxious.' He shuffled the papers before him. 'How might I help you, Miss Dobbs?'

'Was Catherine Saxon your patient?'

Chester took a deep breath – a breath that sounded resigned to what might come next. Maisie wondered if he had anticipated a visit from the police. 'Yes, she was. She came to see me soon after arriving in London.'

'I understand she came from Spain.'

'Well, via a couple of other countries – and I saw her before she moved in across the street. She told me she had seen my name on the door here when she first came to view the rooms to let in the house opposite.' He rubbed his chin. 'I'm not supposed to be talking about her, you know.'

'Given the circumstances, I would be grateful for any information you are able to provide within the bounds of laws governing your practice. A young woman has been murdered, and she is owed every effort to find her killer. Anything you tell me will be held in the strictest confidence.'

'What about when you catch the man? What then? Will details of her private life be emblazoned across the front pages of the gutter press?' Chester's colour had heightened.

Maisie leant forward, resting a hand on the doctor's desk. 'There has been and will be minimal reporting of the crime. It is a delicate situation, so I am in the same boat as you, in that I can tell you little more beyond the fact that I am investigating the case. Suffice it to say, Miss Saxon is not only the citizen of another country, but she is also the daughter of a prominent man in America – hence the need for confidentiality. He was a man who did not approve of his daughter's line of work.'

'Frankly, Miss Dobbs – I don't blame him. War is no place for a woman, no place at all – which is why she was in trouble.'

'What sort of trouble? Was she expecting a child?'

Chester shook his head. 'No.' He pushed back his chair, stepped away from the desk, and moved to the window. 'Not when she saw me, anyway.' He continued looking out, his hands clasped behind his back.

Maisie said nothing, waiting for Chester to turn around and take his seat once again. A moment later, he shook his head and sighed, looking down at his feet. He returned to his chair on the other side of the desk.

'Miss Saxon came to me because in Spain she had given birth in very difficult circumstances. Apparently the child was stillborn. The body was taken from her and disposed of – I don't think a decent burial would have been possible, though who knows what the situation was like over there. She had not received any medical care – and though it could be argued that we doctors are only on hand to twiddle our thumbs while midwives, women and nature do the work, she experienced continuing pain stemming from the nature of the delivery, and – dare I say it – not least from the psychological distress, given her situation.'

'That's rather, well, interesting. It's unusual for a doctor in your position to voice an opinion on "psychological distress". Don't many doctors steer away from such a diagnosis to avoid dealing with a hypochondriac – or to sidestep having to treat a difficult condition outside their bailiwick?'

Chester lowered his chin and regarded her over his spectacles. 'I was a junior doctor when I was sent to France in the early days of the last war, Miss Dobbs. And I was one of those who identified very troubling symptoms in young soldiers who had been in battle – and officers, I might add – and I drew attention to my observations, which amounted to naming what I believed to be some sort of shock caused by the constant exposure to both the sound and impact of constant shelling, and witnessing death from the most terrible wounds. Among other medical men in the field hospitals and casualty clearing stations, I was very clear about what I was seeing, and I was – I suppose – not very subtle in my reports. Therefore I know what a deep wound to the psyche an experience of this order might inflict upon a young woman who expected to give birth to her first child, even though the circumstances of motherhood might have presented her with another set of problems.'

Maisie looked away, feeling her eyes sting.

'Oh – oh my dear, I am sorry – I had not meant to distress you.' He leant forward, looking into Maisie's eyes as she brought her attention back to him. 'Clearly you've had an accident, and here you are, soldiering on while not feeling terribly well. I should have taken account of that – can I do anything to help you?'

Maisie shook her head, and reached into her bag for a handkerchief, fumbling with the linen. 'No – no it's not that, Mr Chester. Just give me a moment and I'll be perfectly all right.'

'I suppose in investigating a person's death, someone in your position becomes quite close to the subject. I would imagine you have to know the deceased as you would a close relative.'

'Yes, that's it,' said Maisie. She cleared her throat and composed herself. 'So, to recap – you said that Catherine was experiencing some pain and discomfort as a result of the delivery.'

'I examined her and found there to be nothing that would cause pain, which led me to conclude that the death of the child had weighed heavily upon her – and I would expect it to have done so. And whilst I am on the one hand an advocate of taking up the reins of life again following a loss such as this, I also counsel my clients to accept that recovery takes time.'

'Did Miss Saxon suffer any other medical conditions of note?'

Chester sighed. 'She was aware that pregnancy would not be possible in the future. Of course, I could be wrong, and I am the first one to admit to being surprised at the ability of the human body to endure all manner of abuse – but it was unlikely she would ever have conceived, or managed to carry a child to full term again.'

'But you said there was no reason for her to feel pain.'

'A distinction, Miss Dobbs. She had scarring, and there had been trauma to the uterus, but it had healed. Another pregnancy was unlikely, and I considered it inadvisable to try.' He shook his head. 'You see, the problem with so many young women is that they expect everything to go so smoothly, yet childbirth might as well still be in the Stone Age. The birth of a child is arguably the most dangerous time in the life of mother and baby – and I cannot see that changing, even with the level of medical care I can offer, and any advances one might imagine in years to come.' Another pause. 'She confided in me that she was in love with a man, but did not feel she could continue seeing him or make the commitment of marriage if she could not bear his child – so she threw herself into her work. There, I've told you too much already. The poor girl poured her heart out to me, and I had to be brutally honest with her or cause even more disappointment in the future, when she could either not conceive, or have to endure miscarriage or another stillbirth – or die in the process.' Chester allowed a pause, before a final comment. 'This might all sound like Greek to you.'

Maisie gave a half-laugh, though she did not smile. 'I was a nurse, Mr Chester – in the last war, so the medical information is far from Greek to me. I saw young men suffering shell shock, and I had the misfortune to be wounded myself. And while in Spain a few years ago, I had to take on the mantle of midwife when I delivered a baby in a small clinic run by a nun – I had never assisted at a birth before, because my work had been with soldiers. The mother was wonderful and trusting, so between us, we did all right.' She held up her begloved hands. 'And until a couple of days ago I wasn't doing such a bad job with the Ambulance Auxilliary. My best friend was terribly burned saving the lives of two children. So you see, I must disagree with you on one count. Women will always be part of war, whether fighting, tending the wounds of soldiers, reporting – as Miss Saxon did so very well – and even when we're the ones left waiting. And as you probably know, most soldiers would tell you that waiting is the hardest part of war to endure.'

'And now criminal enquiry is your line,' said Chester.

'It has been for many years. I'm sure when you telephone Andrew Dene he'll tell you more.' Maisie gathered her bag. 'Did Miss Saxon ever name the father of her child?'

'I know he was her husband.'

'Her husband?'

'Killed in Spain when she was just a few months along. I think he was with the International Brigade. Both of them young and idealistic – but I've made an assumption there, I suppose, based upon my experience in the last war, having been a young, idealistic doctor at the time. When I returned home to Blighty, I found that bringing life into the world was much more rewarding, if sometimes fraught.'

'But I had no idea she was married,' said Maisie.

'Hmm,' said Chester.

'What do you mean, "Hmm"?'

'It occurred to me that she might not have told anyone. That the union had been kept something of a secret.'

178

Maisie nodded. 'Did she tell you anything else, anything in confidence that might help me find her killer?'

'No, I'm sorry. I didn't actually encourage her to speak to me in so frank a manner, but perhaps Americans are different. Having said that, I've worked alongside doctors specialising in neurasthenia, so I think I might have helped her without trying particularly hard. Given what you've indicated about her family, and reading between the lines, perhaps it was soothing for Miss Saxon to speak to someone detached, someone who would not cast judgement upon her. And above all, someone who was bound by the Hippocratic oath to keep her secrets.'

'What might she have been judged for?'

'For a start, remaining in a country torn by war when she was expecting a baby.'

Maisie nodded again, though she neither agreed nor disagreed with Chester's summation. She wanted to leave the physician's office, and she wanted to go home. But the home she wanted to go to was not her flat in Holland Park. She wanted to go to Chelstone. She wanted to hold the child she loved in her arms, and she wanted to be close to her family. She wanted to go to Priscilla, to care for her friend's sons, and to offer support to Douglas. Yet Catherine Saxon was as real and present to her as if she were in the room, listening.

'Thank you for your time, Mr Chester. I appreciate your candour and your willingness to discuss this confidential matter with me. I know you are acting in the interests of helping me find Miss Saxon's killer – and to that end, please do get in touch if you think of anything else.'

'Of course.' Chester escorted her to the outer office, where Miss Handle was slipping a sheet of paper into a typewriter.

'Would you see Miss Dobbs downstairs, please, Miss Handle?'

'Yes, certainly. Do come this way, Miss Dobbs.' Handle offered only a cursory 'Goodbye' when they reached the door, and did not wait for Maisie to reply or extend her thanks.

As she turned away, Maisie regarded the house opposite, casting her gaze from floor to floor, while considering the path Catherine Saxon had followed before reaching England. So much loss and yet she had an abundance of energy, of wit and charm – and she was brave, with a passion for her work. Now unexpected information was starting to be revealed, rendering Saxon something of an enigma. Maisie focused on the windows, and observed several things that interested her. Pamela Lockwood must have returned from work early, for Maisie was sure the figure who backed away from the second-floor window was the well-dressed widow. And at the same time, Polly Harcourt was looking down at the street. Maisie's attention was then drawn to the ground floor, where Mrs Marsh could be seen adjusting her curtains. Maisie looked at her watch. She was sure she would soon hear the air raid warning, but if she was not mistaken, she had just enough time to go to Broadcasting House – then she would go home, to rest.

Having asked if an engineer named Bob Walkinshaw was available, and showing the police identification card to a receptionist, it was only a few minutes before Walkinshaw appeared to speak to her.

'Mr Walkinshaw, you must be terribly busy, so I'm grateful for your time.' Maisie lifted her hand to take his, then drew it back, afraid the light throbbing pain would escalate with his touch.

'You've come to talk about Cath, haven't you?'

'I have – I understand you were very friendly with her.'

Walkinshaw nodded, and pinched the bridge of his nose. 'Sorry. We're all still shocked about it.' He looked around him, then brought his attention back to Maisie. 'Look, you're right, I have got my hands pretty full, but I can talk for a bit. Do you mind coming with me? I'm in a soundproof area, so no one will hear us.'

'Of course – it's probably better insulated than the interview rooms at Scotland Yard.'

'Yeah, but people leave here with all their teeth,' said Walkinshaw, leading the way along a windowless corridor.

Maisie raised an eyebrow, but did not reply, though she took stock of Walkinshaw as they walked. Of average height – perhaps a couple of inches shorter than Mark Scott – Walkinshaw wore grey trousers and a pale grey shirt topped with woollen sleeveless pullover knitted in a Fair Isle pattern of greys and blues. He carried his grey herringbone tweed jacket. Maisie wondered why so many men seemed to be wearing grey. Was it a fashion she had missed, or was it an easy colour to wear when there was so much debris in the air? She'd noticed that even during a short walk from Warren Street Underground Station to the office, she had seemed to be a magnet for smuts of ash and dirt that adhered to her clothing.

'You look like you got into something bad yourself,' said the engineer, pointing to her hands.

'Too long a story,' said Maisie.

Walkinshaw opened a door to a small room, revealing what Maisie assumed was a controllers' domain of some sort. Wires led from one end to the other, and then to a panel of knobs and buttons which took up an entire wall. Sound was indeed muffled; she could not hear anything beyond the room.

Walkinshaw hung his jacket on a hook behind the door, took out a chair for Maisie to be seated, and looked at his watch. 'Right then, what do you want to know?'

'Tell me about Catherine,' said Maisie.

'Cath was a great girl. Everyone here liked her from the minute she walked in the door. She was energetic, affable, and she got the story – and Mr Murrow saw that, which is why he gave her a chance. And if she hadn't been killed, she would be one of the boys.'

'I heard you were a rather special friend,' said Maisie.

Walkinshaw laughed. 'No, let me put that right, and I'll be honest with you though you'll probably think I'm a right one. I'm a married man but I liked Cath's company – she was a laugh.' He blew out his cheeks and for a second cast his gaze away from Maisie. 'And Cath wasn't interested in me, but I'll be honest with you – might as well be honest in a murder investigation, eh? The truth is, I might have been persuaded to stray if she'd been interested. I'm not a saint – got married too young for that, and at the end of a shotgun, if you know what I mean. So, yes, we went out a few times, but I will tell you right now, she kept her work and her private life separate, and I wouldn't know anything about the latter.'

'When you went out – where did you go?'

'For a drink. Sometimes a bite to eat. But the fact is that our hours are not exactly set up to encourage fraternisation. She was new working here, but I met her when she came in one day – snooping around to see if she could get in with the broadcasting reporters. I took her out for a drink, and we kept in touch.'

'Did she talk about her work – I mean, the stories she was writing?'

'A bit here and there. Over the summer, when there were all those dog-fights going on, before the London bombing really started, she was out in Kent and Sussex, talking to airmen and to the people who'd been watching it all happening from their back gardens, and in the villages where bombs had been dropped.'

'I understand she was working on a story about American airmen who were flying with the RAF and Canadian air force.'

Walkinshaw nodded. 'She was, yeah.' He laughed. 'I tell you, everywhere Cath went, you can bet some bloke with a puppy-dog smile would try it on with her.' He held out his hands, palm up. 'And look at me – I was one of them!' He paused, pinching the bridge of his nose again, as if to stem the emotion reflected in his eyes. 'But she became my friend. We were mates and we had a laugh together – though she was that much younger than me. I used to tease her about needing a pa. She thought that was funny. "I've got one of those, and two big brothers – and I'm glad I'm over here and they're over there," she said.' Walkinshaw looked from his hands to Maisie. 'Here – has anyone from her family been over since it happened?'

'Not as far as I know,' said Maisie.

'She wasn't keen on them, that's one thing I knew about Cath. She didn't like her people at all – though she talked about her mum. Said she was more like that side of the family than her father's lot.'

Maisie scribbled in her notebook.

'Mr Walkinshaw, do you have the names of anyone she was acquainted with here who might be able to give me some more information about her?'

'Not getting very far?'

'I have a lot of information,' Maisie paused. 'But in my line of work there's always that snippet, that little nugget that spills out, and it's a bit like a hook – once I have that hook, the fish seem to become more plentiful.'

'And you think I've got the hook,' said Walkinshaw.

'I thought you might have it,' said Maisie.

Walkinshaw leant forward. 'And I might. But I work with reporters, Miss Dobbs, so I know you have to be careful, even though the reporters are supposed to check and recheck their sources if they've got a big piece of news under their hats. I am guessing you have to check and recheck too.'

'Probably more than your average reporter,' said Maisie. 'If I get it wrong, an innocent person could go to the gallows, or at least be incarcerated for a long time at His Majesty's Pleasure.'

'That's true of a newspaperman too,' said Walkinshaw. 'They can put people away.'

Maisie leant forward, lowering her voice as if someone might overhear whatever might come next. 'What do you want to tell me, Bob?' said Maisie, using the engineer's Christian name.

Walkinshaw took a deep breath. 'We'd gone out to the pub one night, and came back – not late, because Cath didn't like a late night, not when she had to get up early in the mornings. As we walked along the street – I always insisted on escorting her to her door, even though I live in Islington – anyway, as we walked along the street, there was a bloke standing outside the house where she lived. She stopped, took another look at him, and said, "Bob, you go home now. I can see the house, so I'll be OK from here." I asked her if she was all right, and whether that bloke would be a bother, and she laughed. "No," she said. "It's work – a lead on a story." Now, Miss Dobbs, I can tell you now, I didn't believe a word of it. I let her go, and heard her say, "Scotty, don't you ever take no for an answer?"'

'His name was Scotty?'

Bob Walkinshaw shook his head. 'No, it wasn't – well, it was, but I found out who he was.'

184

'I'm not following you,' said Maisie. 'How did—'

'I followed him. I hung around until he came out, and I followed him. Now, I'm no spy, but I managed to stay back and I kept a bead on him. I was surprised he didn't go by cab, but perhaps he wanted a bit of a walk – and he walked all the way to Oxford Street and then over to Park Lane, where he walked right into the Dorchester.'

'The Dorchester?'

'Yes, all very nice if you can afford it.'

'And?' prompted Maisie.

'He goes to get his key, and I didn't even have to eavesdrop much – I heard the bloke on the desk say, "Good evening, Mr Saxon – I trust you had a good day."'

'Mr Saxon? But—'

'The older brother. Name of Clarence, like the dad. Only his middle name is Scott, and in the family they called him Scotty, so father and son didn't both answer when someone shouted out, "Oi, Clarence." It's his nickname.'

Maisie leant back in the chair. Her eye was throbbing and her hands hurt. Now she felt as if she had a brass band tuning up inside her head. 'Scotty is her brother.'

'You knew him?'

'No.' She shook her head. 'But I should have known about him – I've spent a few days pinning the name on someone else.'

'Another suspect?'

'No.' She paused. 'Well, to tell you the truth – I don't know.'

'Was that the hook though?' asked Walkinshaw.

Maisie exhaled, feeling as if she had held her breath from the split second Walkinshaw had uttered the word 'Scotty'. 'It might be the hook – the line is certainly worth following.'

She was about to ask another question, when a sudden knocking at the door startled both Maisie and Walkinshaw. The door opened.

'Oh, sorry, Bob.' The young woman gave a brief smile. 'The air raid siren's just started.'

'The buggers,' said Walkinshaw. 'All right, Rosie. I'm going down to get the studio ready.' He looked at Maisie. 'You'd better come with me – you can't go anywhere now.'

Maisie looked at her watch. 'I lost track of time.'

'Happens around here – that's why there are clocks everywhere. Come on.' He led the way out of the room. 'Follow me – and you never know, you might find it interesting, because the Americans will start broadcasting this evening – not many people are in the studio when their bit goes out.'

Later, seated in the corner of a tiny studio, close to Bob Walkinshaw as he worked, Maisie listened to the American broadcaster read his prepared message to his fellow countrymen. He held several sheets of paper before him and leant in close to a square black microphone. Looking up, he waited for a sign from the engineer, and began to read from his prepared report, ending with the words 'Goodnight, and good luck.'

If we talk at times of the little flashes of humour that appear in this twilight of suffering, you must understand that there is humour in these people, even when disaster and hell come down from heaven. We can only tell you what we see and hear . . . Between bombing one catches glimpses of the London one knew in the distant days of peace. The big red buses roll through the streets. The tolling of Big Ben can be heard in the intervals of the gunfire . . . In many buildings tonight people are sleeping on mattresses on the floor. I've seen dozens of them looking like dolls thrown aside by a tired child. In three or four hours they must get up and go to work just as though they had had a full night's rest, free from the rumble of guns and the wonder that comes when they wake and listen in the dead hours of the night.

It was almost five o'clock in the morning when Maisie was shaken awake by a young woman holding a cup of tea. At some point in the evening, Walkinshaw had called out to that same young woman, asking her to show Maisie to a room with mattresses cast across the floor, rendering it a dormitory for those who worked through the night at Broadcasting House. Though it was pitch-black, she heard people coming and going, and the occasional illumination from a match or a torch as another member of staff looked for a place to lie down, or to swap with someone just getting up. She had remained awake for a long time, feeling the building shake when a bomb came too close, or a distant *crump-crump-crump* of falling bombs that permeated even the many soundproof areas of the British Broadcasting Corporation. Her thoughts ricocheted between worry for Anna, her father and Brenda, and pain from her hands reminding her time and again of pulling Priscilla away from the flames, of the weight she could not bear on her own and, against her better judgement, the constant nagging *what if . . . what if . . . what if*. And now, awake to face another day, Maisie's attention was again focused on the death of Catherine Saxon. Her brother had been in London, and it appeared his presence was not welcomed by the reporter. But when did he leave? And what if he had not left England, but was still in the country? What did that mean? Was Walkinshaw trustworthy? And was the information he'd given her a hook? Could she start to wind in the reel and bring in the killer? Not without bait – and she had to find just the right bait. Mark Scott might have it, but so might Jenny Barrington – Catherine's friend from college was a missing link thus far.

Maisie sipped the hot, sweet tea. She would see Jenny Barrington today. And Mark Scott. Then she would go home – to Kent, home to those she loved. Home to the people she thought about constantly and who were causing her to reconsider everything she might have assumed about her future. But first, she would make her way to a small Italian restaurant in Marylebone Lane where a man named Pete would be serving hot food for people who had not slept, people who now had to go to work as if today was another normal day in the life of a Londoner. People who, for just a few hours until the next blitz, would be free from the rumble of guns and the dread that enveloped them when they lay awake and listened in the dead hours of the night.

CHAPTER ELEVEN

'Hello, madam – I can't remember your name, but I remember you were here with Mr Scott. What would you like this morning? We don't have bacon, but we can fry an egg or two for you, and serve it with our own bread, toasted.' Pete stood before Maisie, his smile broad as he waited for her order. 'And can I bring you some ice for that eye? Believe it or not, we have ice.'

'A couple of scrambled eggs on toast would really be lovely. And some coffee – strong and no milk.' Maisie lifted her hand to brush hair from her eyes. 'And my name is Maisie Dobbs.'

'What have you done to yourself, Miss Dobbs?' He pointed to her hands with his pencil, and *tut-tutted*. 'And that eye's looking a bit dodgy. Come with me – here, I'll tip the chair against the table so no one else will be given your place.'

The kind restaurant owner who had served Maisie and Mark Scott lunch only a few days earlier escorted her to the back of the restaurant, and through the kitchen to a storage room where there was also a sink. With a gentle touch he removed the gloves and the dressings, turned on the tap, and asked her to hold her hands under the running water.

'Keep the water running – I'll be back in a minute.'

Maisie remained alone in the room, feeling as if she had been left to languish in a broom cupboard. She wondered how many people would have to help her with her hands before they were healed. Pete returned clutching a glass jar filled with a bright ochre cream.

'My granny makes this and she won't tell anyone what's in there, which is a pity as she's getting on – she'll probably spill the secret when she's on her deathbed and we'll all be rushing round looking for a pencil and paper to write it down sharpish before she goes! But it works – we get a lot of burns and scrapes in the kitchen and this always does the trick. You'll be right as rain in next to no time, and with hardly a scar.' Pete took each of Maisie's hands in turn and dried them on a clean towel, which he then threw into a basket for soiled laundry.

'Mr Scott seems to be one of your best customers – how long has he been coming in?' Maisie spoke while watching Pete apply the cream to her hands.

'Oh, I reckon since he found us. He was walking around the area – probably soon after he arrived in London. I bet he told you it was only a couple of months ago. I've learnt with Mr Scott that he probably forgets how long it's been – and I distinctly remember it was before Christmas that he first came in, because we had the decorations up. We might be at war, but life goes on and you've still got to have a bit of a party when you can.' He reached to a shelf above his head and drew down a box marked 'Kitchen Medical'.

'Does he always come alone?' asked Maisie.

Pete laughed as he began dressing Maisie's hands using a fresh gauze pad and light bandage. He looked at Maisie and grinned. 'Ah, so you want to know how many lady friends he brings here?'

Maisie blushed. 'No, actually, I was just curious.'

'Hmm.' He grinned again. 'Let me think. No – never a woman, but I've seen him in here with a bloke or two. Probably fellows he works with over at the embassy. And I can tell you he lives alone – I had to take his coat to his flat once. He left it here after coming in for a late supper.'

'How did you know where he lives?'

'There was an envelope in his pocket with the address.' He tied a knot in the bandage, then took a pair of scissors from the red box to snip away excess material. 'It was a bit of a walk over there—'

'Over where?'

'To where he lives – sort of round the back of Knightsbridge. Nice flat – small from what I could see. He was very pleased to see his coat!'

'I bet he was,' said Maisie. 'I've only seen the flat from the outside – in fact . . .' She frowned to appear thoughtful. 'Gosh, I don't even think I can remember the address.' She reached up with her right hand to sweep hair away from her eye again.

'Don't do that, miss – you want to try to ignore it or you'll get an infection. I'm going to get some warm salt water and bathe that eye for you. It's not too bad at all, though I bet it was a lot nastier yesterday.'

'Oh no, really – you've done enough, and I am very hungry now. Scrambled eggs will set me up for the day.'

'Right you are, miss – but we don't run to gloves, so you'll have to buy a new pair if you want to keep the dressings clean. And here –

take this aspirin powder. Make sure you eat something first though.'

'Pete, you missed your calling – you should have been a doctor!'

The young man laughed as he escorted her from the stockroom, back to her seat. And it was more than scrambled eggs on toast and a large mug of black coffee that he brought to the table later. He gave her a scrap of paper with Mark Scott's address.

'After all,' he said, giving a conspiratorial wink. 'It's not exactly a top secret address, is it? Can't be, not if I know it!'

Feeling better for having had a good breakfast, Maisie walked to her office in Fitzroy Square – yet having reached the square, she decided to linger. The disturbed night in unfamiliar surroundings had left her with tired, gritty eyes. It was still not yet half past eight, and she wanted time to gather her thoughts, alone. Seated on a wooden bench, she closed her eyes and felt the morning sun begin to heat the day. Shafts of light cast shadows of tree fronds across the square, and she could feel the warmth touch her face, then become at once cooler, then warmer as clouds passed overhead. In snatches – a second here, a second there – she could imagine London before the war. It was a London without the vaporous smell of burning in the air, a London without barrage balloons overhead, without sandbagged buildings, and barbed wire around government offices. Now it was a London where tension was threaded into the fabric of life, just as London's oldest rivers ran beneath her streets, silently winding their ancient way under the thoroughfares of a city where people prided themselves on their ability to carry on as normal. After some twelve days of blitzes across the city, and following a summer of war fought in the skies above southern England, moments of peace on a sunny day seemed so fleeting, and anything approaching normal had ceased to exist.

Mark Scott had lied to her. He did not live in Manchester Square, or anywhere near the restaurant on Marylebone Lane. He lived closer to the place where Billy had seen him in South Kensington. He had been in London for longer than he had indicated in their early conversations. He was with her in the investigation, but absent – that was the truth of the matter. She was on her own and she was on the path of a killer, and as she assembled the disparate pieces of information – nuggets that seemed valuable but at the same time were slow to lead her to the solid ground of a case closed – she felt as if she were getting closer to discovering the identity of Catherine Saxon's murderer. She sighed, trying now to clear her mind, because every time she endeavoured to plan her next move, every time she thought she was focusing on the case, she saw flames licking up around Priscilla's body as if to consume her. Indeed, the vision was so strong, it had displaced another recurring image that filled her with fear – that of standing before the committee who would decide if she could legally become Anna's mother. *But she's already yours.* She felt herself hold on to those words in her heart, as if she were putting them away for safekeeping while she went about her business. But wasn't that what the people of Britain's cities were doing each and every day? Burying the fear and getting on with the next job to hand? And right now, at this moment, her business was itself giving her cause for doubt. Yet she was sure of certain things, the first being that doubt was a reality in every investigation she had ever embarked upon. She employed doubt as her servant, the one who would continue pressing her to check and recheck, to be sure of herself until the moment the servant was no longer required, because she had uncovered the truth and her work was done.

She was sure Mark Scott was not working on the case in any tangible fashion, yet he wanted someone or a group of people to think he was. She was sure Catherine Saxon's death had given him a useful cover – but what was he up to, and should it concern her?

Could she trust him? Again the question nagged her. In her line of work, people often lied – she had done it herself. The irony in any investigation was that lies were often protectors of the truth – unless they became too powerful, in which case lies were like worker bees who turn on their queen.

And she was sure that, concerning Mark Scott, MacFarlane was as much in the dark as she was – but at the same time, MacFarlane had respect for the other man's work, because his own role within Britain's secret service was equally covert.

So, who could she trust as she delved deeper into the life of Catherine Saxon? And could the murderer's motive be found in greater knowledge of the worlds the reporter had occupied before coming to London, or within the tight cadre of acquaintances she had made since her arrival in the city? Maisie sighed. Had Saxon allowed her head to be above the parapet for too long? Had she offended someone to the extent that an argument had taken place? Was jealousy involved? Was it a premeditated murder, or a crime of passion – *crime passionnel*, as the French might say? Saxon had been strangled and her throat cut – with the weapon possibly a knife she kept on her desk. And while Maisie thought it most likely the killer was known to Catherine, what if someone else had been sent to intimidate her, and being not easily intimidated, there was an escalation of words so she was killed to ensure her silence?

Yet Catherine Saxon was also a woman in love – a woman who had already given birth, who was now barren as a result of an improperly aided stillbirth, and who could have been about to end an affair because she was not able to bear a child with the man she loved. Who was the man? Bob Walkinshaw had rebuffed any suggestion that it was him, although he was right about one thing – Maisie needed a bigger hook on her line.

'Miss? Miss? Are you asleep?'

Maisie opened her eyes, squinting to focus in the sunlight.

'Blimey, Sandra said you'd have a bit of a shiner, but – well, I suppose I've seen my boys with worse, and it's only down one side of your eye, below that cut. As soon as that heals a bit more, it'll all look a lot better. It's a bit yellow round the edges already – which, believe it or not, is a good sign.' He pointed to the space on the bench beside Maisie. 'Mind if I join you?'

'Please do, Billy. I was just lingering for a few minutes.'

'Have you been bathing it with warm salt water? You don't want to get an infection in there, and salt water will help.'

Maisie laughed. 'I wonder if your prescribed treatment is a metaphor for dealing with this case – flushing out the bad bacteria.'

'What, miss?'

'Nothing, Billy – take no notice of me. And no, I haven't bathed my eye with salt water, but I will later. I'll be going down to Chelstone at the end of the day. Luckily I keep clothes at the house, along with everything else I might need, so I won't have to go back to the flat. And hopefully these dressings will last all day.' She held up her bandaged hands.

'You heard anything about Mrs Partridge yet?'

'She was transferred to another hospital yesterday – I'm hoping to see her tomorrow – I had wanted to go today, but . . .'

'This case will go cold if we don't get a move on, miss.'

'I know, Billy – but about Mark Scott—'

'I've been thinking, miss,' Billy interrupted. 'I've been thinking that he might not have told the truth about where he lives – I mean, I know that if he was on or near Manchester Square, I would have found his gaff.'

'Funny you should say that.' Maisie looked at Billy, reached into her pocket and pulled out the slip of paper given to her by the man she knew only as "Pete". 'Here's his address – as you can see, it's over in Knightsbridge, and though I'm not so familiar with that area, I believe it's very close to the place where you saw him.'

'That's interesting.'

'To a point – after all, who knows where the embassy has leased or owns property in London? They've probably got flats all over the place for their staff and this is just one.'

'Yeah, but, miss – he lied about where he lived, didn't he?'

'Yes, he did, Billy, which means—'

'He doesn't want you to know where he lives. You want me to go over there?'

'Yes, I do. And remember what I said before – be very careful. I don't think for a moment you're at any risk – I can't see Mark Scott coshing you for being on his street – but he's very, very observant and I don't want him to see you. Just do the usual – see what you can find out without giving cause for curiosity.'

'Right you are, miss. Anything else?'

'One more thing – and it means taking your mate on Fleet Street for yet another drink. He seems to know a fair bit about what's going on across the Atlantic, and he knows something about who's who in terms of their politicians. Ask him if he's ever come across anything about Catherine Saxon's older brothers, particularly one known as

"Scotty" – it's his middle name. The first name is the same as the father – Clarence.'

'Consider it done, miss.' Billy looked at his watch. 'I'm going over to Kensington for a couple of hours now, so by the time they've put the afternoon editions to bed, I'll get along to Fleet Street and in the Punch Tavern before they've pulled my mate's first pint.'

'I'll leave it to you, then,' said Maisie. 'I'm going in now – I've to telephone MacFarlane and then I'm off to visit Jennifer Barrington.' She stood up, reaching for Billy's arm as she did so.

'You all right, miss?'

'Just a bit dizzy – a cup of sweet tea will help. I slept on the floor over at Broadcasting House last night. I didn't leave before the first air raid sirens sounded, so I had to stay there.'

'Meet anyone famous?'

'No, but I heard the American correspondent make his broadcast.'

'I wonder what Mark Scott thinks about all that.'

'Good question, Billy. The thing is, we know Americans over here at the moment are with us – they can see Britain's holding the line against a possible invasion. But what are Americans thinking in their own country? What do they think of these warcasters – and especially when a woman is the one reading her report?'

Billy nodded. 'I daresay we'll find out soon enough, you know, whether they're with us. Because I suppose if they're not – then who are they with?'

'I have a distinct feeling Mark Scott is one American trying to answer that question. Anyway – I won't be returning to the office after I've seen Mrs Barrington, so would you telephone me later at Chelstone?'

'As soon as I've done my blackout rounds, I'll be on the blower to you.'

'Thank you, Billy.' She stopped and rubbed her forehead again. 'Look – I know I keep saying "just one more thing" – but there is something else.'

'What is it, miss – I can see something's bothering you, and not just those hands.'

'Bob Walkinshaw leaves Broadcasting House in the morning and comes in for his shift later in the day. Could you keep tabs on him, just for a day or two. See where he goes, who he talks to. He says he lives over in Islington, but I don't know—'

'Consider it all done, miss. Now then, you watch yourself today, all right?'

'Yes!'

'MacFarlane. It's Maisie Dobbs here.'

'Any news yet?' A shuffle of papers accompanied MacFarlane's brusque question, followed by an expletive as the echo of a heavy tome dropping off the desk reverberated down the line.

'None of note,' said Maisie, making no comment on MacFarlane's language. 'I have questions though.'

'You would have.'

'Yes, I would – but first of all, I have hardly seen our friend Mr Scott since he met me at the hospital, and according to the briefing, we are supposed to be on this case together.'

'Missing him, are you, Maisie?' said MacFarlane.

'No, and to be fair, he said he had other responsibilities, but I am not entirely at ease.' Maisie twisted the telephone cord around her fingers – already she was debating how much to take MacFarlane into her confidence.

'Go on, lass – what're you thinking?'

'Robbie – I know I've hinted at this before, but I believe this investigation has given Mr Scott a cover for something else.'

'So what if it has? None of our business. And it leaves you to do what you do best, which is work alone. Think of it as an advantage – you can move faster if you don't have to keep slowing down, after all, we both know murder isn't exactly his forte, though I am sure he's very good at whatever his job is.'

'He's lied to me already, Robbie.'

'Playing devil's advocate here, Maisie – why would he not lie to you, if he has other fish to fry? He doesn't want you sniffing around his work, and as far as I can see, he's letting you proceed with yours.'

Maisie was silent.

'Still there, lass?'

'Yes – but Robbie, what if the fish he is frying has something to do with the investigation, and . . . let me think here.' She paused. 'What if he's controlling my enquiry to make sure I don't get in the way of his, and I'm on the case because if it were Scotland Yard investigating – someone like Caldwell, for instance – then he wouldn't be able to exercise as much control? As I have been given to understand, if Scott tells me to go in a different direction at any point, then I have to go – even if that direction is away from where my nose is telling me I must go.'

'Hmm,' said MacFarlane.

'"Hmm", what?' asked Maisie.

'Maisie, continue with your investigation. Get on with the job, and find out who killed Catherine Saxon. The sooner you bring the killer to me, the sooner you're off the case and you can see the back of our American friend.'

'All right – I just wanted to tell you what I believe is happening.'

'You've indicated as much before, so I thank you for the telephone call to recap. And I forgot to ask – how are you? I heard about what happened to Mrs Partridge.'

'She's in good hands, Robbie – but not out of the woods. And me? My hands hurt and I've a slight black eye – it's because the cut is draining, but I'm on the mend.'

'All right, then. I'll telephone you later, at Chelstone. Give that little girl of yours a kiss from her Uncle Robbie.'

Jennifer Barrington's home was part of a substantial red-brick mansion on Green Street in Mayfair, more of an apartment than a simple flat. Having made a swift diversion to Selfridges to purchase a pair of light cotton gloves, Maisie had arrived at the house shortly after twelve noon, and presented her identification card to the housekeeper, who led her to a ground-floor drawing room. The apartment extended from the lower ground floor to the first floor of the mansion. Maisie imagined there would be a number of reception rooms, including a dining room and library, as well as a morning room and drawing room. While making her way across the entrance hall with the housekeeper, she saw a maid exit a door to her left, which she suspected led to a back staircase into the kitchen and scullery. It was indeed very spacious accommodation for just two people, even by the standards of their station.

As she entered the drawing room, Jennifer Barrington turned away from the front window, where she had been looking out at the street, and smiled at Maisie.

'Miss Dobbs – I had heard a woman was leading the investigation into Catherine's murder even before you made an appointment to see me. I am so very glad you've come. I wanted to call you, but Miles –

my husband – said not to. He said that enquiries are very systematic, and that you would be in touch in due course.'

Maisie smiled in return, somewhat intrigued by Barrington's mid-Atlantic accent – she could not place it as either British or American. Indeed, the cadence of her voice reminded Maisie of the Devonian accent, with a gentle rolling of the *r*'s and a longer vowel sound. And Barrington had something of Catherine Saxon about her – an ease of movement that was, Maisie thought, distinctly American, though this had not occurred to her before when she'd visited Boston some years earlier. Like the reporter, Jennifer Barrington seemed to own the space she stood up in. Her fair hair was pulled back in a low chignon, and she wore light linen trousers pleated at the waist, and a white silk blouse. A single row of pearls adorned her neck, and on her feet she wore brown sandals; nails on her toes and fingers were manicured and painted with a deep red polish.

'Please take a seat, Miss Dobbs – may I get you some tea?'

Maisie shook her head. 'No, thank you. I don't want to take too much of your time, Mrs Barrington.'

'Don't mind my saying so, but you look as if a building fell on you,' said Barrington.

'That's not quite what happened,' said Maisie. 'But I am going to the country for a couple of days. I've been volunteering as an ambulance driver, and we had an emergency a couple of nights ago that led to this.' She pointed to her eye with one gloved finger. 'And my hands are burned, so picking up a cup is a bit of a job. Anyway, if you don't mind, I have some questions for you.'

'Fire away,' said Barrington.

'You'd known Catherine for some years, I understand.'

'Inseparable from our first day at Vassar.' Barrington began twisting her wedding ring around and around. 'We just clicked. We loved the same books, we loved walking for miles in the countryside. We loved plays, art, horses – you name it, and we mirrored each other. The other girls said we even looked like twins – in fact, it was a big joke, that we'd been separated at birth. Perhaps that's always the same with the best of friends.'

Maisie smiled, thinking of Priscilla. 'Oh, sometimes it's the opposite – my very best friend and I are quite different. She's very beautiful – plus she has a good inch or two on me, and I'm not short. And she has lovely, rich coppery hair and mine's almost black. But I know what it is to have a very good friend.' Maisie felt her throat catch, for she had almost added 'and to fear losing her'. She put her hand on her chest.

'Is everything OK?' asked Barrington.

'Oh, yes . . . yes. Let's continue. So you were very good friends. Were you familiar with Catherine's family? Did you spend time with them – in the college holidays, for example?'

'She usually came to us for the summer.' Barrington shrugged, and looked down at her hands again, then brought her attention back to Maisie. 'I feel as if I'm talking about her behind her back, and I would never have done that to Catherine.'

'I understand,' said Maisie. She leant forward, resting her elbows on the arms of the chair. 'But any information you can offer helps me to see Catherine, to get more of the measure of her – it's part of my work to look back at her life.'

Barrington nodded. 'It's like this . . .' She took a deep breath and exhaled audibly. 'It's like this – she didn't look forward to being at home, though she absolutely adored Amelia – her mother.'

'I understand her relationship with her father was troubled.'

'You probably know all this, but she wasn't wanted by her father; however, as soon as she was part of the family, he thought he could use her.'

'You're going to have to explain all that to me – do you know why this situation existed?'

'Oh, sure I do. Catherine told me everything, and I don't think she ever told anyone else. Here's how it was – the senator – and by the way, that's what they called him, even in the house. Never "Daddy" or "Father" – he was "Senator". Can you imagine that? Amelia was his second wife. The first, Angelica, was killed in a riding accident, hunting in Virginia. They'd had two boys – Clarence Junior and Walter. Then being a good senator, old Clarence needed a wife by his side, so he married the daughter of a wealthy newspaperman, and they had Catherine. It was the senator's idea that she should be called Catherine Angelica – and boy, did she hate that! Amelia and Catherine were tight – in fact, I am shocked she isn't here, to tell you the truth. She was much younger than the senator, and so much fun – she came to stay for a while one summer, because Cath – Catherine – wouldn't go back home, and of course her mother missed her.'

'How did Catherine get on with her brothers?' asked Maisie.

'Not very well. They were a fair bit older. I think Scotty – that's Clarence Junior – was about fifteen when Catherine was born, and Walter was thirteen, so she didn't really know them, not like you'd usually know your brothers. And I can tell you, Catherine didn't like them much either – probably because she was brighter than either of them, and especially Scotty. That irritated the senator no end, because he wanted his number one son to follow in his footsteps, which I understand he is trying to do, though without much success. The goddam Nazi!'

203

'Nazi?'

'Oh yeah, you bet. He's part of a committee, they had a big old jamboree in New York with swastikas and everything. It was all about bringing proper so-called values to the people.'

'And did Catherine object to her brother's affiliation with this committee?'

'She most certainly did! And she seemed to go out of her way to rub the family's nose in it too, looking for ways to write about fascist regimes. Probably why Amelia and the senator are all but divorced.'

'I see . . .' Maisie had ceased taking notes. The information coming from Jennifer Barrington felt more like a tidal wave of grief threaded with whitecaps of anger and a deep desire to unburden herself – as if everything she had ever known about her dead friend was a weight she could no longer bear. Even as she spoke, Maisie could see the result of Barrington's revelations in the way she carried herself – her back was becoming straighter, her cheeks flushed. 'Tell me,' Maisie continued. 'I'm now getting a picture of Catherine's home life – and you say that Amelia Saxon is separated from the senator?'

'She lives in her parents' house, though her mother is now dead. Catherine's grandfather – Bartholomew Flannery – is still very much alive and running his newspapers.'

'Did Catherine ever work for her grandfather?'

Barrington shook her head. 'No. She wanted to make her own way, though I am sure Flan would have given her a job. He's had to be very careful with his newspapers – he's a Roosevelt supporter, but he knows the senator most definitely is not, so he's been circumspect, though his newspapermen have been given more slack in the past year, I would say,' said Barrington. 'My mother sometimes sends me the papers from home,' she added. 'Though the war seems to have put paid to that. But I can usually find one in London anyway.'

Maisie took time to frame her next questions. 'Tell me, what happened after college? What did you do? How did you keep in touch?'

'We both landed jobs in New York,' said Barrington. 'Mine was with a women's journal, and Catherine's with a newspaper. We lived in a women's hotel – the sort of place our parents would not have thrown a fit about, though we had some freedom to enjoy ourselves. And we both started writing stories and sending them off to other places. Catherine really liked the more political subjects, whereas I was better at writing about the latest this and that, and the kind of people you saw listed in the *Social Register*.' She shrugged. 'I suppose you could say I was good with commentary that was comic and just this side of caustic. I liked reporting on fashion and people and yet at the same time showing it for what it was – basically indulgent, especially when there were still thousands lining up at soup kitchens.'

'And Catherine?'

'Oh well, that's when she had to get away, wasn't it? Her father was after the marriage made in political and commercial heaven, and to please her mother rather than the senator – it was clear Amelia was getting the blame for having a so-called wayward daughter – she became engaged to Sanderson Brown. That's "Sandy" to his friends, and he was such a bore. But she just couldn't go through with it, which is hardly surprising. That's when she said to me, "Sorry, Jen – I'm off to Europe, it's calling my name." By then I was seeing Miles – he was working for his family's bank in New York at that point – and around the same time he asked me to marry him. So I said yes.'

Maisie nodded. Jennifer Barrington had married because Catherine was leaving, and she hadn't known what to do next – of that she was sure.

'And this happened in – what – 1935?'

Barrington nodded. 'Yes, I was married in December 1935 and we came here to live in London almost immediately afterwards. As I mentioned, Miles is with his family's banking concern.'

'Did you see Catherine while she was in Europe?'

'Briefly.'

'When was that?'

'Oh, it must have been 1936 or '37.'

'So that would have been in Paris, or Spain.'

Barrington nodded. 'Yes. Then of course she was in touch as soon as she came to London, earlier this year. Since then we've seen each other once or twice a week. It depended more upon her work than mine.'

'Oh, I see – and what do you do now?'

'I'm a correspondent for a couple of journals back home. Not the sort of thing that Catherine would write. I keep the ladies abreast of what the king and queen are doing, and how the princesses are coping with the war. The nearest I've been to Catherine's sort of writing was reporting the bombing of Buckingham Palace, and the queen saying she could now look the East End in the face. They love all that "bravery on the upper-class civilian front" rhetoric.'

Maisie nodded, and looked around the room. 'Where do you go when the air raids start? Down to the kitchens?'

'I go down there with our son, Charlie – he's still young enough to think it's a grand adventure he's embarking upon with his teddy bear. But Miles stays in the library. Each to their own. I do not have any reticence regarding spending the evening with the household staff, whereas my husband would rather meet his end with a shot of whisky and a good book. He doesn't mind us going down though, so it's not

English snobbery – probably more to do with being in a trench back in the last war – he gets claustrophobic.' She sighed. 'He's rather older than me, so he's seen it all before. Hates the sounds, but to a greater degree he cannot bear being cooped up downstairs, though he does worry about us, and we've been going to our country house when we can – that's where we were when you called. We like to be together, as a family though. It's so important.' She glanced at a photograph on the mantelpiece, of herself with her husband and son, then brought her attention back to Maisie. 'Do you have children, Miss Dobbs?'

Maisie met Jennifer Barrington's gaze, feeling herself falter.

'I'm terribly sorry. It looks like I've trodden on your toes again – I shouldn't have asked,' said Barrington, her hand to her throat as if she wanted to drag back her words. 'And I'm sure it's difficult, with your job.'

'No, it's all right – and yes, I do have a child. My daughter is almost six years of age – in fact, I will be seeing her in a few hours. She's in Kent, with my parents.' Maisie opened her notebook again, her hands shaking. 'It's just as well I have a good memory, because I fumble every time I start to write.' She closed the notebook without writing, and regarded Jennifer Barrington. 'Mrs Barrington, did you see Catherine on September the tenth?'

Barrington nodded, and glanced down at her hands, pressing back her cuticles as she looked up. 'I thought that would have been your first question – whether I'd seen Catherine on the day she died – or from what I understand, it was probably in the early hours of the following morning. In fact, I did see Catherine on the tenth – she came here in the morning, just to have a cup of coffee and to talk.'

'Was she concerned about anything or anyone?'

'No. In fact, she was very excited – she was going out with an ambulance crew that evening, and she was scheduled for her first broadcast. It was going to be her big break – that's what she called it. Her big break.' Barrington's eyes filled with tears, and she pulled a handkerchief from her trouser pocket. 'I don't know how I've kept this back while talking about her. I can't believe she's gone. I keep expecting to get a call and hear her bubbly voice saying "Hey, Jen, how about we go along to Fortnum's for tea like good little English ladies!"' She rubbed her nose and eyes and, clutching the handkerchief with one hand, she pressed the other to her chest. 'She was everything to me – my sister of the heart. I don't know what I'll do without her.'

'I'm so sorry, Mrs Barrington – I hate to ask all these questions, but it's necessary for me to know as much as I can. I want very much to bring Catherine's killer to justice.'

'I know – and I absolutely understand you've got to do your job. I'll do anything I can to help.'

'Look,' said Maisie, coming to her feet. 'I will leave you now – I've taken a good deal of your time. If you think of anything that might help me, please do telephone me at the number on my card.' She took one of her calling cards from her bag, and passed it to Barrington, along with a pencil. 'In fact, please write down this number – it's for my house in Kent. Chelstone seven-three-eight-seven.'

Barrington wrote the number as instructed and returned the pencil to Maisie, who fumbled, and dropped it at her feet. Barrington reached down to pick it up, slipping it into Maisie's bag. When they reached the door, Maisie thanked Barrington for her time before departing. Consulting her watch as she walked along the road, she realised she had spent more time with Catherine Saxon's best friend than anticipated. Now she would have to hurry to catch the coach to Tonbridge. But there was much food for thought. She had notes to go through, names to consider. In silence she would reflect on each person she had met, would close her eyes and reconsider every move they had made as she asked each question. Her work was twofold – searching for the killer, while at the same time waiting for the killer to make the error that would reveal his or her identity.

CHAPTER TWELVE

'Auntie Maisie. Auntie Maisie – you're a big sleepyhead!' Anna rushed into the room, her adopted Alsatian dog, Emma, following at heel.

Maisie had moved into the bedroom next to Anna's, relinquishing her larger bedroom so that Frankie and Brenda would be more comfortable, now that they were staying at the Dower House full-time.

She rubbed her eyes and sat up. 'Ouch! I shouldn't have touched that eye.'

'Auntie Brenda said I must on no account disturb you, that you had a long journey to get back here, and you're really, really tired.' Anna leant forward and brushed Maisie's hair away from her face, then clambered under the covers. 'But I thought I would just come up and go to sleep again, and then you wouldn't be disturbed.'

'Anna – I don't mind you climbing in, but you've left your shoes on,' said Maisie.

The child chuckled, kicked out her feet and slipped off one shoe after the other.

'And you know what Uncle Frankie says about not untying your laces first, don't you?' warned Maisie.

Anna nodded. 'Yes – he says new shoes don't grow on trees, and I must undo the laces so I don't tread the backs down when I put them on again.'

'Be sure you don't,' said Maisie, putting on a frown, but laughing instead. 'Now, Miss Anna, what do you want to do today?'

'Auntie Brenda said you'd be going to see Auntie Pris. Can I come too?'

Maisie shook her head. 'Not today, my love – perhaps another time, when she's a little more on the mend.'

'She'll be better soon. That man Auntie Brenda told me about will look after her – that special doctor.'

'I hope you're right, Anna – she's not been very well at all.'

'Oh, I'm right – I can see her when I go to sleep at night and dream. She'll have a mark on her face, and where you can't see it on her leg and shoulder, but she'll be all right now.'

Maisie smiled, pulling the child to her. 'If you're sure, then that's all I need to know. But I think I should get up – it's almost ten, and it's very late. In fact – oh dear me, Anna, you should be at school! I completely forgot! Come on, let's hurry, or I'll be in horrible trouble with your headmistress.'

Anna shook her head. 'There's a bomb in the playground. Uncle Frankie took me on time, and a soldier turned us back.' She giggled. 'Uncle Frankie said he'd have to give me jobs to do instead.'

'Let's get up and start them, shall we?'

'Oh, and a man telephoned just after we got back from school. He wants to talk to you – Auntie Brenda said I mustn't forget to remind her to tell you.'

'Oh, that must be Mr Beale – I missed hearing from him yesterday.'

'No, it's not him – he always makes Auntie Brenda laugh, and she didn't laugh. But she did go a bit red though.'

Maisie pushed back the covers and stood up, reaching for her dressing gown. 'Auntie Brenda blushed?'

'Yes, and when she came off the telephone, she said, "That man sounds just like Clark Gable."'

Maisie stopped tying the belt, and regarded Anna. 'First of all, how does she know what Clark Gable—Oh, I remember. I took her to see *Gone With the Wind* when it first came out. Auntie Pris came too, and we went to the picture house in Tunbridge Wells. Yes, she swooned a bit then, and Auntie Pris told her that Uncle Frankie looked just like him when he was younger.' She continued tying the belt, then held out her hand. 'And was this man called Mr Scott?'

Anna frowned. 'No. I don't think so. I think it was Mr Something Else.'

'Come on, let's go and see Auntie Brenda and find out who it was, then I must have a bath and face the day – oops, mind my hand, my darling. It's still a bit tender.'

With Anna dispatched to join Frankie on a walk with the dogs down to the paddock, Maisie asked Brenda about the telephone call.

'I wrote it down here, love,' said Brenda. 'Yes, a Mr Saxon. He's an American, and he said he was staying at the Connaught Hotel, and would you please telephone him as he would like to speak to you as soon as possible.'

'I wonder how he found my number. And I suppose he didn't leave the Connaught number because he thinks we know the numbers for all the expensive hotels off by heart!'

Brenda tutted in agreement. 'He just rung off as soon as he said he wanted to speak to you.'

'All right. I'll be in the library this morning, Brenda – I've some reports to read and telephone calls to make. And what's all this about a bomb at the school?'

'The Germans dropped it on their way back over to France,' said Brenda. 'Lucky it wasn't daytime, as that school would have been full of children. Terrible to think of human beings killing innocent little children. Look at what happened in Canning Town. And some of those shelters they've put up in a hurry could be blown down in a gale, never mind having a bomb land on top. As for the trench shelters in the parks – I wouldn't want to be under there during a blitz. It's bad enough going down to the cellar. All it does is make you feel safer, though truth be told, we'd be goners if a bomb dropped on the house.' She breathed in and exhaled a deep sigh. 'But I suppose we've all just got to get on with it and keep the little ones happy so they don't have nightmares.'

'That's all we can do, Brenda.' Maisie went to her stepmother and put an arm around her. 'And in this house we'll all be happier when the adoption hearing is over and Anna's future is settled, one way or another.'

Brenda nodded her head and turned away.

'What is it, Brenda?'

Brenda gave another deep sigh, turning back to face Maisie. 'I suppose this war is making me think a lot more about things than I used to. I've had my tragedies, as have you and your father, and what with all this bombing business, it makes me wonder what it's all about. And what I think it's all about is just being with the people you care for most.' She took up a cloth and began wiping the draining board, back and forth, back and forth, as if the rhythm of movement would give power to her words. 'Which means, Maisie, that if you are given leave to proceed with adoption, and you become that lovely little girl's mother – you have to make a choice. You can't go running around doing a job like yours when you've responsibility for a child. You will be her mum, and we will be her grandparents – which means she will need all of us, just like a person needs a roof over their heads to feel safe. We'll be the castle walls protecting her – and you'll become the standard bearer, the most important person in her life. There's no part-time motherhood, you know.'

Maisie moved towards Brenda and put an arm around her shoulders again. 'I've been thinking about it a lot too, Brenda. There are the hours Anna is in school, and I certainly won't be sitting here doing nothing, or arranging flowers – we both know that's not like me. And there are other ways for me to continue my work without compromising Anna's family life. I'm here four nights of the week and I intend to make it more – and in the meantime, she's doing so well.'

'But you don't see her eyes fill up when she comes home from school on a Monday and you've already gone back to London. And then she's on tenterhooks until you come back here on a Thursday evening – you should see her, sitting at the window with Emma, both of them looking along the path, waiting for you.'

'I didn't—'

Brenda placed her hands on Maisie's shoulders. 'Don't you see, Maisie? She never knew her mother, and she lost her granny, that lovely woman who brought her up as well as anyone could have. Anna's terrified of losing you – that's what the tantrum was about when you and Priscilla left early last week. And goodness knows

214

you were both brave and didn't shirk your duty when you were called back there. But she knows what you do when you go out on that ambulance, and she imagined all sorts of terrible things going on.' She shook her head. 'The only good to come of what happened in that building is that you and Priscilla won't be driving any more ambulances.'

Maisie nodded, rubbing her forehead, then pulling her hand away. 'I'm doing my best, Brenda – but I'm afraid too. I'm afraid Anna might be taken away, and then what will happen to her?'

'If you must know, I don't believe for one minute that'll happen. You've got a lot on your side, Maisie, so pulling back at this stage of the whole business isn't going to stop your heart from breaking.' Brenda's voice took on a firmer tone. 'Do your work, finish this case you're working on, and then let's look forward to the hearing being out of the way so we can all concentrate on getting through this war.' Brenda placed her forefinger under Maisie's chin, forcing her stepdaughter to look into her eyes. 'Now then, chin up. You're a grown woman who's come through enough in your years to start feeling sorry for yourself now. Yes, you've just had a nasty injury, you're worried sick about your best friend, and goodness knows what else – and as always, you've got a big case on the go. I don't think Dr Blanche would have soldiered on through all that without a bit of a rest.' She shook her head as she spoke of the man for whom she had once worked as housekeeper. 'Have yourself a nice bath, Maisie, and I'll bandage those hands again before you telephone that man and get some of your work done. We'll all have a nice lunch together, and then you can go off to see Priscilla. People do best with a plan, and there's the plan for today. Anna will be occupied, because as soon as Lady Rowan heard about the bomb in the school playground, she sent word that she'd like her to go over this afternoon to read to her – that'll wear both of them out, mark my words! And while I'm on the subject of Lady Rowan – there's someone else who'd like to see more of you. Lady Rowan and Lord Julian aren't getting any younger, and you're the only one left who can talk to them about James – and they worry about you too.'

'Thank you, Brenda – consider my marching orders issued.' She kissed her stepmother on the cheek, and turned towards the staircase.

'Oh, and Maisie – will we be doing a lunch for everyone on Sunday? Those Partridge boys and their father could do with sitting round for a good meal, and I've got all our ration books, so I could put on a fair spread with a bit of help from Cook over at the manor.'

'Yes, let's do that,' said Maisie. 'And we should probably invite any of those Canadian officers who are still billeted there.'

Having steeped herself in a hot bath, Maisie was dressed and about to pick up the telephone to place a call to the Connaught Hotel when it began to ring. She lifted the receiver.

'Dower House,' she said, by way of greeting.

'Maisie Dobbs – how the heck are you?'

'Mr Scott, I—'

'Mark.'

'Yes, Mark – I might well ask you the same question. How the heck are you? And more to the point, where the heck have you been?'

'You're beginning to sound like me. Embassy business kept me busy.'

'I see. Look, I should brief you on the investigation,' said Maisie.

'How are those hands of yours? Feeling better? I heard Pete gave you some of his granny's miracle cream.'

'Yes, and it is indeed doing miracles on my burns. I should be able to take off the dressings in a day or so.'

'Great. So, have you found the killer yet?'

Maisie rolled her eyes. 'You make it sound so easy, as if it were a board game.'

'Like Monopoly?'

'Like what?'

'You really do live a sheltered life, don't you, Maisie?'

'Anyway, Mr Scott – I do not have the name of the person who took the life of Catherine Saxon, but I have conducted some fruitful interviews,' said Maisie. 'I would hope I can close this case within a week or so,' she continued. 'Though a bit of luck might help, and a ceasing of the blitzes on London, which would mean a personal petition to Herr Hitler. Perhaps I can ask Mr Clarence Saxon Junior if he can put in a word for me.'

'What do you mean?'

'I thought that might get your attention,' said Maisie. 'Clarence "Scotty" Saxon left a message for me this morning – here at my home in Chelstone. It appears he is in London and would like to speak to me. I'd already suspected he was in England, so it would seem fortuitous that he called me first.'

There was silence on the line, and then a tone indicating it was time for the caller to place more coins in the slot for the conversation to continue.

'Hello?'

'I'm still here, Maisie.'

'Are you in a telephone kiosk?'

'Yes. I'm in a place called Tunbridge Wells. And a little lost.'

'What are you doing there?'

'I thought I'd venture out of London to see something of the countryside, and seeing as I had dibs on an embassy automobile, it seemed like a good idea to drive on into Kent and surprise you. I guess I missed the part in my briefing about all the road signs being removed in case of an enemy invasion. Anyway, how the heck do I find Chelstone?'

'You're coming here?'

'Might as well – you're not that far away, are you?'

'Mr Scott—'

'Don't start that again. Just tell me how to find you. I'm hoping I'll be in time for a bite to eat.'

Maisie gave directions to Mark Scott, with landmarks to observe along the way.

'So it's true – you people really do give directions based upon the pub on every street corner. I'll be drunk by the time I get there.'

'You don't have to actually stop at the pubs, Mark – just keep following my directions until you get here. And seeing as you have the motor car, you can take me to East Grinstead after lunch. Now, if you don't mind – I must return Mr Saxon's call. I've also more of Catherine's notes to read before we talk again.'

'Maisie – one thing before you hang up.'

'Yes?'

'Don't call Scotty Saxon.'

'Why?'

'Just don't make that call. Trust me.'

Maisie paused, turning to look at Maurice's chair – the chair she had never moved from beside the fireplace after inheriting his home. She had left the chair in place as if to remind herself of every lesson he had ever taught her through the years of her growing and of her apprenticeship. Whenever she looked at the chair, she could imagine him sitting there, talking to her, pressing her with his questions and advising her with his wise counsel.

'All right. I won't call him,' said Maisie, turning back to the desk. 'I'll wait until you get here – the drive should only take you about twenty-five minutes at most. Unless you end up in Hastings, that is.'

'Don't worry – I'll battle my way through it, like they did in 1066.'

'Oh for goodness' sake, Mark – don't you ever stop trying to be funny.' She replaced the receiver, smiling to herself as she ran to the door then along to the kitchen. 'Brenda – Brenda – we've one more for lunch. An American. His name is Mr Mark Scott.'

'Oh my goodness—' Brenda wiped her hands on her pinafore. 'Does he look like Clark Gable?'

Royal Air Force Flight Officer James 'Jimmy' Trahey is an Indiana farm boy now fighting alongside Britain's finest aviators in the skies ~~across~~ above ~~acres of hedged fields~~ farmland spread out like a ~~grand~~ patchwork quilt across southern England. Flying in the face of American policy regarding Adolf Hitler's march through Europe – a policy ~~formulated designed~~ put forward to appease the Führer and ~~with luck to~~ keep America safe from the fascist foe – Trahey ~~is one among a~~ joined a cadre of his fellow countrymen who are up there among the British boys of whom Prime Minister Winston Churchill has said, 'Never have so many owed so much to so few.' ~~They are doing their bit to protect this small island and its freedom from the tyranny of attack.~~ Trahey, 32, said his first ever flight was in 1920, when he was just twelve years old. One of those aviators from the last war, a man who had flown with the Lafayette Escadrille, landed in a field close to the Trahey farm. He was a barnstormer ready to give anyone with a few cents in their pocket a ride up into the clouds. Jimmy Trahey had the precious few cents, and from that time on he was hooked on the aviator's line . . .

'So, where do I find you, Jimmy Trahey?' asked Maisie. She rubbed her eyes, flinching as she scratched her skin with the bandage Brenda had just wrapped around her hand. 'Why do I keep doing that?' she asked herself. There was no one else in the room.

She leafed through the pages again, the first raw draft of an article Catherine Saxon was writing about an aviator she had met, an American now fighting with the RAF. Another clutch of notes appeared to have been made while in conversation with Jimmy Trahey, and were attached to the essay with a dressmaking pin.

'Ah!' she said, lifting one sheet of paper. 'At last – a break in the clouds of unknowing. I've found you, Flight Officer Trahey, and would you believe it, you're at Hawkinge.' She reached for the telephone. 'I just hope you're still alive.'

She was about to dial the number for the cottage Priscilla and Douglas were renting in Chelstone, when Brenda knocked on the door.

'Maisie – it's your American. He's here – and he's in the kitchen!'

'It's all right, Brenda – he won't bite you!'

'I didn't think he would – but please hurry. Don't leave your father and Anna with him.'

'Brenda, we really don't have to panic. Look, I must make this one telephone call, and then I'll be out. Ask him if he would like a cup of coffee, and make it strong, like you would have for Maurice.'

'Oh dear—' Brenda turned away, closing the door behind her.

Maisie began to dial again, and waited for the call to be answered.

'Yes?'

'Tim? Is that you?'

'Tante Maisie! I'm sorry – I would have said hello if I'd known it was you. Are you here, in Chelstone?'

'Yes, I am – and I'm going to see your mother today. Have you seen her yet?'

'No. Tom's been. So's Tarquin, and Dad of course. Tom's going back to Hawkinge after he's seen Mummy later.'

'Why haven't you seen her, Tim?'

'She won't want to see me.'

'Of course she will – I know she would want you by her side. Come on, Tim – you want to see her, I know you do.'

There was silence on the line.

'Tim?'

'Yes, Tante Maisie?'

'Tim, everything will be all right. Look, why don't you come with me today? I'm getting a lift from a friend, so you only have to say yes, and I'll take you in.'

'Tante Maisie, I can't help it. I – I do everything wrong. Ever since – you know – ever since Dunkirk, and my arm, I just don't know what to do any more, and it's all my fault. If I hadn't been horrible to her, she would never have been injured, I know it, and—'

Maisie heard her godson begin to weep, his wracking sobs echoing in the telephone receiver.

'I can tell you now, Tim, that your mother's injuries have absolutely nothing to do with you. She was injured because she risked her life to save two little children. She was injured because it was just our turn to be on that particular street at that time.

We were doing our duty, and your mother was injured as a result. Nothing that happened is your fault.'

'But if she dies, all she'll ever remember is me shouting. She's terribly hurt, and I'm the one who shouted at her.'

'Oh, Tim, love – she knows how difficult it's been for you. And she is so very proud of you. She talks about your bravery to everyone, and she keeps the newspaper cuttings about what you did for those soldiers from Dunkirk. She will want to see you very much – I am sure of it.' She waited for a response, but only heard Tim sobbing. 'Tim, where are your brothers and your father?'

'They went to the hospital this morning, and they stayed for lunch in the town so they could go in again later this afternoon, though I'm not sure about the visiting times because of the air raids.'

'All right, this is what we'll do. We're having an early lunch, so we should have finished by one o'clock – we'll pick you up at about half past, and then off we go to East Grinstead.'

'They won't let us all in, you know – we'll have to take it in turns.'

'I know. Remember, I was a nurse, Tim, so I'm familiar with the rules. Now, have a wash, put on clean clothes – a nice shirt – and I'll see you in an hour. Can you manage?'

'I'm good at buttonholes now, so I'll be all right.'

Maisie replaced the receiver, left the library and made her way along the hallway to the kitchen. Mark Scott was sitting at the kitchen table, talking to Frankie while Anna sat on his lap, sucking the first two fingers of her right hand and watching Scott's every move. Emma and Jook, the two dogs, lay on the floor with noses to front paws, their eyes appearing to follow Anna's as the American waved his hand in the air while describing how he flagged down someone in the village to get final directions to Chelstone Manor.

'And wouldn't you know it – it was the pastor. Do you call them pastors here?'

'No, you would have spoken to the Reverend Hartley, our local vicar,' said Frankie.

'Except he's a canon,' said Anna. 'And he's really old. He comes to our school to teach us about Jesus.'

'Ah, she speaks!' said Scott, raising an eyebrow in Anna's direction. The child giggled, snuggling farther into Frankie Dobbs' arms. 'I thought a canon was a weapon – so this canon guy is a weapon. Going to church must be fun around here.'

Frankie and Anna laughed, which seemed to please Mark Scott.

'Good coffee, Mrs Dobbs – I never expected that here in rural England. And the only place I've found it in London is in an Italian restaurant. Maisie knows it – don't you, Maisie.'

Maisie pulled out a chair, taking a seat at the kitchen table. 'Yes, and they serve very nice food too.'

'Well, it might not be Italian, but I hope my lunch is good enough for you, Mr Scott,' said Brenda. Scott was about to respond when Brenda turned to Maisie. 'Shall we have our meal in the dining room?'

'Let's eat in this lovely kitchen, Mrs Dobbs,' said Scott. 'You don't need to get the dining room all gussied up for me. This is good – it reminds me of home.'

'I think Mr Scott has made the decision for me, Brenda. Come on, sit down for a minute or two, then we can get lunch on the table.' She turned to Scott. 'And I don't think you've ever told me about your home, Mr Scott. I'm sure we'd all like to know.'

Scott laughed. 'Not very interesting. I'm from the state of Illinois. My grandparents had a farm, so I spent a lot of time there. Loved it.

My dad travelled a lot, so my sister and I, we were always at the farm.'

'Why did your daddy travel a lot?' asked Anna, taking her fingers from her mouth. She wriggled from Frankie's lap and moved to Maisie, clambering up to hear the answer to her question.

'He was a doctor, and he went to different hospitals because he was a sort of specialist. My mother went with him. I joined the army in 1917, and made it into the air. And your county reminds me of home, though there are more hills – Illinois is flatter. But it's green, just like Kent.'

Brenda scraped back her chair. 'I think I'd better get on if Maisie's to get to the hospital in time for visiting.'

'Mark – let's go to the library.' She kissed Anna's head. 'Better get down now, poppet – help Auntie Brenda set the table for our lunch.'

'Nice family you've got there, Maisie,' said Scott, opening the door to the library allowing Maisie to go through.

'My father married Brenda only a few years ago – she's made him very happy, and they love Anna.'

'I can see that – you all love her, and she loves you back.'

'I just hope it all works out so she can remain with us,' said Maisie.

'I'm rooting for you.'

'Thank you, Mark,' said Maisie, smiling. She held out her hand to a chair set next to hers at the desk. 'Right, let's get down to work, shall we?'

Maisie briefed Scott on her meetings with the other residents at the house on Welbeck Street, together with her findings with regard to Catherine's health problems following an emergency delivery of a stillborn child. They discussed Jennifer Barrington, and Maisie recounted her visit to Broadcasting House.

'You have been busy,' said Scott.

'As I said before, not easy when you consider people are rushing off to a shelter as soon as the air raid warning is sounded. Among my plans for next week is a visit to the Tuckers – they're the owners of the house. Really I should have seen them earlier. And I want to go back to Jenny Barrington again.'

'Why do you want to see her a second time?' asked Scott.

'Just to clarify some aspects of her recounting of events, and I left some questions out because I wanted to visit her again – it's always good to return with new questions when you're about to ask previously answered questions a second time, and you would be amazed how much more information you get, and people answer the question in a different way. She was tired and quite distraught by the time I left. Talking about her best friend's death was a strain – they were very close.' She tapped the notes she had been reading just prior to Scott's arrival. 'And I want to find this James Trahey. I think he could be important.'

'Why?'

'For a start he's another American, and according to the other women renting rooms at the house, he was a visitor, possibly a suitor.'

'You sound like my granny. A "suitor".'

'You know what I mean, so my comment landed on target, I would say,' said Maisie. 'Now then – why can't I speak to this Clarence "Scotty" Saxon? If he was in London when his sister was murdered, he's of interest to me in this investigation.'

'You just can't talk to him, I'm afraid, Maisie.'

'And will you tell me why not?'

Scott stood up and went to the window.

'Look at that view out there – if this were my house, I would never leave. I'd be a farmer like my granddaddy and spend every day in the fresh air. I can just see myself on a tractor ploughing that field.' He turned back to Maisie. 'And it's nowhere near as cold as it gets in Illinois, or even in DC.'

'We have our moments; we get a lot of weather here,' said Maisie. 'Tell me why I mustn't speak to an obvious suspect.'

'Why do you think he's an obvious suspect?'

'All right, I might have over-egged the pudding there, but—'

'"Over-egged the pudding"? What the heck—'

'Exaggerated – I may have exaggerated, Mark. But I'm curious about him, given the fractious relationship Catherine had with her family. I believe he might well have been leaning on her to cease her work as a wartime news reporter. From what I understand, she was an embarrassment to the family. I also understand that the father and his namesake have taken their beliefs about American isolationism to another level.' She paused, tapping the pages in front of her. Scott said nothing in reply. Maisie looked up. 'Of course – you're investigating him. You're looking into any political activities he might have been engaged in while in this country. But were you doing that before or after Catherine's death? And Mark – why are you really here at the embassy in London? At this moment, you're under my roof and a guest in my house – I think it's time you gave me an answer or two.'

Mark Scott shook his head. 'No, I can't. But I can tell you I have spoken to Clarence Saxon Junior because it's my job to talk to any important person from the United States upon their arrival in Great Britain. Saxon landed here again after his sister's death, and he is in this country on business in connection with his political as well as commercial interests. He will be leaving in a few days, flying from Southampton to Lisbon, then on to Newfoundland en route to New York and Washington, DC. There, now you even know the flight path.'

'It seems he goes back and forth from New York to London with some regularity.'

'I cannot comment on that.'

Maisie nodded. 'Will you be seeing him again?'

'No.'

'But you're watching him, aren't you?'

'I am an officer attached to the United States consular service. It's my job to know when our citizens arrive in this country, and when they leave.'

'Mark – you're forgetting something. I already know you also work for the Department of Justice Bureau of Investigation.'

'Maisie – stop right there. Clarence Saxon had nothing to do with his sister's death.'

A knock on the door was followed by Anna skipping into the library.

'Auntie Brenda says to come to the table otherwise the lunch will get cold, and she's not warming it up again.'

Scott came to his feet, leaning forward to salute Anna. 'Yes, ma'am! I reckon I'd better not get on your bad side.'

Anna giggled, putting both hands to her face.

'Tell Auntie Brenda we're on our way,' said Maisie.

The girl turned and ran from the room, calling out as she ran to the kitchen, 'Auntie Brenda – they're coming!'

'Great kid you've got there,' said Scott.

Maisie shuffled the papers before her into a pile and slid them into an envelope.

'Yes, she really is, isn't she?'

'Don't worry, Maisie. It'll all work out for the two of you. I can tell.'

Mark Scott placed a hand on Maisie's shoulder, and before she could stop herself, she had covered his hand with her own.

CHAPTER THIRTEEN

After lunch, Maisie chivvied her father and Brenda away for an afternoon rest in the conservatory while she began to clear the china and cutlery.

'Time for the guest to help,' said Scott. 'And you can't get those hands wet anyway.'

Maisie was about to speak, when Anna ran into the kitchen. 'The telephone's ringing in the library, Auntie Maisie,' said Anna. 'Can I answer it, please?'

'You may, Anna – but remember to say "good afternoon" and then ask who's speaking.'

The child turned and ran along the hall towards the library. Mark Scott rolled up his shirtsleeves.

'Really, Mark – just leave them—'

'It's Mr Beale,' said Anna, running back into the kitchen.

Maisie turned to Scott. 'I won't be a minute,' she said, slipping knives and forks into the hot water. She added washing soda, and stepped towards the hallway. 'And don't use that red soap for the plates, it's for clothing.'

'Take your time,' said Scott.

And as Maisie walked away, she glanced back to see the American looking down at Anna and saying, 'I guess it's all on our shoulders now, Miss Anna – we're the kitchen crew.'

Maisie smiled, then hurried along to the library hearing Anna's chuckles echoing from the kitchen, punctuated by Scott's deep tones.

'Billy – I thought I'd hear from you yesterday evening,' said Maisie, holding the receiver to her ear.

'Aw, miss, what with one thing and another, I couldn't phone. Young Bobby was home from his college for a few days – I reckon he'd be safer back there, to be honest – and then I was on ARP patrol, but I've got some information.'

'Just a minute,' said Maisie. She checked the library door was closed, and came back to the telephone.

'Go on, Billy.'

'First of all, like we thought, there are quite a few flats around the South Kensington area used by the embassy, so they've got more than just the big house where the ambassador lives. The properties are all on a long lease to the American government.'

'How did you find this out?'

'Talked to a publican and a couple of shopkeepers. There's all sorts of staff at the embassy – everything from secretaries to clerks, people who look after stranded Americans and the ones who get into trouble. And they also have what they call political officers – they're the bods who make connections, you know, get to know what's going on in the host country, who does what and who's important.

230

Anyway, Scott's flat is in one of them converted mansions. Just as well they built all them big houses years ago, because if they hadn't been changed into flats by now, where would everybody in London live?' He cleared his throat. 'I tell you, miss, what with all this blimmin' smoke and soot in the air, if the Germans don't kill us with their bleedin' bombs, they'll give us all terrible chests and the whole country will be in hospital with pleurisy come the invasion, you can bet on that!'

'Let's hope not,' she said. 'Did you find out anything else?'

'Not about your Mark Scott, no. Seems everything about him is very close to the bone. But you've got to look at it like this – these people don't exactly socialise with the neighbours, do they? Unless they're other Americans, and I've always wondered why people sit down for a drink and a natter with people from work, but if they've got no one at home I suppose—' He stopped speaking. 'Now, don't take that the wrong way, miss.'

'I won't, Billy – but can you confirm he definitely lives at the address I gave you.'

'You don't see names on the doorbells, just initials, so I reckon that, yes, he's the "MS" with the second-floor flat.' He sighed. 'It made me wonder about these people, the ones who work at the embassy – I reckon they're probably all a bit lonely, being a long way from home. And especially now, what with the blitzes.'

'You could be right there, Billy. Anyway – what about the other task? Did you see your pal on Fleet Street?'

'Like I've always said, Fleet Street is a drinker's lagoon – and you can bet on them all rolling out of their offices at around twelve, straight into the pubs. That's where I saw him, in the Punch, and he had a few things to tell me.'

'Go on.'

'Turns out the eldest Saxon son – the one they call Scotty – has been here in England a couple of times in the past year or so. And it's not like people have to sit around on a ship any more, though if you ask me it's a long time on an aeroplane, which is how he's been coming over here. There's this thing called the Pan Am Clipper – it's down to two crossings a week now, on account of the war. It flies from New York to a place called Botwood in Newfoundland, then to Foynes in Ireland, and the passengers can get on another flight from there to Bristol. Or they can fly to Lisbon and get on a BOAC aeroplane to bring them into Southampton. It probably only takes a day and a half, two days, to get to London, what with having to wait in Lisbon or Foynes.'

'Billy, that's all very interesting, but do you know why he's been coming over here so much?'

'Meetings with people – the American ambassador for a start.'

'Quite a few roads seem to be leading to the ambassador's residence at Prince's Gate. I wonder why he was making that journey just to see the ambassador. I would have thought such important people have telephone connections.'

'Well, I'm sure he was seeing more than just the ambassador, miss. But my mate says he has "political aspirations" and is looking to increase his associations over here too. But the best bit was that this Scotty Saxon takes after his father and believes in America staying on its own side of the Atlantic, and not helping us to hold the fort against Hitler. Mind you, we've got this far without them, and we're fighting back and taking down a lot more of the Luftwaffe bombers and fighters than anyone expected. Bobby tells me it's all about strategy and tactics – and we've got better aircraft. He said the Hurricane is the workhorse of the skies, and the Supermarine Spitfire is the one all the pilots want to go up in, because it's fast. I suppose that's boys for you.'

Maisie understood that Billy would take any opportunity to talk about his family, as if bringing them into the conversation lessened his worry, turning the light on in the dark room of fear he could slip into with ease. 'And I take it Bobby hasn't changed his mind about becoming an engineer on the bombers.'

'Changed his mind? He's worse than ever. I never saw that coming round the corner at me, really I didn't.'

'Hmm,' said Maisie, keen to move back to the main point of the call. 'Did anything else emerge from the conversation with your friend?'

'Sort of – he said that Scotty Saxon was an advance guard working on behalf of his father and these other men who are for the America First Committee and that they want to get the broadcasts from London stopped. They reckon the warcasters are building up the stories about us getting bombed, that it's not really as bad as they say. They want to prevent the news reaching the American public, because most of the American public are with us.'

'They want to stop the news? That's like trying to close the stable door after the horse has bolted, isn't it?'

'He says all these men like Scotty Saxon – and more than a few women – are connected with big money, and that a lot of the editors and newspaper owners over there could be bought off, persuaded not to publish or broadcast anything that affects people in a way that men like old Mr Saxon don't want them affected. He reckons certain men have been trying to get something on every newspaper editor, so they can manipulate the news. That's what he said – manipulate the news. Apparently Scotty Saxon has said that the reports of little children dying in the air raids isn't news that Americans want in their homes, and it's being exaggerated by the reporters. Well, we both know otherwise, don't we?

'Miss?'

Maisie said nothing.

'You still there, miss?'

'Yes, Billy – I was just turning a few things over in my mind. Anyway, I know you've had a lot to do, but did you find out anything of note about Bob Walkinshaw?'

'Went over there this morning – I found out what time he leaves Broadcasting House, and watched him leave. I had a description of him, and as he shouted goodbye to someone, I heard that accent of his.'

'And?'

'He may live in Islington, miss, but he went home to a place not far from Camden Lock. And I don't think it was his wife who opened the door to him.'

'Really?'

'I don't know anyone whose wife opens the door dressed in a pink silk dressing gown, with her hair down in curls across her shoulders, and her face on. She had the door open ready for him and just about strangled him with her arms around his neck. And looking at that description of Miss Saxon you wrote on the case map, I would say old Bob Walkinshaw likes a lady with a certain look about her. I reckon this one came out of the same mould.'

'See what else you can find out about him on Monday, Billy. And thank you – you've put in some legwork over the past few days.'

'All part of the job, miss.' Billy cleared his throat. 'Blimmin' dust everywhere. Sorry about that.'

'Are you all right?'

'Yeah, no worse than anyone else. Anyway, I was going to say, I reckon you can see this whole picture better than I can, and it's a few days since we sat down to look at the case map, but as I talk, I think there could be a few more pieces of the puzzle just slipped into place.'

'Me too, Billy. Yes, definitely – I think so too. Look, I must dash – believe it or not, Mark Scott is here and he's going to give me a lift over to the Queen Victoria Hospital to see Priscilla.'

'Mr Scott is there? At Chelstone?'

'I know how it must sound, and I'm still trying to work out what he really wants.'

'Oh, I think I know very well what he wants, miss.'

'And by your tone, I believe I know what you're thinking, and I'm also sure you're very wrong. Have a lovely time with Bobby, and give my best to Doreen. You've done good work, Billy. I'll see you on Monday – I'll leave as soon as Anna's off to school – that's if the bomb has been removed.'

'UXB?'

'Yes, it landed but didn't detonate, so they brought down the Royal Engineers bomb disposal squad.'

'Wouldn't want their job. And that's something coming from me, considering I was handling explosives in the last war.'

'I don't think anyone in their right mind would want that job. Anyway, look, I must ring off now, Billy – mind how you go.'

Maisie replaced the telephone receiver and returned to the kitchen, where Mark Scott was holding the bar of red laundry soap and showing Anna how to blow bubbles.

* * *

235

Tim was waiting outside the cottage when Scott and Maisie came along in the motor car to collect him. He was dressed in his best trousers with a shirt and tie, and carried a jacket over his remaining arm.

'Can he manage?' asked Scott, in a low voice.

'It looks like he won a battle with the tie, so don't help him.' She turned to Tim as he clambered into the back of the motor car and closed the door.

'Tim, you look smashing! Your mother will be so pleased to see you.'

'Is my tie all right, Tante Maisie? I had to use my teeth to help my hand.'

'Your tie is perfect, Tim – well done!' She gave Tim a broad smile of encouragement. 'This is Mr Scott – he's kindly taking us to East Grinstead, and he's going to bring us back.'

Tim nodded and blushed.

'I understand you're the bravest young man around here.' Scott turned to greet Tim. 'I'm proud to meet you.' He held out his hand, which Tim grasped in return.

'Not very brave really – I just lost an arm, that's all. My dad's the same – runs in the family, I suppose,' replied Tim, adding, 'What sort of motor car is this?' as Scott pressed down on the accelerator and set off, following Maisie's directions.

Maisie watched as Mark Scott looked in the rear-view mirror to respond to Tim's question. 'It's a Buick, son – we've a few over here, and thankfully they put the steering wheel on the right side, otherwise I'd be in real trouble trying to see around the corners out here!'

Maisie was relieved as the journey to East Grinstead passed with friendly chatter – she had feared Tim would be sullen and melancholy, the dread of seeing his mother enveloping all other feelings. But Scott managed to bring Tim out of his shell, and – to Maisie's shock, rather than surprise – engaged in a discussion about automobiles, and then sailing. And for the first time since before his wounding at Dunkirk, Tim seemed animated, talking about the boats he'd been aboard, and how his friend's family had taught him to sail.

'I'll wait here for you,' said Scott when they reached the hospital. 'I've a batch of files in the boot to read, so I'll be well occupied.'

'Thank you, Mr Scott,' said Tim.

'We probably won't be long, Mark,' said Maisie. 'Visiting times are strict, and Tim's mother will be tired.'

Priscilla's middle son and Maisie walked side by side, entering the hospital and stopping at a reception desk so Maisie could ask the way to those wards under the purview of a doctor named Archibald McIndoe.

'Your son an airman, is he?' asked the receptionist. 'And you've come to visit him?'

'No, we're here to see my mother,' interjected Tim before Maisie could answer, his voice bordering on terse. 'She saved two little children and was burned a few days ago, so my brother – who *is* an airman – had her brought here. Some of his friends are in ward three.'

The nurse raised an eyebrow and looked at Maisie, who gave an almost imperceptible shake of the head. *Please, just let it pass.*

The nurse smiled. 'Ah yes – you must be one of the young Mr Partridges. Your mum is a very brave lady.' She picked up a pen and pointed them in the direction of the ward. As Tim marched on his way, Maisie turned and whispered, '*Thank you.*'

Priscilla had been placed in a small room alongside the main ward, not only for her privacy – most of the other burns patients were young men – but to protect her from infection. Tim came to an abrupt halt at the door, and stared through the glass window into the room. Maisie linked her arm through his.

'Do you think they're happier without me?' said Tim.

Maisie looked through the window. Douglas was seated on one side of the bed, with Tarquin on the other. One side of Priscilla's face and head was bandaged and a cage had been placed over her left leg, to relieve the weight of a blanket.

'Never in a million years, Tim.' She looked up at the young man, who was now almost as tall as his father. 'I've never told you this, but I hope you know that you are your mother's son in every way – you have become more like her with the years, and you have her sharp intelligence, her wit, her charm and you have every single ounce of her bravery.'

'I think I could do with one of her gin and tonics, to tell you the truth, Tante Maisie.'

'Now I know you're ready to see her,' said Maisie, pushing open the door.

'Tim!' Priscilla's voice was compromised, and her son's name came out as 'Bim' – but as she lifted her arms both Douglas and Tarquin stood up and moved their chairs back, making way for Tim and Maisie. Maisie kept her distance as Tim moved to the side of the bed and leant down towards his mother, resting his head on her chest with great heaving sobs.

'Oh my darling,' said Priscilla, circling her bandaged hands around his back.

Maisie turned and left the room, followed by Tarquin.

'The staff are actually pretty good about visitors here,' said Tarquin. 'So I don't think we'd get into too much trouble if we were all in there with her. Apparently the doctor says that his patients get better if they're treated like human beings and not specimens. But of course, there is the worry about infection.'

'How has she been?'

'Oh, this visit will probably knock her out. She gets very tired – they gave her some morphine for pain. She refused to have too much though. She told the nurses that she didn't want to be lying there like a dead grilled fish when her family came in.' He looked at Maisie, frowning. 'You all right, Tante Maisie?'

Maisie nodded, wiping her eyes with her handkerchief. 'The last time I saw your mother was when I brought her into St Thomas' hospital – as you said, it was only a few days ago, and already she's had another operation.'

'Oh, that one in London wasn't much – just to take away the bad skin, and when she got here the doctor said thank God they didn't put this stuff on her that they use for ordinary burns – it's a sort of coagulant with tannic acid, and it's called Tannifax. Mr McIndoe said the stuff is a disaster for these really terrible burns he's been seeing in airmen, and makes his job all the harder. Anyway, he examined her, and then they wheeled her in for what he calls grafts – they took some skin from her back, I think, and put it on her face. Or it might have been from her other leg. I wasn't really listening. I felt a bit queasy, to tell you the truth. The doctor said he would let us know after the next trip to the theatre how many more operations she would need.'

'Where's Tom? Did he go back to Hawkinge?'

'Oh no – he's here somewhere. He said he wanted to see some of his muckers – pilots he's flown with. I think they've gone down the pub, actually.'

'Gone down the pub? But . . . but aren't they supposed to be here in the ward?'

Tarquin's eyes widened. 'Well, you would have thought as much, Tante Maisie! But this doctor says that the men get better if they have normal lives, so if they're well enough to go out, they can go to the pub, to the shops or for a walk. Some of them will even go back to duty between operations. And Dad says they certainly seem a lot happier than the men he saw in hospitals when he was wounded in the last war. Tom says the local publicans and the people are just marvellous – no one stares, but they get a lot of drinks bought for them, which probably means they wake up with a headache.' He touched his face. 'And you know, some of the men have very, very bad scars. I've seen them – you wouldn't believe it. There are two in there without ears or noses, but the doctors graft on their own skin and it looks like they've got an elephant trunk.'

'It's called a pedicle,' said Maisie. 'They shape it in later operations, when the graft has taken.'

'I'm glad Mum still has her nose, and her ear.'

Maisie looked out of the window at the very moment a group of young men were walking along the path, returning to the hospital. Tom was among them, laughing and joking as if all were well in the world along with his friends, young men with faces ravaged by fire, men who would be facing more skin grafts, more invasive operations and more pain as time unfolded. And from the opposite direction another man walked towards them, a doctor with his white coat flapping behind him as he hurried along, his head forward. He stopped and greeted the patients with a smile, putting his hand on one young man's shoulder. Maisie watched as the group spent a few minutes in conversation, and the doctor appeared to have made a joke, because the airmen laughed, and waved to him as he went on his way.

'Do you know who that man is, Tarquin?'

'Oh yes – it's the doctor. McIndoe. He's from New Zealand, and he's the surgeon Tom was going on about – that's why Mum's here. Tom's become very pushy since he joined the air force. He's still Tom, though.'

'And what about you, Tarq?'

Tarquin shrugged. 'Me? I'm almost fifteen now, and I'm a pacifist. I know it's not the thing you're supposed to say, but all I want is peace, and I'm ready to fight for it. But I won't fight like Tom and Tim. Not that Tim can fight much any more, though he's done his bit.'

Maisie looked at Priscilla's youngest son, a boy who was now as tall as herself and fast gaining on his brothers. 'Tim's fighting every single day, Tarquin. And the fight you take on might well be bigger than anything either of them have faced.'

'Ah, I've found you,' said Douglas, approaching along the corridor. 'You can go in now, Maisie. Tim's still with her, but I've told him you'd want some time alone with his mother.'

'Hello, Pris, my darling,' said Maisie, nodding to Tim as he vacated the chair next to his mother.

'I'll be back in before we go, Maman,' said Tim, smiling at Maisie as he left the room.

Maisie sat down as Priscilla turned her head towards her. Pressing the back of her hand against Priscilla's undamaged cheek, she said, 'You really are the bravest woman I have ever known.'

'Probably the stupidest too – but I'll take what I can get, especially as you've known your fair share of brave women.'

'Maurice once told me that in Hebrew there is a phrase for a woman of valour – so you, my friend, are an *eshet chayil*.'

'I'll make sure the doctor knows that before they wheel me in for the next operation. *Eshet chavil* should go on my medical notes.' Priscilla coughed, the tears filling her eyes an indication of painful congestion in her chest. 'How are those little children, Maisie?'

'They are both alive and very well. They've been reunited with their mother and the family has been evacuated to Suffolk, as far as I know.'

Priscilla pressed her lips together. 'I never was a cook, Maisie, but I seem to have roasted myself to perfection.'

'Why didn't you jump, Pris? You could have jumped – why didn't you?'

'I – I don't know. I can remember holding the children out of the window and just hoping you had the blanket in the right place, because I couldn't look down. And then the last thing I remember thinking – and you'll have to excuse me – but I thought, "Bugger this, I'm going back the way I came in." Foolish, foolish, foolish of me. I put us all at risk.'

'I had to ask you, Pris.'

'Fear started to plague me when Tom left, and after Tim was wounded it became worse. If I hadn't run into the building when I did, I would have become frozen to the spot. Every time we went out in the ambulance, I was terrified, and acting as if I was really brave was the only way I knew to counter it. Perhaps Tom had something to do with it – he's told me that when the alarm goes, you just have to run to your aeroplane, get in and up in the air and start fighting before you can let fear enter your head, and any thoughts of what might happen if you're hit. So that's what I did – I went in for the fight without thinking, and when I was too scared to jump, it seems strange but it was easier to run back into the flames. The doctor says I am lucky it wasn't worse. I've a few more grafts to go through. He says my hands will have some scarring, and down the side of my leg, but my face won't be too bad. Might have a bit of a bald patch though.' She coughed again. 'It'll take about a year or so, all told – but I can come home and have a normal life between the operations. Trouble is, I'm not sure what a normal life is any more. I don't even know if I've ever had one.'

'Tom made sure you're in the very best hands, Pris,' said Maisie, trying to reassure her friend.

'I know – he's quite amazing really. You go through their childhood thinking you've got to fight all their battles, and suddenly there they are – and they don't need you any more.'

'I wouldn't go that far,' said Maisie.

Priscilla reached for Maisie, resting a bandaged hand on her arm. 'They are such wonderful young men, aren't they? I know I've done an awful lot of things wrong, but I did something right, didn't I, Maisie? I married the right man and we brought up three really quite lovely sons.'

'Yes – you did the very best thing, Pris – and since I've known you, you've always done the right thing.'

'You saved my life, my friend – if you hadn't helped bring me out of that house, and then taken me to the hospital, I would have died.'

'No, you wouldn't. I knew you would fight on.'

Priscilla closed her eyes and nodded.

'You've to rest now,' said Maisie. 'I'll be back soon – perhaps tomorrow, if I can.'

'Mmm—'

With Priscilla slipping into sleep, Maisie stood up and lifted the chair to avoid disturbing her friend, and began to step away from the bed.

'Tim said you came here with an American,' mumbled Priscilla.

'Just a friend who was able to give us a lift over here.'

'Hmm,' said Priscilla. 'Just a friend. Pity.'

Maisie waited to see if Priscilla would add anything more, but she had fallen into a deep sleep.

Douglas and his sons were outside the hospital in a cluster talking to Mark Scott when Maisie emerged from the building.

'All right?' said Douglas.

'Thank you for allowing me to spend precious time with her,' said Maisie.

'You're family, Tante Maisie,' said Tom. 'Mum always says you're really her sister, only you were separated at birth.'

'She said that?' queried Maisie.

'Of course – and when we were young, in Biarritz, if we were naughty she said she would leave us to it and go back to see her sister, our Tante Maisie.'

'We were a bit worried until you actually turned up in Biarritz and you weren't a terrible ogre,' added Tim.

'I didn't know that,' said Maisie.

'All true,' added Douglas.

'Are we ready to roll out of here?' said Mark Scott. 'Who needs a ride, and where to?'

'Um – would you mind if I have a word with Tom?' said Maisie. 'We'll just have a quick walk along the path while you discuss getting home with Douglas.'

Maisie exchanged glances with Tom and they began to walk away from the group.

'Is this about Mum?' asked Tom.

'No – it's to do with my work, Tom. I think you might be able to help me.'

'Me? Gosh, that's a stretch, Tante Maisie.'

'Do you happen to know an American airman by the name of James Trahey?'

Tom stopped walking and looked at Maisie. 'Jim Trahey?'

'That's him.'

'What's he done? I can tell you he is as straight as a die – really good man.'

'Ah, so you know him.'

'Yes, he was at Hawkinge. Now at Biggin Hill, though he might have moved on because I think he was earmarked for training new pilots. He could be in Northumberland by now.'

'I take it he's good at his job.'

'Better than good – but that's not why he was earmarked for training,' said Tom. 'Jim is older than most of us. We're all nineteen, twenty, twenty-one, that sort of age, and Jim's about – oh dear – I think he might be about thirty, or even more. We call him the old man! But he's the very best fighter, and he's been like a rock for us; given us all backbone when we needed it. Jim will have a joke with the boys, and he'll take some real ribbing, but he'll come back at you laughing. And when he was at Hawkinge, Jim always managed to get us going again when one of the boys was lost.' He looked at the ground. 'We try not to think about it, but we've all seen a good bloke go down in flames, and you just try not to wonder who's going to be next.'

Maisie allowed a few seconds of silence as they strolled on.

'Tom, could you find out where I might be able to reach Jim? I'd like to speak to him – and as soon as I can.'

He nodded and brushed his hair back where it had fallen forward, and in that moment, Maisie saw the lines across her oldest godson's forehead, and more lines alongside his eyes and around his mouth.

'Of course I can, Tante Maisie. I'll get him to give you a telephone call once I've found him. Shouldn't be too hard, because he'll be with the other Yanks next time around. The RAF has just started a new Eagle Squadron for the Americans who've been fighting for us, and there's been more of them coming over to help. You see, they risk losing their citizenship at home for taking up arms on behalf of another country, and a handful of them have given their lives. So it's only right they have their own squadrons. Mind you, when I've spoken to Jim about it, he told me that some of the Americans are commercial pilots at home who just wanted a chance to fly a Spitfire – fastest aircraft in the world, and we've got it! I'm happy in a Hurricane though.'

'You're all daredevils, that's what you are.'

'Like Uncle James, I suppose.' Tom looked at Maisie. 'I shouldn't have said that – but you know I looked up to Uncle James. That's why I joined the RAF – I wanted to be just like him. He made flying sound like such amazing fun. And even though he died in that awful crash, he was testing a new aircraft on behalf of his country. He was so brave, Tante Maisie.'

'Yes, I know, Tom. And thank you for helping me out,' said Maisie, without revealing surprise that Tom had spoken of her late husband with such passion. She took her godson's arm. 'Let's go back and join the others now.'

'Jim was pretty pleased about his transfers, actually,' said Tom as they walked.

'I'm sure he was, if it meant he was going into training American pilots on new aircraft – he could still get to fly, but I imagine passing on his knowledge and preparing them for what's to come is quite a responsibility.'

'Most of us wouldn't mind it at this point – but for Jim there was something else. He had a girl and he was head over heels for her.'

'Really?'

'Trouble was, he had only known her for a few months, and I don't think he'd told her about his true feelings.'

'Oh dear,' said Maisie. 'Do you know who she was?'

'He didn't say much. But here's what I think – I reckon she was out of bounds.'

'What does that mean, to a young man in the RAF?'

'Could be anything – her father's the air vice marshal, or she's engaged to someone else, or heaven forbid, she's a married woman with a husband overseas. Of course, the worst thing is that she's already lost her love and she's inconsolable; you've got to be careful with a rebound bride.'

'A rebound bride?'

'That's what one of the boys said about Jim. "Perhaps he's found himself a rebound bride."'

'Remember to ask him to get in touch with me, Tom,' reminded Maisie.

'It's as good as done. But can you tell me why you're interested in him?'

'In confidence – his name came up in an investigation. He was acquainted with someone who is now deceased and I think he can help me with some information. Nothing more spicy than that.'

*   *   *

Tom was given a lift back to Hawkinge by a fellow airman visiting a friend, while Mark Scott offered to take Douglas, Tim and Tarquin home to their Chelstone cottage. After they had dropped off the boys and their father, Scott drove Maisie to the Dower House.

'Do you hear that noise?' said Scott as they entered the driveway and turned left towards the Dower House.

'It's the bombers on their way towards London. We should get indoors quickly – I daresay the air raid warning was sounded while we were in the motor car.'

'They won't drop a bomb here though, will they?'

'Not on their way to London – but if they've anything left on the way back towards the Channel, they might take a chance on hitting a village; after all, they want to break our morale. Look at the bomb at Anna's school.'

'I must get back to London,' said Scott.

'You'll be stopped by the local police or an air raid warden. You'd best stay until the all-clear. We'll be going down to the cellar soon.'

'The cellar?'

'It might not be safer, but it feels like it – put it that way.'

'I'll stay on ground level, if you don't mind,' said Scott.

Allowing time for the bombers to reach London and then begin their return, Maisie and Brenda prepared a light meal to be enjoyed in the kitchen, and packed sandwiches and a flask of tea to take to the cellar. Mark Scott maintained he would be perfectly comfortable in the conservatory, so Maisie gave him a blanket and pillows.

'I can pretty much sleep anywhere – all part of my training,' said Scott.

'Your training for what?' asked Maisie.

'For almost everything I've done in my life,' said Scott.

'You were very kind today, Mark – taking us to the hospital meant that Tim hardly had time to reverse his decision, and travelling with him on the train would have been very difficult, given his feelings about seeing his mother. And it would have taken ages. You distracted him, which I thought served him well.'

'They're a good family.' He sat down on the sofa in the conservatory. 'I enjoyed meeting them, though the circumstances could have been better. I don't meet too many people outside my work, so it was a break.'

'Yes, well, thank you.' Maisie stood for a second, then turned to leave.

'It was good to see you out of your working armour too, Maisie. You know – meeting your folks, and Anna, then Tim and his dad and brothers. They're all your people – you're lucky.'

'Don't you have people?'

'Parents are dead. Sister was killed in an automobile accident when I was away in the last war. I married my high school sweetheart before I went over to France, but she fell in love with someone else while I was away being a flyboy and getting a few medals pinned to my chest. So much for that. I took up with the government when I had the chance, and now I get to see the world.' He shook his head, looking out of the window at the gaining dusk. 'And this place reminds me of home – like I said, home's a bit flatter, but it's still farm country, and I'm a farm boy at heart, despite having had the run of a few cities around the world.'

'Well, if you've time tomorrow morning, we can take Anna for a walk across the fields.'

'I'd like that, Maisie.'

Maisie nodded and made her way to the stairs leading down to the cellar.

'Is he all right up there, Maisie?' asked Frankie Dobbs.

'Oh, I daresay he'll survive,' said Maisie.

'He's a very nice fellow,' added Brenda.

'And he makes me laugh.' Anna giggled, having offered her assessment of the American.

It was later, when Frankie, Brenda and Anna were asleep, that Maisie decided to venture upstairs to the kitchen. She was restless as her thoughts ricocheted from the death of Catherine Saxon, to images of Priscilla surrounded by flames, to thoughts of Tom in his Hurricane taking on Luftwaffe fighters sent to protect the bombers, and Tim struggling with his tie. Without a sound she took a glass from the cupboard and filled it with cold water. She sipped the water and stared out of the window, mesmerised as she gazed upon fields illuminated by what the people called a Bomber's Moon – a full moon so high in the sky that it illuminated the way for enemy aircraft to find their targets with ease. She watched a fox steal across the pasture, and at once felt compelled to walk out into the garden, to be in fresh night-time air and to be unafraid in the face of an invasion that sometimes seemed all too imminent. She unlatched the back door and stepped outside, meandering a short way so that all the land before her was laid out as if it were a reminder, a gift worth fighting for.

A light breeze picked up. In the distance, Maisie heard the sound of bombers returning. Having dropped their payload of slaughter upon London, the Luftwaffe were on their way back to Nazi airfields in France. In that moment, she knew she was not alone. Mark Scott was standing next to her, and soon his arm was around her shoulders and she leant into him. As the V formation of bombers droned overhead, they looked up to see moonlight glinting off metal. He pulled her to him and wrapped his arms around her.

'Mark—'

'Life's way too short, Maisie. Just stand here with me, that's all I ask.'

And as they remained in that place, both looking across the land, they heard a shot and a gun fire at the perimeter of the paddock before them, and the voice of an elderly man was almost, but not quite, drowned by the engines. 'Just you take that, you buggers! And again!' Another shot rang out. 'You Nazi buggers!'

'Well, I'll give you this – your people are really making sure Hitler is given a good run for his money.'

Maisie laughed. 'That's Mr Avis,' she said, turning to Scott – who lifted her chin and kissed her.

I've just had a message from an American friend, concluding with this cry: 'What a great race you are!' But I shall tell him that our men wouldn't be so fine if our women at this fateful hour were not so magnificent. There isn't an airman, submarine commander, or unnamed heron in a bomb squad who hasn't behind him at least one woman, and perhaps half a dozen women, as heroic as himself.

J. B. PRIESTLEY, DURING HIS *POSTSCRIPTS* BBC BROADCAST,

22ND SEPTEMBER 1940

Mark Scott left Chelstone at dawn on Saturday morning, as soon as the all-clear sounded, and before Frankie, Brenda and Anna were awake – he had decided not to remain for a morning walk across the fields. The day unfolded in an easy fashion, with Maisie, Brenda and the cook from Chelstone Manor gathering to work out what could be prepared for Sunday lunch at the Dower House, given the rations allowed, and consideration regarding foodstuffs required for the coming week – they couldn't use everything to hand in one fell swoop. Fortunately, Canadian officers billeted at the manor were able to contribute to the feast.

Tom Partridge telephoned the Dower House just before lunch.

'Hello, Tante Maisie – I've found Jim for you.'

'Oh, good news, Tom – I'm so grateful. How can I get in touch with him?'

'He's still at Biggin Hill, but due to go somewhere he won't say tomorrow afternoon, and surprisingly not on an aircraft – he has a travel warrant for the train. He said he could meet you in London, if you like, at about half past two. I told him you were always happy to give a young airman a good tea somewhere, so he only had to name the place and time.'

'And I bet he chose the Ritz,' said Maisie.

Tom laughed. 'Can't blame the man, can you?'

'No, I can't – and it will be an honour to treat an American airman fighting with a brand-new RAF Eagle Squadron to tea. Tell him to ask for Miss Dobbs when he gets there, and I'll be waiting for him.'

'I asked him to telephone me back, so I'll vector him in. I'd better be off. Consider it all arranged.'

'Thank you, Tom.'

'Oh, and by the way, I liked your gentleman friend.'

'He's a work colleague, Tom.'

'You might think as much, Tante Maisie, but if I may say so, I think he has other ideas.'

'That's enough, Tom,' said Maisie. 'Are you on ops today?'

'I'll be going up as soon as we know Goering's flying circus is on the way.'

'Safe landings, Tom.'

'See you soon, Tante Maisie.'

The telephone line disconnected.

'Yes, see you soon, Tom,' whispered Maisie.

CHAPTER FOURTEEN

83 CHILDREN DIE AS HUNS SINK LINER IN STORM

Eighty-three out of a party of ninety children being taken to Canada died along with 211 other passengers and crew when a British liner was torpedoed and sunk by the Huns in an Atlantic storm. Seven out of nine adults who were escorting the children were also drowned. A U-boat committed this crime against civilians when the liner was 600 miles from land. The ship sank in twenty minutes.

THE DAILY MIRROR,

MONDAY 23RD SEPTEMBER 1940

Maisie left the Dower House directly after Anna was taken to school by Frankie Dobbs. The two elderly dogs, Jook and Emma, joined them for the ride, sitting on the back of the governess cart, tongues lolling as they were drawn along by Anna's pony, Lady.

While changing trains at Tonbridge, Maisie purchased a newspaper. She read no further than the headline story, leaving the newspaper on her lap and staring out of the window as the journey progressed. She could not pull her thoughts back from the terror those children must have felt – such innocent little children being sent to safety overseas, the grand adventure turning to horror with one order from a submarine commander who might well have children of his own. Several times she had to fight to stop herself getting off the train at the next station and boarding the train going in the opposite direction, back towards Tonbridge, and then on to Chelstone and home. She imagined going straight to the school, to take Anna in her arms and tell her how loved she was, and how she would always keep her safe.

It was eleven o'clock before Maisie reached the office, and picked up the telephone to make her first call of the day.

'Oh, good morning. May I speak to Mr Tucker?'

'Speaking,' said the man who answered the call.

'My name is Miss Maisie Dobbs, and I am investigating the very tragic circumstance of Miss Catherine Saxon's death at your property on Welbeck Street.'

'We've already spoken to *men* from Scotland Yard.'

Was it Maisie's imagination, or had Tucker placed emphasis on the word 'men'?

'Yes, that's right,' she replied, with no change of tone to her voice. 'And, of course, I have the notes from your very brief meeting with Detective Superintendent Caldwell. However, along with a representative of the United States consular service, I am conducting an additional enquiry. The consular officer's involvement is necessary given Miss Saxon's nationality. So it's really a formality. I'd like to visit you at your earliest possible convenience, if I may.'

There was silence on the line, then a gruff response. 'Tomorrow morning, ten sharp. You'd be best advised to catch an early train, because I won't be here if you're late. Do you have our address?'

'Yes, I have your address and look forward to seeing you tomorrow at ten. I shan't be late.'

Maisie replaced the telephone and rubbed her eyes. 'I miss the Alvis,' she said, thinking of her motor car, now retired to the garage at Chelstone for the duration of the war.

'What did you say, miss?' said Billy, entering Maisie's office with two mugs of strong tea. 'There's no more of that coffee in the bag, so I just made the tea as strong as I could without it being too bitter. I don't like to see the spoon standing up in it. Mind you, what with the tea ration just gone down to two ounces a person per week, I don't know how I'll get myself going of a morning.'

'I'll take the tea however it comes, Billy. Anyway, I've just spoken to Mr Tucker, the owner of the Welbeck Street property – he wasn't terribly welcoming, but they probably thought the whole investigation had been drawn to a close.' She looked up at Billy. 'Let's get out the case map. I've to be at the Ritz by about quarter past two – I want to get there before a certain Flying Officer Jim Trahey, an American serving with the RAF.'

'God bless the boy, that's what I say,' said Billy, placing the mugs of tea on the table and rolling out the case map. 'Terrible about those poor little nippers, on that ship.'

'I can barely think about it,' said Maisie. 'And I wonder why we're only just hearing about it – it happened five days ago. I suppose it took a while to effect a rescue of those who were saved, and to gather the names of the dead.'

Maisie set a jar of coloured pencils between them, and began to add names, which she linked to others on the map. Billy added brief notes of his own, circling them with coloured crayon and linking them where he saw a relationship between pieces of evidence. They worked for a while in silence before Billy spoke again.

'Looks like someone just threw the names up in the air and watched them land. I reckon any one of these people could have killed Catherine Saxon.'

'Motive? What would be the motive, though?' asked Maisie.

Billy sighed. 'From everything we know, I reckon it was to do with something she said, or was about to say – or write – that would upset someone.'

'I'm not so sure,' said Maisie.

'What do you reckon then, miss?'

Maisie tapped Catherine Saxon's name. 'This is a woman people fell in love with. She had a certain magnetism, but she wasn't overwhelmed by it – what I mean is, she doesn't appear to have used it, as some might.'

'But what if someone was in love with her and another person wanted to stop it?' Billy shook his head. 'No, that sounds like one of those penny dreadfuls. I still reckon she upset someone with that writing of hers. There's her family for a start – we've heard enough about them, haven't we? And what about that American agent? I bet he could kill someone and not look back.'

Maisie held her breath, and exhaled deeply. She shook her head. 'If I had to make an assessment of Mark Scott, I would say he could very easily kill someone who represented a threat to his life or the life of someone important to him personally or to his work. But by the same token – he would not have done so with a knife used to sharpen pencils.'

'So you definitely think that's what was used?'

'Yes, I do. But even if I find it, it might not point to the killer.' She studied the case map, taking up another coloured pencil and linking more names. 'These are possible associations we must have more information on. There might be something more between Polly Harcourt and Catherine Saxon, and between Pamela Lockwood and Saxon. I believe Jennifer Barrington is keeping a secret, and I am trying to find a reason not to follow my instinct on what that secret is. And then there's the man wearing grey, but as I walked down the street this morning, every man I passed was wearing shades of grey. I mean – look at you. Even you're wearing grey!'

'Now we both know I didn't kill her, miss!' Billy leant forward. 'Are you going to tell me what you really think?'

'I don't want to muddy your observations. Once an idea is in the head, it's hard to see the other possibilities. I do want to speak to Jennifer Barrington's husband, though, and I have yet to speak to those final two lodgers. Harcourt was at the club where she works at the time of Saxon's death, and Pamela Lockwood was in a shelter at her work because she could not get home that night. Isabel Chalmers was in a shelter too – underneath the building along Whitehall, and she did not get home until after the time of death. Mrs Marsh was there too – but we think she was asleep.' Maisie sat back. 'Or was she?'

'You reckon the old lady lied to you?'

'She appeared to be hard of hearing, yet I wonder . . . I wonder if she might have suspected I was testing her when I dropped that book on the floor.'

'I reckon you'd better see them girls at the top of the house.'

'Come with me when I go, Billy.' Maisie looked at her watch.

'I'll have finished tea by half past three, and can be at the house by four. Could you meet me there? I want you to keep Mrs Marsh occupied while I go up to see the young women.' She sighed. 'I do hope they're at home – fingers crossed. And let's ask if you can visit Catherine's room – you could well notice something important that I didn't see.'

'Right you are, miss. And this morning, we had two new enquiries, so I'll nip over to see one of them in the meantime. I'm on duty at half past six tonight, so I'll be on my way as soon as we're finished at Welbeck Street.'

Flight Lieutenant James Trahey attracted some attention as he was brought to the table where Maisie had been waiting. She came to her feet to greet him, shaking his hand and inviting him to be seated. Trahey was almost six feet tall, with reddish-brown hair combed away from his face to reveal eyes that seemed at first blue, but as he turned his head the changed angle of light rendered them grey. He gave an appearance of athleticism; indeed, Maisie thought she would not have been surprised if he'd told her he was also a sprinter.

'It's very good of you to meet me here, Flight *Lieutenant* Trahey.' She emphasised the officer's title while pointing to the very new stripe on his jacket cuff indicating his promotion. 'I'd been informed by the staff to expect a Flying Officer.'

'Thank you, ma'am. It's good of you to invite me, though I'm not sure how I can help you.' Any smile of greeting seemed to drain from his face. 'Tom told me a bit about you, so I guess you wanted to talk to me about Catherine – Miss Saxon.'

'Yes. I hope you can help me, James.'

'It's Jim. Much better than James, unless I'm trying to impress your aristocracy, and as I haven't met any yet, I guess it doesn't matter.' He blushed. 'Oh heck – I've just remembered. Tom told me you're a lady. And your late husband was—'

'Let's forget Tom's briefing for now, shall we, Jim?' Maisie smiled. 'I've ordered a good tea for you, and I thought you'd prefer coffee with your sandwiches, scones and cake.'

'Tea and coffee?' enquired Trahey.

Maisie laughed. '"Tea" can mean the food as well as a drink – so you can eat your tea and drink your coffee. I thought you would have known that by now!'

Trahey blushed as they took their seats. 'I have to learn it all over again every time someone asks me if I want coffee with my tea. But this is just terrific, Miss Dobbs – or do I have to call you by a special name?'

'If you're Jim, then I'm Maisie. All right?'

Trahey nodded. 'Fire away, then. If I can help, I will – Catherine was a wonderful girl. Really wonderful. I couldn't believe it when I heard she'd died.'

'And how did you find out?'

'Read it in the newspaper. I was surprised it was so small – "*American News Reporter Found Dead*". It caught my eye right away. I didn't know what to do – I thought I should call someone, but I realised I didn't know who to call.' He looked away, then back at Maisie. 'I was . . . I was in a state of disbelief, but then I was out on ops, and – I hate to say this – I had more on my mind. I figured her folks would come over and take her home. Or her ashes. And because she never liked them – apart from her mum – I knew it was no good finding out how I could be there, how I could say goodbye.'

'You first met Catherine when she came to Hawkinge – is that correct, Jim?'

'She wanted to talk to American airmen over here. Some of us are hard to find – the ones who joined the Canadians before they came to England are listed as citizens of Canada, so not identifiable as Americans. I came over and enlisted as an American, though I had to swear to serve Great Britain, and when my folks found out, they said I'd never get back in again when the war's over. Or I'd be executed for treason or something else terrifying.' He shrugged. 'But where there's a will, there's a way. When it's time to go back, I'll get in.'

Maisie nodded, then took a moment to pour coffee for Trahey, and tea for herself, pointing to the sandwiches. 'Eat up – you need your strength.'

'Sure do,' said Trahey, filling his plate.

Maisie waited until he'd consumed two more of the small sandwiches – which seemed to vanish in a couple of seconds – before asking another question.

'So, Jim, I take it Catherine was interested in how you felt about being over here, what you liked about the people, that sort of thing – and she probably wanted to know something about where you came from, so she could interest Americans at home.'

'To a point. She was interested in the fact that I'd left home to learn to fly – I went out west to a place called Mines Field, in California. Good place to learn. Lots of flyboys there, and some really good ones. I learnt the ropes from the best. And the weather was great, flying over orange groves, farms and mountains, especially in spring.'

'I'm sure it was wonderful,' said Maisie.

'But England's good too – not when you're trying to kill Germans so much, but on the way home from France, when you see those White

Cliffs at Dover, and you know you're coming in to land, it's perfect. Like being a seagull.' Trahey was quiet for a moment, thoughtful – then reached for a scone, upon which he slathered jam and clotted cream. 'This is how you do it, isn't it?'

'It certainly is. And make the most of it – you won't get that anywhere else, you know,' said Maisie. 'What else did Catherine ask you about?'

'Um, well, she wanted to know how I felt about the folks at home who don't want Americans to get into the war.' He pressed a table napkin to his lips.

'And what did you say?'

Trahey put down the slice of cake he'd just picked up, and took a sip of coffee. 'I told her we're all going to be in this war together sooner or later. It won't be long now. I'm not sure what will bring my country in, but I can feel it here' – he pressed his hand to his heart. 'It won't be pretty. It'll take something big – maybe a flotilla of those U-boats cruising up the Charles River or something like that. But like I said to Catherine – we Americans know how to do the right thing, and the sooner we do it, the better we'll all be.'

'I think Winston Churchill said something along those lines.'

'Well, he's half-American – he knows how it is.'

'So you told Catherine all this – and do you know if she reported it? I have read notes about your interview that were found among her belongings, but I wasn't sure if she'd published anything based upon your meeting. And I didn't see notes reflecting the conversation you've just recounted.'

Trahey shook his head. 'No – she didn't send it in.' He looked at Maisie, as if gauging her trustworthiness.

'Tell me what you're thinking, Jim – this is no time to keep anything to yourself.' Maisie kept her eyes on his. 'You must realise, I am trying to find a murderer and any evidence I have to hand is getting colder by the minute. Tell me as much as you can and help me find her killer.'

Trahey pressed his lips together. He leant back in his chair, rubbing a hand across his forehead. Maisie thought that in increasing the distance between them, even for a second, Trahey was bolstering his resolve.

'I saw Catherine again you know, after she'd come to Hawkinge. I came to her place, and we went out a few times. As many times as we could, I'll admit it. She was gorgeous, a real lady and so very, very charming and intelligent. She was the girl you wanted to take home to Mum and Dad, and you knew that every moment with her for the rest of your life would be amazing.'

'You were in love with her, weren't you?'

'I was, Miss Dobbs – Maisie. I was in love with her, and yes, we'd talked about the future, and yes, we were . . . we were having what you might call an affair, though that sounds like adultery and we weren't married to other people. But I guess I just was not her guy, not the one she wanted to marry. She told me she was in love with someone else.' Trahey picked up his cup of coffee, appeared to have second thoughts, and set it down again. 'But she was good about it – she let me down as light as a feather, saying that in any other time and place, she would fall for me like a rock, but she had fallen already, and was in love with another man.' He shrugged. 'And what could I offer her? Every day could be my last. With some luck my risk will come down for a while, because I'll be training the new guys. I'll still be out there, though – but I plan to be a squadron leader before you know it!'

'Was that why she didn't file the story about you – she wanted to protect you in some way?'

Trahey shook his head. 'No – it was because of her brother. She has two – I'm sure you know this. The older one – they call him "Scotty" – he came over here, and while he was visiting her in her rooms, he saw her notes on the desk and threw a fit. She told me he lost his temper, said that she would ruin their father and him, and that he would rather see her dead than file this or any other story.'

'She doesn't sound like someone who would have been easily intimidated.'

'She wasn't. But he threatened to kill her career – and frankly, Maisie, he could have done that. A senator has a lot of power in America, and a senator with the Saxon money behind him has even more power – and even though her grandfather was in the business, the senator could have bought any news editor he wanted, and I am not sure he didn't do just that. I think that's why her mum came over here – to let her know she was on her side.'

'Catherine's mother was in England?'

Saxon nodded. 'I didn't see her – but I met Catherine for a drink one evening, and she said her mother was coming over. I asked her if that was safe, because you never know with those U-boats, and she said she was coming by air to see her.'

'When would she have arrived in England?'

'I guess about three weeks before Catherine died. Maybe four. I know Catherine was worried about it, after all there have been air attacks and bombings all through the summer. We lost a lot of boys – not as many as the Germans, but we've lost a lot.'

'When did she go back?'

Trahey shook his head. 'I don't know – but I think she planned to return home by the end of August.'

'Do you know where she stayed? There's hardly any room for her at the Welbeck Street house.'

'She stayed in a hotel at first, I think – the Dorchester, somewhere like that. And I can't remember the exact details, but Catherine said that while she was in London one of the other tenants at the house was planning to be away, and she'd offered the rooms to Catherine's mother, so they could be close by each other.' Trahey glanced at his watch. 'Do you think it's important?'

'I'm not sure – but I'm glad I know. It could be nothing, but it's very sad that her mother returned just before Catherine's death. She must be terribly upset about it.'

'Um, look, Miss Dobbs – Maisie – I really have to be on my way. I've a train to catch.' He pushed back his chair and came to his feet at the same time as Maisie stood up. 'It's really good of you to treat me to this spread. You don't know how good it all tasted.'

'Oh, I most certainly do! I was once away from home during the last war, and I remember what it was like to have a plate of something that tastes like real food put in front of me for a change.' She held out her hand. 'I've enjoyed meeting you, Jim. Take care, and safe landings.'

Flight Lieutenant Jim Trahey of the newly formed Eagle Squadron left the tea room, stopping to wave to Maisie one more time before leaving. She took her seat again and poured another half-cup of tea for herself. She wanted a moment or two alone before leaving for Welbeck Street. She was cutting it fine on time, but she would go by taxicab.

* * *

Jim Trahey was a rather more ebullient character than she'd imagined, but she countered that with an understanding of how his work as a fighter pilot might affect his demeanour. Tom Partridge would always assume a happy-go-lucky persona when he was with his family, as if to say, 'Look at me, I'm all right – don't worry about me.' She was sure the young aviators seldom allowed anyone to know their true feelings – perhaps drowning sorrow with a beer at a local pub, giving the dead a collegial send-off knowing it could be their name repeated by every man as he raised his glass the following day. But there was something else about Trahey. Had she seen him before? No, she knew they'd never met. Yet there was a certain familiarity about him, and she could not put her finger on it. But she knew he had loved Catherine Saxon.

And what about Saxon's mother, Amelia? Why had no one mentioned her visit to England? Perhaps it was not deemed important, though surely she would have had to register with her embassy, and considering the possible connection between two powerful men – Senator Clarence Saxon and the American ambassador – would she not have received an invitation to call at the embassy? It would have been recorded, surely – though perhaps marital separation rendered Mrs Saxon persona non grata at the ambassador's Prince's Gate residence.

One piece of 'evidence' she was sure she could dismiss with regard to Jim Trahey was the tattoo she had seen etched between Catherine's toes. It just did not seem to fit the affair between the two – the more she thought about the tattoo, the more she considered it to be something a less mature person might have done. And as Maisie mulled over what she had learnt about Saxon and Trahey, so she imagined them to have had an earnest love affair, despite the fact that she had confessed to falling for another lover. In the circumstances, and with Catherine's understanding of war, Maisie wondered if Saxon had deliberately scuttled an intense relationship to save them both from heartbreak – neither was guaranteed to emerge from the war alive, given their work. Could that be why the reporter had not kept any reminder of the airman, beyond the notes pertaining to their initial meeting? On the face of it, Jim Trahey's importance to the reporter had been reduced to the subject of a searing piece she planned to write and possibly broadcast – yet her powerful brother had prevented her from doing so, and with a threat that was not at all idle.

Maisie paid the bill and left the Ritz, allowing the doorman to hail a taxicab for her. As the vehicle meandered through London traffic that seemed undiminished by the Luftwaffe blitzes, her thoughts drifted to Mark Scott. Was his affection a mark of passing interest, or did he have deeper feelings for her? Were they just two people swept together by the tides of war? She shook her head. Wartime love was foolish for a young girl, let alone a woman who had seen it all before, a woman who now had responsibilities, not least to a child and elderly parents. Besides, when his work was done, Mark Scott would return to a country some three thousand miles away, and she had no intention of leaving England.

'There you are, madam,' said the driver.

'Oh, are we here? Sorry, I was miles away,' said Maisie.

'Don't we all wish we were, eh, madam?'

'Indeed we do,' said Maisie, as she stepped from the taxicab and paid the driver.

She stood for a moment outside the building, and then caught sight of Billy Beale running along the street towards her. Thoughts of Mark Scott still lingered, and she wondered what on earth she was going to do. The problem with her resolution to keep him at arm's length was twofold. One, that it warmed her heart every time she reflected upon Anna laughing at his jokes, and the little girl's chuckles when he taught her to blow bubbles – how she loved hearing Anna's laughter and seeing her filled with joy. The second was that, regarding her resolution, the door was already open – for she had entered into the affair she wanted to avoid.

CHAPTER FIFTEEN

It was to Maisie's and Billy's good fortune that Mrs Marsh and the two women who lived on the top floor of the Welbeck Street house where Catherine Saxon was murdered were all at home when they called. Mrs Marsh accompanied Billy to Catherine Saxon's quarters, while Maisie made her way to the top floor and knocked on the door.

Elizabeth Drake and Helena Richardson were in the midst of packing.

Maisie introduced herself as the door opened, and stated her business. The woman who had answered the door smiled and invited her to enter.

'We heard you'd been here to talk to Mrs Marsh – well, we didn't know it was you, but we knew a woman had been round to the house, and that she would want to speak to us. Hang on a minute.' The woman turned and called out in the direction of the second room. 'Lena – Lena, come here. It's the woman from the police. About Cath.'

She brought her attention back to Maisie. 'I should have introduced myself – I'm Elizabeth Drake. My friend who was in the other room is Helena Richardson. Here she is. Lena, this is Miss Dobbs.'

Maisie greeted Richardson, noting that the two women mirrored each other, and could have been siblings, though not twins. Drake had dark hair, while Richardson's was light brown, and both stood about five and a half feet tall. They were of equal medium build, and Maisie thought they probably shared clothes, for they were each wearing linen skirts with cotton blouses and plain brown lace-up shoes. Neither wore stockings.

'Hello, Helena,' said Maisie, shaking hands with both women. 'It appears I've caught you in the midst of moving.'

'Finally!' said Drake.

'Off to the Wrens,' said Richardson.

'So you were both accepted – Mrs Marsh told me you'd applied.'

'Best uniforms.' Richardson winked at Maisie. 'That's what all the girls say, anyway. We just liked the idea of the Wrens more than anything else.'

'And we certainly weren't going to shovel manure with the Land Army!' said Drake.

Maisie laughed with the women, but was anxious to proceed with her enquiries.

'I'd like to ask you some questions about Miss Saxon, and about the morning of her death.'

'Let's sit down – sorry, we should have shown our manners,' said Elizabeth Drake, gesturing towards a small dining table. She pulled out a chair for Maisie, Richardson took a place opposite her friend.

'First,' said Maisie, 'tell me about Catherine – when did you meet her? How well did you know her?'

'Cath was terrific,' said Richardson. 'A real sport – and she made sure she introduced herself to us the very day she moved in.' She glanced at Drake, and then continued. 'We'd heard some noise downstairs – you know, the sound of footsteps going up and down the stairs, and when I looked over the banister, I could see this woman coming up with a box.'

'She was making a bit of a racket, like you do when you're moving in. Pam on the floor below was looking over the banister at the same time,' said Drake.

'Mrs Lockwood?' enquired Maisie, taking notes on a small pad.

Drake continued the story. 'Yes, she was at home that day. Then the noise stopped and before you knew it, there was a knock at our door and Cath was standing there—'

'Brandishing a bottle of wine,' finished Richardson. 'Apparently she'd knocked on Pam's door, but she'd declined the invitation to celebrate Cath moving in, so she worked her way up. Polly was out, so it was just the three of us – and Cath was great fun!'

'What did you talk about, during that first meeting?' asked Maisie.

'Well, first off we asked how she found out about the flat,' said Drake. 'And it turned out she'd known someone in Paris who'd told her about the house, so she wanted to look it up. That's what she said – "look it up". Then when she did her looking up, she saw the sign in the window, that there was a room for rent, so she jumped at the chance to live here.'

'Interesting,' said Maisie.

'She told us she was a news reporter, and that she was writing about London and the war – of course this was before the blitzes started, but as we all know, there had already been a lot of bombing following Dunkirk, when we were all expecting the invasion at any minute. I suppose nothing's changed there, has it? The Germans could still walk all over us tomorrow.' Drake looked at her friend to take up the story.

'It sounds so brave and exciting, doesn't it? Being an American in London, and writing about the war for the people over there. We asked her about her job, and how Americans felt about the war here, and she said people's minds were changing, and she was going to do her part to make them see the truth of what was happening,' said Richardson. 'In fact, I can remember exactly what she said, Miss Dobbs – "Opinions are ready to be changed back at home, and I'm going to do my part to make sure Americans know what's really going on in Britain and how people are bearing up, fighting Hitler with their spirit."'

'Really?' said Maisie.

'She told us all about the other American newsmen – and a woman or two, I think – who were over here and bound and determined to make sure America came to the aid of Britain, at the very least with supplies, despite their neutrality acts,' Richardson continued.

'And she said she would do what Mr Murrow was doing – reach the people through stories *of* the people, but she would do it from a woman's point of view,' added Drake.

'It sounds as if you really admired her,' commented Maisie.

The women exchanged looks. 'I suppose we did,' said Drake. 'But it's not as if we saw much of her after that. She was so busy, and working at unsociable hours. Just like Polly. When we had a get-together out in Isabel's garden, we joked that Polly and Cath were the only ones to pass on the stairs, because they would both be coming in late, though I don't think Polly ever went out early. Not like Cath.'

'Were you aware of any friends who visited, or family?'

'There was Stage-Door Johnny – an American airman,' offered Drake. 'I bet Polly's already told you about him. He was a bit of fun, if we saw him, but I was never sure about them – not that I saw them together much, but I always thought Cath had more feelings for him than she let on.'

'Oh, and there was that awful American – wasn't he her brother or something? Or perhaps a cousin. Anyway, he was a relation,' said Richardson. 'And he was shouting – talk about broadcasting!'

'Was it about her work?' said Maisie. 'Did you hear or—'

'Did we hear?' interrupted Richardson. 'The whole street must have heard him, going on about her letting her father down, running off and getting into all sorts of trouble in Paris and Spain and then going to Germany, where her father had business interests. He went on and on about the family name, about how their grandfather didn't struggle to come to America with nothing in his pocket so she could squander it.'

'He might have been upset because of the German ancestors, something like that,' said Drake.

Maisie looked up from her notes. 'German ancestors?'

'Saxon – Saxony. I mean, we don't know for definite,' said Richardson. 'Cath never said anything, but we were up here getting ready for an exam – we've been students, you see – and that's what we suspected, that she had German ancestors. Though I suppose they could have been Anglo-Saxon. I read somewhere that the officials in America changed the names of an awful lot of people who went over there to build a new life in the last century. They did it so people fitted in. Or they might not have understood them and just wrote down something that sounded familiar.'

'I hardly think Cath's family were descended from an Anglo-Saxon village idiot, Lena, so I am sure they were understood,' said Drake.

'I suppose it's a possibility there was a German connection,' said Maisie, wondering if the supposition was pertinent to the investigation. 'In any case, do you know if this Mr Saxon visited more than once?'

'I think it might have been more than once – what do you think, Lena?' said Drake.

'Oh no, you're getting him mixed up with that other man – the one in the good suit,' replied Richardson.

'You certainly see a lot from up here,' said Maisie. 'Can you tell me more about the other man?'

'I bumped into him on the street, as he was leaving the house,' said Richardson. 'I saw Cath waving him off. I was coming back from working in the college library. Oh dear, I hate to admit this, but it was about half past six in the morning. To tell you the truth, I don't think the librarian found me because I'd fallen asleep at a desk behind a bookcase where I couldn't be seen. It's a wonder I managed to get out of the place when I did. The caretaker had to unlock the doors first thing, so I gave him sixpence not to report me! Anyway, this man I saw was very well dressed – you know, he was the Savile-Row-suit type. Nice hat, carried a mackintosh – even though there wasn't a drop of rain.' She shrugged. 'I told Liz, after I'd seen him, that it wasn't for me to pass judgement because Cath can walk out with who she likes when she likes, and more power to her for managing to get him past Mrs Marsh.'

'Who, if truth be told, probably likes having her palms greased,' said Drake. 'Nothing like a pound or two to keep someone quiet and happy, and Lena said he looked as if he had a pound note or two to spare.'

'More like the sort to have two hundred to spare! Anyway, I saw him a couple more times,' added Richardson. 'Once when he was leaving and getting into a taxicab, and another time he was arriving at the house. I let him in, actually – I knew he was visiting Cath, so what was the point in him ringing the bell and waiting? I suppose that was about six in the evening, not much later. And I'm sure he visited her more often than that, if I saw him twice and we're usually out all day.'

'And you don't know his name, by chance?' said Maisie.

The women shook their heads.

'And on the morning of Catherine's death?' asked Maisie.

'We'd been at a shelter,' said Drake. 'When the blitzes first started, we ran down to the cellar here on the first night – it's through a door next to Isabel's rooms. No one ever used it, and it was very tight in there, but we knew it would be safer than being on the top floor, what with those bombers going over our heads. But it was also full of spiders and generally horrible, so we've been at different shelters since the blitzes got worse.'

Maisie asked a few more questions, and confirmed that Catherine Saxon's mother had indeed paid a visit some weeks before her daughter's death. Having exhausted the well of information offered by the friends, she took her leave, wishing the two women the very best of luck in the Wrens. As she made her way down the stairs, she glanced up and saw them looking over the banister. They reminded her of two young owls, wide eyed, peering down from their nest.

Maisie made one stop before departing the house. Passing through the ground-floor entrance hall, she descended to the lower ground floor and just before reaching the door to Isabel Chalmers' rooms, she opened another door to the right. A length of string brushed against her face, so she pulled it and a single light bulb came on, illuminating a very small, musty storeroom – only at a stretch could it be called a cellar. A couple of blankets had been pushed into a corner, and she estimated that no more than three people could lie down for the night, and it would be a tight squeeze. An old bicycle frame had been left propped against the wall, which was damp and indeed home to a few spiders. But people were bearing up in equally uncomfortable circumstances on the Tube platforms and in trench shelters. She was sure Isabel Chalmers would not use the cellar – after all, she was already in her lower-ground-floor rooms, and Mrs Marsh would not come down. Polly often remained at work until the all-clear, and Pamela Lockwood also sought refuge at her place of work, for the most part – and besides, Maisie could not imagine the very particular Mrs Lockwood sharing such a confined space with any of her fellow lodgers. She took one final look around the cellar before turning to leave, when her shoe kicked against the bicycle frame and it fell against her leg. 'Ouch!' she cried, and pushed it away. She bent down to rub her ankle and felt her fingertips brush against another piece of metal. Believing it to be part of the bicycle, she was about to pick it up and throw it to one side to join the rest of the frame, when she stopped and instead pulled out a fresh linen handkerchief from her pocket. Covering her fingers, she reached for the item. The shape was unmistakable. She departed the cellar, closed the door behind her, and joined Billy, who was waiting for her outside the house.

'What is it, miss?' said Billy.

Maisie opened the handkerchief and studied her find.

'I have a terrible feeling I have just found the weapon used to kill Catherine Saxon,' said Maisie. 'It was in a small storeroom. The women upstairs told me about it, though they called it the cellar, so I thought I'd have a look.'

'Blimey,' said Billy. 'Are you sure it's the weapon?'

Maisie shook her head. 'No, I'm not at all sure. But it looks like the sort of knife you would sharpen pencils with and it's a very sharp knife indeed – I can feel it through the handkerchief.'

'What's it doing down there? Why would a murderer put a knife in a storeroom – I mean, you found it easily enough, didn't you?'

Maisie shook her head. 'It wasn't that easy, but I will add that it's fortunate the bandage on my hand does not extend to my fingers. And I don't know why someone would throw it in there – or leave it in there. I can only imagine that, if it is indeed the murder weapon, the killer panicked, and just wanted to be rid of it.' She passed the handkerchief-wrapped knife to her assistant. 'Billy – could you hang on to this for me? I just have to run upstairs to talk to those girls again.'

Maisie tried to open the door, but it had locked behind her. She was about to raise the brass ring to knock on the door again, when it was opened by Mrs Marsh.

'Left something, did you, Miss Dobbs?'

'I did – my notebook, would you believe? I would forget my head if it wasn't screwed on! I just have to run up and get it.' Maisie rushed past the landlady.

'And I have to ask you, Miss Dobbs,' Marsh called out after her, 'will you be finished with your enquiry soon? Mr Tucker wants to rent out Miss Saxon's rooms again and he's getting a bit anxious about it all. Doesn't like to lose rent money.'

'Soon, Mrs Marsh – soon,' said Maisie, without turning.

She was breathless by the time she reached the top floor, where the door was wedged open by a box of books.

'Hello! Elizabeth. Helena,' she called out, her hand to her chest.

The young women came from the bedroom, both carrying boxes.

'Did you leave something, Miss Dobbs?' said Drake.

Maisie shook her head and tried to catch her breath.

'That's how I feel every day!' said Helena. 'Puffed out! Give yourself a minute, we're not leaving for a few days.'

'I'm sorry to bother you, but can you confirm something for me – and I apologise for going over this ground again – but did you retreat to the cellar just the once, on the night of the first blitz?'

'Only that once – too many spiders, though I suppose a spider isn't as dangerous as one of Hitler's bombs! So it was only on the seventh that we went down into the spiders' lair! Since then it's depended upon where we are – the college has a big cellar if we're there late, and Isabel lets us bunk in with her if she's at home, so no, we haven't been into that nasty little cave since, though Mrs Marsh said she would leave some blankets in there, just in case, but I don't think anyone's used it. Mrs Marsh always says she'll take her chances in her own rooms – you'd never get her out.'

'Did you take any utensils in there with you? A fork, knife, or anything?'

Both women shook their heads. 'Just ourselves and a blanket each. Didn't even stop for a flask of tea,' said Elizabeth. 'If you're going to look, be warned, there's an old bicycle frame propped up against the wall, and it's a bit rusty – you don't want to fall over it and get tetanus.' She looked at Maisie's ankle – she had worn trousers that morning so the bandage on her leg would not be visible, but now a small rivulet of blood could be seen running into her shoe. 'Oh dear. Warning came too late. Come on – let's do our first aid bit, shall we?'

It seemed that in a minute a kettle was boiling, a bowl produced and salt mixed with hot water, and Drake was bathing the cut while Richardson prepared a bandage.

'There – all done,' said Richardson. 'And you look a bit unbalanced. What with your hands and now one leg, perhaps you should put a bandage on the other leg, so everything's equal! How did you do that to your hands anyway? We didn't want to be rude and ask when you came up before, but we did wonder.'

'It's nothing really,' said Maisie. 'Now I feel rather stupid, because having other people tend my wounds is becoming quite a comical habit.'

'Have you found out something important, Miss Dobbs?' asked Drake. 'I mean, the way you came running up here again made me wonder.'

'No. I ventured into the cellar and it occurred to me to confirm when you'd been in there, that's all,' said Maisie. 'Thank you very much.'

She smiled, pulled her notebook from her bag and held it in her bandaged hand as she ran downstairs again, knowing the two owlets would be watching her leave.

Running past Mrs Marsh, she waved her notebook and called out, 'All's well that ends well, Mrs Marsh. I'll be back again soon.'

'What's going on, miss?' asked Billy. 'And I don't think I should even ask why your ankle is bandaged – I can see it from here.'

They began walking along Welbeck Street. 'I cut myself and the girls upstairs helped me out – that dressing can come off as soon as I get home. I went back up there because I wanted to confirm

279

when they had used the cellar as an air raid shelter. Fortunately, it was before Catherine Saxon was murdered. And it hasn't been used since – too many spiders and too small. If this is the knife used to kill Catherine, I'll find out from the pathologist.'

'I had a glance,' said Billy. 'It looks pretty clean to me. And if the killer had time to wipe it off, then he had time to think of a better place to get rid of it.'

'Not necessarily,' said Maisie. 'If it was done in the heat of the moment and he was shocked by his actions, he might have wanted to dispose of the weapon as quickly as possible.'

'That means the killer knew the house – knew there was an old cellar there, and it was not used,' added Billy. 'But there are only women living in that house.'

'I know,' said Maisie. 'Come on, let's get back to the office. Then I want to go over to the Barrington Bank, pay a surprise visit to Jenny Barrington's husband.' She consulted her watch. 'But I wonder . . . I'll see if I can book a telephone call to Amelia Saxon. I'll have to find out her number, and I do hope MacFarlane can help me there.'

'Haven't the government stopped all trunk calls out of the country? Even if you can do it, you won't be able to get a trunk call in until tomorrow, I shouldn't wonder – I bet the lines are all spoken for. It's going to cost you about ten quid for three minutes – and we know you'll need more than that.'

'I'm not worried about the money, Billy.' She paused as they crossed Great Portland Street. 'But back to you – did you notice anything?'

'I'd like to know one thing, miss. Did you take Catherine's letters with you?'

'What letters? And no – I didn't take any letters.'

'Are there any in the briefing notes from MacFarlane?'

'No – no letters. What are you getting at, Billy?'

'I don't know much about being a writer, but when I came to think about it, I suppose I reckoned writers would write a lot of letters – and therefore, miss, they would get a lot of letters back from other people. If I was a writer, I think I'd want to keep letters. I mean, after all, there's all sorts of belongings you like to have with you, especially if you're a bit of a gypsy – which she was, you've got to admit it, miss. She got herself around a bit, travelling to Paris, Madrid, Barcelona, and Berlin, then London. I bet she kept people's letters, and yet there wasn't a letter to be found in her rooms.'

'You're absolutely right, Billy, and—'

'And if someone killed her because of something she knew – or even *someone* she knew – what would they have done? They would have taken letters before anything else, either to read or destroy. Or both. And there might have been something about the killer in those letters.' Billy shrugged. 'I dunno, I just think that in this case the fact that any letters addressed to her weren't in the rooms means they were taken to protect someone.'

'It's a fair observation,' said Maisie.

They had reached the square. 'Let me have that knife now. I've just looked at the time. I'm going to try to find out more about Amelia Saxon, and where I can telephone her. You'd better be off, Billy – you'll be late for duty.'

Billy handed Maisie the knife, and went on his way with, 'See you tomorrow,' and a wave. Maisie proceeded to the office, and was a little disappointed to find it had not been broken into and a man named Mark Scott was not waiting with a witty comment about security at her place of work. She realised that she missed him.

Robert MacFarlane listened to Maisie's request, and the information regarding Amelia Saxon's living arrangements, which were apart from her husband. 'And you say she was over here?' said MacFarlane.

'I do hope you're not trying to pull the wool over my eyes, Robbie,' said Maisie, holding the telephone receiver awkwardly in her bandaged hand.

'No – by now I would have added a quip. I'm as surprised as you are. Perhaps our friend – well, should I say your friend – at the American embassy will have more information regarding Mrs Saxon's sojourn with her daughter.'

'What was that supposed to mean, Robbie? The emphasis on "your friend"?'

'Nothing, Maisie. Nothing, hen – but you probably know that we know he was in Kent for a day or two.'

'And he stayed at the Dower House because he left it too late to drive back to London – he slept in the conservatory, which I know you've seen before.'

'All right, all right – keep your bonnet in place. My, my – the lady doth protest too much!'

'Robbie – I want to make a telephone call to America – it's crucial I speak to Amelia Saxon. I can't do it because as we both know, trunk calls out of the country have been stopped. But you can make the call.'

MacFarlane was silent.

'Robbie?'

'I'm here, I'm here. Just thinking. I'll arrange it for you – but remember they're a bit behind us, over in America. And I suppose you could say in more ways than one, when it comes to this war. We have to allow five hours. Go home now – I'll telephone you later with the arrangements.' There was a pause. She heard him yawn. 'Sorry about that, hen – long days are catching up with me.'

'You're not as young as you were, Robbie.'

'Ah, but what I've lost in stamina, I've made up for in wisdom. And before you say it – I know I've gained a few inches around the girth too. Are you going to brief me on your investigation?'

Maisie summarised her most recent findings, and voiced her frustration.

'Process of elimination, Maisie. Who can you rule out?'

'I think I can rule out Isabel Chalmers.'

'That's a relief. I don't know what we'd do without that one – doing a good job for us.'

'I didn't know she worked directly for you, Robbie.'

'I've a finger in a few pies.'

'I'm sure you have. Anyway, I would say the girls on the top floor – they were useful though, giving me some very vital information.'

'How vital?'

'I believe I have the murder weapon – and it's right here on my desk.'

'You what? Why didn't you say?'

'I'm taking it over to the pathologist right now. I believe he's working late, as usual.'

'I'll telephone to tell him to stay where he bloody well is. And I'll see you there. Does the Yank know?'

'I have no idea where he is.'

'Probably keeping an eye on his ambassador.'

'What do you mean, Robbie? What's going on?'

'Nothing. You've got enough on your plate. I'll see you at Ferguson's.'

* * *

The air raid siren had already sounded by the time Maisie and MacFarlane arrived at the pathologist's office. Maisie handed over the knife.

'Hmm, shorter blade than I might have expected.'

'Does that rule it out?' asked Maisie.

He shook his head. 'Not at all – in fact, it makes it easier to handle, and it's still sleek.' He turned away from her, crouched a little, and with the knife in his hand struck out into thin air, sweeping the blade from right to left.

'You still think the killer was left-handed,' said Maisie.

'I do. And if he used the knife in a motion such as the one I've just demonstrated, he'd get more heft because he's using the outside muscle on the upper arm, and not the inner muscle. It's instinctive,' said MacFarlane.'

'Yes, I know that. I just wonder if that's how he used it.'

Ferguson nodded. 'Always room for error, Miss Dobbs.' He held the knife under a long-stemmed magnifying glass screwed to the desk. 'It's a nice, easily controlled knife and it's been sharpened a lot, which of course suggests it was used for pencils, as you suspected.' He sighed, and pushed the glass away, balancing the knife with one finger at the midpoint between the silver handle and steel blade. 'Pity she left it on her desk – it's the perfect murder weapon for someone who'd just lost their temper.' He turned to MacFarlane and Maisie. 'And I believe it was a loss of temper – because in my experience, the murderers who plan ahead bring a different kind of knife with them. Something a professional would use – a flick knife, or a knife with a longer blade, something sharpened up for the Sunday roast, or a shorter knife with a serrated edge. People who plan to kill will use a knife they feel a sort of comfort with. A fishing knife's another one. And remember, killing someone with a knife isn't as easy as the pictures make it look – takes strength.'

'But here's the other thing – the blood,' said Maisie.

'There was plenty of blood,' said MacFarlane.

'There wasn't much spray. And if the killer was in front of Miss Saxon, as Dr Ferguson has just demonstrated, then he – or she – would have been drenched, surely.' Maisie looked from one to the other. 'I'm sorry to come back to this, but there is the question of an attempt to kill her perhaps just seconds before the stabbing – someone had tried to strangle her. Would that have reduced the blood sprayed?'

'If she were already dead or almost dead, it could have,' said the pathologist. He rubbed his chin. 'Or if she had monumentally low blood pressure exacerbated by fear.'

'She didn't sound like the fearful sort to me,' said MacFarlane.

'She was doubtless good at controlling it,' said Maisie. 'She'd been in some scrapes in her time, Robbie, so I daresay she was used to carrying on despite being terrified on many occasions.' She looked from one man to the other. 'Given the amount of time that has now elapsed between the death and this very moment, I think we have to make a few leaps of faith. We are assuming that this knife is the murder weapon. We are also considering the fact that she may have had a lowered blood pressure leading to a reduced – by just enough – loss of blood. And I am going to suggest her killer had a motor car outside, so he could leave without anyone seeing blood on his clothing or hands, because I doubt there was time for a wash and brush-up.'

'But the blackout—' said MacFarlane.

'Wasn't so black, because London was burning, and at about half past four in the morning there were a few motor cars on the roads – not many, but they were there. The killer might have gone only so far – perhaps to Regent's Park – before setting off for another place, though I suspect his destination would be home. After all, an animal is always drawn back to the lair when in trouble. And there's another scenario.'

'What's that?' asked MacFarlane.

'Perhaps the killer only had to run upstairs, or downstairs, or across the road, or up the street to be home.'

On the instructions of Robert MacFarlane, Maisie was taken to her flat in Holland Park by his driver in a government vehicle. The night-time blitz continued, with the sky illuminated by fire and searchlights. She thanked the driver and was taking the key from her bag as she walked towards the front door, when she realised the blackout curtains in her downstairs flat had been drawn. She stopped for a second or two, then walked on, slipping her key in the lock and entering her home, knowing she would not be alone. The low sound of a blues number playing on her gramophone seemed to come in waves from the sitting room overlooking the garden, though no garden was visible in the blackout. She walked into the room, then stepped back into the hallway to the small kitchen, where Mark Scott was pouring two glasses of wine.

'I thought your record collection might be missing a beat or two, so I brought something of my own along. And some good wine, and with it a whole meal from Pete's – he wrapped it for me and gave me very strict instructions about warming it for us.' He looked up at Maisie. 'Please don't ask me how I gained entrance to your castle, fair lady.'

'I wasn't going to. If they ever kick you out of the Justice Department or the embassy, you could do well as a cat burglar.'

'At least I have a certain skill in knowing which house is worth breaking into,' said Scott, as he took her in his arms.

And as they kissed, Maisie felt unsteady. Whether she was prepared for it or not, Mark Scott had broken into her heart.

CHAPTER SIXTEEN

A railway journey could be a double-edged sword, thought Maisie as the train passed through Clapham Junction. There was something about the rhythm, the side-to-side movement, and the pace of the journey that seemed to facilitate deeper thought. If she harnessed those thoughts and only allowed consideration of the Catherine Saxon murder case, the opportunity to reconsider all possible scenarios leading to the attack on her life could be fruitful. But this morning, it seemed she had no dominion over her mind, which seemed to be filled with the question: what should she do about Mark Scott? And of course, Anna was at the heart of her concern. Beyond the window, smoke was rising up above barrage balloons, and she admonished herself for selfishly considering a dilemma of a personal nature when so many civilians had been killed and injured and thousands were without a roof over their heads.

If she was to prepare for her visit to the Tucker home in Haywards Heath, she would have to concentrate. And to do that, she would write down her feelings about Mark Scott and then put them aside and not favour him with another thought for the rest of the day. She remembered Maurice, after the Armistice, asking her if she had planned to visit Simon, her first love, a young man who was expected be in an 'old soldiers' hospital for the rest of his life, his mind shattered following a brain injury sustained when the casualty clearing station where they were working came under attack. Maisie had recovered from her own physical wounds, though those to her soul still ached at times. When she demurred, deflecting the question, Maurice had said, as if to himself, 'War has such a strange alliance with the heart's deepest feelings. It can make people fear the intimacy of love, and it can lead them to search for it, as if the poor heart clamours to be held through the worst of times, yet is paralysed through the fear that the pain of separation will be more unbearable than death.'

Were she and Scott being pulled together by war? By death and destruction seen every single day? Was whatever they felt an affirmation of life itself at a time when so much was being lost? Or were they romantic conveniences for one another; emotional crutches grabbed to get them through the war, while it lasted? And what right did she have to fall in love when she was claiming responsibility for a child, a wonderful, dear child she adored? Already Anna had enquired after him. 'Is Mr Scott coming with you on Thursday?' she'd asked when Maisie telephoned the house that very morning. And she had replied that she doubted it, as he was someone she worked with, and was not a friend – and he was terribly busy.

She had to put a stop to this affair right now. There was too much at stake, not least Anna's happiness. And what game did she think she was playing, entering into an affair with a man who would be upping sticks and moving back to a country thousands of miles away just as soon as whatever it was he was doing in England was done? She would speak to him that very evening. Put her foot down. This fledgling affair must end. Now.

Maisie looked out of the window at fields and farms. She began to reflect on questions she had planned to ask the Tuckers, but was interrupted by a nagging thought, one that now repeated itself time and again. *What right do I have to fall in love?* Had she really asked herself that question? Yes, she had, and now she had made a confession to herself, using the words that counted – she was in love with Mark Scott. Perhaps she always had been, in a way, even when she first met him in Munich, and put a gun to his throat.

'Miss Dobbs. Glad to see you're on time.' Mr Tucker answered the door, stepped aside for Maisie to enter, and having extended the chain of his gold watch as if to very visibly demonstrate a certain respect for punctuality, he replaced the watch in his waistcoat pocket. 'As you might imagine, I would usually be in my London office, so it's fortunate I have taken a day off and we were able to meet. I have only a short time to discuss this business with you, as I have another pressing appointment. Please, follow me.'

A housekeeper stepped aside as Tucker led Maisie to the drawing room, and having invited her to be seated on a sofa covered with a fabric printed with red and gold cabbage roses, gave the housekeeper instructions to find Mrs Tucker and also to bring a pot of tea and some biscuits, refreshment for the visitor.

'The tea will doubtless be weak and insipid, given our adherence to the mere two ounces we're allowed per person, per week, but it will be wet and warm, as the saying goes.' Tucker took a seat in a wing chair opposite Maisie.

He was a man who at first seemed tall, but when she had stood beside him, Maisie realised it was his slender frame and choice of clothing that gave the impression of height. Tucker – she did not yet know his Christian name – wore a pinstripe suit of dark blue, with a waistcoat, white shirt and navy tie. His shoes were polished to a shine. His hair had receded to reveal a high forehead, and his eyes were dark blue. Lines around his eyes and mouth, and loose skin on his cheeks seemed to suggest a man who had known illness in recent years, but had never regained the weight of previous good health.

'I'm so sorry, dear – I was in the greenhouse, and completely forgot Miss Dobbs was coming.' As Mrs Tucker entered the room, Maisie stood up to greet her and formally introduce herself. 'Scurrying' was the word that entered Maisie's head as the woman approached her.

'It's so good of you to see me, though I should perhaps have come sooner,' said Maisie, taking a hand that was still damp, as if the women had hurriedly washed her soiled hands and had no time to dry them properly.

'Well, it's probably difficult, what with the bombs dropping on London right, left and centre,' said Mrs Tucker.

'Yes, quite, though I would certainly have appreciated an earlier meeting, because we're anxious to let the rooms out as soon as possible,' said Tucker. 'And do sit down again, Miss Dobbs – you, too, Beryl. Sit down.' Tucker unbuttoned his jacket and took his place in the armchair again.

Maisie was just about to put her first question to Beryl Tucker and her husband, when the housekeeper entered with a tea trolley. Tucker sighed audibly and, crossing his legs, turned away from the women as if to demonstrate his frustration. After the housekeeper left and Beryl Tucker had furnished her husband and Maisie with cups of tea, Maisie took a sip and placed her cup and saucer on the side table next to the sofa.

'May I begin by asking you how long you've owned the house on Welbeck Street?'

Beryl Tucker spoke first. 'Yes, of course, it was twenty years ago, I inherited it from my uncle, so it was—'

'It was only seventeen years ago, Beryl, so if you're going to answer the questions, probably best to get them right,' said Tucker, still not turning towards Maisie or his wife.

'But – oh, anyway,' said Mrs Tucker, 'it was when John and Eunice were children, and I would not wish to contradict you, dear, but it must have been twenty years ago, because Eunice is thirty now, and she was about ten when we moved in.'

'Beryl—'

'Yes, I'm glad you mentioned your children, Mrs Tucker,' said Maisie, circumventing the sharp rebuke she anticipated Tucker was about to aim at his wife. 'You have two, is that right?'

'Yes,' said Beryl Tucker, before looking down at her hands. 'Well—'

'We *had* two children, Miss Dobbs,' interjected Tucker. 'But now we have one. Jeremy, our son, died several years ago, I'm afraid. An event still very difficult to bear in this household, so it's one we do not linger upon in conversation.'

'Quite, yes, I understand,' said Maisie. Then, as if to inspire an element of connection with Beryl Tucker, she added, 'I am a widow, Mrs Tucker. My husband was killed in a flying accident several years ago, so I understand something of how you must feel.' She paused. 'And I also lost a child.'

Beryl Tucker's eyes filled with tears. She took a handkerchief from the sleeve of her cardigan and dabbed her nose.

'But let's continue,' said Maisie. 'So, you inherited the house – and it sounds as if you lived there, at least for a while.'

'I decided to take advantage of living in London whilst I became more established in the banking industry, Miss Dobbs,' said Tucker. 'We moved to Haywards Heath ten years ago. As you know, there is a very good train service to London from here – when there are no bombs dropping, anyway. Furthermore, I decided to make arrangements to let the rooms out on each floor, and to that end our housekeeper, Mrs Marsh, remained there as the de facto landlady – she rather preferred to live in London – and a firm of accountants deal with the rent. Such an arrangement is to my advantage.'

'I see,' said Maisie. 'And to recap, the house was in fact your wife's inheritance.'

'That is so, but I am a banker, and head of the household, thus certain decisions fall to me. And in addition, my wife's uncle made certain stipulations in the will, so I was unable to sell. The area is subject to some quite antiquated land laws, as I am sure you have discovered.'

'Indeed,' said Maisie. 'I own a property on the same street.' She would not as a rule have revealed such a detail, but she felt a certain pleasure in seeing a sharp raising of the eyebrow on the part of Tucker, indicating his surprise. 'May I ask when you first met Miss Saxon?' she continued.

'She applied to rent the room,' said Mrs Tucker.

'Beryl,' cautioned Tucker. 'You do not deal with the day-to-day running of the property, so let me answer.' He turned to Maisie, uncrossing his legs, turning his body towards her, and resting his hands on the arm of the chair. 'Miss Saxon submitted her application to Mrs Marsh in the form of a letter of enquiry. She gave the information required and references, and after my accountants had checked all elements of the letter, I instructed them and Mrs Marsh accordingly, and Miss Saxon moved in.'

Maisie judged Tucker's position, and leant forward, knowing that in so doing she had moved into an area that he considered his domain simply by dint of his posture. 'Mr Tucker, this is very interesting, because I believe Catherine Saxon came to London from France, having already travelled from Spain. Do you know how she might have heard about a room to let at Mrs Tucker's house?' She was well aware of her breach of conversational protocol, as Tucker had made it clear that he considered the house to be his property, and his alone. 'Do you have any idea, Mrs Tucker?' she added, leaning back and turning to Beryl Tucker.

'No, she doesn't. As I've indicated, my wife does not have a hand in administration of the property.'

'But do you, Mr Tucker? Do you know how Catherine might have learnt about the rooms for rent?'

'I don't. But you must consider her work – she was a reporter, so I am sure one of her American friends had seen the sign in the window, or read our advertisement in *The Telegraph*, and let her know. There are a number of them working only a few streets away, at the BBC.'

'Hmm,' said Maisie. She let the sound hang in the air before continuing. 'I wonder, are you familiar with Miss Saxon's family connections?'

'I am now – it was mentioned in *The Times*. She's the daughter of an American senator.' Tucker flapped his hand as if to dismiss the connection. 'As soon as I read it, it was easy to see how she had gained such a reputation so quickly – her father obviously got her the jobs!'

'Actually, that's not the case, Mr Tucker. Catherine's father was rather the opposite – he did everything he could to stymie his daughter and prevent her from continuing her work.' Maisie allowed only the slightest pause before moving on to the next question. 'Did you ever meet her?'

'Well—' began Beryl Tucker.

'No, never.' Once again Tucker cut off his wife as she was about to speak.

'Mrs Tucker?' encouraged Maisie.

The woman shook her head. 'No, I never met her, though I heard from Mrs Marsh that she was a lovely young woman. Quite lovely. It's very sad, especially for her parents – her mother at least, if she'd upset her father.'

'Where does your daughter live?' asked Maisie.

'She lives overseas,' said Beryl Tucker. 'Canada.'

'Oh, really – how interesting,' said Maisie. 'I lived in Canada for a while. Not terribly long.'

'She's a teacher, Miss Dobbs,' said Tucker. 'My daughter chose to teach English and took up a position in Canada.'

'I do miss her,' said Beryl Tucker. 'But then you do, especially after—'

'I think you've probably asked enough questions by now, haven't you, Miss Dobbs?' said Tucker, standing up. 'I know little about your trade, but it would appear to me that if you haven't reached the end of your enquiry by now, surely you stand little chance of discovering who killed Miss Saxon.'

Maisie came to her feet, the words 'your trade' echoing in her mind; the attempt at humiliation writ large. 'Yes, indeed, I have asked enough questions. As you have no doubt realised, concerning Miss

Saxon's death, I am trying to put pieces of the puzzle in their correct place. You see' – she extended her hand to shake her host's as she spoke – 'if the murderer of a fine young woman is not found soon, I want to ensure I have done all I can before we consider the case cold. And at the present time it may be cool, but not cold – to my touch anyway.' She turned to Beryl Tucker, taking the woman's hand. 'And thank you so much for your time, Mrs Tucker. I do, however, have a favour to ask of you – you have an absolutely gorgeous rose in your grounds at the front of the house. Would you be able to give me the name? My father has an enviable rose garden, and I would like to find one just like yours to give to him.'

'Let me get my secateurs, my dear – I'll get you a cutting,' said Beryl Tucker. 'If your father's a rose man, he'll know exactly how to propagate it.'

Maisie met Tucker's frown with a smile and followed Beryl Tucker from the room.

'Ah, that one is a favourite of mine,' said Beryl Tucker. 'A Bourbon rose – and I do love the traditional cabbage roses.' She leant towards the pale pink rose, her gloved hands holding the secateurs steady as she took several cuttings.

'This is very kind of you, Mrs Tucker,' said Maisie. 'My father will be delighted.'

'I'll just wrap them for you – I'll prepare some damp newspaper to keep them fresh.'

Maisie watched as the woman led her to a potting table at the side of the house, where she wrapped the cuttings in damp newspaper, and placed them in a small bag made of sacking.

'There you are.' She handed the bag to Maisie, but as she did so, she touched Maisie's hand. 'And please forgive Jonathan, Miss Dobbs. My husband has not been quite the man he was since our son died. This business with Miss Saxon has upset him no end. Of course, he doesn't show it, but I know it concerns him – as it has both of us. You don't like to think of someone being murdered on your property. I'm sure if we could sell, we would. But the house will go to our daughter. And I doubt she'll ever return home now.'

'It is a long way to come for a visit,' said Maisie.

'Eunice and her father don't really see eye to eye. That's why she went off in a huff and applied for a job in Canada. And she was so terribly upset when her brother was killed. But I am sure she's happy over there, teaching in a girls' school. She seems to have a very nice life, so I would imagine that, when we're gone, she'll just rent out the property again.'

'How did your son die, Mrs Tucker?'

Beryl Tucker sighed, brushing soil from the potting table. 'He died being a young man with a passion, I suppose. He was in Paris – he wanted to be an artist, you see. And you can imagine how his father took to that idea! Jonathan sees the world through very narrow glasses, Miss Dobbs, and he wanted Jeremy to be either a doctor, a barrister or a banker. Jeremy loved drawing as soon as he could pick up a pencil. I think Jonathan would have settled for an engineer or architect, but our son would not be fenced in. Off he went to Paris – about five years ago now, I would say. He would have been thirty years of age this year.'

'So he died in Paris?'

'Oh no – sorry, I must have confused you. No, Jeremy died in Spain, fighting with the International Brigade. He had made friends with a group of young people about his age, all of them artists of one sort or another and they decided to go to Spain to fight for the

Republic.' She sighed. 'And he was killed in Barcelona. But look at what's happened here. Who knows what fate might have held for him by now, what with France invaded and young men going off to fight? I doubt he would have been an artist today – he might have been one of those boys killed at Dunkirk, or in the air, or with the navy.'

'I am so very sorry.' Maisie clutched the cutting, feeling the thorns against her palm, still so sensitive from the burns it was as if there was nothing between her skin and the rose. 'Mrs Tucker – do you by any slight chance think your son might have known Catherine Saxon in Paris?' She saw the woman's brow furrow and her eyes reveal confusion, as if she could not countenance a new thought regarding her son's death. 'I'm afraid I must ask you this – you see, Catherine was in Paris a few years ago too, and then she went from there to Spain. Did he ever mention a young woman in the group? Some people call her "Cath". Does that help?'

'Oh dear—' Beryl Tucker leant against the table.

'Mrs Tucker – are you all right?' Maisie reached for the woman, steadying her.

'What on earth is going on here?' Jonathan Tucker approached the women from the front garden. 'I wondered where you'd gone, Beryl, and there you are, playing with your infernal flowers again.' He pointed at Maisie. 'And I hope you haven't bloody well upset my wife. You police and enquiry agents are all the same. You should have solved this case days ago, and here you are on my property when I told you I had nothing more to say.'

'But Jonathan—'

'Beryl – do go inside, wash your hands and make yourself presentable,' said Tucker. He turned to Maisie. 'And I would appreciate it if you left my property immediately.' He pulled his pocket watch from his waistcoat, and squinted at the dial. 'If you hurry, you'll catch the twelve o'clock train. Good day.'

'Thank you for the cuttings, Mrs Tucker,' said Maisie. 'And to you, Mr Tucker, I thank you for your time. I will be in touch.'

Maisie turned and began walking along the path towards the gate, though she looked back once to see Tucker take his wife by the arm and lead her to the back of the house.

Once on the train, she consulted her own watch. Yes, she would have time to visit the Barrington Bank, where she wanted to speak to Jennifer Barrington's husband. But in the meantime, the seed of an idea had been planted in her mind – that Jeremy Tucker might well have been the man whose initials Catherine Saxon had tattooed between her toes, where no one but herself and someone very close to her would see them.

The Barrington Bank was encased with sandbags to protect the large panes of glass used in construction of the building, which was situated close to the Aldwych Theatre. Lights were on in a reception hall that would, before the war, have been flooded with natural illumination. Now it was like entering a cave. She approached a reception desk formed in the shape of a half-circle, beyond which was a curved staircase of wood and stainless steel.

'I'd like to speak to Mr Miles Barrington, if I may,' said Maisie. She gave her name and added, 'Please inform Mr Barrington's secretary that it's regarding a Miss Catherine Saxon's estate.'

The receptionist placed a call to his office, and without a noticeable delay Maisie was informed that his secretary would be down shortly, and to take a seat.

'Thank you very much,' said Maisie, smiling at the receptionist.

'Would you mind doing me a favour before I go up to Mr Barrington's office? I'd appreciate it if you could look after this for me. It's a rose cutting. A business associate just gave it to me as a gift, so I would not want to mislay it – or kill it.'

The woman looked at Maisie and took the small sacking bag with her forefinger and thumb, as if it held a substance emitting a pungent smell. 'Don't forget it,' she said. 'I'll have to throw it out if you don't collect it.'

At that moment a woman descended the staircase and, standing on a landing, summoned Maisie to join her with a curt, 'Miss Dobbs? This way, please.'

The staircase curved up and around to a corridor on the left. The secretary opened another door to the right, whereupon they were in an outer office. The secretary, who had not introduced herself, knocked on double wooden doors framed with stainless steel, and entered.

'Miss Dobbs for you, Mr Barrington.'

Barrington turned away from the window where he had been standing, looking out, and smiled at Maisie.

'Thank you so much for coming to see me, Miss Dobbs,' he said, stepping from behind his desk towards Maisie, ready to shake her hand. He looked up at his secretary. 'That will be all, Miss Barker.'

Barrington was an imposing man, not tall, but broad in the shoulders, and with a stance indicating he was used to being in control of all he surveyed. Yet there was something else about him that Maisie had seen often in men of his age – his was the face of a man who had known pain, grief and disillusionment; a man who had lost something of himself on the battlefield, and had never quite regained the blind optimism that had accompanied him into war.

She wondered if the fact that his dark hair was longer than the accepted norm for men might be a mark of rebellion against all that had been expected of him, even, perhaps, his position at the helm of the family business.

Maisie shook Barrington's hand, hearing the door close behind her. 'I'm very grateful for your time. No doubt your wife told you about our meeting, and that I am conducting an enquiry into the death of her dear friend, Catherine Saxon.'

Indicating a leather armchair situated to one side of the desk, he waited until Maisie was seated and sat down opposite her. Maisie noticed his position was an open one – legs crossed in an easy manner, arms on the arms of the chair, hands not clenched, but at rest. His charcoal grey suit was well cut and his shoes expensive. His tie indicated he had studied at Cambridge, and his shirt was starched. If she had wanted to invest her money, she might have chosen the very dour Jonathan Tucker before Miles Barrington, for she suspected he was a gambler with other people's funds, a banker for those who could remain calm while treating investing as something akin to roulette.

'Now then – fire away, how can I help you? Jenny has been absolutely shaken to the core about Catherine's death, as have I, so we're both anxious to see whoever killed her at the end of the hangman's rope.' He began to drum his fingers on the arm of the chair.

'This hasn't been a straightforward enquiry, Mr Barrington, as you can imagine. Catherine was a vibrant young woman, accomplished, and she knew a lot of people. She was not on good terms with her father – or her brothers – so there was family discord, and—'

'And it wasn't hard for them to get over here – think upon that, Miss Dobbs. Think upon that! Those Saxon men saw Catherine as a thorn in the side. I wouldn't put it past the old man to arrange for someone to scare her, and then it all went wrong. Is that something you're looking into?'

Maisie inclined her head, 'Well, it's interesting you should mention her father and brother – do you know them well?'

Barrington nodded. 'Oh, I've met them socially. Jenny was Catherine's very best friend – they were like two peas in a pod, those two. Sisters not of the same blood, that's what Jenny said. So of course our paths crossed at a party or two when I was over there, in New York.'

'Your wife told me you'd met in New York – you seem to have picked up as much of her accent as she has of yours. And regarding the Saxons, I would imagine your family name was attractive to them.'

'Yes, I suppose it was. Connections are important to those sort of people. Even Catherine was not shy about using connections – but in her work, that's what you have to do, I suppose. Rather like my work, if I'm to be perfectly honest – perhaps that's why I picked up a bit of an American accent.' He raised his eyebrows. 'Perhaps I should watch that so our son doesn't pick it up – otherwise he'll be in for a dreadful ribbing when he starts school. Anyway, in terms of using contacts, Catherine wasn't much different from the men in her family.'

'It would seem not,' said Maisie. She noticed him begin to knead the back of his right hand with the fingers of the left, and saw that an ink stain where he had held his pen had rubbed across the opposite knuckles. 'I know you're a very busy man, but could you tell me anything at all about Catherine that I might not know? How often had you seen her since she came to England? And what did you think of her?'

Barrington rubbed both palms together. 'Gosh, let me see. Hmm.

First of all, I've only seen her a couple of times since she came to London – of course, she saw Jenny more than me, but she came to dinner once or twice, and as you know, she was a very, very committed news reporter. Wanted to make her name, did Catherine. And what did I think of her? She was ambitious. Incredibly witty, and of course an attractive woman. I know very little about her men-friends, though I know she had seen an Australian a few times.'

Maisie nodded. *Was this the right time? She would chance revealing Catherine's secret.* 'Did you know, Mr Barrington, that Catherine had delivered a child, some three years ago?'

He rested his hands on the arms of the chair again. 'Oh yes, of course. I was sure you would know about that. Jen told me about it. The child was stillborn, in Spain. Those two told each other everything, and Jenny must have cried buckets about it – her best friend, losing a child. She protected Catherine's reputation, though – she only told me because I insisted upon knowing why she was so upset.'

'What did you think about it?'

He shrugged. 'To tell you the truth, my main concern was for Jenny. Sometimes I thought she was more like a mother to Catherine than a sister figure, and she was so worried about Catherine, I thought it would make her ill. And what did I think of the situation? Frankly, the loss of the child was probably a godsend. I know that sounds rather strong, but she had no husband, and she refused to tell even Jenny who the father was – so what would she have done? Lugged a child around the world while she reported from every embattled city on her way to fame?'

'So Jenny had no idea who the father was?'

'None – I believe she would have told me. We don't have secrets in our marriage, Miss Dobbs.'

Maisie looked at Miles Barrington. 'Mr Barrington, I know you've mentioned Catherine's brothers, but if you had to take a stab at who might have taken Catherine's life, who do you think might have done such a thing?'

'I wish I could say – and goodness knows, Jenny and I have talked about it, gone through everyone we know who Catherine also knew. And we've considered the people she talked about, who she'd met through her work. Neither of us could name one person we'd suspect. I mean, there are other women tenants – they're the only ones who can come and go to and from that house as they like, aren't they? And dear old Mrs Marsh watches the place like a hawk, plus there's always one of the women around anyway.'

'Oh, so you've been to the Welbeck Street house,' clarified Maisie.

'With Jenny – I waited in the motor car for her while she ran in to take a dress up to Catherine. She had to go to a party or something with her brother – oh yes, that's it – it was at the American ambassador's house, over in South Kensington. She hadn't a gown with her, so Jenny took one of hers over. Catherine hadn't been here long, so it must have been in May or June – yes, that was it, because it was probably a hair before France fell, or she would never have got out. Knowing Catherine, it was probably touch-and-go and an adventure-filled journey.'

'I see.' Maisie gathered her bag, which she had set on the floor beside the chair. 'I think that's all, Mr Barrington.' She came to her feet. 'Once again, thank you very much for your time.'

'Absolutely,' said Barrington. 'And please do not hesitate to be in touch if you have any additional questions – I'll do anything I can to help. I'd like to see the end of your investigation as much as you, because all the time the killer is at large, Jenny won't rest.'

'I understand,' said Maisie.

Barrington led her to the door, but as he opened it and was about to summon his secretary, Maisie turned to him.

'I am sorry – one last question. Do you know Jonathan Tucker, by any chance?'

'Tucker? Oh yes, of course – *that* Jonathan Tucker. He's with a bank over on Threadneedle Street, isn't he? I've seen the man a few times – at my club, I think it was. He came in once or twice with a colleague, if my memory serves me well. Can't say much more about him. Seemed a bit of a stuffed shirt, if you ask me – old-school type. Not the sort to set the investment world on fire, after the war's over.'

'But you know he and his wife own the property where Catherine died, don't you?'

Barrington raised his hand to his forehead. 'Good Lord, I had forgotten all about that. I remember Catherine mentioning the same thing.' He shook his head. 'Terrible of me, forgetting that one. But has he said anything to assist you?'

'I met Mr Tucker and his wife this morning, actually. Lovely woman, I must say – the wife is a dear. But no, he didn't give me any information that might really help.' She allowed a pause. 'But the thing is about my business, every case is a puzzle, and sometimes one person will say something that suddenly' – she snapped her fingers – 'that suddenly changes another person's innocuous comment into a vital clue. It's what makes my business a strange one, I suppose. People in my line of work depend upon that alchemy.' She rested her hand on Barrington's forearm for just half a second. 'Do assure your wife that I will find Catherine's killer, come what may.'

Having collected the rose cutting from the receptionist – who held the bag between finger and thumb while looking the other way – Maisie walked along the Strand and at Trafalgar Square caught a bus to Tottenham Court Road. She had taken off her gloves prior to the meeting with Barrington, but now her fingers hurt where she had snapped them – deliberately, at the time – because she wanted to make Barrington jump, if not into the air, then at least out of his well of self-assured complacency.

A message from Robert MacFarlane taken in Sandra's neat handwriting awaited Maisie at the office. A trunk telephone call had been booked for the following day from his office to the home of Mrs Amelia Saxon in Boston. She was instructed to be at MacFarlane's office no later than half past three in the afternoon, which was half past ten in the morning in Boston. Mrs Saxon had been informed and would be waiting for the connection.

Boston.

Following the death of her husband, when she was finally well enough to leave the hospital in Toronto, the city where she and James had made their home, Maisie began a quest to put as much distance as she could between herself and the tragedy. So much of that bitter time was a blur of memory now, a gauzy film through which she tried to identify who she had been as she navigated the early days of widowhood. She had stayed at the Boston home of Charles Hayden, the doctor Simon – her first love – had become friends with in France, and his wife, Pauline. They had three daughters, one of whom she had heard was now an army nurse. Then she'd left, sailing for India – to the place where she had accepted James's proposal – until, finally, it was time to return to England. Brenda had summoned her home in a letter telling her in no uncertain terms that it was time, that her father was not getting any younger, and she should not be afraid because she would be loved and cared for as she endured her lingering grief. Her penultimate stop was Gibraltar, where her courage had failed her, and she knew she could not face England – and that sojourn had led her to Spain, and to the convent where she had become a nurse in another war. Then she came home, and there was the assignment in Munich.

She remembered the comment the obstetrician, Chester, had made, and her response. Yes, she was right – war might be considered a man's game, but women always ended up where there were wars, and suffered the lingering scars. It appeared she might have been in the same orbit as Catherine Saxon, yet not at the same time. But it was the mention of Boston that inspired Maisie to go to the filing cabinet where notes on old cases were kept. She pulled out one in particular, not because it had immediate bearing on the case in hand, but because there was a resonance, a sense of being in a certain place before, with only a slight alteration in the landscape.

During her apprenticeship, Maurice Blanche had taught her that it was a strange phenomenon, but sometimes cases appeared to come around again. In the same way that styles of women's clothing were repeated over the seasons, there were subtle differences with each incarnation, and he advised her to consider such cases with increased interest. 'A case that mirrors another should command our immediate attention to both that which is past, and the present investigation – there is possibly something for us to learn beyond enhancing our skills of detection, of enquiry. If a case has that resonance – and you will know it, because you will hear its echo in your questioning mind – then take heed. Go back to the notes, and most particularly, remember how you felt during the process of that earlier investigation.'

On the desk before her, she opened the file pertaining to the murder of Michael Clifton, a young Bostonian who had travelled almost six thousand miles to England from land he had purchased in California, when he had read news of the outbreak of war in August 1914. His remains had been discovered in France some eight years previously, in 1932, and Maisie had been approached to find out what had happened to him. Her enquiry had revealed all manner of family disruption, and ultimately the truth of what had come to pass after Michael Clifton had fallen in love with a married woman, in Paris. She would never forget this case because it was during the course of her investigation that her beloved mentor had died, and she had not begun work on a case since that time without asking herself how he would have approached the enquiry, and what advice he might offer her. There were times when she felt alone in her work, and only memories of Maurice – imagining he were with her, pressing her to use every tool at her disposal, giving her a confidence that guided her as she brought a case to a satisfactory conclusion – sustained her in the most difficult of endeavours.

Michael Clifton's people had come from Boston. Another coincidence. But that was not why she was drawn back to the case. She wanted to read her own notes, to identify what she had felt at the point at which she knew how the love affair that Michael had embarked upon had come to an end – and yet Michael's story had not quite concluded there.

She sat back, leafing through the file, studying notes and photographs. She checked her watch. She dare not telephone the Tucker household until the morning, after Jonathan Tucker had departed for his train to London. She would wait until nine. Then, having made the call, she would visit Jennifer Barrington. She closed the folder, but as she lifted it to take back to the filing cabinet, a small sheet of paper fell out. It was a copy she had made of a poem – the poem she had found in Michael Clifton's belongings, which had helped her close the case. It was also the poem that at the time seemed sent by Maurice, a warning not to tarry when it came to matters of the heart. The verse was by Elizabeth Barrett Browning, and at this moment there was one line that seemed to command her attention, as it had upon that first reading.

Love, when so you're loved again.

She slipped the sheet of paper back into the file, and replaced it in the filing cabinet. But the words remained with her as she collected her bag, closed the office and made her way downstairs. She was repeating them to herself as she stepped out into the square, hearing the heavy door slam behind her.

'Does the lady need a ride home?'

Maisie turned to see her partner in the investigation leaning against the black Buick. 'Oh, Mark, how on earth do you know where to find me all the time? I could have been out with a client, and gone directly back to the flat.'

'I'm paying attention, Maisie. I'm just paying attention. Come on, let's get a bite to eat and I'll take you home.' He put his arm around her shoulder and opened the automobile's passenger door. 'Really, I should kiss you now – give MacFarlane's boys something to report on.'

'MacFarlane's boys? Where?' said Maisie, beginning to pull away.

'Don't bother, Maisie – he probably knows about us already, because he's always got someone on your tail. The last thing he wants is to lose you.'

'What on earth do you mean?' asked Maisie.

'MacFarlane's got plans for you – professional, I mean – and the last thing he wants is someone valuable to his cause leaving for the other side of the Atlantic.'

'But I'm not going anywhere, Mark.'

'I know. And neither am I.'

She looked at Mark Scott as he started the motor car and pulled out onto Warren Street.

'And before your eyes completely pop out of your head at what I just said, did you make any progress on the case today?' said Scott. 'I mean, we might as well do some work now we're here together.'

'Actually, yes, I did. I made some progress.'

'Tell me about it, then.'

'I believe I know the *why*, and I know the *how*. I just want to make sure I have the right *who*, and that all the other players are in their correct place, so to speak. It's like a game of chess.'

Scott braked hard. 'You know that much? Last time we talked, you said you had some pieces and were still trying to fit them together.'

'And as I just said, I made progress. It's what I do. I take a few steps every day, and I wait. I throw hooks out into the wild mysterious sea and I wait. I don't have the fish on the line, but I know I have the right hook. And I'm rather sure I know the fish.'

'Let's go over to Pete's – see what he's got on the menu. That OK with you?'

'You're a creature of habit – but that would be lovely. Thank you.'

'And you can tell me everything, Miss Dobbs.'

'Perhaps not everything, Mr Scott.'

He reached across, took her hand and lifted it to his lips.

No, she would not tell him everything. Some aspects of the

case she would hold close until she was ready to bring the killer to justice. There were other arrangements to be planned before she made her final moves. Eight years ago the Michael Clifton investigation was closed with one element of unfinished business over which she had no control. She would not let it happen again.

CHAPTER SEVENTEEN

Today I walked down a long street. The gutters were full of glass; the big red buses couldn't pull into the kerb. There was the harsh, grating sound of glass being shovelled into trucks. In one window – or what used to be a window – was a sign. It read: SHATTERED – BUT NOT SHUTTERED. *Nearby was another shop displaying a crudely lettered sign reading:* KNOCKED BUT NOT LOCKED. *They were both doing business in the open air.*

EDWARD R. MURROW, BROADCAST TO AMERICA,

25TH SEPTEMBER 1940

'Hello, may I speak to Mrs Tucker, please? My name is Maisie Dobbs – I wanted to ask her a question about the rose cuttings she gave me.' Maisie suspected Jonathan Tucker questioned the housekeeper about telephone calls made to the house during his absence.

'Just one moment, if you please.'

There was a hiatus of several minutes before Beryl Tucker came to the telephone, breathless.

'Hello – Miss Dobbs. How very lovely to hear from you! Did your father like the cuttings?'

'I'll be taking them to him tomorrow, but in the meantime, I'm treating them as if they were newborn babes, and they seem to be doing very well.'

'As long as they're kept in water, they should survive – and remember to swaddle them in damp newspaper and the sackcloth bag for the journey. Is there anything else I can help you with, my dear?'

'Yes, in fact there is one thing, Mrs Tucker, though I must ask that this request be kept between us, at least for the meantime. And I am afraid I am going to have to leave you with more questions than answers; however, I wonder – would you be able to find a couple of photographs of your son for me? I'd like one from childhood, if possible, taken when he was a little boy of about three or four. And another as a young man. Might that be possible?'

There was silence on the line.

'Mrs Tucker,' said Maisie. 'I know this is a very strange request and I am going to have to ask for your absolute trust. I am at a very delicate point in my enquiry, and to reveal my reasons for asking for the photographs would be foolish, because I am only acting upon a . . .' She faltered in her explanation. 'I'm acting upon a feeling I have, that I really must see those photographs of your son.'

'Do you think—' Beryl Tucker began, then continued in a manner suggesting she had bolstered her resolve. 'Of course. I have no idea why you might want these photographs – well, let me correct myself – really, I am frightened to even think about why you might want the photographs, but I know exactly which ones I can send, and I will do so as quickly as possible. If I set to it now, I can catch the ten o'clock post, and you might even get the envelope later this afternoon.'

'Thank you very much indeed, Mrs Tucker. And again, I would rather you didn't speak to your husband about this – as I said, I am at a very sensitive stage in the investigation.'

'I think I understand. And even if you had not made that stipulation, I would not have told Jonathan. I have many secrets from my husband, Miss Dobbs. Now then, I had better get on with the task. I have several letters to take to the post office, so one more won't elicit any undue interest from my housekeeper.'

Maisie thanked Beryl Tucker, and realised that in keeping certain confidences from her husband, the woman who had seemed downtrodden was in effect drawing a line in the sand only she could see, and it had made her bear an otherwise untenable marriage.

Maisie checked her watch and revised her plan for the day. She would wait until tomorrow to see Jenny Barrington a second time, but she would visit Pamela Lockwood today. Then she would go to MacFarlane's office for the telephone call to Amelia Saxon. She closed her eyes, leant her elbows on the desk and rested her forehead on her hands. What if she was wrong? Was she taking what amounted to a wild guess and trying to make it fit what she knew so far about the murdered Catherine Saxon? There were so many unanswered questions, and she knew that at this point she had to go forward with a good deal of trust in her heart. She knew that death unsettled any family, but a murder was akin to a bomb dropping – the living were cast this way and that as debris from the investigation fell around them. Secrets would be revealed that were meant to remain buried; secrets that, perhaps, had little to do with the untimely death which would be uncovered despite all best efforts to wield the truth with a gentle hand. Those whose lives had intersected with the deceased might never be able to continue on as they were – people moved to another town, or a different country; they chose new paths, they grieved and they cradled their shock, never to be the same again. Was it any wonder that Maurice emphasised time and again the importance of a certain type of meditation – quieting her mind so that she might create a shield of protection around herself. 'The onus is on you to be right, Maisie. To be absolutely correct in your conclusions because you will never be forgiven for an error, and you will cause a maelstrom of terror from which you, acting on behalf of the dead, will never recover.'

And when she closed her eyes, she could see images of the London that greeted her every day as she left her home and made her way to the office, and along the streets of the city as she went about her business. She knew what a maelstrom of terror looked like, and she knew what it felt like in the heart, and she prayed that she would be given the means to minimise any suffering the next twenty-four hours might bring.

Pamela Lockwood was, once again, dressed in a manner that seemed to underline her level of authority in the accounting offices of Derry & Toms, this time wearing a navy costume with pale lavender silk blouse and navy blue shoes. A brooch of amethyst stones was pinned to her lapel. Her greeting was cordial, despite there being no prior appointment made, and she pointed out different offices as she led Maisie to the same room where they had met before, and invited her to take a seat.

'Are you any closer to finding Cath's murderer, Miss Dobbs?' asked Lockwood, closing the door behind her.

'I am. However, as you might imagine, I have to fill in a few gaps around the enquiry that do not necessarily have direct a bearing on the act of murder itself.'

'I'm not sure I understand,' said Lockwood, sitting opposite Maisie. She clasped her hands in front of her on the table.

'Yes, I suppose that does sound rather vague. But you see, I come across all sorts of information about people when I'm engaged in an enquiry, and sometimes it requires clarification even though I have reached a conclusion that it is not a vital piece of evidence.'

'And what evidence have you gathered about me that you could possibly be interested in?' asked Lockwood.

Maisie could hear the woman's foot tapping on the floor, a nervous reaction to the question.

'I believe to a certain extent, and only with regard to one element of her life, you were envious of Catherine Saxon.'

'Me?' Lockwood shook her head and, as Maisie expected, the woman was struggling for composure. She gave a half-laugh. 'I mean, what could I possibly be jealous of?' Another half-laugh. 'Well, I suppose we all had a bit of envy when it came to a hankering for adventure, after all, Cath had it all in that department. But life's pretty adventurous in London just getting to and from work at the moment, isn't it?' Lockwood shrugged. 'No, you're wrong there, Miss Dobbs – I was never envious of Cath. And what do you mean, "one element of her life"?'

'Flight Lieutenant James Trahey.'

Lockwood reddened. 'I'm sorry, I'm not with you – Cath's stage-door Johnny is a boy, nothing but a boy in an RAF uniform, and as you can see I am a mature woman who has about – what? – twelve years on him? At least. I met him a few times, when he was coming to and from Cath's rooms, but no, Miss Dobbs, you're barking up the wrong tree there.'

'James Trahey could have been your late husband's twin.' Maisie inclined her head and, risking rebuff, reached out and placed a hand on the clasped hands of the woman before her. 'On one of my visits to the house, I'd just called to speak to Polly and on the way downstairs I saw Mrs Lockwood in your rooms – she said she was cleaning for you. I took the liberty of stepping into the room to say goodbye, and it was then that I noticed your wedding photograph. You were a beautiful young bride with her very handsome groom. Later, when I met Flight Lieutenant Trahey, I just could not think why he seemed so familiar, and then it came to me. I don't believe for a moment you had designs on Jim, but you could not have looked at him without thinking of your late husband, and how lucky Catherine was to have this man in love with her.'

Pamela Lockwood's eyes filled with tears. She looked down at Maisie's hand covering her own, and did not pull back. 'People don't realise how desolate you feel, Miss Dobbs. How this ache never goes; it's like a weight in the middle of the body, a bad ache in the gut every single day. And the thing is, it's not simply a case of missing a person – it's missing everything that came with that person. This—' She nodded towards Maisie's hand. 'You placing your hand on mine – I think it's the first time another person has held my hand since I was widowed.' She struggled to compose herself, clearing her throat and drawing back one hand to take a handkerchief from her pocket. 'You know, we all had a real affection for Cath, if truth be told, but anyone could see Jim Trahey adored her, and although

I thought that at first it was a diversion on her part, I realised it wasn't, that she was falling in love with him.'

'How many times did he come to see her, do you know?' asked Maisie.

'I saw him a few times – perhaps three, or four. Coming and going. I thought about it a lot, actually, and one day it struck me that she was trying hard not to fall in love with him, that there was something stopping her, and I came to the conclusion that it was her work, that she really wanted to prove something. And of course you know, what with flying Hurricanes, any day could have been his last.'

'I see,' said Maisie.

'But I confess, you're right,' said Lockwood. 'Yes, I was envious. I – I suppose I felt very alone, very old and very desolate. A woman of a certain age who goes to the pictures on a Saturday afternoon just to pretend – to pretend that it could be me in someone's arms, as someone's lover. Do you know how many times I've seen some of those pictures?' She laughed. 'They don't make enough films for me, I'm afraid, so I see the same ones over and over again.' She shook her head. 'I wish I could talk to the people who make these pictures, because I'd like to see more *Wuthering Heights* and less in the vein of *The Wizard of Oz*!'

There was nothing said between the two women for some moments, though it was not an uncomfortable silence.

'Miss Dobbs, I want you to know I didn't kill Catherine. I might have felt a stab of envy, but I would never have taken her life – she had too much life to give.'

'It's all right – I know you're not her killer, Mrs Lockwood.'

'And I don't think it was Jim Trahey either.'

'Neither do I, but there are some elements of any investigation I have to double-check,' said Maisie. 'Hence this visit – for clarification, if you will.'

'Do you know who it is?'

'I believe I do, and it makes sense to me why Catherine would have tried not to fall in love with James Trahey, and I think both of us would understand.'

'And why is that?' said Lockwood.

'Because, like both of us, she had lost a love in another war, and she probably wondered if she could suffer the heartbreak all over again. And I suspect there was another reason too, though I cannot discuss it at the present time.'

Lockwood nodded and looked at Maisie as if weighing up the investigator. 'Do you make mistakes, Miss Dobbs? I mean, you must, but do you worry about making mistakes, in your job? If I make a mistake, the books don't balance and I end up here half the night toiling with the adding machine until I find a loose thruppence ha'penny. But what about you? What do you do?'

Maisie pushed back her chair. 'It's about the same – the books don't balance, but in my case it's not money, it's a life that has to be accounted for. And yes, I do make mistakes, which is why it's important for me to follow every single little niggle, every tiny seemingly insignificant question that has not been answered.' She smiled as she stood up, gently pulling back her hand. 'You see, I knew Catherine was in love with someone, but until our conversation – and that clarification – I had to keep an open mind and entertain the notion that it might have been another man entirely. If I had followed that piece of so-called evidence any further it would have made something bad even worse for everyone concerned. This meeting has helped me no end – to avoid a very serious loose thruppence ha'penny, I suppose.'

Lockwood nodded. 'I'd rather have my job than yours. At least I get a staff discount!' She stood up and stepped towards the door.

'One moment,' said Maisie. 'Did you let Mrs Saxon – Catherine's mother – stay in your rooms recently?'

'Yes, in August. I went down to visit my parents – they live near the coast. Bit worrying, actually, because they'll be rather close to the front lines, if it comes to an invasion. But I go down to do my spinster daughter duty, so I offered Catherine's mum the use of my rooms. She was a very good guest, though I am sure it was very much below par compared to what she's used to. Catherine said it would be fine. "Mother's a sport," she said. The irony of course is that Mrs Saxon isn't that much older than me, so I went away feeling very despondent when it occurred to me that at a push, I could be Catherine's mother.'

Maisie smiled, and having assured Pamela Lockwood that she could pass for thirty, she thanked her and went on her way.

Maisie arrived at MacFarlane's office at quarter past three, ready for the transatlantic trunk call to be placed.

'Good timing, Maisie. Not too early, not too late.'

Maisie pointed to the black telephone with a distinctive green receiver. 'I see we're using a scrambler for the call.'

'Can't be too careful, lass – and we want it private, don't we?'

Maisie nodded.

'Care to bring me up to date?'

Maisie outlined the most recent elements of her investigation, including the fact that Mark Scott had spoken to Clarence 'Scotty' Saxon, circumventing the need for her to respond to the message Catherine Saxon's brother had left at the Dower House.

'So, he doesn't want you speaking to the brother?' said MacFarlane.

'I daresay he has his own reasons,' said Maisie.

'Hmm.'

She looked at MacFarlane. 'What is it, Robbie?'

'Far be it from me to interfere in your personal life, Maisie, but you have surprised me. I mean, I thought you were setting your hat for our friend Richard Stratton, formerly of Scotland Yard – not someone I'd peg for you anyway – but along comes this American and now it appears you're keeping company.'

'I know what I'm doing, Robbie – and it is my personal life. My work has not once been compromised.'

'I would never employ you if I had any doubts about you, so I'm on your side. But Maisie – I just don't want to see your heart broken. Not again. Not when you've got so much at stake, what with the wee bairn, and that panel hearing coming up.'

'I've thought of that, Robbie, and—'

'Be careful, Maisie, that's all I'm saying – and just to let you know, I've a wee bit of intelligence for you. Tuesday, October the fifteenth at County Hall. Half past eleven in the morning. Your adoption hearing.'

Maisie's eyes widened. 'How did you know? I mean – I haven't had a letter yet.'

MacFarlane smiled. 'Little birdie told me – I have to admit, I got on the blower to someone and told them it was not good enough, making a woman wring her hands and wait until next year for a decision on something so important as a child's future. I thought it was worth chivvying them along, and I had a favour to call in anyway.'

'Robbie—'

'Save your thanks for later, hen.'

The telephone rang.

'Here we go, lass. Pick it up and have your word with Mrs Amelia Saxon.'

Maisie picked up the green receiver and held it to her ear.

'Hello, am I speaking to Miss Dobbs?'

'Yes,' said Maisie.

'This is the operator, connecting you now.'

She heard the operator speak to an American operator, followed by the voice of Amelia Saxon accepting the call and saying she was ready.

'Go ahead, caller,' said the operator.

'Hello,' said Maisie. 'Hello – Mrs Saxon?'

'Yes, I'm here.' Amelia Saxon cleared her throat. 'Is this Miss Maisie Dobbs?'

'Yes. Hello. Mrs Saxon, thank you very much for agreeing to this call. I'm the investigator looking into your daughter's death. I realise this is a very difficult time for you, but I wonder, may I ask you a few questions?'

'I want to find out who killed her, Miss Dobbs – you can ask me anything you like.'

There was a catch to the woman's voice, and Maisie wondered if she had been weeping. She smiled, as if Amelia Saxon could see her. 'Thank you, Mrs Saxon. Now, I understand you were in England for a few weeks to see Catherine, about a month or so ago.'

'That's right. But just for two weeks. I stayed at the Dorchester for about six nights, and then in her friend's rooms. I never met her, the friend, but her name was Mrs Lockwood.'

'Yes, I've spoken to her. During the time you were with her, did

Catherine give any indication that she was worrying about something or someone?'

'Catherine always talked about her job a lot – I'm sure you know that by now. I'd supported her from the beginning, though her father didn't. And I suppose I took her side even more because of his attitude. I should add that my husband and I are now separated, though not divorced – it would not look very good for him. I think Catherine was worrying about my situation. The senator and I live separate lives, Miss Dobbs, though I will be seen with him at various political functions. I'm not making a secret of it to you.'

'Thank you, Mrs Saxon. I must ask, did Catherine confide in you regarding anyone she might be seeing?'

'She didn't – but she had a glow about her, and she didn't get it from Maybelline, that's for sure. I had an idea she was seeing someone, but I will admit I was always very careful with my daughter. I never pushed her to tell me about her personal life, because that's all her father did. He never wanted her to be anything but married well, and so he poked his nose into her affairs from the time she was old enough to have affairs. Young women like their privacy.'

MacFarlane tapped on the table to attract Maisie's attention, then tapped his watch. Maisie nodded.

'About Spain. Did she tell you anything about her life there?'

'Not really – not anything personal, though she told me about everything she witnessed. And I—' There was a crackling on the line.

'Yes? Mrs Saxon – are you still there?'

'I'm here. I was going to say that she was quite down after Spain, not herself. And she didn't sound well – I know my daughter, and

I worried she'd picked up something from the water or the food. We'd talked on the telephone, and I know even her father was concerned enough to send Scotty over, though Scotty was always heavy-handed and I believe did his best to drag her back here. Of course, Jenny saw her in Spain.'

'Did you see Jennifer Barrington while you were here in London?'

'No – no, I didn't. Catherine said she was busy. But I'd spoken to Jenny on the phone when she first came back to London. She confirmed that Catherine had been ill. That's why Jenny – being the wonderful friend that she is – had rushed over there to see her. Very brave. Very brave indeed.'

MacFarlane tapped the table again.

'One more thing, Mrs Saxon, and I know this is going to sound incredibly strange a request, but I wonder, would you be able to make arrangements to travel to Lisbon on the Clipper and then from there to London? I think in about a week, if you can.'

'Oh my – my goodness. I never expected that.'

'I can't explain at the moment, Mrs Saxon. I can only say I really hope you can do it – for Catherine's sake. I'm asking you to trust me.'

'Then expect to hear from me. I believe I can reach you through a Mr MacFarlane.'

'Yes, that's right. I'll be in touch. Thank you, Mrs Saxon.'

'Thank you, Miss Dobbs – and I take it this is all confidential.'

'Very,' said Maisie. 'Goodbye, Mrs Saxon.'

Maisie replaced the telephone receiver.

'Just as well you don't have to pay for that one, Maisie.'

'It's for both of us, Robbie – not just me.'

'Sometimes you can't tie up the loose ends, Maisie.'

Maisie shook her head. 'But you know why I'm trying, don't you? You've just arranged for my adoption hearing to come sooner rather than later because you realised it was important for people to be settled, especially when everything has been torn asunder. I may not be able to tie the loose ends on this one, but I'm going to give it my best effort, and there's a very vulnerable person I want to see settled, as far as that might be possible.'

CHAPTER EIGHTEEN

Maisie was in the office early on the morning of 26th September. It was a Thursday, and if all went to plan, by the time she reached Chelstone in the evening, the lives of at least six people would have been changed for ever. It would not have been the first time she had embarked upon this stage of an investigation feeling as if giant moths were at large inside her. It was a far more intense sensation than the feeling of 'butterflies' she had described for Anna on the first day of school following the summer holidays, when the child had said, 'I can't eat my porridge, because I have something crawling in my tummy.' Maisie understood the child's feelings were a blend of excitement, anticipation, and perhaps a little fear. There was no excitement when she imagined her own day ahead, but she recognised the fear of making a terrible error. Yet this was the enigma of a duality that often emerged at this stage of an investigation – despite that fear, she knew, in every fibre of her being, that she was right, and it made her heart ache.

The buff envelope sent by Beryl Tucker arrived with the first post at nine o'clock. Maisie stared at the address, studying the name written in Mrs Tucker's flowing hand. What was she looking for in the script? Kindness? Understanding? Empathy? Compassion? A good heart? She slipped a paper knife into the edge of the sealed flap, opened the envelope and took out the photographs. Beryl Tucker had done more than Maisie could ever have expected. Instead of two photographs, she laid out three on the desk. The first revealed Jeremy Tucker to be a bonny child, one who might be depicted on an advertisement for the sort of hot cereal considered to be good for children. A blonde curl dropped forward on his forehead, and he was clutching a toy train. The second photograph was of a boy on the cusp of manhood, dressed in shorts and a rugby shirt. His hair was darker now, and swept back, apart from the curl that still fell forward, and he was laughing, holding the ball on his hip as if he had scored the game's final winning try. The third photograph was the unexpected gift, and was enclosed in a separate note.

Jeremy sent this one from Paris – if you look on the back, you'll see he says it was taken on a day out with his friends. You can see the Eiffel Tower in the background. They seem such a happy group, don't they? Jonathan was most disapproving. He wrote to Jeremy expressing his displeasure, telling our son he would amount to nothing and unless he came home immediately to follow a gentleman's profession, he would cut him off. Sadly, my darling Jeremy never wrote to his father again, and only corresponded with me, sending his letters to the post office for collection because he didn't trust his father.

Maisie looked at the photograph and uttered the words 'Thank you' aloud.

'What's that, miss?' said Billy, who had just walked into the office.

'Talking to myself, Billy. Everything all right?'

'Still got a roof on the house, so nothing to worry about,' said Billy. 'What've you got there, miss?'

'Have a look at these.'

Billy took up the photographs and studied them while Maisie rolled out the case map and with a red crayon began making final links from one person to the other. Still holding the photographs, her assistant joined her.

'Makes me wonder what people like us did before cameras,' said Billy, placing the photographs on the case map.

'Several possibilities, I suppose. Investigators had to find even more clues to elicit a confession, or to give the prosecuting counsel enough evidence. Or, indeed, the perpetrators of crimes walked away free, either by dint of a jury conclusion or simply escape. Or the wrong person was sent down. I'm sure there are many other variables. And it's the same for many of the tools we and the police have at our disposal today – fingerprinting has been with us for a while now, for example.'

'Hmm. You might have these, but you've still to get more solid information, and a confession.'

'I know.' Maisie turned to Billy. 'That's what I'm going to endeavour to accomplish today. And I would like you to do something for me too.'

'That's what I'm here for,' said Billy.

Maisie took her notebook, scribbled a name and a London address, and tore out the leaf of paper. 'It's the tedious end of the job, actually.

I want you to go to this address and to keep tabs on this man. I'll brief you regarding his appearance – he's quite distinctive. You will know when your job is done – but while you're there, you'll have to keep your eyes peeled.'

Billy took the note, glancing at the information. 'Makes it easier with those buildings covered in sandbags, because you can see people going in and out – they're like rabbits climbing out of the burrow. And I'll be the wily fox!' He looked up, grinning at his own joke, then became more serious. 'What about Mr Scott? Is he going to be there?'

Maisie shook her head. 'He has embassy business to deal with, so I would think not. However, dependent upon how this morning proceeds, his presence will be required sooner or later.'

'You off now, miss?'

'Yes, I am.'

'And what about Mr MacFarlane? Anyone can get nasty when they're backed into a corner, so I hope he's going to be with you.'

'MacFarlane will be close to hand – that's the plan anyway.'

'All right, then.' He paused, fingering the note Maisie had given him bearing a London name and address. 'You take care of yourself, miss – remember little Anna.'

Maisie met Billy's gaze. 'I never forget her, Billy. Not for even one minute of the day.'

Maisie believed fate to be on her side when she arrived at the mansion in Green Street. The family's nanny was just leaving the house, having placed the little boy in a pushchair for their morning walk. Maisie wondered again why the family – or at least mother and son – had not been sent to the country, but perhaps they had not wanted to be apart from the father. Taking the opportunity, Maisie approached the nanny before she had a chance to move off along the street.

'Oh, hello – I was just about to knock on the door, when I saw you with little Charlie. How is he today?' Before the nanny could reply, Maisie knelt down and smiled at the child. 'Are you taking your teddy to the park for a walk?'

'Master Charlie takes Teddy with him everywhere,' said the nanny.

'His leg's gone,' said the child, holding out the toy.

'Oh my goodness – where did he lose it?' asked Maisie, still kneeling alongside the child.

'He's a soldier,' said the boy, pushing fair hair out of his eyes with a dimpled hand.

'And a very brave soldier he is too! You'd better take him to the park now,' said Maisie, standing up. 'Sorry to keep you,' she said to the nanny. 'Have a lovely walk.'

'Oh, we shan't be long now, just enough to tire him out a bit,' said the nanny, wishing Maisie good day.

Maisie watched the nanny as she pushed her charge along the street and, feeling the unwelcome flutter of nerves in her stomach, held her hand to her waist, took a deep breath and turned to the door. She rang the bell and waited.

Jennifer Barrington answered the door herself, greeting Maisie with a smile that went no farther than her lips.

'Miss Dobbs – what a surprise. Have you news?'

Maisie nodded. 'Let's go into the house – we can talk about it there.'

'Of course.' Barrington stepped aside for Maisie to enter, and having closed the door led her to the drawing room. 'Please take a seat,' she said, indicating a chair opposite her own – the morning newspaper was draped across the arm. 'Now, tell me what's happened.'

Maisie looked at Jennifer Barrington, and for one second thought she might simply get up, say it was nothing, she was mistaken, and then she would walk out and never have to see the woman again. But she had come this far, and it was better she be the person to do this job than MacFarlane. MacFarlane could be heavy-handed.

'Mrs Barrington – Jenny, if I may.' She took a deep breath. 'I have a job that at times is very difficult, as you know. Some murder cases are the result of what we might call a *crime passionnel* – a person is killed in a moment of anger, of passion – and some are murdered by a person with a premeditated intention to end a life.'

'I'm sure I don't require a description of your work, Miss Dobbs,' said Barrington, her smile tight. 'I know the business of reporting as much as Catherine, and while I did not leap into exploits quite as adventurous or dangerous as hers, I am fully aware of what might inspire a person to kill.'

Maisie nodded. 'Yes, I believe you do. Jenny, let me tell you what I have concluded. You loved Catherine very much, as if she were your sister – and indeed, you said as much yourself, that you were often taken for sisters, even twins, weren't you? You would have gone to her aid anywhere in the world, if she needed you, and she would have come to your side if you were in trouble, I'm sure. And you went to her in Spain, when she was about to give birth. The child's father had been killed, and Catherine suffered quite serious illness in the latter months of pregnancy following his death.'

'Please—'

'Let me finish, Jenny. Let me finish because if it's not me recounting this story that you know so intimately, then it will be someone else. It's much better if it's me, now, before you have to hear or repeat it again, which will happen in due course.' Maisie paused, gathered her thoughts, and continued. 'Catherine had a difficult birth and was very unwell following the delivery. The baby's health was compromised, but you would not let him die, because you had held him in your arms, you'd felt his little body against yours, and you did everything in your power to keep him alive. But Catherine was tired, already drained from the loss she'd suffered, and from the delivery, and she was not in a position physically or emotionally to care for her son, and she told you she didn't want the baby. Indeed, I would imagine she believed she would never be able to so much as hold her boy, and I can see her turning away from him, such was her state of mind. So you came to the conclusion – because you knew her – that when she recovered, she would be the same old Catherine, seeking adventure, not in a position to mother a child. And this dear boy was a gift for you, in a way – wasn't he? I suspect because your husband could not father a child. I believe you made the decision to remain overseas at that point – you had to give Catherine a chance to change her mind, after all, though she continued to be more focused on making a name for herself. Catherine still wanted to prove herself in a realm other than motherhood. And your husband – who saw this as his opportunity to provide an heir to the family business, as well as to assuage any comments from other men regarding his ability to sire a son – arranged for you to bide your time abroad until you could come home with a babe in arms. Was it Switzerland, Jenny?'

Jenny Barrington nodded.

'I thought it might have been. The problems really started when Catherine came to London, didn't they? Yes, she was still suffering from some lingering health concerns following the delivery, but life had moved on apace, and you had this delightful little boy who completed your marriage, and who everyone thought was the image of his mother – not surprising, given the similarities between you and Catherine. And of course, people are always looking for the reflection of the parents in a child. You idolise the boy, I know that. But Catherine began to want more than just being the delightful maiden aunt, didn't she? And then she fell in love with a man she'd met, which I am sure you thought would strengthen your position, but it didn't because Catherine knew there might not be more children, given the damage she'd suffered giving birth to her son. And she began to want him back. I'm sure she had worked out how she would introduce the child to her parents – especially her mother, who would help with the financial aspects of raising a child – and although I have not yet had a chance to speak to the man in question on this specific subject, I am sure, had he known about the boy, her lover would have embraced fatherhood, because he had fallen deeply in love with Catherine. But perhaps she wasn't quite sure about that herself.'

'I don't know why I don't have you thrown out this very minute. I could call the police on you.' Barrington stood up, took a cigarette from a carved box on a side table, and lit it with a silver lighter placed alongside. She walked to a window overlooking a walled garden, drew on the cigarette and then came back to Maisie, who had not moved. 'So what if that is all true – it doesn't mean I would take a knife and slit Catherine's throat, for heaven's sake!'

'I hadn't quite reached that point, Jenny – but now you've mentioned it, here's what I think happened. Catherine had put even more pressure on you – she was trying to push you into relinquishing the child, and she was – I would imagine – coming up with all sorts of scenarios whereby you could both come out of the situation without everyone trying to second-guess what really happened. You had tried to reason from your point of view, and even your husband had visited her to try to get her to change her mind, and to leave Charlie well enough alone. It was all to no avail, and you couldn't take it any more, could you? And no one could blame you for the way you felt. So after you'd listened to her broadcast, you went to her home and you waited for her outside. Together you went to her rooms, and you talked for a long time, and perhaps you even dozed a little together, because it was just like the old days, when you were at college. Then the conversation started again, the pull and push. Once again you pressed your case, and then you became angry. You became so angry, you did not know what to do with yourself. Catherine probably told you to keep your voice down – but who was there to hear? Mrs Marsh is hard of hearing, and the other women in the house were out, sheltering from the bombs.'

'You have a strong imagination, Miss Dobbs, I'll give you that,' said Barrington.

'Then indulge me, just for a little longer,' said Maisie. 'It was probably about this time that your husband came along, wasn't it? How did he get in? At first I wondered if someone had climbed up into the room from the street, but no, that was rather fanciful, though it's my job to entertain every possibility. Did you or Catherine creep down to open the door?'

There was no answer. Barrington pressed the half-smoked cigarette into an ashtray.

'Right, so however he gained entrance to the house, he came into the room, and the conversation about the boy's future and Catherine's demands became even more heated. You walked away towards the window, yet you lost your temper, didn't you? And although people talk about losing their temper, few really know what it's like when every element of control evaporates because the situation is lost. It's a powerful sensation that starts in the feet and it rushes through you like fire, and then you don't know what you're doing. The next thing you know, you've gone for Catherine's throat, because you want to shut her up, you want her to stop talking about *her* son, about *her* boy, when really he's your son, your boy, and you have raised that child.'

'Stop it! Stop it, stop it, stop it!' Jenny Barrington put her hands over her ears. 'For God's sake stop it!' She turned to Maisie, her eyes wide. 'You don't know what it was like – what Cath could be like. Yes, she was wonderful, she was brave, she was – oh, for goodness' sake, yes, she was the writer I could never be. But she knew what she wanted in life, and she never stopped until she had it in her hands. She was more like the senator than anyone knew, that's for sure. And yes, Charles was her son – by birth. Her son by that English artist who couldn't draw to save his life, who ran off to Spain in a cloud of stupid idealism when his daddy told him to get off his butt and do something useful. And yes, you can bet I lost my temper, Miss Dobbs, and it was a long time coming. I grabbed her by her hair and put my hands around her neck, because I just wanted her to shut up and go away and be a reporter somewhere else, and not think she could follow her muse and drag that darling child around with her and her flyboy lover at the same time. And so would you lose your temper, so would anybody. Did she think I was going to leave that poor little baby in Spain when she turned away from him? Not on your life, I wouldn't. I took him, and we have raised a fine child as our own. We love him. But I didn't kill her, I didn't cut her throat.'

'I know,' said Maisie. 'I know you didn't. But I pressed you because I wanted to know I was on the right path.'

'What do you mean?'

'There were three of you in the room when Catherine was murdered, and the other person was Miles. When you failed to take Catherine down, and in the heat of the moment, he grabbed her knife – the one she used to sharpen her pencils; it was there on her desk – and he swiped the blade across her throat.'

'But—'

'I'd never told you how Catherine was killed, Jenny.' Maisie's voice was low, almost a whisper. 'Yet you knew. And it wasn't an idle guess, was it? You knew because you saw it. I daresay there was a certain reduction in the amount of blood loss due to you clutching her throat from behind – the marks under her ears were roughly where your thumbs would have been. That was still visible.'

Jenny Barrington fell to her knees, clutching her stomach while a violent keening came from deep within her throat. 'I never meant it. I truly never meant it. I loved her, and I love Charlie, and it was all so terrible.'

Maisie stepped across to Jenny Barrington and knelt down beside her, wrapping her arms around her shoulders.

'I hate him. I hate my husband for what he did,' said Jenny Barrington through deep, wracking sobs. 'Now I've lost everything, everyone who ever mattered to me.'

'It's all right, Jenny – it's all going to come out right in the end.'

Within five minutes of Maisie's call, a police vehicle arrived at the Barrington house. A policewoman in plain clothes attire accompanied MacFarlane.

'All right, Maisie?' asked MacFarlane. 'We were waiting around the corner for your call and the Yard to alert me. And I won the bet

336

with Miss Hawkins here, I said we'd hear at bang on twelve noon, and she thought nearer to quarter past.'

'Oh, Robbie – how could you make bets at a time like this?' Maisie shook her head. 'Jennifer Barrington has just made a verbal confession regarding her involvement in the death of Catherine Saxon – and she's absolutely at the end of her tether. What about Miles Barrington?'

'Caldwell's got him – he tried to do a runner, but that Mr Beale took him down. He only got a few yards out of the building, and the next thing you know, Beale belted across the road like greased lightning, and old Miles Barrington was on his face, screaming blue murder.'

'Oh dear – is Billy all right? I asked him to keep an eye on the building because I was afraid Barrington would leave before Caldwell arrived at the allotted time.'

MacFarlane consulted his watch. 'An American bloke in a flash black Buick will be coming down the road in a minute or two. Do you want to wait, or leave it to me? He'll have to come along to the Yard as the consular representative of an American citizen, and you'll have to make your statement.'

'Please ensure Mrs Barrington has legal counsel present, won't you, Robbie? She might not have to go down, in the circumstances. Losing your temper isn't a criminal offence, is it?'

'It is when you've kept quiet about someone else committing a murder, so you'd better stop the wishful thinking, or I'll think you've gone soft – you know the law as well as I. But it looks like you've got it all sorted, haven't you? You've done your best to make sure the boy won't suffer, and the people who should have known about him all along will know about him soon.'

Maisie nodded. The policewoman came from the drawing

room into the hallway, her arm around Jennifer Barrington.

'I'm so sorry, Jenny – that it's come to this,' said Maisie.

Barrington nodded. 'Me too – but it had to happen, didn't it? This sort of secret would have come out one day. They always do, don't they? Secrets. And it's really strange, but I feel as if a weight has been lifted. It was always there, see – always there. Catherine was like a dog with a bone when she wanted something – and most of the time she wanted a story. I think I always knew she'd demand him back, that I was a mother on borrowed time.'

'And you're a good mother, Jenny.'

At that moment the door opened and the nanny entered holding the little blonde boy on her hip. She licked her hand, using her damp fingers to brush back an unruly curl that had dropped across his forehead.

'Oh, I'm sorry – I didn't know you were expecting visitors, Mrs Barrington.'

Little Charlie held out his arms to Jenny Barrington. 'Mummy. Mummy – we saw fire engines!'

Jenny Barrington reached for the child and held him to her. 'Mummy's going to a very important meeting with some very important people. Be a good soldier until I get home, won't you?'

As if he felt the tension in her body, the child clung to the only woman he had known as his mother and began to whimper.

'Now, now, let's be a big boy,' said the nanny, reaching for her charge. She took young Charles Barrington, who buried his head in her neck. 'I'll give him a spot of lunch, Mrs Barrington, then put him down for a nap.'

Maisie remained at the house to talk to the nanny and housekeeper, informing them that Mr and Mrs Barrington would be away from home for some days attending to an important family matter. She took one last look at the photograph on the mantelpiece, of a happy Miles, Jennifer and Charlie Barrington, and left the house. As she walked down the steps leading to the pavement outside the Barrington residence, a black Buick drew up alongside the mansion. Mark Scott emerged from the back of the motor car and opened the passenger door for Maisie.

'I figured I wasn't such a great driver in London, so it seemed a good idea for me to get the pro on the job,' said Mark Scott, nodding towards his driver as the vehicle moved off along Green Street. 'We're on our way to Scotland Yard. Mac says he'll need a statement from you, and I'll be handing over all matters concerning Jennifer Barrington to another embassy employee. It's a formality now.'

'Mark – it was always a formality for you, wasn't it?'

'Maisie, I'm sorry, but—'

She cut him off. 'It's all right, Mark – I'm not blaming you. I'm not upset with you, and I didn't really expect you to tell me what you're doing here, but perhaps at some point you could see fit to trust me.'

'It's been a very delicate assignment, Maisie, but I can tell you something in the meantime. And more later – in a couple weeks' time.'

'You don't have to, you know, I—'

'I'm working directly for the president of the United States of America,' he said in a low voice. 'He's my boss – and not just because he's everybody's boss if you work for the government. I mean, he's my boss for what I'm doing now.'

'And then what – what happens in a couple of weeks' time? If your work is at an end, what happens then – to us?'

*　*　*

339

Maisie telephoned the office just before leaving Scotland Yard. Mark Scott had departed earlier, after officially introducing the consular officer who would be their point of contact in the case of Jenny Barrington, an American citizen charged with the crime of accessory to the murder of Catherine Saxon.

'Are you all right, Billy?' said Maisie.

'The old gammy leg is a bit more gammy – that fellow wasn't exactly like a feather to take down. Pity it wasn't Walkinshaw, he would have been easier. I hoped this one would be a nice soft cushion, but I whacked my knee on the pavement. I reckon I'll be as right as rain though, given time.'

'Billy – go down to Hampshire early to see Doreen and Margaret Rose. No need to come back until Monday afternoon, at the earliest. I don't know about you, but when a case like this ends, I just want to sleep.'

'It's over, then, miss,' said Billy.

'More or less. There are a few *i*'s to dot and *t*'s to cross, then it'll be done – and we'll be onto the next thing.'

'I'd be happy just to work on some nice, easy cases for a while, wouldn't you?'

'I would, Billy – let's see how it all goes.'

'Right, miss – see you Monday afternoon, then.'

Frankie and Anna were at Chelstone Station to meet Maisie.

'That poor pony can't pull all of us along, can she?' said Maisie.

'She's a strong little thing,' said Frankie.

'Tell you what, Dad – you take my bag and go back with the dogs, and Anna and I will wander along the lane. Ask Brenda to put the kettle on.'

Frankie Dobbs instructed the dogs to stay aboard the cart, while Anna clung to Maisie's hand. They waved Frankie on his way, while Emma and Jook looked back, tongues lolling.

As Maisie and Anna walked along the lane to Chelstone Manor in the balmy early evening warmth of late September, they were flanked by fronds of cow parsley moving back and forth along the verge, caught by a breeze spiced with the smell of hops lingering on the air from the recent harvest, and with the sweetness of late varieties of Kentish apples still to be picked. Maisie closed her eyes for a moment, listening to the sound of the child beside her skipping along while giving a running commentary on what happened at school today, and how the soldiers who took away the bomb came back with some sweets, and all the children were very excited because they didn't get many sweets. Every stored thought bubbled up to the surface from Anna's mind to be laid before Maisie – and Maisie felt every word as if it were a jewel to be held and cherished, to be encouraged and rewarded. This walk, this place was her home, and in that moment she knelt down and swept Anna into her arms and held her tight, an image of Jenny Barrington in her mind's eye, and her commitment to Catherine Saxon in her heart – she had revealed those responsible for Catherine's death, but at what cost? She knew, then, in the deepest part of her being, the lengths to which she would go to keep her child, and her heart bled even more for Jenny Barrington – and for Catherine Saxon and the child they both loved.

Maisie and Anna arrived at the Dower House to see Brenda waiting at the kitchen door.

'Anna, Uncle Frankie is at the stables,' said Brenda. 'He said you're to go down there now to help put your pony away. Emma can go with you, so get along there now, there's a good girl.'

Maisie could see Anna was torn, not wanting to leave her. 'Go on, Anna – I'm not going anywhere, and besides, I've got to help Auntie Brenda anyway.'

The two women watched as Anna ran down the path to the stables, flanked by Emma.

Brenda held out her arms to Maisie. 'Hello, love. Your dad said you looked all in.' She stood back for Maisie to step into the kitchen, and pulled an envelope from her apron pocket. 'This came today, Maisie – from the Ministry of Health.'

'I think I know what it is – my hearing is set for October the fifteenth.'

'Not long to go now, then,' said Brenda.

Maisie read the letter, confirming the news MacFarlane had already given her.

'I think I've prepared so much, I'll get it all wrong.'

'We'll be there for you, waiting outside.' Brenda's voice was soft, reassuring. 'And I almost forgot – your American friend telephoned. He said he would telephone later, but he wanted to know if it was all right to invite himself down for lunch on Sunday. I didn't know what to say, I mean, I know they can be awfully familiar, these Americans.'

'So – what *did* you say?'

'I hope I did the right thing. I didn't want to offend him, so I said yes, of course, the more the merrier.'

Maisie nodded. 'And that was exactly the right thing to say, Brenda – everything's all right. But do you think we have enough food to go round, because I'm sure Douglas and the boys will come?'

'Oh, there'll be enough. We always manage, don't we? And we'll keep on managing. Now, why don't you go along to the library and have another five minutes to yourself before our little whirlwind comes back up here.'

Maisie followed Brenda's instructions and made her way to the library. Having been Maurice's housekeeper for years before his death, Brenda understood without being told that it had been a tumultuous day, a day when the heavy lifting on a case had been completed. Yet there were still questions to be answered, not least whether she was doing the right thing in trying to do her best for little Charlie Barrington.

'So you see,' said Maisie, supporting Priscilla's head so she could take sips of water from a cup with a long spout. 'Catherine Saxon's father managed to block any newspaper reports of her death in the American newspapers. At first blush it might seem like something he would encourage to further his cause. Initially, I imagined he might make a statement along the lines of, "My daughter was killed in London, look how bad it is over there, so let's keep America well out of it." However, apparently the senator was canny enough to realise that other unwanted news could well be revealed about the daughter he considered to be something of a liability, and it might reflect poorly on him.'

'I'm amazed you're telling me,' said Priscilla, the bandages rendering 'amazed' to sound as if she'd said 'amaved'.

'I'm keeping you entertained,' said Maisie. 'And besides, by the time you've had a nap and then come round again, you'll have forgotten everything.'

'You mustn't make me laugh. I've had skin gwafts,' said Priscilla.

'Make her laugh all you want!' The voice came from behind Maisie. The doctor with a discernible Antipodean accent had entered the room and was now standing next to Priscilla's bed, the ward sister at his side. 'You can go home in a week, if you're good, Mrs Partridge, and we'll line up the next round of grafts. You're doing well – and laughter is always the best medicine.'

'Hard to laugh, Mr McIndoe, when your flight lieutenant son could be in the ward next door at any time,' said Priscilla.

The doctor took a clipboard hanging at the base of the bed and made a few notes on Priscilla's progress, speaking as he wrote. 'I've never had two patients from the same family before, so I expect I'll only see him when he comes in to visit his pals and proceeds to lead them away from the straight and narrow down to the pub.' He replaced the clipboard. 'I would imagine in a year, eighteen months, you'll have seen the back of me, and in the meantime, life can go on as normal between your operations.'

'He doesn't know what my life's like,' said Priscilla as Archibald McIndoe left her room. 'It's not normal, and I can't laze around all day doing nothing.'

'That's exactly what you can do, and when it's time for you to stop languishing, you'll have plenty of people to chivvy you along,' said Maisie, rising from the chair. 'And you've more company coming in now, so I must be going.'

'Maman!' Tim Partridge entered the room, followed by his younger brother. The boys took up places on either side of their mother's bed, reaching down to kiss her.

'You'll fuffocate me, boys!' said Priscilla.

'Tarq, we're going to have to remember that one – fuffocate!' said Tim.

Maisie turned as she reached the door, to see Priscilla trying to attract her attention by waving one bandaged hand.

'What about the Amewican?' said Priscilla.

'Nothing to report there, Pris,' said Maisie, giving one last wave as she left the ward.

* * *

344

Mark Scott telephoned the Dower House that Saturday evening, a call Maisie took in the library.

'Maisie, I am so sorry, but I can't make lunch tomorrow. I know I talked my way into it, but I – I've to report to DC. I'm heading out soon, flying via Lisbon.'

'Is your work finished here, Mark?' asked Maisie.

'Pretty much – but there's another assignment on the table. That's what I'm being summoned back to discuss. Not something to be dealt with in a diplomatic bag, or a trunk call from the embassy.'

'Then it's goodbye, I suppose,' said Maisie.

'I – I can't say anything.'

'Can you tell me about this assignment of yours, the one you've almost finished?'

'Soon.'

'Mark – what do you mean? Soon? Don't toy with me.'

'It's not over, Maisie – we're not over. But – but trust me.'

Maisie took a deep breath. 'Frankly, Mark, I have more pressing things to worry about. There's still work for me to finish on the Catherine Saxon case, and there's a little girl who's more important than anything else. Anyway – look, I have to go now. It's Anna's bedtime. Goodbye, Mark.'

'Maisie—'

She replaced the receiver, standing still for a moment before walking across to the table that held a bottle of sherry and another of single malt whisky, the latter having been Maurice's tipple. She poured herself a glass of the whisky, and sat in the wing chair alongside the fireplace. Looking across to the opposite chair, where her mentor would sit in the days when she sought his counsel during work on a case, she raised her glass and took a generous sip, brushing away tears with her fingers.

'Well, Maurice, I suppose if you play with fire, you deserve to get burned, don't you? I can't say I went into that without knowing how it might end.'

CHAPTER NINETEEN

Maisie sat at the head of the long table in her office, with MacFarlane and Billy on either side of her.

'So Miles Barrington was the man those other ladies had seen coming and going a few times at the Welbeck Street house,' said MacFarlane.

'And that's why at one point I wondered if Miles Barrington was having an affair with Catherine,' said Maisie. 'But he wasn't, was he? I went back to Pamela Lockwood again to go over some ground I'd already trodden during an earlier meeting – and was able to confirm I'd taken a leap in the wrong direction. He was coming to the house time and again trying to get Catherine to drop the whole idea of getting Charlie back, or at least to agree to some other arrangement that would allow the child to remain with them. He'd come at odd times, hoping to catch her off guard, and for her part, apparently at one point she'd even suggested sharing the child, which would never have worked, would it?'

MacFarlane nodded. 'I had a word with the doctor across the street – what's his name?'

'Chester.'

'Right, him. He said Saxon was troubled not only by some lingering physical ailments following the birth of her son – and I told him I didn't want to know any more of that personal women's business than was necessary, no female details – but he said she also suffered with a sort of severe neurosis he'd seen in only a few new mothers. All up and down they are, and off kilter, though most people only ever saw Catherine Saxon when she was on the up, because she was carried along by her work.'

'What did the Barringtons say about leaving Catherine's rooms, after she was dead?' asked Billy.

'Miles Barrington was wearing a mackintosh, which caught some of the blood when he killed the poor lass. So he took it off and bundled it up. Then he cleaned the blade, but Jennifer Barrington was in shock and just staring at the thing, so he knew he had to get rid of it and pronto. He was careful to wipe any surface either of them touched – his silk handkerchief came in handy – but he left the kettle to burn dry. Catherine had put it on the gas when he arrived, to make some tea. Or most likely coffee.' MacFarlane sighed, as if recounting the chain of events was exhausting him. 'Then he picked up a pile of letters from the table and checked the drawers for more, because he knew a good number were from his wife, and would likely include a plea not to take Charlie away. Anyway, he managed to get Jennifer out of the house without making a noise which would wake Mrs Marsh. On the way out, he flung the knife into that dingy old room, the one they call the cellar.'

'How did he know there was even a room there?' asked Maisie.

'He didn't – but let's face it, we've all been in houses with exactly the same rooms in exactly the same place, and we know a cupboard or the entrance to a cellar when we see it.'

'And I suppose it was missed by the police because Scotland Yard handed over the case quickly after Mrs Marsh found her, and any search was curtailed.'

'Apparently a young constable was sent in to have a look around that room but missed the knife, probably because it was under the rusty old bicycle frame. In his defence, the lad had been up on duty all night, and it's not as if you get a lot of light in there, and he probably didn't have a torch on him. All those things add up.' MacFarlane shrugged. 'But I can see what you're getting at – it should have been found before you laid eyes on it. I can't argue with you there.'

'Then what did they do? How did the Barringtons get home?' asked Billy.

'Mr Barrington had his motor car parked around the corner, so they went straight home and disposed of the coat. Not hard to do, when you think of it, what with great piles of rubbish everywhere. Just throw it in a sack on top of all the other sacks. But we've got people looking for it, all the same.' He shook his head. 'More importantly, we've everything we need in the way of confessions. Those two were so beaten down by worry about losing the boy, that by the time Miles Barrington went for Catherine Saxon's throat with a knife, I'm surprised they didn't walk over to Scotland Yard and confess then, if only to get it off their chests. And it helped that you thought he was left-handed.'

'That was a guess – I didn't see him pick up a pen, but it was the way he rubbed his hands together, smearing an ink stain from his fingers.' Maisie shook her head, weariness settling upon her. 'I feel sorry for everyone involved. It's a piteous situation, and it has no satisfactory ending.'

She looked up from her hands, feeling MacFarlane looking at her. The bandages were off and the cream given to her by Pete at the Italian restaurant had worked wonders, though now the scars itched.

'You're doing your best though, miss,' said Billy.

'Aye, you're doing what you can,' added MacFarlane.

Maisie stood up and walked to the window. She stared up at the barrage balloons, then turned around.

'You don't know about the case of Michael Clifton, do you, Robbie?' She went on without waiting for him to reply. 'It was a case we solved – if that's the word – about nine or ten years ago, and it concerned an American who'd come to fight for Britain in the last war. I received the assignment through an old friend who lives in Boston – a doctor. You see, the parents of the young man – who were getting on, as you would imagine, and who knew only that, during the war, their son was "missing, presumed dead" – had received word that his remains had been found when a French farmer managed to plough up an old dugout. The ground began to fall in as the plough went across. They did not suspect murder, but had given the post-mortem report to our mutual doctor friend to have a look at, and really to interpret it for them – you know how convoluted these things can be. He said nothing to them about his suspicions, however, when the couple decided to come to England, he referred them to me, knowing that as soon as I saw the report I would spot certain inconsistencies.' Maisie paused, pressing her fingers to the bridge of her nose. 'Right from the beginning, the mother had a strong feeling – an intuition, if you will – that her son had fallen in love before he died, and a child had been the result of the union. All she really wanted was for the child to be found, if she was right – and she was. The mother of Michael Clifton's son had raised him as her husband's, and the American went to his death not knowing he was to be a father. I was tormented because there was nothing I could do about the situation.'

'What could you have done, hen? You can't play God with other people's lives.'

'But there was a boy who would never know who his true father was. There were grandparents who would never see their grandson – a grandmother who would never know that she was right. Even Michael Clifton's wartime lover knew that morally it would have been the right thing to do, to let the Cliftons know their grandson. But do you know what kept her from taking that leap?' Maisie looked at both men, from one to the other. 'Billy remembers, don't you, Billy?'

'I do, miss. Tricky case, that one.'

'She could not reveal the truth because if she did so, then her son would lose his inheritance, and indeed his name, and hers would be affected too. The name was important. So you see, I have brought the Catherine Saxon case to a close, to all intents and purposes – but there is a child who will now be without both parents. I almost walked away from seeking a confession from Jennifer Barrington – I knew very well that I would get it, but I was so doubtful about the situation with the boy. And look at it – Miles Barrington may well go to the gallows, though if they have the best defence counsel money can buy, then he will be incarcerated for the rest of his days. Jennifer Barrington will go to Holloway Prison – but again, they can afford the right counsel, so it might not be for too long. And in the meantime, what happens to Charlie? Well, we'll see – because as soon as Amelia Saxon arrives, I will apprise her of the situation, with nothing omitted. She will be informed that there are other grandparents, and particularly another grandmother, Beryl Tucker. I have a distinct feeling – perhaps it's simply hope, I'll give you that – that those two women will put Charlie's well-being before everything, and he will be provided with the very best opportunity to grow into a fine young man.'

'It's funny though,' said Billy, 'how Catherine Saxon met Jeremy Tucker, and there they were with all the same things bothering them. I mean, look at it – both got mums who've been married to men who aren't exactly what you'd call respectful towards them. Powerful, but not your friendly types. Both of those kids had fallen out with their fathers, and it sounds like Beryl Tucker could quite happily walk out on her husband tomorrow, just like Amelia Saxon left that senator bloke.'

MacFarlane stood up. 'Well, all this is never going to get the eggs cooked, is it? Can't be sitting around chatting all day when I've solid work to be getting on with, and not your funny psychological hocus-pocus either. I sometimes think there's too much of that going on when I visit this office.' He looked at Maisie and placed a hand on her shoulder. 'I still think you should leave well enough alone now, Maisie. You can't account for what people do, and you can't save everyone.'

'It's the child, though,' said Maisie.

'I know,' said MacFarlane.

With Amelia Saxon expected to arrive on Saturday 5th October, Maisie knew it was time to begin her final accounting, a process by which she revisited the people with whom she had crossed paths during the investigation, and the places where the most important aspects of the case had come to pass. She started with Mrs Marsh, at the Welbeck Street address where Catherine Saxon had lived.

'So, can I let out the rooms yet? Mr Tucker is very anxious to know, and it doesn't make my life any easier,' said the landlady.

'You should wait until the police give you final permission. I cannot tell you any more than this: a suspect is in custody and has been charged. I am sure you will know more in due course,' said Maisie.

Marsh brought a handkerchief from her apron, which she pressed to her eyes. 'I did like her you know, Miss Dobbs – I mean, you couldn't help but have a soft spot for Catherine. As I said before, I knew she'd had a young man in her rooms, but I turn a blind eye to these things as long as everyone's discreet. I mean, the way things are going, you've got to live your life as if every day were your last.'

'I'll be honest, I never expected you to say that, Mrs Marsh, but I think you're right,' said Maisie, who enquired after Helena and Elizabeth, the two women on the topmost floor.

'Funny you should mention them, Miss Dobbs. They've gone now, off to the Wrens. They said they'd come back and visit me as soon as they could, because they wanted to show off their uniforms. Lovely girls, those two – very fond of each other, so it worries me what might happen when they're sent off to different jobs.'

'I'm sure they'll take it in their stride. And do give them my best.'

Maisie caught Pamela Lockwood as she was leaving Derry & Toms, and walked with her to the Underground station. Already people were making their way down into the depths of the station, many straight from work but with blankets under their arms, and bags with a packed supper, and a flask of tea.

'I came to the conclusion I was safer down there than in a cellar under the store. I feel as if I've been run over by a tractor in the morning, but if I can't get back to my rooms before work, I keep a clean blouse in my office, and just have a quick wash in the ladies' facilities at the shop.'

Maisie thanked Lockwood for her time and her help, adding that she could not divulge any information regarding the death of Catherine Saxon, but was sure the trial would be in the newspapers in due course. In truth she knew better – the trial would not be covered by the press on either side of the Atlantic; Senator Clarence Saxon had seen to that.

Less than a month later Maisie would write to Pamela Lockwood, letting her know that Flight Lieutenant James Trahey had been killed in action over the English Channel while protecting his adopted country from German bombers. But she would not send the letter, deciding instead to rip it into small pieces, and allow the woman to have her dreams every Saturday afternoon at the picture house.

Polly Harcourt was in the early stage of rehearsals for the Christmas pantomime when Maisie found her at the theatre. She sat at the back of the house, watching the actress read her lines, then ask the director a question, then read the lines again. During a tea break, an assistant delivered the message that a woman named Miss Dobbs was waiting to see her.

'Miss Dobbs! How are you? Do you have news?' Harcourt sat down alongside Maisie. 'It's quiet at the back here; no one can hear us, so we can talk.'

Maisie gave Harcourt the same information she'd offered Mrs

Marsh and Pamela Lockwood. Doubtless the women would talk about it – she could imagine them sitting in the garden with cups of tea, discussing Catherine's death – so Maisie was careful to ensure they were all given identical details.

'One question, Polly – I wondered what happened to those children you told me about, the siblings being sent to America for their safety. I was worried when I heard about that ship being torpedoed – the SS *City of Benares*.'

'So was I – but would you believe it, Miss Dobbs? My sister told me that at the last minute, right at the docks, their mother said, "That's it – they're staying at home. I'm not having my children going over there on a big boat." And that was that.'

'My goodness – they had a lucky escape,' said Maisie. She smiled at the young actress. 'What's next for you, Polly?' asked Maisie.

The young actress shrugged. 'Oh, heaven knows – my future and fame are in the lap of the gods. But this panto will go on until the new year, and I've almost finished writing my own play. Oh, and I'm working on a novel, plus I'm still serving drinks at the club. You can't let go of a paying job, can you?' She gave an impish smile. 'So let's see what 1941 brings!'

'Yes, we've still a few months of this year left, but let's see what 1941 brings,' echoed Maisie as she stood up to say goodbye to Polly Harcourt.

Today I think is the first quiet night we've had since the Blitz started on September 7th. Somehow the absolute dead silence is more disconcerting than the noise of the guns . . . Ah, there's the siren. It's three-thirty. It's a pity to have to wake up six or seven million people just because one Jerry may be up there. But of course there may be five hundred Jerries up there.

And there are the guns. Comforting sound. Things are
normal again. Now I can sleep.
QUENTIN REYNOLDS, AMERICAN JOURNALIST,

IN A LETTER TO HIS FATHER, 6TH OCTOBER 1940

On October 6th Maisie met Amelia Saxon in her suite at the Dorchester. The woman who approached Maisie to take both hands in her own seemed to be an older version of her daughter. She was tall and slender, wearing a matching jacket and skirt costume of fine black wool, with a diamond brooch pinned to her lapel. Her hair was brushed back and fell in waves around her shoulders, and she wore pearl earrings and a pearl and diamond necklace. There was something in her bearing that led Maisie to believe that in other circumstances Amelia Saxon might be a wry social observer.

Following an exchange of niceties – Maisie enquiring about the journey, and Mrs Saxon commenting that she was a keen follower of Mr Murrow's broadcasts, so she knew what she was flying into when she booked her travel to London – Maisie described the situation to Catherine Saxon's mother, informing her that Miles and Jennifer Barrington were in police custody, with Miles charged with her daughter's murder, and her best friend accused of being an accessory to the crime.

'Would you like a moment to digest all I've said so far, Mrs Saxon?'

'No, no, that's OK, Miss Dobbs – you go ahead, and I'll tell you if I need a break.'

'Right you are. I'll continue.'

Maisie described the affair between her daughter and Jeremy Tucker, and the outcome – that she had given birth to a son, and the child had been brought up to believe Jennifer Barrington was his mother. She waited again, allowing Amelia Saxon a moment to absorb even more troubling information.

'And what about the boy's people – do they know?'

'I was getting to that, Mrs Saxon,' said Maisie, continuing with her story, and describing the current situation with Jonathan and Beryl Tucker.

Amelia Saxon leant back on the well-stuffed sofa. 'Seems to me that two young people who kicked the traces laid down by their fathers found each other.'

'My assistant made a similar observation,' said Maisie.

'The first thing I want to say is that I would like very much to see my grandson. I was always very tolerant of my daughter, though my husband was angry at me for what he thought was complete indulgence. But I was glad to see her grow up to be a young woman with a robust brain and some muscle in her character. Then of course, I lost her – lost her to everything she wanted to do and become. And don't get me wrong – I was prepared for it, and I knew it would happen, because you can't encourage independence of spirit and expect a child to remain hanging on to your skirts.' She was thoughtful for some moments before speaking again. 'You haven't said as much in so many words, but I think this Beryl Tucker and I are probably of the same ilk. Have you told her everything you've told me?'

'Not yet – you were first. And I have to prise her away from her home – she has an overbearing husband, if I may say so.'

'Hmph – she's a lot like me!'

'Actually, I believe she is becoming so,' said Maisie.

'Speak to her soon, Miss Dobbs,' said Amelia Saxon. 'I'll remain in England for as long as it takes for me to decide what I must do for

Catherine – and for Jenny, I must admit. I feel for my daughter – for her memory, for what she must have gone through. She must have endured so much pain and exhaustion, and in a complete fog of grief. I cannot fathom what a terrible, confused time it was for her – perhaps her ambition was the only route out. But what I cannot get to grips with more than anything else, is the fact that she was prepared to cause such harm to someone she loved. And she loved Jenny.'

Maisie invited Beryl Tucker to join her at a tea shop in Haywards Heath, and was surprised when she took the news in a calm, dignified manner.

'I knew it was something like this, Miss Dobbs. I mean, you asked for a photo of Jeremy as a child, and there could be no other reason for wanting such a thing. And tell me if a mother doesn't see the writing on the wall when she receives a photo from her son of a group of friends in Paris, and straightaway she can spot the girl he would have fallen for.'

'Mrs Saxon wants to meet you, if you're willing, Mrs Tucker.' Maisie took a breath before continuing. 'I would ask, however, that you do not take your husband into your confidence in this matter at this stage. I know I am asking for a secret to be kept between man and wife, however—'

Beryl Tucker held up her hand, interrupting Maisie. 'That's a given, Miss Dobbs. My husband is a difficult man, and I would be the first to admit it. And I will take that into account when Mrs Saxon and I put our heads together regarding our grandson.'

'Right you are – Mrs Saxon can meet you at any time. Shall we say sooner rather than later? Perhaps tomorrow?'

'Yes. Absolutely, yes. Tomorrow at noon, at her hotel – the Dorchester, you said?'

Maisie smiled, and felt compelled to take Beryl Tucker's hands in her own. 'I am so grateful to you – and to Mrs Saxon. You've both shown such remarkable willingness and . . . and courage. And in the face of so much sadness.'

'But hers is still acute, Miss Dobbs. My grief has settled into me like a constant dull ache. It's different. We'll do what's right for Charlie – and for Mrs Barrington. How is she, by the way? Poor woman.'

The only person Maisie could not see was Isabel Chalmers, but she extended her thanks for the young woman's cooperation, to be passed on by Robert MacFarlane. With her final accounting almost complete, Maisie spent more time at the Dower House, travelling to London as required for her work. It was not until Wednesday 9th October before she was able to visit Bob Walkinshaw at the studios of the BBC – and once again she was caught at Broadcasting House due to an air raid. This time she slept fitfully, seated in a corner of a control room. It was Walkinshaw who woke her, beckoning her to accompany him into a studio where the American newsman Mr Murrow was beginning his broadcast to the United States.

This is London, ten minutes before five in the morning. Tonight's raid has been widespread. London is again the main target. Bombs have been reported from more than fifty districts. Raiders have been over Wales in the west, the Midlands, Liverpool and the south-west and north-east . . .

Maisie listened to his account of the air raids, and how he had joined the men and women of the London fire service that very night. He concluded his broadcast describing a scene he had witnessed, of a man copying the names of dead firemen in a big ledger.

'You can see why he's getting a reputation over there, can't you?' said Walkinshaw. 'I mean, we think he's a good bloke here, but there's some people on the other side of the Atlantic who don't like the way he tells a story. He goes straight to the heart of it, see. Every time he broadcasts, the Americans listening can hear what's happening on the streets of London – he tells it so they can see it. If it wasn't for him, it would all just be words on the page.'

Maisie agreed and slipped out of the studio. It was a brisk Thursday morning. She would go into the office for a brief visit to clear her desk, and then home to Chelstone, and she would remain there until the fifteenth of the month, when she would come to London again with her father and stepmother, and with Anna. And if Anna asked her if she was feeling all right when she arrived at the Dower House, she would just have to explain that she had butterflies inside her.

'Now, Miss Dobbs – we understand that you do not use the title bestowed upon you by marriage to the late Viscount James Compton, is that correct?'

'Yes, that's correct, sir. I have been a volunteer with the Auxiliary Ambulance Services until quite recently, and I have always believed using my maiden name is more conducive to a positive . . . a more positive . . .'

'Miss Dobbs?'

'Yes, more positive . . . a more positive time at work . . .' She felt sick. Her mind was racing and she knew the words leaving her mouth had little connection to the answers she had practised over and over and over again.

'Quite, I see. Might you have not wanted to intimidate people, perhaps?'

Maisie straightened her back. 'I have always prided myself on my approachability, sir.'

A woman looked at Maisie over half-moon glasses. Her hair was permed into tight curls, and she wore a cameo brooch on the high collar of her lavender silk blouse.

'Let's get down to brass tacks, shall we, Miss Dobbs?' said the woman. 'We have a lot of ground to cover, and I for one do not want to waste time on titles.' She glanced at the man who had asked the previous questions, then looked down at the folder on the desk in front of her. 'Now, you first met the child, Anna, when she was billeted with you in early September last year, is that correct?'

'Yes,' said Maisie.

'Right. And it seems you went to great trouble to locate the child's grandmother, a sick woman who had placed her on the evacuee train even though she was not a member of any school party departing on that train.'

'Yes.'

'I can also see you made extensive enquiries through diplomatic channels with the Maltese government to find the child's father – a man she had never met, given the very brief liaison between the child's mother and this man, who was a merchant seaman.'

'Yes, that's correct – I thought I should try to find him,' said Maisie.

The woman looked over her glasses at the men on either side of her. 'Good, we're getting somewhere – this is progress.'

Maisie drew a deep breath. *Here we go*, she thought, as it occurred to her that the questions would now come at her thick and fast – and she was ready for every single one.

An hour and ten minutes later, she emerged from the hearing room. Frankie and Brenda stood up. Anna ran towards her.

'Tell me . . . tell me . . . tell me,' she said. Anna tended to repeat her sentences three times when she was excited. She jumped into Maisie's arms.

'Not quite there yet,' said the woman who emerged from the room behind Maisie. She held out her hand towards Anna, and looked at her over her half-moon glasses. 'Miss Anna Mason? We'd like you to come in and have a little chat with us.'

'Go on, my lovely one – go with the lady,' said Maisie. 'We'll be here in this very spot waiting for you.'

Anna left Maisie's side, and reached for the woman's hand. Looking back with wide eyes, she placed the first two fingers of her left hand in her mouth.

'Oh dear,' whispered Maisie. 'She does that when she's worried.'

'The littl'un will do well by herself, just you see,' said Frankie.

'I suppose all we can do is wait, can't we?' said Brenda.

Maisie nodded. 'I feel as if I've been waiting years.'

EPILOGUE

The letter was delivered on Friday 25th October. Maisie was in the kitchen buttoning Anna's green school mackintosh when the first post arrived; they could hear the sound of envelopes being pushed through the letter box and landing on the mat.

'Letters!' squealed Anna, as she pulled away and scurried along the hallway to fetch the mail.

She ran back into the kitchen. 'There you are,' she said, placing several envelopes on the table in front of Maisie, who picked them up and leafed through them. She stopped at the envelope bearing the return address of the Ministry of Health.

'Oh—'

'What is it, love?' asked Brenda, coming into the kitchen.

Maisie held up the envelope so Brenda could see who it was from. 'I'm going to the library.'

Anna moved to follow, but Brenda held her back. 'Let Auntie Maisie go on her own – it's something to do with her work. And you're going to be late for school – where's your satchel?'

Maisie reached the library, hearing her stepmother call her father up from the cellar, where he had been endeavouring to stem rainwater leaking in from outside. She closed the door behind her, and sat at the desk. She looked at the envelope, then took up a paper knife and slipped it along the fold for a clean cut. She removed the letter, unfolded it and skimmed down the page until she reached the part she was looking for.

'. . . *therefore you have been given leave to formally adopt Anna Mason, age six.*'

Maisie closed her eyes and held the letter to her chest. Everything seemed to stop around her, with the exception of the grandfather clock, which continued its steady *tick-tock, tick-tock,* as if to remind her that the earth had not ground to a halt and that it was still necessary to breathe. At that moment the telephone began to ring. She picked up the receiver, her hand shaking as she fought back tears.

'Maisie – Klein here.' It was the deep voice of her solicitor, Bernard Klein, the man who had navigated so many legal waters on her behalf since the day she had learnt of her inheritance.

'I just received the letter – I – I – I can't believe it.' Maisie began to weep.

'My dear girl – I know how this must feel. I received a copy of the same letter and I wanted to offer my most heartfelt congratulations immediately. She's yours, Maisie. You're a mother now, and you should celebrate. Only a couple of formalities, nothing troubling – I will complete the documentation for you to sign this week, and that's it. Anna's adoption papers will come through in due course.'

'Thank you so much, Mr Klein – you've been an absolute tower of strength through all this.'

'Maisie, dealing with the transfer of Maurice's estate to you, and now the adoption of Anna, have been among the most rewarding work I've done since I started out on the legal path. Now then, I'll have my clerk start on the paperwork. You must go to your daughter. You're both safe now.'

Maisie thanked her solicitor again, replaced the telephone receiver and ran to the door, opening it and calling out, 'Anna! Dad! Brenda!' only to find the three beloved members of her family standing outside the door. Anna stared up at her, two fingers in her mouth.

'It's all right, love – no need to shout, we can hear you,' said Frankie.

'Maisie?' said Brenda, her voice shaking.

Maisie nodded, for words had escaped her. She reached for Anna, who was already holding out her arms.

'Can I call you "Mummy" now?'

'Yes, my love,' she sobbed, picking up her daughter. 'Yes, you can. You can call me Mummy.'

A celebratory Sunday lunch was planned for an assortment of guests, including Priscilla, who had been discharged from the Queen Victoria Hospital in East Grinstead to recover and gain strength prior to her next operation. Douglas and all three sons came to the house, plus a friend of Tom's who was also on a twenty-four-hour leave. Lord Julian and Lady Rowan were at lunch, as were Sandra with her husband and baby son – they had been looking at another cottage that had become available on the estate. Billy, Doreen, and their daughter, Margaret Rose, were not present – Frankie and Brenda had offered use of their bungalow to the family for as long as required, so they were in the midst of packing for the move. A group of Canadian officers completed the table, which was decorated with paper stars made by Anna. Glasses were raised, and Anna was the belle of the ball, having been taken into Tunbridge Wells to buy a new dress on Saturday morning before the shops closed. The guests lingered long into the afternoon, with Tom and his friend the first to depart, announcing that they had to get back to Hawkinge because their leave was almost up.

Maisie stood with her godson at the front door, while his friend turned the motor car around.

'We're not quite out of time, Tante Maisie, but we wanted to get back because there's a gang of us getting together at the Cat tonight – you know, the Red Lion, in Paddlesworth. We're raising our glasses to Jim Trahey.'

'Just a minute,' said Maisie. She ran into the house, returning with a pound note, which she pressed into his hand. 'Raise one or two from me too, Tom. I liked Jim Trahey very much.'

They both looked up at the sound of another vehicle approaching along the gravel drive towards the Dower House. A black Buick.

'Looks like your friend is back, Tante Maisie.'

Maisie stared at the motor car.

'Tante Maisie? Hello!' Tom waved a hand in front of her eyes. 'Well, I suppose I'll be off now.'

'Sorry, Tom – oh dear, I am sorry.' She reached up and kissed him on the cheek. 'Safe landings – and don't drink too much, will you?'

'Ha! You can't stand a couple of rounds for the chaps and then tell us to go easy! See you soon, Tante Maisie.' He turned to get into his friend's motor car, waving to the man now emerging from the driver's seat of the black vehicle. 'Hello, Mr Scott! You missed the celebration!'

'That's me, son – always a day late and a dollar short!' Mark Scott waved to Tom Partridge and turned to Maisie. 'Hello, Maisie – I was going to call, but then I thought, "Heck, I can find my way down there again." So I managed to snag an embassy automobile. I followed the same roads from pub to pub, and here I am.'

'Here you are,' said Maisie.

'What's the celebration?'

'It's for all of us, really – but especially for me, and for Anna.'

Mark Scott gave a broad smile as he reached for Maisie, taking her in his arms. 'Congratulations. And I know I've some explaining to do.'

'Yes, you have,' she pulled back. 'But I've an apology to make – I was short with you when we last spoke.'

'You had every right to be.'

'Not in wartime, Mark – there's too much to lose. And people like us don't have ordinary jobs, do we? I should have been more understanding.'

'No, we don't have ordinary jobs, but one of mine has come to an end. And I want to tell you about the new one.'

'Tell me later, Mark – come and see Anna. In fact, apart from Tom and his friend, there's quite a few people still here, including some Canadians who look as if they would jump at the chance to give someone from the other side of the border a bit of a roasting!'

'With good reason!' said Scott. 'I can take it on the chin though.'

* * *

Later, when all guests had left the Dower House, Anna had finally fallen asleep on the sofa in the drawing room, while Frankie and Brenda settled in to listen to the wireless. Maisie and Mark Scott took their drinks into the conservatory.

'You know you can't drive back to London now, don't you?' said Maisie.

'That's OK, your conservatory is as good a place as any for me to put my head down.'

'You're welcome to join us in the cellar – I'll be taking Anna down in a little while.'

'Your daughter.'

'Yes – my daughter.'

Mark Scott cleared his throat. 'I don't know why people do that when they're about to tell a story. I guess the words get caught up in your gullet and you can't help coughing. Anyway, here goes – I can tell you about my work now.'

'It certainly wasn't helping me find Catherine Saxon's killer, was it?'

'No, but that poor girl's death came along at the right time, though that sounds like a terrible thing to say. Has it all worked out OK with the two grandmothers? I heard you've been doing a bit of amateur diplomacy yourself.'

'It appears to be going well – and without doubt, Beryl Tucker discovered her backbone. It transpired that not only had the Welbeck Street property been part of a legacy in her favour, but the house in Haywards Heath was also hers, and as much as her husband considered it all down to him to make the decisions, her late uncle's trust was watertight, so Jonathan Tucker ultimately had no power because the uncle had taken a dislike to him when he was courting Beryl – everything is firmly in her name. Beryl has now instructed her husband to go to his club and remain there – she's definitely become the mouse that roared. She invited Amelia Saxon to stay at the house in Haywards Heath, and they worked out a plan for Charlie. The nanny is still employed, and the little boy will be enrolled in school locally when he comes of an age. I believe Mrs Tucker and Charlie will be spending summers in America with Amelia, who maintains she'll "take care of the senator"! And the grandmothers have also discussed Jenny Barrington, and how they can ensure she remains part of Charlie's life, if and when she is released. It's rather hard for Amelia, but they both know it's the right thing to do.'

'Grannies to the rescue.'

'You could say that – but now, Mark, tell me what's been going on.'

Mark Scott took a last sip of whisky, and poured another. 'My work will remain a secret in government files for at least fifty years, then I doubt anyone will notice because I'll be long gone and I won't be mentioned by name anyway. The government line is that I came to London officially as another embassy worker bee with the job of writing reports on the security of American citizens in Europe – to most of the staff there, I was a Bureau of Investigation man being redeployed.'

'I'm surprised no one guessed there was more to your role – being a worker bee wouldn't keep you occupied, would it?'

'Not by a long shot, although security in general became part of my eventual official account. For months now I have been reporting directly to the president of the United States on the activities of our ambassador to London, Joseph Kennedy. My work ended a few days ago when Kennedy boarded an aircraft home, and I would be surprised if he ever set foot on British soil again.' Scott cleared his throat again. 'Joseph Kennedy was always an isolationist, and he was an appeaser. Not only that, his rhetoric in support of Adolf Hitler, and suggestion that Britain capitulate to the Nazis, did not reflect the impression President Roosevelt wanted to give to the British – that we may not be over here, but our hearts are with you and we'll do what we can while retaining our neutrality. The work of broadcasters like Murrow's Boys and your Mr J. B. Priestley have led the American people to realise that Britain is on its uppers, and that you're the last country holding the line against the Nazis – and your people are dying while keeping their chins up. And that photograph in *Life*, the one by your Cecil Beaton of the little girl bombed out of her house, sitting in her hospital bed with her head bandaged clutching her raggedy toy – that has been seen on all the news stands at home and it's gone straight to the hearts of Americans nationwide. But back to Kennedy – and there's a long list of diplomatic infractions, even within his own departments. He upset the State Department, and he interfered with their efforts to get American citizens home by trying to send them out of England first, when our folks in France, Germany, Austria and all over Europe have been in much greater danger. And some of our Americans over here didn't want to go back – they wanted to see it through in London, or they went to the country. Then he commandeered valuable space on US registered ships to get stock from some liquor company he had financial interests in out of Britain, so he wouldn't lose any money.'

Scott sighed. 'Ambassador Joseph Kennedy had it all in the palm of his hand when he came over here – his family were treated like movie stars, and it would have been so easy for him to make Anglo-American relations shine as never before. But he threw it all away – and then he fell before he was pushed, though there was pressure at his back. Next time around – and it won't be too long – the president will be sending a statesman over here to be our ambassador, and he won't be a guy known for his sleight of hand in business!'

It was a long time before either Maisie or Mark Scott spoke. It was Maisie who broke the silence.

'It's all falling into place – Billy seeing you in South Kensington, and those absences. And why you couldn't tell me the reason for your return to Washington.' She pulled a blanket from the back of the sofa, wrapping it around her shoulders. 'So, what's next for you, Mark?'

Scott reached for her hand. 'I get to stay here. I don't have a fancy title or anything right now, but I'll be a special political attaché at the embassy, preparing for the new ambassador's arrival, keeping tabs on what's going on in Britain – reporting back to DC with the things I'm allowed to know, and finding out about the things your people would rather I didn't know. And I'll be continuing to work in London until at least the end of the war – however long that will be.' He shrugged. 'And seeing as I'm not getting any younger, though I hate to admit it, this might be my last posting before they put me out to grass.' He reached for Maisie's hand, brought it to his lips and kissed her scars. 'And I have to say, Maisie, I really like the grass here.'

'I'm glad you're back, Mark.'

'I'd hoped I'd get a bit more than that.'

'Give me time.'

'OK, but—'

'Shh!' Maisie put her finger to her lips. Leaving the sofa, she stepped across to the windows and looked out beyond the sweeping view across Wealden countryside. 'That's the air raid warning – they're coming over again.'

'Let's go.'

Mark Scott ran to the drawing room and lifted the sleeping Anna from the sofa, as Frankie opened the cellar door and Brenda collected a basket from the kitchen. Maisie watched as the man she had come to love rested her daughter on a mattress, and tucked a blanket in around her. He helped Brenda get settled, and Frankie to stem rainwater that had found another way to enter the cellar.

'Would you like a cup of tea, Mr Scott?' asked Brenda, pulling a flask from the basket.

'Oh no, thank you, Mrs Dobbs. I think I'll go upstairs – I'm not a cellar kind of guy,' said Scott.

'I'll be back in a minute, Brenda, Dad,' said Maisie, following Scott to the conservatory.

Maisie and Mark Scott watched the V formation of German bombers flanked by Luftwaffe fighter pilots in the distance, crossing the land in the direction of London. Over their heads a squadron of RAF aircraft was on its way to greet them. And once again old Mr Avis could be seen shaking his fist and shouting at the sky, before aiming his rifle towards the bombers.

'You know, you've gotta love you Brits,' said Scott, turning to Maisie.

You burned the city of London in our houses and we felt the flames that burned it. You laid the dead of London at our doors and we knew that the dead were our dead – were mankind's dead. Without rhetoric, without dramatics, without more emotion than needed be . . . you have destroyed the superstition that what is done beyond 3,000 miles of water is not really done at all.

POET ARCHIBALD MACLEISH, FROM A TRIBUTE
TO EDWARD R. MURROW, NEW YORK, 1941

AUTHOR'S NOTE

'The Blitz' is the name given to the period of intense bombing on London and other British cities that began on 7th September 1940, and continued until 10th May 1941. For those unfamiliar with this part of British history, it is important to note that Britain suffered Luftwaffe bombing from the early summer of 1940 until the end of the war – in later years heavy bombs, together with incendiary devices and V1 and V2 rockets were used by the Germans. What distinguishes the period known as 'the Blitz' is the very intense nature of the attack, the sheer number of bombers flanked by fighter aircraft, and the formation employed. Aerial combat known as *blitzkrieg* – the German word for 'lightning' – was the brainchild of Hermann Goering, head of Hitler's Luftwaffe. It had been successfully tested during the Spanish Civil War on behalf of General Franco, and subsequently destroyed resistance to Nazi invasion in Poland, Belgium, the Netherlands and France. While the Blitz was in progress, people often referred to 'another blitz' or 'last night's blitzes' – because there was obviously no prior knowledge of when the intensive bombing campaign might end, although some overseas journalists, in particular, referred to 'the Blitz last night' (with a capital *B*) for example. During this time, Britain was also bombing German cities.

When I began writing *The American Agent*, I was aware of the position of Joseph Kennedy, who took up the role of ambassador to Britain in 1938, and left England in October 1940. He had a reputation for supporting appeasement, and predicted that Hitler would be in Buckingham Palace within two weeks of war being declared. He was an isolationist and was believed to have Nazi sympathies, likely as a result of his anti-Semitic rhetoric and business relationships he had forged in Germany – relationships he was loath to lose. I decided to 'invent' a situation where he was being investigated by a special agent – mainly because I wanted to bring back Mark Scott, a character in *Journey to Munich*. While writing the novel, it therefore came as a surprise to read a press article pertaining to the declassification of reports filed by an unnamed agent sent to London to monitor Kennedy's activities during World War II until his resignation in October 1940. When he first took up his post, Joseph Kennedy and his family landed in London to the sort of fanfare accorded film stars – and it is known that his daughter, Rosemary, who had learning difficulties, fared particularly well while living in England, and even more so after her siblings had been sent back to America at the outset of war, and she had more of her father's attention. But by the time he left Britain, Kennedy's rhetoric and activities had – according to some accounts – rendered him an unpopular figure. Others – especially those US correspondents who liked the ambassador, and who were regular visitors to his home – suggested that the British were sorry to see Kennedy go. He was most certainly also being investigated by the British Foreign Office. Personally, speaking to family members and friends who were in London during the war, it appears people didn't really care either way – whatever might be lost during a given night's blitz was of greater importance than the arrival or departure of an ambassador. Kennedy's successor, John Gilbert Winant, had much ground to make up when he arrived in London in March 1941 as the new ambassador, yet became much admired for his willingness to go into the streets to talk to and try to help ordinary people suffering the effects of constant bombing. He remained in office until March 1946.

There is sometimes confusion regarding use of the word 'wireless' in historical fiction set in Britain, especially as the word has a quite different meaning today. In 1930s Britain, a radio was referred to as the 'wireless' simply because it did not need wires. Many homes were still without electricity well into the 1960s, so in the early days of radio – which became a popular entertainment and communications tool – a type of battery known as an 'accumulator' was used. The accumulator had to be taken to a local garage or similar shop on a regular basis to be 'topped up'. There are still people of a certain age who refer to listening to the wireless, and not the radio – though whatever name the device is known by, the importance of the wireless as a means of social influence in the twentieth century cannot be underestimated.

Finally, a word about 'Don' to whom this story is dedicated. On the one year anniversary of my grandfather's death, my parents, brother and I visited his grave in London, taking with us armfuls of flowers brought from our garden in Kent. I was almost twelve years of age, my brother four years younger. When we arrived, the grave was already overflowing with flowers left by other family members, but we added some of ours, and walked away still carrying a massive bouquet of bright magenta Alexander roses. As we walked among the gravestones, my father stopped alongside one that was overgrown with weeds. The inscription was simple, indicating that the deceased was a twenty-two-year-old RAF pilot killed during the Battle of Britain, in June 1940. His name was Don. There was no surname, and nothing to indicate that his parents had been laid to rest in the same place. Without a word spoken, the four of us began to clear the weeds, and working together we made Don's resting place worthy of him again, finally placing the Alexander roses at the head of the grave. As we walked away, those roses seemed to take over the whole cemetery – we could see them from the gates as we left. Decades later, I used the idea of a grave with only a single name in my first novel, *Maisie Dobbs*, so it seemed only right to dedicate a novel set during the most terrible months of 1940 to Don, and with such deep gratitude for his service.

ACKNOWLEDGEMENTS

With each new novel published, it is in these pages that I express my gratitude to many of the same people I thanked the last time a novel was published – and will do so again here. I am extremely fortunate to have worked with the team at HarperCollins in the US and with Allison & Busby in the UK for some years now, and I have forged relationships that I have come to cherish.

Amy Rennert has been my agent from the very start of my career as a novelist, and in that time has become a very dear friend – I am an incredibly blessed recipient of her wise counsel. And when it comes to being blessed – my long-time editor, Jennifer Barth, is one of a kind, and I am so very grateful for her insight, valuable advice, and direction. An editor who listens is a gift, and Jennifer has always listened and heard. Katherine Beitner has planned my book tours and promotion for some years now, and has been a supporter on every level. Thank you, Katherine – for your friendship, and not least for bringing my attention to the beautiful Hebrew phrase *eshet chayil*.

Thanks must go, as always, to Stephanie Cooper, who is a marketing wizard (and I'm sure I've said that before!). She amazes me with her new ideas and sheer enthusiasm for every project.

I've worked in sales, so I know how hard sales teams work – and how easily it is for that 'behind the scenes' endeavour to go unrecognised. Josh Marwell and his team at HarperCollins have my deepest thanks for everything they do, and for continuing to bring the Maisie Dobbs series to an even broader audience. Thank you, Josh. And for being such a constant Maisie Dobbs supporter – thank you, Jonathan Burnham, publisher and senior vice president at HarperCollins.

Susie Dunlop and the brilliant team at Allison & Busby in the UK have my most sincere gratitude for their infectious enthusiasm for my novels, and their very hard work on behalf of the Maisie Dobbs series in the UK and across the Commonwealth. And thank you all for the welcome I receive every time I cross the threshold of A&B's London offices.

The covers that grace the Maisie Dobbs series have been described as 'iconic' – indeed, they're just amazing. I have loved every cover, but the artwork for this book took my breath away. Thanks must go to the unbelievably talented artist/craftsman Andrew Davidson in the UK, and to creative director Archie Ferguson in the US. Andrew and Archie, you outdid yourselves on the cover for *The American Agent*. It is stunning.

My husband, John Morell, is at the head of my A team on the home front, aided and abetted by Maya, the dog sleeping at my feet as I write this.

SOURCES

Excerpt from *Der Rundfunk als achte Großmacht* © 1938 by Joseph Goebbels
English language translation © by Randall Bytwerk. Reprinted with permission of Randall Bytwerk

Quote from Vernon Bartlett in the BBC's *North American Service* used with permission of BBC and author's estate

All quotes from Edward Murrow in the *London Calling* broadcasts used with permission of CBS News

Quote from J. B. Priestley in BBC broadcast *Postscripts* used with permission of United Agents and author's estate (Permission pending)

15. — Through the K. 0. 16

JACQUELINE WINSPEAR is the author of the *New York Times* bestselling novels featuring psychologist and investigator, Maisie Dobbs. She has won numerous awards for the series, including the Agatha, Alex, and Macavity. In addition, Jacqueline's standalone novel, *The Care and Management of Lies*, was a finalist for the Dayton Literary Peace Prize. Originally from the United Kingdom, Jacqueline now lives in California.

jacquelinewinspear.com